CAMBRIDGE BLUE

Some hide the truth … some hide from it…

Lorna Spence knows she is clever. She thinks she is in control – and she's sure that she is loved… She believes each of these things until the moment she realises she's going to die.

DC Gary Goodhew is the youngest detective at Cambridge's Parkside Police Station. When the body of a young woman is discovered on Midsummer Common, Goodhew, intelligent and intuitive, feels ready for the challenge of his first murder investigation, but he finds that flushing out the killer could mean risking his job and revealing the truth about the one person he hopes will be innocent.

Cambridge Blue

by

Alison Bruce

Magna Large Print Books
Long Preston, North Yorkshire,
BD23 4ND, England.

0900608

British Library Cataloguing in Publication Data.

Bruce, Alison
     Cambridge blue.

     A catalogue record of this book is
     available from the British Library

     ISBN   978-0-7505-3077-4

First published in Great Britain by Constable,
an imprint of Constable & Robinson, 2008

Published in Large Print 2009 by arrangement with
Constable & Robinson Ltd.

Magna Large Print is an imprint of Library Magna Books Ltd.

Printed and bound in Great Britain by
T.J. (International) Ltd., Cornwall, PL28 8RW

For Jacen, Mum,
Natalie, Lana and Dean

Prologue

Jackie Moran opened her eyes and stared at the underside of her duvet. Pulling it over her head had been the final thing she remembered of the previous night.

One of her pillows now lay cocooned with her, and that seemed to be the only sign that she'd moved in her sleep.

Unless someone else had put it there.

The faint orange glow of her night light leached through the bedding, unchallenged by any hint of daylight, and she guessed it was still some time before dawn.

She kept herself motionless and watched the graduated shades of ochre and grey, trying to persuade herself that there was no movement on the other side of the covers, but scared to look out, sure that someone would be waiting for her if she did. She listened, but the more she strained to hear the more convinced she was that someone was breathing quietly in time with her rhythm. She held her breath and listened. Nothing. But if she was holding her breath they could just as easily be holding theirs.

She waited until the sound of her heart palpitating blocked her ears to the chance of hearing anything else, then began to breathe again.

If she moved slowly she thought she could just about turn her wrist enough to see the fluorescent glow of her watch face. The trick would be to do it without disturbing the bedding.

It was 4 a.m.

It was no surprise; every night without sleeping pills went this way. The same fear and paranoia. The same cold sweat that drenched her neck and breasts. The same feeling that her world was flat and she was sliding ever closer to the edge.

She shut her eyes and hoped it wouldn't take long to go back to sleep. She counted her heart-beats and tried to ignore the familiar uneasy feeling that hovered above her and the knowledge that today it had become far more intense.

She'd woken again at 6 a.m. with her hair tousled, tangled at the back like she'd wriggled her head from side to side in her sleep. Her duvet lay on the floor and she couldn't remember what she'd dreamt. As always she refused to dwell on her nocturnal self-torture.

By six thirty Jackie Moran had been out of bed for the full half-hour. She still wore her nightshirt; it was grey and cut like a thigh-length T-shirt with the words 'Personal Trainer' across the front in pink lettering. She'd chosen it firstly for comfort and secondly for the amusing idea that she could be fit enough to work in a gym just by wearing it.

Her cottage had originally had two bedrooms but she had decided to have the second refitted as a bathroom. She kept the first floor warm throughout the night – it was one of her luxuries in life, allowing her to pad around with bare legs and feet. Pulling on her jeans and thick socks was always the last thing she did before going down to the unheated lower half of the house.

She made up the bed, drew open the curtains, then crossed the small square of landing between the bedroom and the bathroom. She called downstairs, 'Bridy, walk in five minutes.' She turned a blind eye to the dog spending nights on the settee.

In the sitting room the border collie uncurled herself and slid on to the stone floor. She took her place at the bottom of the stairs and waited for her mistress.

Jackie's fresh undergarments were draped in an orderly left to right queue on top of the radiator. They too were pink and grey and had come from the same home shopping catalogue as her nightshirt. It was only the second time she had worn them and already she could see that the quality wasn't great.

She ran the basin's hot tap until the water steamed then dropped the polished plug into place and left the basin to fill. She pulled off her nightshirt, folding it as she made her naked way back to the bedroom to leave it under her pillow. She glanced at herself in the dressing-table mirror; she had no objections to her figure. She had long since accepted that it was her lot to be boy-like rather than womanly and her once-over was just to make sure there was no quiet shift towards flabbiness. There wasn't. She moved on. Perhaps she would have paused longer if there was anyone else who was going to see her naked. But again, there wasn't.

At 7 a.m., dressed in her ski jacket and jeans, she opened the cottage's side door on to the Fen Ditton morning and checked the weather for the first time. Not that it mattered: barring a change of boots for floods or unexpected snowfall, there was no British weather that would prevent her from taking Bridy on her morning walk.

A damp chill hung in the air, looking like a dirty net curtain, but feeling like a wet one. She put Bridy on the lead, and the dog trailed at her heels, grey muzzle always close to her left hand.

This was the village at its best; fresh with a new morning and thankfully few people. Not that she disliked people, but they did take up thinking time, and she liked to think.

Bridy paused to snuffle in the verge. Jackie rattled the choke chain and made a clicking noise with her tongue against the roof of her mouth. 'Not yet, Bridy.'

Bridy responded with a sneeze, then continued to trot alongside her.

Jackie cast a concerned eye over the war memorial too. That had suffered from a different blight: a delinquent who'd defaced the 'Lest We Forget' by changing the 'L' to a 'B'. The press had inevitably jumped on the bandwagon. The *Cambridge Evening News* had surveyed local schools and reported a 'commendable knowledge of the two World Wars amongst local teenagers'.

Words are cheap.

Mr Mills at the post office had actually done something about it. He had campaigned for a custodial sentence, which apparently had scared the lad witless in the process. She walked past the post office, its windows polished and paintwork immaculate; she had a great deal of respect for Mr Mills and his determination to care for the

10

village. The idea of standing up in public like that was impossibly daunting and she'd been glad when the press's brief interest had died.

She checked herself. Wasn't she suddenly sounding middle-aged? The point of her whole routine had been to make her daily life more efficient, but she could see it had left her set in her ways. Now she was touring the village complaining about other people when it made more sense to look at her own life with the same critical eye.

She wasn't about to dwell on all the things she'd once thought she'd be able to accomplish by the age of thirty. She didn't need to list them to know that she'd ticked none of them, and with only one month to go they were most likely to remain unrealized. But was this it?

Damn. What if it was?

At the Plough public house the road curved to the right with a tractor-width mud track to the left. She let Bridy off the lead and followed this trail for a few yards to the river path, walking between the tyre tracks on the raised strip of stones and divots.

Once clear of the pub and its family gardens she enjoyed her favourite view of the village. The mercurial Cam flowed on her left, grey and swift today; like cold molten metal – had such a thing existed.

On her right, beyond the paddock stood a telegraph pole fanning cables to houses. Joining them. A reminder that villages were still supposed to be places of community, even if the neighbours didn't know one another any more. For the umpteenth time in her adult life she wondered how different it would have been if her mother had lived; the cottage could have been less of a comfort and more of a joy.

She diverted her attention away from the houses. And in the paddock itself a grey and a roan wore matching royal blue head collars and New Zealand rugs. The grey raised his head and watched them pass.

She paused to pat Bridy.

It started to drizzle, the tiny rain droplets making silent dimples in the river, adding to the waters surging through from Cambridge and out towards Ely and eventually the Wash.

Two eight-oared boats nosed around the bend ahead, pulling upstream, rowing back to the college boathouses. They had come and gone in seconds, each man puffing warm white breath and breaking the peace with grunts of coordinated exertion. The oars skimmed and creaked past Jackie and she knew that they were concentrating far too much to notice the figure she'd just glimpsed as he stood in the shadows.

He waited in the drizzle, a quarter of a mile further along the banks of the Cam, leaning on the fence that ran beside the footpath, sheltering under the bare branches of the overhanging trees.

As far as she knew she was the only one who'd ever noticed him. The first time she'd passed him she thought he looked strange, standing alone under a tree. He looked like a labourer waiting for the gang van. Except there was no road and she happened to know he had his own van.

That had been three weeks ago and she'd heard him trying to start it as she walked back home; it had taken several disruptive attempts before the van's starter motor stopped rasping like a distressed saw and reluctantly allowed the engine to fire. It had driven past her as it whined and pinked its way back out of the village, puffing oil-tinged blue smoke from its exhaust.

She'd written the registration number on her memo board, where it had stayed until she'd over-written it with the date of her dental appointment.

She was less than a hundred yards from him when he looked towards her. Today he had his black woollen hat tugged tight over his cropped ginger hair. In fact all his clothes were dark and somehow that made him loom larger on her path ahead.

She turned to Bridy; it gave her an excuse to look away. Bridy snuffled in the hedgerow, inter-ested in the smells drawn out by the rain.

'Come on, Bridy.' Her voice sounded unnatur-ally bright, brittle even. 'It's too cold to stop.'

Britain, she decided, had become a country full of women looking for rapists and muggers down every alley and she wasn't about to become the next victim of a nation's raging paranoia. But goosebumps still rose on her neck and scuttled up on to her face. Suddenly she wanted to go home.

He stared at her as she approached; he'd never made eye contact before but, she reminded her-self, he'd never done any harm before either.

His face glowed moon white, punctured by dark dilated bullet holes for eyes and nostrils exuding short blasts of steam.

She ignored the way her heart was thumping like it wanted to escape her chest.

13

Besides, she was not prepared to change her routine for anyone.

Jackie forced herself to keep walking even though every instinct told her to turn and run. She drew deep breaths, hoping they'd calm her, but the harsh chill in the air had felt like an in-draught of terror. Her muscles seemed to have atrophied. Her head felt giddy and all she could think was *run, run, run*. She thought it until she was too close to change course.

She passed within two feet of him and heard a sharp crackle of movement from the hedgerow. She didn't turn to face him, but the first wave of fear arrived even before she felt his hands at her throat. It paralysed her. Sucked her inside herself to a place where her body was no longer her own and her last seconds would be torn from her as easily as tearing paper. His grip was ferocious, compassionless, crushing her windpipe, making the pain scream in her ears and silencing the rest of her world.

She saw Bridy, just a tumble of black and white. Then a second wave washed over Jackie, but this time it was adrenalin that flooded her. And Bridy rushed again. Barking and buffeting his shins.

'Shut up,' he snarled, and lashed out with his boot. Bridy was faster and dodged the kick. His grip slipped. Jackie threw herself sideways, grabbing at the undergrowth; anything for escape. She needed to roll away, but his hands fell on to her legs, grabbing her at the knees, bringing her to the ground. One hand reached up and his fingers grabbed the belt buckle on her jeans; he hauled himself on top of her, working his way up her

14

body. His face drew closer to hers, his breath hot and mouldy. She had no room to manoeuvre now and for one long moment it seemed that neither of them moved. His weight pressed down on her, chest to breast, pelvis to pelvis, pushing her legs apart.

With one free hand he reached downwards, and she expected to feel his fingers tugging at the zip on her jeans, but instead he felt for something in his own back pocket.

Bridy renewed her barking just as Jackie saw the knife in his hand. He lashed out his leg once more. This time the dog launched herself, grabbing the hem of the man's trousers between her teeth. She pulled. He extended his foot and attempted another kick. 'Fuck off,' he yelled but Bridy held tight and growled as she yanked at his outstretched leg.

The knife sprang from his fingers, landing silently in the long grass. As he reached to grab it Jackie wriggled one arm free, slipped her hand into her jacket pocket and grabbed for Bridy's collar and lead.

Still on the ground, the man hauled himself towards the knife, heaving the weight of Bridy along with him. His fingertips brushed the handle, but still not close enough to take hold of it. She knew that if he reached it he would finish the job.

The choke chain still ran in a loop and with one movement Jackie hooked it over his head. His reaction was delayed: it seemed several seconds before his body jerked, then he let go of her and his hands shot up to his own throat.

She dragged on the lead and he pulled it back

15

towards him, slackening the chain momentarily. *It's him or me. Him or me.*

His eyes were still wild, but now they bulged with fear. Jackie kicked out. One leg, then the other, pulled free of him and the hard toes of her boots drove into his abdomen and chest. He hung on to the metal links of the lead, but she also refused to release her grip. Then her knee connected with his jaw, cracking against the bone and sending his teeth into his tongue.

Finally she found the foothold she sought and pushed hard on his sternum. Her body flexed rigid and she pulled the lead tight until the links slipped out of his fingers and the chain had disappeared into an engorged welt around his purple neck.

Bridy let go first, but by then the man had been dead for six minutes.

Jackie Moran retreated. Standing with her back in the hawthorn she stared down at the body. Two questions screamed at her, spinning past until they merged into one hideous banshee of a word. *Whowhy. Whowhy. Whowhy.*

Bridy looked up at her, waiting for her to decide what to do.

Just then something bright caught her eye. She stepped past Bridy and looked down at it. It was his knife, its blade poking up at the angle of a shark's fin. She knelt beside it and considered its presence; it was a kitchen knife, not the folding pocket kind that some men carried in the normal course of events.

She picked it up, holding it with the tip of its blade between her forefinger and thumb, before

16

taking it by the handle and testing its sharpness. It would have been an efficient murder weapon. She stroked the flat of the steel. This man had deliberately brought it for use on her. She wasn't surprised when a familiar nausea began to stir inside her. This had been no random attack. This had been the lingering and diseased finger of the past clawing at her just when she'd dared to think about the future.

The edge of the water was about eight feet away. Heavy tufts of grass topped the bank and from there she knew that the eroded sides dropped sharply into the deep river. She threw the knife and watched it disappear with no bigger ripple than a dace could have made.

She could have handed it over, of course, but she pictured the familiar doubtful expression, and that look it turned into: part pity, part disgust. She closed her eyes and when she reopened them she couldn't locate the spot where the knife had disappeared.

The river had remained deserted and she guessed a body could be buffeted some distance before it was eventually discovered. Then she shook her head, not fully believing the decision that she found herself making.

She rolled him over and over, reminding herself of a single truth: it was too late to look for help.

He slipped in head first, making a wave of water which slopped back against the bank. He descended gradually, turning from man to ghostly shadow to nothingness. She stepped back from the edge and reached out for the warmth of Bridy. She rubbed the soft fur at the base of Bridy's ear.

'Good girl, we're safe now,' she whispered in a shaking voice. 'It's all over,' she added. But in her voice she heard the unmistakable sound of a lie.

Chapter One

Rolfe Street was only a short walk from the heart of Cambridge, a perpetual backwater, no accidental visitors and few daytime inhabitants.

A lone man stood on the pavement waiting to speak to Lorna Spence, the woman who was spying on him from her first-floor window. So far he'd knocked twice but she had no intention of letting him know she was at home.

She stood behind a carefully placed ruck in the curtains. She knew he couldn't see her but even so kept perfectly still in case he glanced up and caught the flicker of her shadow.

Lorna Spence had gone to bed in yesterday's knickers and that was all she wore as she studied the top of his head.

He took a few short steps towards the door and then a few towards the street. He ran his hand in an impatient foray through his hair, completing the gesture by clasping his hand across the back of his neck. He faced the front door, leaning in towards it and listening. Listening. His hand, still on his neck, massaged the rigid muscles which locked the top of his spine.

He was stressed.

She imagined him swearing under his breath.

He took a step back and his gaze shot up to her window, boring into the gap in the curtains. He seemed to stare straight into her face, but she didn't blink.

A tingling sprang across her bare skin, racing in waves across her shoulders and trickling across the freckled skin of her small breasts and on to her nipples. Only her chest moved, rising and falling ever quicker; trying to keep pace with her heart.

Lorna waited for him to knock again but instead he stepped away and out of sight of her little spyhole. She moved closer to the gap and crept around forty-five degrees for a view of the closed end of the cul-de-sac.

She located him again.

He stood on the edge of the kerb with his hands on his hips and his leather-soled shoes planted wide and facing in opposite directions.

She whispered down towards him: 'Go away. Go on, get in your car and drive away.'

His attention had settled on the rows of parked vehicles flanking each side of the road. She knew he wouldn't recognize any of them.

Then he left, walking briskly towards his own car at the end of the street. He'd accepted what she already knew: that he had no reason to believe she was at home.

She waited. He started the engine and let the postman pass without cross-examination. He pulled away and drove out of sight. But she waited further still, and watched the road until she'd counted to one hundred and was sure he wouldn't return.

And then she exhaled with a long puff. Her heartbeat slowed and her pulse steadied.

The letterbox creaked as it opened and gave an echoing snap as it shut. The junk mail made a heavy thud as it hit the hallway's tiled floor. She leant over the handrail and checked in case an unexpected letter looked tempting enough for a dash downstairs.

A holiday brochure lay face down, obscuring any other post that may have been underneath. A photo of a caravan park and the words 'Family Entertainment' jumped out through the clear plastic envelope.

'Why me?' she groaned. Last week the mail had been sit-in baths and stair-lifts. What a waste of time.

Her dressing table was a wide antique pine chest of drawers with a reproduction pine mirror on top. She only owned the mirror, and the battery clock next to it which told her it was eight thirty-five and she was going to be late for work.

In the circumstances late would be a good thing.

But not too late, she couldn't afford trouble at the office too.

She padded into the bathroom, pulled off her knickers and threw them into the corner with the rest of the week's laundry. She ran the hot tap until the water flowed warm and damped down her short ash-blonde hair, working her fingers through the feathered strands at the back so they lay close to the nape of the neck.

She dressed quickly and chose Warm Mocha lipstick. She ran it back and forth across her lips then dabbed it on to her cheekbones, rubbing it in to give the approximation of blusher.

That would do.

She checked her reflection; she knew that a skim of freckles across each cheek and a lucky gap between her two front teeth gave her face more character than any layer of make-up.

She grabbed her bag and hurried downstairs. As she reached the bottom stair she could see other letters under the brochure.

Five pairs of her shoes were lined up beside the door; in two-inch heels she made five foot five. Just.

She reached for the post, slipping her feet into her highest shoes as she turned the envelopes over. There were four of them, and the brochure.

She flicked through them. Mobile phone bill, bank statement, credit card bill. Then the fourth. White, A5 and emblazoned with an advert for a bank loan. But it was the addressee's name which caught her eye.

'Miss H. Sellars.'

Lorna frowned. A chill tickled her scalp, then vanished. How strange, she thought. She shook her head and smiled. What an amazing coincidence.

She suddenly wondered whether the holiday brochure was similarly addressed. She moved it from under the other post.

Instant fear washed the smile from her lips.

The black print on the white label jumped out at her. She recoiled and the post scattered, tumbling from her fingers on to the floor. The corner of the clear envelope hit the mat; it bounced and landed, slapping down flat on its face.

She hurried away down the street. Behind her the hall tiles stayed cold, rebuffing the uanswered ring of the telephone that called from upstairs.

Chapter Two

The punting station was quiet. A few ducks paddled on the river but the punts themselves were stationary and so tightly moored to one another that they looked more like an extension to the jetty than individual craft.

Most of the buildings around the cobbled quayside square had been converted into cafés and restaurants. Some had flats above, luxury apartments with romantic views of the river and discreet street-level entrances. One of these doors, however, bore a chrome plaque which read 'The Excelsior Clinic'.

As Lorna crossed the quayside she was already forty-five minutes late for work.

The wind blowing along The Backs made it too cold to sit outside, but tables and umbrellas cluttered the pavement. No doubt trying to entice people inside. Lorna knocked over a chair as she hurried through. It clattered on to its side, then clattered again as she paused to haul it back on to its feet.

The outer door was unlocked and Lorna hurried up the steps. A prematurely grey woman with a prematurely middle-aged haircut sat behind the reception desk. She wore half-moon glasses and her blouse was buttoned up to the top.

Lorna slapped her hand on the oak counter-top. 'Morning. Are you from the agency?'

The woman nodded and introduced herself as Faith. That figured, nothing more glamorous would fit.

Lorna smiled, reached over and shook her hand. 'I'm Lorna, I do the accounts through there.' She pointed at the frosted glass panel behind Faith's chair.

'Oh good, I have more messages for you than anyone.'

Lorna swung up the hinged end of the reception counter and slid back the glass partition which led to her office. She worked alone in the twelve-foot-square space with two desks, two phones, two chairs and one kettle. 'Give me a minute to sort myself out and I'll be with you. Tea or coffee?'

'Not for me, thanks. I'll wait until eleven.'

The corner of Lorna's mouth flickered with the hint of an ironic smile. That made a change; a temp with a work ethic.

Faith sat on her side of the open door and Lorna chatted to her as she organized her morning drink. 'When I first worked here I thought Excelsior sounded like a brand of condom, and of course that is exactly what it sounds like. After a while I realized how appropriate it was too.' Lorna stole a quick glance at Faith's ring finger and saw that she wore a wedding band. 'I think it's all about sex,' she added.

Faith raised an eyebrow. 'Is it?'

'Yup. I've been here two years and nearly every treatment is cosmetic. The dental department does caps and whitening, the eye clinic does laser treatment so people can chuck out their glasses, and that's nothing compared to the cosmetic surgery lot. Have you heard of Botox?'

Faith shrugged. 'I've heard the name.' She sounded vague.

'It costs three hundred and fifty quid for a ten-minute session. And for that Mr Moran injects them, paralysing their facial muscles with shots of purified botulism. It's nearly all women and they roll out of here feeling like sex kittens.'

Faith picked up a notepad and tore off the top sheet. 'Dr Moran is one of your messages.'

'It's Mr, not Dr,' Lorna corrected and carried on cheerfully, 'I think there's nothing like tossing money around to boost a woman's libido.' Mr Moran's schedule lay on the top of her in-tray. She checked it. No cancellations. She ran her finger down the list, making a rough total of the bills to be issued. Almost £12,000. 'Same tomorrow. Twelve grand for one day's work.'

Faith shook her head. 'I don't think I need to know all of this.'

Lorna paused. 'I'm sorry, I didn't mean to sound indiscreet. But I find it so fascinating. Besides, you work here now. And I'm not saying he doesn't deserve his success, he often works ten-hour days so he can see people who travel up from London after work. And everyone says he's very good.'

She looked across at her post tray, deep from a single delivery. Her job included issuing neat bills in crisp tamper-proof envelopes and banking the personal cheques which, in his case, arrived by return of post. No one kept Mr Moran waiting for payment, not when his diary was full two months ahead and trustworthy consultants were so hard to find. 'Very, very good,' she added.

Faith nodded. 'Don't mind me, I just have some old-fashioned views and I'm sure they don't count for anything in the world of business.'

They turned to their respective desks. Faith's note was written in her own style of shorthand with names and words separated by commas. 'Dr Moran, moran, redhd.'

Lorna frowned, rolled her chair towards Faith and passed back the note. 'What does it mean?'

Faith glanced at it, and spoke, stressing the word 'Mr'. 'Mr Moran rang twice. Wanted to know where you were and said you had to ring the second you arrived.'

Lorna cut in. 'What did he say?'

'Just that. And then a nurse stopped by.'

'Victoria?' It was a redundant question since Victoria was the only person in the building who looked remotely nurse-like.

'Again, I don't know. To be honest she was pretty rude. She looked rather out of sorts when I said you weren't in. Swore several times in fact.'

'A slim redhead?'

Faith nodded. 'Skinny and rude.'

'She's all right, she just gets stressed and makes a drama out of things. So, what did she want?'

'I'm sorry, I have no idea.'

Lorna didn't respond to any of the messages. She raised invoices until she took an early break at ten thirty. She closed the door between herself and reception, had two cups of coffee and a packet of salt and vinegar crisps, then composed a two-word text on her mobile. 'Miss you.'

Her phone bleeped twice almost immediately. 'Where are you?'

'Here.'

She put her mobile to one side and positioned herself with her fingers poised over the keyboard and an alert gaze fixed to the centre of her screen. She estimated he'd be in before she'd counted to thirty. She'd reached twenty-seven when she heard the office door opening.

She didn't turn; she could imagine he still looked as stressed as he had from her bedroom window. 'Good morning,' she said brightly.

'Where were you?' His words were clipped, tight with an anger he was fighting to keep screwed up in a ball of reason.

'Sorry, I was late in.' She spun slowly in her seat and gave him an easy smile. 'I overslept.'

'I called by your flat this morning, you weren't there.'

She kept the smile going, warming her face with it, letting her eyes glow. 'Today?' she queried. She saw stubbornness in his face. 'I just told you, I overslept.'

'You would have heard me.'

'I didn't. Perhaps I was in the shower?' She tilted her head to one side and stayed patient.

'You weren't there,' he insisted.

'Where was I then?' She glared.

He glared back. 'That's what I want to know, Lorna.'

'No,' she snapped. 'I'm asking you where you are accusing me of being. Are you saying I was screwing another man?'

'Keep your voice down.'

'Are you?'

'Just tell me where you were.'

'And if I was with a friend? Isn't that OK? Do you suddenly have a right to dictate what I do in my own time?'

'Of course not.'

'So you think I was with someone else?'

'Lorna.' He reached out to grab her arm but she squirmed away from him. Finally she heard the first note of defeat in his voice. 'Please stop.'

'OK, I'll tell you. I was there when you called and I saw you from my window.'

He looked doubtful.

'You parked at the end of the road and the postman walked by just before you drove away.'

'Then why...?'

'Because you were checking up on me again. I was at home. Alone. And I'm not going to keep pandering to your jealousy.' She reached forward and took his hand then whispered, 'I love you, Richard, but I won't go on like this.'

At twelve Lorna took lunch, glad to have a break from looking at her post tray. It reminded her of the mail scattered on her front door mat; she was desperate to rush home and open it.

She needed to know if she would find a note inside. Or a threat even.

She pressed her tongue against the gap in her teeth for luck and slipped out past the receptionist.

27

Chapter Three

The previous week's bank holiday had motivated a surge of tourists to descend on the city, and now, although busier than April, the streets were comparatively quiet again. The shops bustled but the tills were slow.

Alice Moran was just over five feet eight and slender; at thirty-nine she still possessed a mix of maturity and girlishness that acted as a visual magnet. Her skin was tinted with a hint of winter tan and she wore well-polished sunglasses.

She held a large paper carrier from one of the better dress shops; it contained a pair of size ten suede trousers and a coordinating rust-coloured blouse. The fact that they were almost identical to the ones which she currently wore hadn't deterred her. Trousers suited her, they were practical and sat better on her narrow and slightly angular frame.

She had used the morning in a deliberately unproductive fashion: she had, she decided, been pushing herself a little too hard. She knew from experience that it only took seventy per cent of the effort to achieve ninety-five per cent of the results and squandering the other thirty on perfecting the filing would do nothing more than turn her into another Richard. God forbid.

Besides, when she became too fussy she knew it took the fun out of working alongside her brother. She liked to think that he enjoyed being supported, not managed.

Alice was approaching the last of the shops. A few yards ahead the Round Church was trying to entice the older tourists with brass rubbing and tea. Probably served in flowered china and accompanied by a sugar-sprinkled slice of Victoria sandwich. Would that be the highlight of her day in another thirty years, she wondered?

Suddenly she wasn't looking forward to the end of her sojourn and, although she knew she'd feel guilty if she arrived any later, she pushed her glasses up on to her head and slipped in through the nearest doorway. The shop was old-fashioned, glass cases displaying pipes and tobacco and model cars. A big boys' nostalgia emporium.

A globe caught her eye; it was football-sized and stood in the window, displayed against a fanned-out selection of postcards depicting the golden age of steam. Bet they didn't know it was a golden age when they were in it, she thought idly.

She touched the globe's surface, her fingers brushing across Europe. She was about to look closer, wondering whether she'd managed to find the Pyrenees by feel alone, when in the street outside a familiar figure caught her eye.

The figure wore black as she always did and walked quickly. Any faster would have been a jog. It was Lorna, her colleague and her brother's girlfriend. Lorna was preoccupied, her expression slightly manic; somewhere between mild ecstasy and bubbling hysteria.

She passed the window without spotting Alice. And as if just the act of walking past had dragged a change of mood along in its wake, Alice felt her reluctance to return to the Excelsior Clinic vanish, replaced instead with a need to reach Richard.

She could always sense when he needed her.

Chapter Four

Alice took the stairs and as she reached the top of the first flight she heard footsteps coming towards her. They were leather-soled shoes which skimmed the steps as they rushed down. She knew by sound alone that they belonged to her brother. He rounded the corner, pulling himself towards the handrail to save himself from careering into her.

'I'm sorry.' He was holding his car keys and mobile phone and trying to keep moving while bundling himself into his jacket.

She smiled. 'In a rush?'

'Yes. I need to catch up with Lorna, she's not answering her mobile.'

'She's already gone.'

'I know. I wanted lunch with her.'

'No, no, I saw her, she's already in Sidney Street.'

He stopped in his tracks and scowled. 'Oh fuck.'

Alice touched his arm. 'Will I do?'

He smiled and it made him look boyish, almost as young as Lorna in fact. 'Anything to avoid work?' he quipped.

She narrowed her eyes in mock annoyance. 'Do

you begrudge me my morning off?' They walked back down the stairs side by side, Alice in her heels only an inch shorter than her brother. She saw their reflection in the mirror-panelled foyer wall and wondered whether they would have been mistaken for twins if he wasn't having a day where he looked at least eight years younger instead of nearly two.

'No. You'll do.'

'Thanks,' she said sarcastically. He held the outer door for her and she was about to return with another barb but as she glanced into his face she saw he really didn't look as good as she had thought. Perhaps the interior lighting had been overly flattering, or maybe the May daylight was just a bit too honest.

She gave him a smile, but it was a sad one, sorry for the stress he was under: bad events took their toll. 'Are you snowed under still?'

'I'm fine.' He looked at her and seemed to know she was worried. 'It's not that, Alice. It's...' He paused. 'Come on, I'll tell you at lunch.'

And so they walked back the way she'd only just come, towards the centre of the city. 'I don't mind where we go. I've just been in town. Here will do,' she added hopefully as they passed the last of the restaurants.

Alice spied her globe in the shop window ahead. And saw the sign outside the Round Church; God help Richard's frame of mind if he were to take her for lunch in there. But he took a right up Trinity Street and led them past the entrances to the colleges. 'I don't need the tourist route, Richard.'

They marched shoulder to shoulder, their

strides matched.

'I do. I think it's good to remember what a beautiful place we live in. How lucky we are.' He passed Trinity without a glance through the ancient gate at the perfect green of the quadrangle lawns.

She always looked. Even now with Richard walking ever faster she stole a glance at the small statue of King Henry and the chair leg he held in the place of a sceptre. What sort of man brandished a chair leg? Hadn't the university establishment realized that leaving it there was mocking a monarch? She knew they were lucky, and she meant it with none of her brother's sarcasm. 'I don't need the tourist bit today is what I meant. Where are we going?'

'By the river.'

Of course, he wanted to watch the water.

Neither of them spoke again until they reached the Anchor pub. Alice chose a table with a clear view of the mill pond and Richard went to the bar and returned with two halves of IPA.

Alice was watching the water, and Richard sat in the opposite seat and watched it too. The river snaked towards them through the flat of the water meadow; in the distance a scattered herd of cows grazed, up to their hocks in rich spring grass.

'Do cows get laminitis?'

Alice shook her head. 'Never heard of it. Probably only an equine illness.'

'Just as well.'

'We could ask,' she pointed out.

He gave a humourless snort. 'I don't think so.'

The water slipped through the sluice gates, calmer and more refined as it tiptoed up The

Backs, probably taught since pre-Tudor times not to disturb the scholars.

Alice was the first to look away from the river. 'Remember when we were children? We all loved the water, but you most of all.'

Richard sipped his beer.

'And if you cried, Mother would say, "Let him see some water," and if we were indoors she'd run the tap and you'd settle down straight away.'

He let her finish the anecdote, though he'd heard and she'd told it many times before. It gave him extra time to put off talking about the present. Those were his best childhood memories; later ones were rarely so fond.

His eyes flickered and made him refocus on the present. Alice was staring at him, not unkindly, just tolerantly, as if she'd been like that for some time. Waiting for him to answer something probably. He tried to remember hearing a question. No. But he could guess what she was expecting and he wanted to tell her anyway. Or at least thought he would feel better if he did.

'Do you think Lorna's too young for me?' he began.

Alice smiled. 'Well, the age gap's the same as it's always been. Are you suddenly thinking of marrying her or something?'

'No. Should I?'

'Haven't a clue. Do you want to get married?'

Richard screwed up his face. 'Sometimes I do, but I'm not sure enough. But then again, I don't want to lose her.'

'And you think you will?'

'She wasn't at home this morning.'

'So?'

'That means she didn't go home last night. But she didn't stay with me either.'

'Perhaps she was up early. Don't start making assumptions, you can't expect to know every move a person makes, that would be unreasonable. You know that, don't you?'

'Uh-huh.'

'Ask her where she was. In a nice way.'

'I did.'

'And?'

'She said she was in the shower but...'

Alice leant across the table. 'Richard, look at me. You can't let yourself start to get possessive, you know that's when it goes wrong. Don't you?'

Richard nodded dumbly. Finally he whispered, 'You're her friend...' His words trailed away but Alice could guess the rest of the question.

'OK,' she replied, 'I'll have a chat with her. But I'm sure you're worrying over nothing. You always feel she's loyal to you, don't you?'

'Yes, but...'

Alice reached over and squeezed his hand. He felt like a little boy again, but it was a feeling of relief not oppression. 'You're feeling jealous again, aren't you?'

He squeezed her hand in return. 'I know it's stupid, but yes, I am.'

Chapter Five

Lorna never made it home. Three times her mobile rang and each time she saw Richard's mobile number appear on the display. When it rang for a fourth time she expected it would be him again, but this time the name 'Victoria' flashed up. Lorna was still tempted not to answer, but she knew that some people were like bills, sooner or later they had to be paid off.

She flipped open the handset and held it to her ear. 'What?'

Lorna wasn't surprised when there were two or three seconds without reply. She could picture Victoria, alone at a table or standing in a corridor, cigarette in one hand, mobile in the other, smelling of cosmetics and letting a languid smile settle on her lips before even thinking about opening them to speak. Victoria's voice was mellow. 'I'd love to take a vacation in your brain – empty space and the luxury of being the centre of the universe for two whole weeks.'

Lorna didn't rise to it and pitched her reply mid-distance between matter-of-fact and uninterested. 'What do you want?'

'An answer.'

This was the conversation she knew she needed to have with Victoria, but despite avoiding her for a week or more she was relieved it was finally here. 'I'm not leaving.' That was easy.

'Then I'll speak to Richard.'

'That's fine because I've told him everything.' She'd put a chirpy note in her voice, hoping it would hide the bluff.

'Even about your latest plan? I doubt it somehow.'

Lorna frowned. 'I have no idea what you're talking about.'

'That's funny, a murdered baby wouldn't slip my mind.' Sardonic as ever.

Lorna's intake of breath was both sharp and audible. It wasn't Victoria knowing about little David that was frightening – after all, they'd both read the same pages, and even though the case was over twenty years old they both saw the potential in a document that turned it from 'natural causes' into 'wilful murder'. It was the mention of him in relation to recent events that made her gasp; she knew that one malicious moment from Victoria could destroy everything.

Victoria added another of her long pauses and when she spoke Lorna guessed it was intended to make her squirm even more: in fact it had the opposite effect. 'Or doesn't he believe it was murder?'

Victoria hadn't exactly got the wrong end of the stick, but was clearly poking it around until she could be sure which was the right end, and Lorna was determined not to give anything else away. They'd both recognised the initial vulnerability in her voice; now Lorna was careful to maintain an air of panic. 'I don't know. We should discuss this.'

'Talking to you never works.'

'Hold on, let me think. Look, Victoria, I can

come up with an answer that will work for both of us, I know I can. Just give me a little time.'

'By tonight, Lorna, or I'll tell them everything. Today is the last day where I get screwed around by you.'

After the phone call Lorna changed direction. She wandered into the city centre, casting an unenthusiastic eye towards the shop windows. At least she knew there was no rush to reach home, that much made sense. But beyond that she had no idea what to do. After almost ten minutes of deliberation she made two calls. She was pleased when her first was answered with 'Hi, Lorna.' At least her number was still stored in his phone's memory.

'Are you around later? I need cheering up,' she said.

Then she phoned Richard's mobile to apologize for missing his calls and found him in a state of post-jealousy calmness. She offered to work late to make up for her late arrival, and instead he offered to buy her lunch. When she hesitated, he added, 'And dessert. Alice is here too.'

She laughed. 'Good.'

'Dessert or Alice?'

'Both.' She strode out towards the Anchor pub, her mind never leaving the dilemma of Victoria. Richard waved when he saw her. She waved back, momentarily wondering whether he really did love her enough to forgive everything. It wasn't worth the risk.

Alice held out a large glass of white wine. 'You look like you need this.'

After the second glass Lorna began to see the

possibility of a compromise, a version of the truth she could tell Richard and the opportunity to make Victoria leave her alone. Jackie was the key. Perhaps, with a little help and a little luck, she wouldn't face losing him.

By the third glass she saw that it was just a question of juggling her plans for the evening and keeping the right people on her side.

Chapter Six

DI Marks reached the top of the stairs and turned down the corridor towards his office. He was reviewing the statement he'd just made to the local paper, turning it over in his head. It preoccupied him, though no one would have known because he had always found it so easy to remain expressionless.

For example, his fifteen-year-old daughter, Emily, currently had a crush on a lad called Pip. Pip was taking GCSEs and liked The Kooks, ice hockey and skateboarding. Marks imagined that Pip would have shoulder-length wavy hair, chewed nails and a total vocabulary of about two dozen varying grunts.

Meanwhile his wife swapped flirty emails with a builder called Gordon, who lived near Inverness and claimed to share her interest in daisy growing. Marks didn't take it too seriously and was pretty confident that his wife didn't either.

But the point was, no one knew he knew, and

whether it was really a skill or just his natural demeanour, it was something he'd often found useful when dealing with both his detectives and his suspects.

This evening he'd used it as a mask for his concern. He'd left the team finishing a three-hour stint in the city centre, handing out leaflets and reminding women that most of the recent spate of rapes had occurred between 5 and 8 p.m. As though they needed reminding. He was sure that every office worker within fifty miles was fully aware that any one of them might become the next target. And unless a swift arrest followed, there undoubtedly would be a 'next target'. Forensics had managed to isolate a sample of the attacker's DNA and Marks had made a statement to the press using words like 'confident', 'imminent' and 'positive identification', thankful that they couldn't read the helplessness he really felt. Yes, he was truly sure that they would catch the man, but without a stroke of luck he doubted that would happen before they had seen the details of at least one more traumatized woman added to their files.

He walked into his office and flicked the light switch, but even by the light slipping in from the corridor he had already spotted a manila envelope which had been left squarely in the centre of his otherwise empty desk. He drew the sharp breath of recognition and flashed back three months to the first time this had happened. Despite the official line he found himself hoping that this might be the same sort of luck that had helped close their last serious case.

Initially he didn't touch the envelope. He

hooked his jacket over the hat stand, walked around the desk and lowered himself slowly into his chair. He paused for several seconds, tapping the desk in indecision. He considered calling a SOCO down to open it, letting them fingerprint it, opening an investigation. Then he considered the next victim and slid it closer. He'd look first, then decide.

He tore open the end, and tipped its contents on to the desk. The first item to slip out was a toothbrush in a clear plastic bag, the second was a single page of white A4. It had been folded in half, just as before, and he could see the shadow of print showing through from the back of the sheet. In his top drawer he kept a pack of sterile gloves and he slipped a pair over his hands before touching the paper. He smoothed it open on the desk.

The text was brief, and to the point. 'This toothbrush belongs to Ian Knott, 205 York Road, Cambridge and will be a DNA match for the Airport Rapist.'

Expressionless failed him and he smiled; he liked the note maker's use of the words 'will be' and liked the way they crushed his pessimism. Next he found his own evidence bag and scooped up the envelope and its contents.

He also realized that the notes had to stop before they began to undermine official investigations. He stopped smiling with the knowledge that the culprit was one of his own team. For all their front and initiative they'd be sacrificing their own job if they didn't watch out.

There wasn't one he wanted to lose, but Marks thought about each of his detectives in turn, silently listing them from the longest serving to the latest to finish his probation. Only the final name stood out.

DC Gary Goodhew. The departmental enigma. The twenty-five-year-old who had reached detective faster than anyone else Marks knew.

Goodhew had been at Parkside for six months, turning up after Marks had informed the team that their new colleague was a high-flying privately educated graduate with a first in maths. Marks had immediately realized that what he'd intended as a build-up sounded more like a warning, and Goodhew was met with a very chilly reception.

It had lasted until about lunchtime on day one. By the afternoon DC Charles had offered him a place on the pool team and PC Kelly Wilkes was referring to Goodhew's slightly unkempt appearance as 'that just out of bed look'.

The word 'fit' had been bandied round the canteen a fair bit too.

In many ways Goodhew came across as just an average bloke: his features a little too sharp, hair a nondescript brown, slim-built and with no discernible accent. But somehow the composite wasn't average at all. Maybe it was his personality that did it, laid-back but serious, intuitive, but unaware of his own appeal. Private enough to be intriguing.

Just as well Goodhew was apparently unaware of the frisson that had crackled through the corridors within a couple of days of his arrival. Marks thought it more likely that the detective was under the delusion that the female staff were consistently that helpful, but there were days

41

when Marks suspected that he had better results when he asked Goodhew to ask someone to do something than when he asked himself.

By contrast DC Kincaide was the peacock of the department, mentally and physically smart but surrounded by an air of fraught ambition and a whiff of insecurity. He still wasn't too warm to the new arrival. Marks liked the idea of pairing them up, figuring that it would give them both an opportunity to develop.

He turned the evidence bag over, and the toothbrush left a wet streak on the inside of the plastic. Kincaide wasn't in the market for sending anonymous tip-offs; he liked his efforts rewarded at every point.

Goodhew was less simple to assess. From Marks's point of view the contradictions he noticed were what defined Goodhew and more frustratingly left him feeling that he had grasped only a superficial understanding of him. He knew DC Kincaide had diverted his initial opinion from 'He's got a degree in maths, he must be a geek,' to 'Women like him, he must be gay.' DI Marks wasn't at all sure how to categorize his new DC, but was confident that it wouldn't be doable in a single word.

Chapter Seven

DC Gary Goodhew had been off duty for forty-five minutes, spending at least half of them walking away from the centre of town. He was slightly later than planned, but he still allowed himself time to stop halfway across the railway bridge. There was a chill in the air, but he didn't hurry. He rested his elbows on the painted steel and watched Cambridge station for several minutes. He wasn't looking for anything in particular, more like everything in general. A single-engined plane curved through the sky, turning away as it left the airport in its wake.

Somewhere below it he knew there would be an arrest soon. Marks would have the envelope by now and soon the streets scarred by the Airport Rapist could begin to heal. Goodhew drew a therapeutic lungful of air; his head had cleared and everything smelt fresher now. He started to walk again. He reached the traffic lights and had to wait for a bike to pass so he could cross the road. The cyclist was a young woman about his own age. She freewheeled for a few yards then rang her bell and called out with a spontaneous 'Hi.'

'Hi,' he smiled, and she laughed then pedalled on.

It took him another ten minutes before the Rock pub came into sight, and he heard it almost as soon as he saw it; it wasn't the sort of venue to book any band incapable of entertaining passing pedestrians. Tonight it was the Vibes plus guest saxophone player. The Vibes were four craggy guys each with more miles on the clock than Keith Richards. It was the guest saxophone player that he'd come to watch.

He pushed the outer door. It tremored with their version of 'Miser Lou', the alto sax doing the whole Dick Dale thing, and opened enough for him to fall into the hot churn of bodies, noise and alcohol partying in the same confined space.

He expected to see just two familiar faces, Mel and the woman he was planning to meet. Of course Mel was easy to find, standing centre stage like that. She was too lost in her solo to notice him but that gave him a moment where he could observe her without making her feel self-conscious. Most distinctive was her hair, bright red and back-combed into spiky tufts; maybe she intended to add the impression of robustness to her slight build, or maybe she just liked it like that. And her dress sense was tomboy meets Debbie Harry: she toned it down for work of course, but even so she was the sole touch of sparkle in the dusty admin department of Parkside police station. In one sense it was amazing they'd given her the job, except that her efficiency was just like her sax playing – pretty damned hot.

Someone called his name then and snapped him from his reverie. He recognized the voice immediately; sadly it didn't belong to the woman he was expecting to see. He began to turn towards it before he had time to consider stepping further into the pub and pretending he hadn't heard. DC

Michael Kincaide was leaning with one elbow on the bar and one foot on the rail beneath it. As usual he wore a suit, and the effect was a pose à la Catalogue Man. Which was actually how he looked most days. Kincaide shouted over the noise: 'It's my local, what's your excuse?'

'I'm meeting someone.'

'Not jailbait from admin, I hope?'

'Mel? No. I'm meeting someone else.'

'Good, cos her fella's over there, and I don't think he likes the attention she's getting. I think it's the way she blows on that instrument. No wonder he's jealous.' Kincaide looked pleased with himself.

Why he thought he deserved to impress anyone was beyond Goodhew and it took no effort to look indifferent as a reply. He scanned the pub again and this time saw her. 'And there she is,' he said, and walked over to his grandmother. She sat towards the back of the pub, in front of the raised area where the band was performing but, typically, just to the left of centre.

'I bought you a pint,' she said and took a sip from her own half of lager.

She wore black slacks and a turquoise lamb's wool sweater. With her usual style she managed to look as though she'd just returned from a day at the salon, as ever cheating her real age by at least fifteen years. Her hair had been styled in a wavy blonde bob. Goodhew had inherited her green eyes, and in turn she'd pinched her smile from Doris Day. 'Did you do it?'

He kept his voice level and his expression inanimate. 'Marks should get it tonight, I left it

45

on his desk.'

'No one saw you?'

'I don't think so. I can't be sure, I guess...'

'Who was that guy at the bar?'

'DC Kincaide.'

'Ah'

'Ah?'

'And he grates on you?'

'Just a bit.'

'You've never mentioned it.'

'He seems to have a good reputation and I don't feel I've worked with him long enough to justify feeling any differently. So I keep it to myself.'

'But I could tell.'

'You know me.'

'You're not as good at lying as you think you are. You're the wrong person to try leading a double life. You really ought to stop now, Gary.'

'We'll see,' he said and turned his attention back to the band.

His grandmother waited until the gap between numbers before she spoke. 'She's nothing like Claire.'

There was no edge to her voice, he knew that stirring trouble wasn't her way, but he just shrugged. 'I'm only here to watch Mel play.'

She touched his arm. 'That wasn't meant in a negative way, just that you don't have a type.'

'I know.' And it was a fair point, Claire was like the clichéd Scandinavian blonde, or as close as possible allowing for the fact that she was born and bred in Derbyshire.

Goodhew had met her in his first week at university and they'd found themselves bowled over by the kind of hit-you-in-the-face, all-encompassing love that exists in movies. Watching old films had been Goodhew's number one hobby through boarding school, but until he met Claire he'd assumed real life romance was never that intense. For three years they had been inseparable, inhabiting each other's lives with an intensity that never soured into claustrophobia or boredom. And ultimately reached a mutual understanding that it wasn't a relationship that would translate to their adult lives: it was more like a three-year-long holiday romance.

He couldn't imagine loving anyone more than he'd loved Claire, but the hard truth was, whatever they felt for each other wasn't enough.

She had ambitions to be an architect in London or anywhere she saw as trendy like Manchester or Newcastle; he wanted to be a detective in what she called the 'museum city of Cambridge'. OK, they could have overcome the geographical obstacles, but he guessed their post-university lives were destined to follow totally divergent trajectories. Their split was one of those rare amicable break-ups, term finished and so did they. But that didn't mean it didn't hurt.

Three years on and he thought about her infrequently now, but on those occasions she still glowed, basking in Color By Deluxe while every girl he'd met before her had long since faded into grainy black and white.

His grandmother was correct: Mel wasn't Claire, and more importantly Mel wasn't monochrome either.

Kincaide drained his glass then leant on the bar while he waited to be served again. Goodhew was still sitting with the woman, who was sixty if she was a day. It wasn't just the age difference that made them seem an odd couple; Goodhew was perpetually under-groomed while she'd clearly been high maintenance her whole life.

The barmaid handed change to the man next to him and Kincaide waved his glass in her direction. 'Foster's.'

He felt his mobile vibrating in his pocket. He had no plans to answer it but took it out anyway, just to see who was calling. His pint arrived. The caller display said 'DI Marks' which probably meant there'd be nothing stronger than coffee for the rest of the night.

Marks just wanted the two of them, Kincaide and Goodhew, back at the station and was pleased to learn that one phone call had found them both.

Kincaide walked towards Goodhew. This was great, he didn't want to be thrown together with some enthusiastic new kid anyway, but being his taxi service back to town really irritated him. No doubt the ride would be filled with inane conversation when all he really wanted to do was wind down for the night.

'Marks wants us back in,' Kincaide announced. He glanced over at the woman but she didn't appear to be listening; probably couldn't hear much over the music in any case.

'Now?'

'No, next Tuesday. Yes, right now if that's not too much trouble.'

'That's fine.'
No surprise there then.

Mel was still playing when Goodhew mouthed 'Goodbye' to her. She didn't smile back which was fair enough considering she was halfway through the Stray Cats' 'Wild Saxophone'. But it may also have been because her boyfriend Toby was two tables away and looking more taut than the top E on the guitarist's Gretsch.

Goodhew said little on the way back to town; he glanced across to the driver's side and weighed up his colleague's mood. Kincaide had never-out-of-place black hair and perfect grooming. He could do neat with less difficulty than Goodhew managed to do marginally unkempt, and for every pair of jeans Goodhew owned he guessed Kincaide had at least two suits. Kincaide's lack of humour didn't bother him, but nor did it motivate him to make any unnecessary conversation.

They were inside Parkside and heading towards Marks's office when Goodhew spoke. 'Why does Marks want us in?'

'Dunno what it's about. He doesn't seem to want to see anyone else, just us.'

'So it's going to be something either really interesting or incredibly dull.'

Kincaide shot him a sideways glance. 'What makes you say that? Have you got wind of some new development, or are you just going on that "average jobs take most people" theory?'

'B,' Goodhew fibbed. 'Anyway, I haven't been here long enough to get anything above mundane, have I?'

'We'll see.'

Goodhew paused and let Kincaide walk first through the doorway of DI Marks's office. The room never changed: an empty, undersized desk that faced the door and stood island-like with enough space to walk around it on either side, the spare chairs in a different shade of olive to the filing cabinet, the water cooler beside the window. On sunny days he could see it sparkling from his own window and it looked turquoise, the way a lagoon looks from twenty thousand feet. The room smelt of sweet lilac air freshener intermingling with the stale whiff of tobacco rising from Marks's jacket.

A dying bluebottle buzzed in the window, the latest victim of an odourless fly killer hanging on the room's only picture hook.

Today, one of the two spare chairs was heaped with documents and a cardboard crate lay half full beside it on the floor. Marks sat at his desk with a pile of other papers on his lap, his head bowed. Something he spotted made him tut and shake his head.

Goodhew and Kincaide waited, and after a few seconds Goodhew began to wish they'd announced their arrival, so he cleared his throat. 'We're here, sir.'

'My deduction skills aren't quite that poor yet, Gary. Sit!' he instructed.

Goodhew wondered whether his boss had ever trained as a dog handler. Probably not a good time to ask. A half-smile reached his lips but he pushed it away.

Marks put the papers on his desk, looked up at

Goodhew then nodded at the free chair. 'I said sit down.'

Kincaide had already taken the chair to the side of the desk so Goodhew settled into the second one, which was directly facing the inspector.

'How many weeks has this rape investigation been running?' Marks looked irritated. Kincaide glanced at Goodhew but neither of them spoke. Just as well, as it turned out to be a rhetorical question. 'Eleven weeks tomorrow.' He patted the pile of papers he'd moved to the desk. 'Do you know what this paperwork is?'

Kincaide looked blank and Goodhew did his best to follow suit.

'The case notes for the rape investigation. Our last major investigation.' He emphasized the word 'last' and spotted Kincaide stiffen. 'Yes, that's right, two rapes near Cambridge airport and this evening we've brought a suspect in for questioning.' He took a breath and his expression settled back to its usual beady-eyed mask, the one that read much and revealed little. The very expression that caused discomfort around the station.

'You're familiar with the case, I take it?' As they'd both been working full-time on it they were definitely facing another rhetorical question. 'I thought we all were, and yet tonight I received another anonymous tip-off. The envelope was hand-delivered to my desk. Yep, this desk, and it contained a letter and a toothbrush. This guy was so accurate last time that I have every confidence that the DNA from that brush will match the rapist's DNA, so we've brought the suspect in. He's an Ian

Knott by the way.' He glanced from one to the other as if hoping for a glimmer of recognition. 'I'm about to suggest to him that he might like to allow a swab to be taken just to eliminate him.'

'He'll say no,' Kincaide pointed out.

Goodhew spoke. 'Not necessarily.' They both looked at him. 'Tell him that there's no DNA from the victims so far, but that we may be lucky if there's another attack. He'll know that refusing will look suspicious and may decide to risk that you're telling the truth. We know he knows how to be careful, he may even think he's not going to do it again – they often do, don't they?'

Marks didn't reply, but studied the top report on the pile.

Goodhew and Kincaide waited for him to speak. 'Michael,' he said finally, 'I'd like you to accompany me while I question Mr Knott. You go down and make sure the interview room's ready and that we have all the kit.'

'Kit?'

'Like chairs for starters,' Marks muttered drily. 'Just use your initiative and I'll be with you in a few minutes.'

If Kincaide was surprised to be ushered out so abruptly he didn't show it. Just before he closed the door he heard Marks announce that Goodhew had drawn the short straw. So it was as Goodhew had predicted, Kincaide had bagged 'the something really interesting' and Goodhew was about to receive 'the something incredibly dull'.

Marks watched Kincaide leave then spent the next few seconds scratching his ear.

'When's my birthday, Gary?'

The question seemed odd but he answered without hesitation. 'July 14th, sir.'

'You're very open about your ability to do that.'

'Do what? Remember dates?'

'Find things out. What is it, a talent or an obsession, or something else?'

Goodhew shrugged. 'I didn't know it was anything in particular, I suppose I just have a retentive memory.'

'Bollocks,' Marks grunted, but without any real sign of anger in his voice.

Silence.

Each stared at the other with a kind of respectful curiosity. Marks strummed the desk and looked like he was trying to read Goodhew's thoughts.

He took a breath and addressed his junior. 'If I were speaking to the person making these tip-offs the first thing I'd want to know is where they get their information and secondly why they can't come to me directly. Perhaps they break the law to retrieve the evidence – if I condoned that, not only would it be inadmissible but they could lose their job over this.'

'If they had a job,' Goodhew pointed out.

'Why am I asking you all of this?' Marks's eyes shone. Unfortunately Goodhew couldn't decide whether he was looking at a gleam of anger or a glint of encouragement.

'No idea,' he replied evenly.

'Because I have a sneaking feeling that you're taking the piss, Goodhew. That's why.'

Goodhew raised an eyebrow. 'Not at all, sir.'

Marks rapped the desk several times with a sharp tap-tap-tap of his index finger, using the sound like a gavel to ensure he had Goodhew's attention.

Which he did.

'These two tip-offs have both occurred in the three months since you arrived.'

Goodhew's eyes widened. 'I had no idea. But I suppose new people start work here all the time, it was bound to coincide with someone new. Just circumstantial evidence then, I guess. Sir.'

'Don't be smart. It is just as well that circumstantial is all I have. I'm going over the files to see what we missed and find out why someone with either a talent or an obsession for uncovering information managed to home in on that obscure group of people called "recently divorced sociopathic wife beaters who can only get a hard-on when they have sex under the flight path of jets taking off from a commercial airfield". I can see how obvious it is now it is pointed out to me. To think the rest of us thought we were clever scrutinizing simple things like sex offenders, plane spotters and disgruntled ex-airport staff.'

Goodhew looked at his boss with concern. 'I sense this is frustrating you, sir.'

The phone rang and Marks mouthed, 'Piss off, Gary,' as he lifted the receiver to his ear. His voice kept its usual unemotional tone and he spoke for about thirty seconds.

He replaced the handset. 'Well, in this particular case I don't care too much how we caught him, assuming we've got the right guy, I'm just relieved we did before it happened again. I'm not saying the means always justifies the end but in this case it's a job well done. Now back to that short straw I mentioned. One of the victims states that the last person she spoke to before she was attacked was a man who sleeps rough who she thinks is called Ratty. He usually hangs round the shops in the daytime. Mean anything to you?'

Goodhew nodded. 'And you want a statement from him?'

'Just a confirmation of time and place if he can. But he's made himself scarce and I'm guessing you'd love to spend some time hunting for him.'

'You can't tell me we're relying on his statement.'

'Absolutely correct, we're not. Just call it belt and braces. And don't moan, I'm sure you'll turn it into something interesting. It's late, I suggest you start first thing in the morning. In fact, just so there's no ambiguity, I'm demanding that you leave it until then, and right now, go home.' Marks stood and Goodhew followed suit. 'And the next time there's a major investigation I would like to think we can at least attempt to solve it faster than an anonymous envelope, eh?'

'Let's hope so,' Goodhew agreed cheerfully as he followed Marks from the room and down the stairs.

Marks waited until they were on the half landing to stop and turn to face Goodhew. The move was abrupt; Goodhew almost piled into his superior and would have apologized had Marks not cut in first.

'No, Gary, it's more than hope so. I don't want it to ever happen again, and if it does I will root out the person responsible and see that they're thrown on the scrapheap – no matter how promising their career seems to be.' And it didn't take an expert to identify the diamond hardness in the inspector's eyes.

Goodhew really didn't believe that Marks knew anything whatsoever about the anonymous letters, but he was curious as to why and how his boss had made such an accurate stab in the dark. Perhaps he would ask him sometime. But then again, perhaps not. Some things were best left well alone, especially if, as his grandmother suspected, he didn't have the makings of a liar.

Chapter Eight

Lorna loved the feeling of midnight, one day complete and the clocks restarting at zero for the next. Twenty-five minutes had passed since Cambridge had travelled through her magic moment: even so she still felt the buzz of opportunity that came with a fresh day.

They'd arranged to meet on the Victoria Avenue bridge, which in itself was unusual, but Lorna chose to take it as a sign that her enthusiasm for night-time walks had finally sounded tempting enough to test. And it was a good evening for it; so still, patches of fog staining the air, hanging between the bridge and the tree-lined paths into the heart of the city. The moon glowed just enough, like its dimmer switch had been turned to minimum. The city was hushed.

Lorna leant on the balustrade and tried to see her reflection in the water below, but the balustrade was too wide so instead she contented herself with a gaze at the rippling reflection of white walls and blue gables on a boathouse further downstream. Her freckled skin looked creamy against the grey stone of the bridge, and behind her the streetlamps dropped pools of light on railings and verges. She held the pose and listened. She guessed that she was already being watched, that two keen eyes were studying her through the mistiness.

Within minutes she heard approaching footsteps. They stopped beside her and she only turned her head when she felt another arm slide alongside her own.

'Why here?' she said.

'I liked the idea.'

'You're strange sometimes.'

'A bit chilly, I guess. Goosebumps yet? Let me feel.' Lorna gave a bemused smile as the hand rubbed up and down the back of her arm. 'No, you're very warm. Shame, because I brought drinks.' For the first time Lorna noticed the two insulated beakers on the top of the wall. 'Coffee?'

She removed the lid and blew into the cup before sipping. 'It's Irish coffee.'

'Is it all right?'

'Absolutely.' It must have been poured a while earlier because it had cooled to the point where it was easy to drink. She drank a third of it immediately before being conscious of being watched. 'I like a good swallow,' she whispered, then giggled.

Her remark went without comment. She pretended to be apologetic even though a suppressed smile twitched at the corners of her mouth. 'You don't approve of my double entendres, do you?' she asked.

'I think they're more a habit than a cleverness. Or perhaps it's your way of showing me you're outgoing; say something daring and I'll think you're confident. Is that it?'

Lorna refused to rise to the dig, and instead just snorted. 'Impressing you isn't something I've ever felt I needed to do. Perhaps I'm trying to bring you out of your shell. Has that ever occurred to you?' Then she reminded herself that she hadn't come out for an evening of even gentle bickering. 'Come on, let's walk.'

They strolled towards the city, with the common on their left and the road on their right. The two figures became synchronized again. Through habit they both noticed the same things at the same time: a taxi in the distance driving from left to right, three students cycling from right to left, the echo of a bell chiming a late half past to the sleeping of Cambridge.

They were halfway to the next junction before there was any response to Lorna's comment. 'No, I don't think you could bring me out of my shell actually.'

'I thought we'd finished with that conversation.'

'I don't think sex is ever far from your mind, is it?'

'You don't let things drop, do you?' Lorna looked huffy 'Nothing wrong with a strong libido, is there?' she asked and then cheered when she saw that she was being smirked at. 'You're funny.'

'First strange, now funny?'

Lorna sucked on her drink and shrugged.

The railings that kept them from drifting on to the common ran like a black-painted railroad track, away from them, curving left on to Maid's Causeway taking them to their destination. Lorna's fingers followed the route, skimming along the horizontal poles and rising and falling at each Victorian dome-topped post.

'Do you know what I want to know?'

'What it's like to have no inhibitions?' Lorna answered.

'Interesting, but no.' Her companion stopped walking. Lorna guessed that they would soon arrive at the real point of the conversation. 'I want to know exactly what you know about David.'

They were quite alone, but Lorna whispered anyway. The little nods and sounds of encouragement she received spurred her into more detail than she had planned. Earlier in the day hearing David's name like that might have startled her, but not now. Now she repeated it with familiarity, as though he'd always been part of their conversations. Her words only dried when she realized she was no longer being listened to. 'And that's it,' she concluded.

'I see.' It was said in a way that told Lorna that that part of the conversation was over. Her companion leant on the railings and Lorna did the same, aware that things between them had become subdued. They both gazed back the way they'd come, towards the far end of the common. There was nothing visible bar the faint glow of the boathouses and restaurants on the other side of the Cam. Nothing discernible. They were alone together and close enough for their elbows to touch. 'Finish your drink and I'll show you something.'

Lorna finished the dregs of her coffee then took the pen that was being held out to her. 'So what am I supposed to do with this?'

The marshy land between them and the river lay motionless, as though it held its breath.

'I want you to write "I'm like Emma" on each palm.'

'I'm like Emma?' Lorna's eyebrows twitched upwards. It seemed like nonsense but she guessed it wouldn't hurt to play along.

'Yes, go on. It's clever, I promise.'

Lorna wrote in Biro on her left palm, the blue ink looking black under the thick light from the sulphurous street-lamp. She used capitals and the letters stretched across, from the heel of her hand to half an inch short of her middle finger.

'Like that?' She held out her hand.

'That's it. Now the same on the other one.'

Lorna gave a short nervous laugh. 'These things always catch me out, even when you get to the punchline you'll have to explain it.' In truth she hated looking stupid and didn't want to take part at all. But the atmosphere between them was curiously fragile; it made more sense to go along with it and avoid anything nastier. She wrote slowly on the other palm in jerky lower case. 'This isn't so good, it looks like a four-year-old's written it.' She forced a grin.

'No, that's fine.'

'Now what?'

They were facing on to Midsummer Common with their backs to the non-existent 1 a.m. traffic.

'I love it here when it's quiet, and once the weather's warmer that's only at night. And in the summer it's never quiet – the fair's here, then the circus and all those hippies camping out.'

'So what about this writing?'

'Hold on.'

Lorna squirmed like a child. 'Can we go?'

'No, please, let's stay here for a minute or two.'

Lorna looked at the ground on the other side of the railings. 'We're standing right next to a load of rubbish sacks. And I'm getting cold.' She sounded sulky.

'I said you'd get goosebumps, didn't I?'

'Clever you.' Lorna sniffed. 'And when are you going to explain this?' She waved her hand, palm upwards. 'Why are you smiling? Have I missed something funny?'

'I guess so.'

Lorna reran her last sentence in her head: she'd slurred and for some reason 'have-I-missed' had coalesced into a single word. She straightened and turned her back to the railings. She gazed in the direction of the Four Lamps roundabout and tried to work out what felt wrong. It couldn't be just cold, fog and tiredness that were making her suddenly disorientated. She wanted to go home but her feet wouldn't move.

Instead of walking away she stood in the same spot, a look of mild bewilderment dawning on her face. 'I feel ill,' she muttered, but her companion never replied. She wanted to repeat herself but was overtaken by the feeling that her brain couldn't connect with her mouth.

She felt giddy and needed to steady herself.

Her left hand moved, it rose from her side and drifted back towards the top rail. And like the slow topple of a felled redwood, the rest of her followed, staggering back, the railing all that stopped her from hitting the ground.

It was then that she had a moment of clarity, an instant where she knew how and why she'd been drugged and the enormity of her fatal miscalculation. She tried to reach out, to beg for her life. She managed to gasp 'I'm sorry' just as two hands flew forward and with a single push to the sternum sent her toppling over the railings and on to the pile of rubbish.

She landed on her back in a crumpled heap, almost parallel to the footpath, with her head nearest the ground and her hair trailing in the mud. The other figure squatted and they stared at each other from either side of the bottom rung. Lorna heard the words hissed at her: 'Do you know why?'

She knew but she couldn't reply. She attempted to nod but her head wobbled through an uncontrolled arc and her arms and legs twitched with a life of their own. She tried to stay conscious, guessing she'd been overdosed and hoping that she would be found before it killed her. She just needed to be left for dead to stand a chance.

But no one was going anywhere. Lorna watched as first a carrier bag, then a length of string were brought out of a pocket. A little more consciousness returned; her eyes widened and her breath came like the little huff children use to steam up windows. A hand reached through the railings and pulled the plastic bag on to the top of Lorna's head, like a swimming cap.

Lorna's heart was beating so loudly that she barely heard the words spoken to her, the words that were intended to add to her suffering. Then the bag was pulled over her face and she felt the string being knotted at her throat.

Inside her head she was screaming out. *Oh God help me.* She breathed in and the bag sucked into her mouth, then out as she exhaled. *I'm sorry.* On her second breath she knew the air was already used. Her chest rose and fell, burning with the effort. *Please no more.* Her heart beat louder. *Please please.* Then it stopped.

Chapter Nine

Goodhew woke at twenty-five past five and hoped that the early bird really would catch the worm; he had no desire to spend more time than necessary trailing around the back streets and squats of Cambridge hunting for the elusive Ratty.

He was pissed off with Marks and too familiar with Ratty's activities to believe that the mission he'd been sent on was any more useful than being sent to stores for the clerk's long stand.

Ratty was about five-five in height and somewhere between twenty-five and forty. Goodhew guessed nearer twenty-five despite the pock-marked skin, receding hair and sunken eyes that argued older. Ratty had once boasted that he'd been on the stage as a child and attempted to prove the point by belting out the first lines of 'Unchained Melody'. He wasn't bad but his liquorice stump remnants of teeth hadn't done him any favours; in the end he'd been cautioned for disturbing the peace.

From time to time he vanished, and on the first few occasions his acquaintances had assumed he lay rotting somewhere after a fix too far. But he'd always reappear and, assuming the role of an oracle for the city's nightlife, he would proclaim to have witnessed virtually every major event that appeared on the station's radar. Often his information was accurate, but Goodhew guessed that Ratty was no more than a top class eavesdropper, sucking up drunken gossip the way some of his cronies hoarded newspapers or carrier bags.

OK, so in this case it was the victim who had identified someone resembling Ratty, but with the DNA match and the victim's statement Ratty, if found and if cooperative, would still be pretty redundant.

Goodhew's face tingled with cold. Clear spring nights sucked the warmth from the flat open streets and left early morning Cambridge encased in a frosty shell. He wiggled his nose, trying to restore the circulation, hoping it would stop running. It didn't, so he dabbed at it with the only square of clean tissue he could find in his jacket pocket.

The 6 a.m. sun stretched over the rooftops and touched the second storeys of the locked shops and cafés. At ground level it wasn't dawn and he walked down the grey slab passageway of Bradwell's Court towards the coach station, the master bedroom for the city's down and outs.

He kept to the centre of the pedestrian walkway, equidistant from the doorways on either side. Only the newsagent at the far end would have any official activity this early, all other signs of life came from the homeless.

No one occupied the blankets heaped at the entrance to East Anglia Pet Supplies on his left. But on his right a blue nylon sleeping bag in the portico of the discount book store stirred and groaned. The black and tan terrier curled beside it scratched, turned, then resettled against its master's stomach. Even with the occupant's head buried under the covers Goodhew knew it wasn't Ratty. Too tall for a start. The man and his dog were the only ones camped out in Bradwell's Court.

Goodhew came out the other side; the bus bays were empty apart from the end space where the first London coach of the day waited for non-existent passengers. Its engine idled.

Logically Goodhew should have turned right, past the first bus, and walked a circuit back to the shopping centre via the smaller edge-of-town stores. He glanced out, past the coach station and over Christ's Piece where tree-lined paths crossed the common land and late daffodils sprouted. The sun had melted the frost and the grass stood bright and dewy in the light.

It was a more appealing prospect than poking at cardboard boxes behind office outbuildings.

He could check for sleepers on the park benches. He never understood how anyone survived outside when the warmth evaporated from the Fens and he expected each curled body to have died in the night, frozen to its draughty slatted bed.

From where he stood each bench appeared unoccupied and he decided to check the public toilets before walking further.

They were an old red-brick square block with individual cubicles along each side and had been recently refurbished with a range of gadgets including cisterns that automatically flushed upon the opening of the doors, and soap and water dispensers that squirted and sprayed without any actual physical contact. It would only take a few more advances in technology and bums wouldn't even be touching seats.

Goodhew checked the doors one by one and found that none were occupied, obviously too compact for even the dispossessed. It was as he turned the final corner that he found Ratty.

Ratty stood tilted back with his shoulder blades against the wall. He was smoking a roll-up, holding it between finger and thumb as it sat in the centre of the tunnel made by his other curled-over fingers. Goodhew felt that Ratty was waiting for him, perhaps resigned to being tracked down and choosing to get it over with.

Even when Goodhew spoke Ratty continued to stare vacantly across Christ's Piece and Goodhew quickly deduced that he hadn't emerged from the cooperative side of the sleeping bag. 'Did you know I was looking for you, Rat?'

Ratty spoke slowly, his voice rasping like bone against bone. 'Course I did.'

Yeah, of course, thought Goodhew. 'OK,' he said, then paused, waiting for Ratty to turn his head to look at him. He didn't. 'We have a witness who saw you.'

Ratty blew out a thin plume of smoke. 'Oh yeah, doing what?'

'Nothing, you were out near the airfield. My guess is heading for that lake off Coldhams Lane, and she walked past. A few minutes later she was assaulted. Did you hear about it?'

This time Ratty looked at Goodhew. 'We've all heard about the Airport Rapist.'

'Did you see a man following her?'

Ratty shook his head.

'That's not an answer, Rat.'

'Why not?'

'Because you have your code. When you mean no you say no – shaking your head is avoiding the question.'

Ratty shook his head again. 'You think you're smart, don't you. Well, you are too. Lucky-fucking-you, that's all I say. I'll tell you about it, Gary.' He had emphasized the 'Gary' and stopped speaking, which word-wise was more economical than saying 'I know stuff you don't know.' Goodhew waited, almost hypnotized by the macabre spectre trying to stare him out.

Despite Ratty's stillness his eyes were dark and hollow. He was less than he'd been the last time they'd met; he'd always been a shell, but now the walls were thinner. Sooner or later the drugs took their toll and Goodhew could see that Ratty now viewed the real world from the other end of an ever-extending tunnel.

Ratty ground the half-inch butt of his cigarette between his fingertips until it flaked to the ground. 'I'm not talking to you. I'm nothing, and when things go bad that's the best thing to be.' He fanned out his nicotined fingers. 'Trouble is like poison. You go near it and you're infected.'

'That's deep.'

'What, coming from someone like me who's never been out of it?'

'That's not what I meant.'

'Well, there's trouble and there's trouble. I have it, but only my own. And I know all about other people's, but there's a line.' He turned his face away and scraped his thumbnail down the wall by his shoulder. 'Can't see it, can you? But it's there, trust me. On one side is me, and what's mine, and over there is other people's shit. What I don't do is anything that takes me over there. I can see what's going on, but I don't visit if you get my drift.'

'You don't get involved?'

'People get possessive about trouble, they only want help on their own terms. And if they don't want it fixed, getting in the middle of it is dangerous, even if it looks safe. That's another problem – it can seem like nothing, but then–' he walked his fingers from his side of the line to the other, then rubbed his hand across the wall in a small circle – 'the line's gone and you're fucked.'

Ratty pushed himself away from the wall, swinging his body round until he faced Goodhew squarely. 'So I look but I don't touch. I don't let it seep over me.'

He didn't seem high, he emanated nothing but stale tobacco and paranoia. 'Touch it and it stains you, Gary. Remember that.'

Getting Ratty to make a statement was not

something to look forward to. Goodhew wondered if he could persuade Marks to drop the idea; this was unlikely to be the witness to swing a court case in any direction it wasn't already headed. He sighed but Ratty didn't seem to notice.

What path had the young version of Ratty stumbled down to end up in such a bleak cul-de-sac? Goodhew stared away and the first person he saw was a distant cyclist, standing out of the saddle and pedalling furiously towards him. He saw a flash of orange swing from behind his back and realized it was the paper boy from the bus station. He was short. He'd noticed him on other mornings, struggling with his sack and unable to reach the seat of his adult bike. Had that been Ratty once, striving to get somewhere?

Ratty was still talking but Goodhew ceased to listen.

The boy's sack swung wildly as his shoulders swayed from left to right in an effort to move faster still. He was about a hundred yards away and his face burnt red from under his mop of blond hair. His mouth was moving. Shouting, or just gulping air?

Goodhew made a single instinctive step in the cyclist's direction, hairs rose on the back of his neck, he knew something was wrong.

At fifty yards he heard the breathy squawk of the boy's voice. All the words, but one, mangled to nothing in the gap between them. 'Quick!' he heard.

At twenty yards the boy was clear. 'There's a body.'

He lurched to a halt next to Goodhew, wobbled

as his foot reached for the pavement. Goodhew grabbed his arm as he toppled from his bike and held the boy upright until he'd disentangled his other foot from the frame. It clattered to the ground and lay with the back wheel spinning in the sunshine.

Sweat pinned a veil of hair flat on his forehead, while the rest bounced up at all angles. He waved his hand back in the direction he'd come. He held Goodhew's jacket with the other hand as he fought to catch his breath. 'You're police, aren't you? Up there,' he gasped. 'Up there, on Midsummer Common.'

'Whereabouts?'

'This end.'

'Hang on.' Goodhew spun round to see Ratty retreating back towards the city centre. 'I need a statement,' he called after him.

Ratty turned and walked backwards for several steps. 'I don't know anything,' he shouted.

Goodhew turned his attention back to the boy, whose right arm was still partly raised in the act of pointing. Most obvious were his trembling hands; beyond that he didn't look too bad. Goodhew peered into his face: not quite ready to pass out, he decided. 'Can you show me?' he asked gently.

The boy shut his eyes for a moment then nodded. 'I touched her,' he whispered.

Goodhew righted the bike and they walked with it between them. 'Don't worry, we'll get it sorted out.'

He radioed in to the station.

'They're sending a car, want us to meet them there.'

70

'I heard.'

Goodhew nodded. 'Sorry, of course you did. What's your name?'

'Matt. Matt Lilley. I do the papers on Maids Causeway.'

They walked quickly towards the end of Christ's Piece, where the aptly named Short Street would take them to Maids Causeway and the southern boundary of Midsummer Common. Goodhew's stomach gave an uneasy churn. 'Tell me what happened.'

'It's bin day, isn't it? And there're sacks outside most of the houses. I'd done the houses near the traffic lights and saw there was rubbish over on the other side of the road, beyond the railings. You know, on the grass. I didn't think anything at the time, it was after when I remembered they were there. So I did the houses on that side then I went back to the lights to cross over and do the houses down Brunswick, you know, the ones that face the Common.' Goodhew noticed Matt's left hand on the saddle of his bike: the fingers gripped the narrow front and a smear of sweat from his palm stained the brown leather liquorice black. 'I don't usually cross there but one of the houses had an extra paper and I'd missed it so I went back and crossed at the lights 'cos that's, you know, where I ended up. There weren't any cars, I just rode across and so I was looking straight on, right where the rubbish was. That's when I wondered which house it came from. It was a big pile of sacks, and it wasn't really light by then, but I saw her straight away.'

They both knew the terrace on their right was

71

the last obstruction to their view of Midsummer Common. Goodhew turned to look at Matt. For the first time he saw tears well in the boy's eyes, and horror sweep his face as he fought the indignity of crying.

Goodhew touched his hand on the lad's shoulder. 'How old are you, Matt?'

The boy's voice trembled. 'Thirteen, and I've never seen a dead person.'

The corner of the building loomed and the first glimpse of the black metal railings surrounding Midsummer Common slid into view.

'How did you know she was dead?'

'I touched her hand. It felt cold, waxy. Not like a person.'

'Did you recognize her?' Goodhew asked quietly.

Mall shook his head and whispered, 'No, her head's in a bag.'

Chapter Ten

As he turned the corner Goodhew had no need to ask Matt to point out the body; it was rubbish day after all and a bright blue dustcart stood with its wheels on the pavement and orange warning light blinking from the roof. Three dustmen, two men and a woman, stood in a huddle at the spot Matt had described. A fourth had returned to the cab of their lorry and Goodhew could see his free arm waving as he shouted into his radio.

'I'm from Cambridge CID. Don't touch anything,' he shouted and hurried forward, but Matt slowed. 'Can I go?' he asked. Fear filled his eyes and he looked more like a ten-year-old than a teenager.

'Not yet.' Goodhew pressed the flat of his hand between Matt's shoulder blades and kept him walking. 'You won't need to see the body again. But I do need your help. Is that OK?' He gave an encouraging smile and Matt nodded.

The fourth dustman dropped from the cab and joined the others. Goodhew and Matt stopped a few feet short of the group and he beckoned the dust-woman over.

'This is Matt. He found the body and he's a bit upset. Can you stay here with him until another patrol arrives in a few minutes?'

'Do the maternal bit?' The woman scowled and straightened her reflective waistcoat.

Goodhew shrugged. 'I just think women are more versatile.'

He guessed he'd just taken the sexist approach and dustmen were probably now known as waste management operatives, especially since one of them was female.

He sighed and approached the corpse. Sirens wailed in the distance.

Strictly speaking the dead body wasn't quite on the ground; she lay heaped on top of a bed of at least a dozen black plastic rubbish sacks piled on the other side of the railings. Two more had been dumped on top of her, covering her torso.

Some of the sacks were split with their innards strewn on the grass. A bloodied meat wrapper lay beside the pile, pilfered by a fox or cat during the night and now directly beneath her outstretched hand.

Her head was furthest from Goodhew, and in a bag, just as Matt had said; but Goodhew was relieved to find it still attached to the rest of the body. The bag was a black carrier, tied at the neck with a length of ribbon-width black cotton. Goodhew leant over the top railing to get as close as he could without stepping on the grass. He could see that someone had poked a hole in it with their fingers. Air had entered through the fluted opening, lifting it away from the dead girl's face.

He held the railing with one hand and gently touched the plastic with the other, expelling the air. The bag sank back against the woman's face. Vein-chased swollen eyes stared out. The lips were blue, drawn back to expose creamy teeth and her tongue still pressed hard against the prominent gap between the middle two.

Goodhew suddenly thought of the stuffed fox in his local pub, bulgy-eyed and grinning. He caught the odour of the meat wrapper; its slick of dried blood releasing the sweet smell of decay.

He averted his gaze and it fell on to the woman's palm. He read the words 'I'm like Emma', or perhaps it was 'I like Emma'. Either way it was odd. And it definitely looked like 'I'm', not just 'I'.

The sirens were closer now, and he wondered who was on the way.

DI Marks, he hoped.

Two cars came into sight. He saw that there were two people inside the first and two further officers in the marked car which followed. Both sirens trailed off as the lead police car swung across the road and parked beside the dustcart. Goodhew waited until the engine died before looking again.

DI Marks stepped on to the pavement. The dustmen moved aside to let him through. His companion was Kincaide who paused to lock up, then followed.

Goodhew greeted them.

'Morning, Gary,' Marks grunted.

Too-cool-for-school Kincaide managed a nod.

Marks said nothing further, but their silent communication must have included a line where Kincaide said, 'I'll talk to the boy,' because he changed direction and walked over to Matt.

Goodhew turned back to face the body and DI Marks stood at his shoulder, studying the corpse for a long silent minute. 'She didn't die in her sleep, that's for sure. Who made the hole in the bag?'

'One of the dustmen.' Goodhew pointed to the driver of the dustcart, back in his cab smoking a roll-up. 'Him. He said he wanted to be sure she was dead, but I think it was a case of morbid curiosity or daring in front of his colleagues because rigor mortis was well under way when I touched her hand.'

Marks nodded. 'What else?'

'The kid over there found her. His name's Matt Lilley, says he's thirteen, but I bet he's about ten.' He watched as Kincaide relieved the dust-woman of her charge and took the boy to sit in the relative calm of the patrol car. 'He's quite shaken, but he seems like a good kid. And at least he worked out she was dead without opening the bag.'

Goodhew hadn't meant to sound sarcastic, that

75

was just how it came out. He smiled, Marks didn't. 'What else?' Marks repeated.

Goodhew turned back to look at the body. 'Her hand has something written on it. From here it looks like "I'm like Emma". I couldn't check the other palm without moving her. She's dressed all in black, that could mean something.'

'Like witchcraft?' Marks asked drily.

'No,' Goodhew snorted. 'Like camouflage amongst all these black sacks.'

Marks smiled a little. 'Good point. Right.' He called across to one of the uniformed officers. 'We need the area sealed off immediately and that includes all footpaths on to the common. This will be a nightmare, especially as rush-hour will be kicking off any time now.' He turned back to Goodhew. 'And you can have the pleasure of viewing the post-mortem.'

Goodhew wasn't sure whether looking pleased and saying 'Thanks' was entirely the appropriate response so he followed Marks back to his car without any comment.

Chapter Eleven

Goodhew drove DI Marks to Addenbrooke's Hospital. He already had questions to ask, but Marks was occupied with making notes on the murder scene. Goodhew had made his before they left and he knew that the post-mortem would take them from a passing acquaintance with the deceased to a most intimate relationship.

He took the most direct route and was surprised when Marks glanced up and directed him down the next right-hand turn. 'Then pull over in the lay-by this side of the lights.'

The car stopped outside the Big Teas Café and Marks had opened his door even before Goodhew had a chance to cut the engine. 'Come on,' he said, 'there'll be at least half an hour before the pathologist is ready for us.'

The café was deserted, but as soon as the door rattled a skinny guy with grey hair and a grease-splattered apron emerged from the kitchen. Goodhew ordered a mug of tea and a bacon sandwich and sat at a table near the door. Marks ordered the same and joined him.

'Let's see if you're still good at keeping your dinner down.'

'Breakfast actually, sir. Any idea who the corpse might be?'

'Female, twenties, that's all I know too. What about the lad who found her?'

'Poor kid, he's really shocked. Kincaide arranged for someone to pick up his mum so he's got company while he makes his statement. He's only ten, he shouldn't even have a paper round, but he lied to get the job. He was worried his boss would be in trouble. But apart from lying about his age he gave clear descriptions of the route he took, and the times too. Hopefully they'll still stack up when it's all written down. I thought Kincaide would view the autopsy.'

'Instead of you?'

'Well yes, but I'm not complaining.'

'Well then, get over it.' Marks suddenly changed tack. 'What did you notice about the scene?'

Despite having seen the body close up, Goodhew began by describing its location in relation to the road. 'Assuming this doesn't turn out to be a bizarre suicide then I'd also think this is a premeditated attack.'

'Why?' Marks asked sharply.

'The attacker was in possession of both a heavy duty carrier bag and something to tie it with.'

Marks tutted and opened his mouth to speak, but Goodhew continued to explain. 'I know, sir. On their own they don't mean much. But it occurred to me that there are plenty of more secluded locations where the body could have been left and there she was, right by the footpath where the first passer-by was highly likely to find her. And that was likely to be at dawn or just after. Headlights would have had trouble picking her out.'

Marks was frowning. 'I still don't...' he began.

Goodhew raised a hand and carried on talking. 'She would have been hard to spot before dawn, she was in the open, but well hidden wearing black amongst those black sacks.'

'I spotted that.'

'Well, I checked, and all the nearby houses had sacks outside so I asked the dustmen whether the spot where the body was found was a typical place for bags to accumulate. They said that it was the first time it had ever happened. Which makes me think someone put them there ready for her.'

Marks's eyes were closed and his head made a

78

small rocking motion, back and forth in a slow rhythm.

Goodhew kept quiet; interrupting the inspector was never a good idea.

Finally Marks raised his eyebrows, which had the effect of heaving his eyelids open. He drew a long slow breath through his narrow nostrils. 'Assuming it is murder – and, for the record, I think it is – I will want you on the team. I'd be pleased for you to take more of a role than you have in previous cases because I think you're ready but–' he paused to pick his words – 'I'd like you to work closely with someone, just so you're not exposed if you find yourself in unfamiliar territory. I hope you get on with Michael?'

'Fine,' Goodhew fibbed and told himself it would be.

'Well, I'd like to pair you with him, but I'll have a word first. Even if he likes you he's probably feeling a little put out because you're here and he's not. But then I would rather he was sick of me than sick in the autopsy.'

Marks checked his watch, stood, drained his mug and clunked it back down on the table. 'He'll be at the station with Matt. Did a lovely job of gathering statements from our rapist's employer. By the way, did you find Ratty?'

'Yes.'

'And?'

'Says he knows nothing.'

'And you got that in a statement?'

'No, I was sidetracked with this. Do you really think it's still necessary?'

'Absolutely. Is there a problem?'

'No, it's fine,' Goodhew fibbed again.

Within five minutes they crossed from the edge of leafy pre-war suburbia to the sprawling sixties development of Addenbrooke's Hospital. Goodhew took the perimeter road around the campus. Two parking bays were reserved for pathology and both stood empty.

'Pull in. We'll wait here until Sykes shows up, there's no point in hanging around inside.' Marks unclipped his seat-belt and shifted round in his seat so his head rested against the window.

Sometimes Goodhew wished he could have five minutes inside his boss's head. But then, on second thoughts, it might be like Ratty had said, healthier to stay on your own side of the line. And therefore leave Marks on his.

Chapter Twelve

The laboratory reminded Goodhew of a show-piece commercial kitchen. Stainless steel appliances hummed, keeping the meat chilled and the cutlery sterilized. The sinks gleamed and the work surfaces were perforated with holes that allowed water and juices to drain from the carcasses. Implements including knives, scalpels and a small tenon saw, sorted by type then size, waited for use.

The room was almost square with a single door over to one corner. It had a window too but only in a partition wall between it and a small viewing gallery. Lighting, bright and white, blazed down from flush panels in the ceiling; plenty of people got more attention when they were dead than they ever did in life, although Goodhew was sure this didn't apply to this particular corpse. Even in the aftermath of her squalid death she held on to neatness. Strands of hair still held the shape of their last cut and not one of her short nails was chipped or broken.

Goodhew felt like a kid on the first day of a new term; the surroundings were familiar but his senses were heightened. He knew his way around but he'd forgotten the detail, the dry air, disinfectant that never quite covered up the rusty smell of blood, and the toe-tag on the body that was always filled in with black ink from a fountain pen.

The girl hadn't been beautiful, but not ugly in any way either. She had a roundish face and features that were in proportion but unremarkable. Her hair was slightly longer than a bob and layered, anything more feminine might not have suited her. She was boyish rather than womanly and that applied to her body too; her breasts were small and her hips narrow, and the overall effect was more like parallel lines than an hourglass, but attractive nevertheless.

She'd taken care of herself too. Her complexion had been flawless, and all over her body her skin appeared blemish-free – even on her feet it was smooth and unchafed. Her legs and underarms were hairless with no sign of regrowth and her bikini line had been waxed to leave just a half-inch strip of pubic hair.

Sykes's first job had been to remove the victim's

81

clothes and personal effects. And the ripped black plastic bag that had ended up looking like a grotesque balaclava.

She lay on their table, naked with blue marbled skin stretched over the stiff tissue. The only colour was in her lower legs where the flesh had turned deep purplish-red. Later Sykes would open her up and the trapped blood would leak, like a side of beef on a butcher's block.

Goodhew pushed the food analogy from his mind. Luckily nothing about Anthony Sykes reminded him of a chef. The pathologist was no more than five foot six, aged around forty, slim and probably lighter than most teenage girls of that height; he didn't look capable of manoeuvring large carcasses of any kind. In reality he was remarkably skilful at lifting and turning the lifeless corpse.

Two anglepoise-style brackets hung down from the ceiling. On one a camcorder was mounted and on the other a rectangular lamp which would act as a floodlight for illuminating Sykes's close-up work.

When he spoke it was slowly and clearly for the benefit of the recording, but in a tone which didn't alter when he addressed Marks or Goodhew.

'Body 8926. Unidentified female.' He wheeled a side trolley into shot. On it was a collection of clear plastic bags, each one sealed and labelled. He took them one by one and held them up to the camera. 'Already removed and bagged are: item 8926-01 black leather left shoe, size four, item 8926-02 black leather right shoe, size four, item 8926-03 black skirt, item 8926-04 black bra, item 8926-05 black T-shirt, item 8926-06 black roll-neck woollen sweater, item 8926-07 hallmarked gold ring, item 8926-08 gold earring set with small white stone removed from left ear and item 8926-09 matching earring removed from the right ear. Each of these items was found on the body. These were the only items discovered at the scene—'

'No knickers?' interrupted Marks.

'These were the only items discovered at the scene, but in isolation this does not indicate sexual assault.'

Sykes pushed the trolley to one side and turned to the body.

'Body 8926. Unidentified female, early to mid-twenties, Caucasian. Height 156 centimetres, weight 112 pounds. External examination of the body...' Sykes paused to position himself at her ankles.

Goodhew wondered why Sykes always started at the feet, especially when, in this case at least, the more interesting information was obviously at the other end.

Sykes inspected the soles, then spread the toes, checking the skin between. He pointed to the dark colouring of the feet and ankles. 'That's not bruising.'

'It's post-mortem lividity,' Goodhew replied.

'Sorry, I forget who knows what.' He took samples from under each of the toenails. 'The feet are both of normal development and they show no visible signs of injury.'

And so Sykes continued, inch by inch up towards her armpits, then down her arm to her fingers where he again took samples from under her nails.

He pointed to a small bruise in the middle of her upper left arm. 'The contusion appears to be recent and while it is only small there is a similar mark on the other arm, possibly consistent with an assailant gripping her and leaving thumbprints.' He lifted each arm and examined it. 'On both arms there are a number of smaller contusions to the rear of the limb. These are, in my opinion, bruises made by fingertip pressure. The distance between the thumb and fingers and the clarity of the marks suggest a person with largish hands and a strong grip. There are no signs of other soft tissue damage to the arms or hands.'

'No defence wounds?' Goodhew queried.

'Exactly,' Sykes replied.

Marks was also keen to get down to the key detail. 'What about her head and neck?'

'Yes, well, I'm coming to that next.' Sykes pulled the inspection light in closer and scrutinized the puckered skin around the throat. 'Already bagged are items 8926-10 and 8926-11, a black carrier bag and a length of black bias binding.' He felt up and down her windpipe, pressing gently with his finger and thumb. 'The marks around the neck could imply strangulation, but with the majority of manual strangulations the use of excessive force causes damage in the larynx area. At first examination neither the thyroid cartilage nor the hyoid bone feels damaged and a more likely use of the bias binding seems to be to secure the bag and cause asphyxiation.'

Marks interrupted. 'Is the ribbon significant?'

'You mean rather than use rope or tights, for example? It's bias binding, used in needlework I believe, so not what most people would have about their person. Of course we don't know that this wasn't the victim's own. As you know, many sexual murders involve strangulation, but this stuff isn't intrinsically strong ... well, who knows? Let's just say that on face value it doesn't tell us much. What is more interesting of course is the fact that, whether strangled or suffocated, the victim did not appear to struggle, so...'

Marks finished the sentence for him: '...she may have known her attacker.'

'Or been drugged,' Goodhew added.

'Or just been unconscious,' Sykes finished. He paused for a few seconds, making sure the attention reverted to the corpse. He took a series of swabs from her mouth and nose, ears and eyes. 'Suffocation,' he muttered, almost to himself. He plucked a few hairs from her head, identifying each by its location on her scalp.

Without asking for assistance he rolled the corpse over on to its belly. It was a deft move that left her symmetrically arranged. Her mouth was partially open and Goodhew had to remind himself that nothing would be dribbling out past her swollen lips, even her tongue would now be powder dry.

'Time to find out about her private life,' Sykes said in a matter-of-fact voice. He flicked a switch on the inspection light and a second bulb lit up.

'What's that for?' Goodhew asked.

'It's a Wood's lamp, fluorescent, used to identify the presence of semen,' Sykes replied before producing a fresh clutch of cotton buds and swabbing the entrance to her anus. Then he reached to his array of sterilized equipment, selected a speculum and obtained internal swabs. 'You haven't seen one before then?'

Goodhew shook his head.

Sykes rolled her on to her back again. 'More likely to pick up something around the vagina.' He parted her legs and swung the light lower, inspecting her labia and clitoris. 'Bingo. Likely presence of semen.' He switched back to the normal light and reverted to studying her skin, working his way up the inside of her legs. 'A few minor contusions on each inner thigh, some recent, some less so.'

He took more swabs and examined the vagina and perineal skin for injuries. With a small metal comb from his instrument tray he combed through her pubic hair and collected the loose ones, then plucked several further hairs for comparison.

Goodhew's gaze wandered back to the instrument tray. The scalpels, saws and drill were lined up on the cold stainless steel. Their turn had almost come.

He knew what was coming next, and knew it didn't bother him. Or it never had in the past. He saw it as an evidence collection process, a key tool for helping the victim and the victim's relatives.

On the scale of things Goodhew had attended few postmortems, only in training and, like now, for the experience. He had never seen a body dissected that had been so close to his own age. Perhaps she had been one of the girls lounging on Parker's Piece just a few days earlier. He looked at the corpse and looked away again, then stared at the clock, concentrating on the second hand slowly stepping around the dial and waiting for his detachment to return.

Then he heard Marks speaking to him. 'Gary?'

'Sir?'

'I said, any questions before we go for the internal?'

'Sorry. No.'

'Everything all right?'

'Fine.'

Marks nodded to Sykes. 'Let's get on with it then.'

Sykes picked up a scalpel. Goodhew always found the first cut the hardest to watch and so pinned his attention on the soft skin near the girl's right shoulder. He needed to know whether he could handle it. His stomach tightened with apprehension.

With firm pressure Sykes made the blade break the skin and drew it across the top of the chest, dipping in the middle to make the cut form a low wide V, like the neckline of a ball gown. The skin parted like silently ripping silk.

He made a second incision, slitting her from the base of the V straight down to her pubic bone.

He reached back to his instrument tray; his next job was to cut through ribs and cartilage and remove the heart and lungs.

Blood began making a metallic plink, plink, plink as drops hit the stainless steel drip trays.

The first waves of smell reached Goodhew's nostrils and the food analogy wafted back with an uninvited suggestion of uncooked pork casserole. Soon Sykes would be cutting deeper and unleashing the thick invasive odour of flesh, faeces and stomach contents; it really wasn't the time to think about dinner.

After a few seconds of thinking about nothing Goodhew relaxed again; the scene wasn't repulsing him. He felt the same as he always had: they needed to know who she was and the cause and time of death, and he was in just the right place to gather information.

Chapter Thirteen

From the corner of his eye Goodhew caught sight of their reflections in the viewing gallery window. He was in the centre and flanked by DI Marks and Anthony Sykes. Twice Goodhew glanced up, expecting to see three other people, instead of the three reflections staring in at the body. After an hour he sensed someone really was watching and looked up to find Kincaide peering in from the other side of the glass.

Kincaide mouthed something and pointed at Marks.

Goodhew touched his superior's arm. 'Sir, Kincaide's here.'

'Better see what he wants.'

Sykes looked up too. 'There's an intercom button next to the window. Turn it on and we'll be able to hear him.'

Goodhew clicked the plastic on-off switch and

slid the volume control up to halfway. He guessed this had been modern technology somewhere back in the eighties.

Kincaide cleared his throat and his short cough came out as a tinny crackle from the single speaker mounted above the booth. 'Your phone's off so I decided to come in and find you. We think her name may be Lorna Spence.'

It was funny how a name made a difference. All four of them turned their attention to the corpse's face: it was an automatic reaction to hearing her name. Lorna Spence. Oval face. Wide mouth. Freckled skin. Hazel eyes. Feathered hair.

It was a bit like dot-to-dot, the name joined them up. It was the missing feature, the thing they'd needed to complete the picture.

'How do you know?' Marks asked.

'Lucky teeth.' Kincaide half smiled and Goodhew guessed he was enjoying his moment of keeping everyone hanging in an expectant pause.

'Lucky what?' Marks asked. 'Teeth?'

Kincaide tapped his own. 'A space between your front teeth is supposed to be lucky, sir. I expect kids are told that to stop them picking on the gappy ones.' He knew just how many seconds Marks would tolerate the suspense and waited until the inspector drew an irritated breath. 'The station had a call from a consultant at the Excelsior Clinic on Magdalene Street. One of their staff, Lorna Spence, is missing from work. She's twenty-three, five foot two with short highlighted hair and a gap between her teeth. The station couldn't get hold of you, so they contacted me because I'd seen the body. I thought it sounded likely so I came straight over.'

'Have you found an address for her?'

'21 Rolfe Street. It's in the centre about five minutes' walk from the Excelsior.'

'Yes, yes, I know where it is.' Marks turned to Sykes. 'We're almost done?'

'Another half-hour at most.'

Then he turned to Goodhew. 'Change your clothes and go with Kincaide to the Excelsior.' He gave a quick nod in the direction of the body. 'If it still looks likely that she's this Lorna Spence call me and I'll get someone over to the girl's house as soon as possible. See if you can find out who knows her, and if anyone lives with her. Don't forget the present tense, it may be the wrong woman.'

Goodhew discarded his gown in the first laundry bin he found. He found Kincaide waiting for him in the corridor leading to the main hospital exit. 'Do you know this Excelsior Clinic?' he asked.

'Only by reputation,' Kincaide muttered. 'It does cosmetic work. It was set up by several specialists and does eye surgery and dental work along with the usual.'

'The usual?'

'You know, boob jobs, nose jobs, tattoo removal. Skin treatments that stretch away wrinkles and shot-blast faces to keep fifty-somethings looking like forty-somethings because forty-somethings are busy trying to look like thirty-year-old Barbies.'

'You don't approve then?'

Kincaide flashed a lopsided smile and it was accompanied by a short snort. 'I'm sure it's the sort of shit that Janice would rather spend money on than use to pay the bills. But there you go. Just not my scene.'

It took about twenty minutes to reach Magdalene Street. They parked in a small car park belonging to the Excelsior Clinic; it had eight staff spaces and eight more for visitors. Four of the staff slots had eight-by-three plaques with two lines of dark blue letters on a light grey background. The top line said 'Reserved For' and the second line gave the name. Goodhew took a quick look at each; R. Moran, A. Moran, D. Shan and P. Norgren. Two Mercedes, one green, one silver, a new 'S' type Jag and a Saab convertible. 'These must be the consultants. Which one rang it in?'

'Guy called Richard Moran.'

Dark green Mercedes saloon. This year's model. 'In person?'

'Seems so. That's what I heard anyway. I don't know how long she's been missing.'

A paved footpath led from the car park through a narrow walkway between two buildings. They stepped from the alley into Magdalene Street.

Goodhew knew the road well: it ran from Magdalene College where leaning Tudor cottages hung over the congested road down a shallow slope to the pedestrianized city centre, finishing at Magdalene Bridge with a knot of pavement cafés.

They stood at the heart of the coffee shops and restaurants.

A stiff breeze threatened rain. It rustled napkins and lifted menus but the tables were full; couples composing postcards, lunchtime meetings of diaries and Danish, and coffee drinkers alone with thick books and slow thirsts. They slipped between the tables and found the entrance to the Excelsior Clinic.

They buzzed the intercom and heard the door being released. Inside, the walls, ceiling and light fittings were plain white. Kincaide was about to press the lift call button but Goodhew took to the stairs and he reluctantly followed.

'It's a bit clinical,' Kincaide quipped.

The landing door opened into a foyer where the all-white theme continued. It was toned down with a beige sofa and an oak floor complete with matching coffee table and reception desk. Apart from being female, the receptionist was about as far removed from a stereotype of the role as Goodhew could imagine. Her fringeless hair – a lack-lustre brown – had been dragged back and pinned at the nape of her neck. Her make-up stopped at her temples leaving her exposed forehead bare of everything except the two deep frown lines which dug permanent tramlines between her eyebrows. Not a good advertisement for cosmetic surgery.

And worse still, she didn't smile. But perhaps that was just because they were police.

Goodhew spoke. 'We're here to see Mr Moran.'

She pushed back her chair and stood. 'He's with a client. I'll let him know you're here but I expect he'll be about ten minutes if that's all right.' She lifted the hinged end of her counter and waved them round. 'Alice Moran is in the office, that will be the best place for you to wait.'

She missed the words 'out of sight' from the

end of the sentence, but they both got her drift. She slid back the opaque panel which separated her area from the room behind. 'Alice, it's the police,' she said by way of an announcement.

Goodhew and Kincaide entered the main office and heard the door slide shut behind them. The office was small with two desks, one heaped with papers, the other bare. Another door on the opposite side of the room stood ajar with an electric fan positioned near it, presumably with the aim of dragging fresh air in from the corridor even though the temperature was already low.

'Alice' sat at the untidy desk adding a list of figures with a desk calculator which whirred and churned out tally roll each time she hit the + key. Adding figures was clearly her forte as the spewing list stretched to three feet and looked to be growing at several inches per minute. Her gaze flashed up to them then back to her list. 'One minute, please.'

It was an instruction, not a request.

She looked in her early or at most mid-thirties. She wore a white man's shirt folded back to the elbows and chocolate brown trousers; her hair was short and her footwear sturdy and by rights she should have resembled a male manual worker but in reality the effect was wholly feminine.

A tiny amethyst pendant hung on a fine gold chain and sparkled in the hollow of skin exposed by the unbuttoned neck of the shirt. It was her only item of jewellery.

She was a woman whose appearance implied great understatement; she knew she could let her bone structure do the hard work for her. High cheekbones and a delicate jawline gave her a face that would turn from above average to striking as the years progressed. She sat upright making the most of being five foot eight.

The calculator gave an extra judder as she finished adding. She copied the final figure from the display then put her pen to one side. 'Sorry to keep you, I was right at the end.' She stood and shook hands with both of them. 'I'm Alice Moran, Richard's sister. I work here part time. Thanks for coming.'

Kincaide spoke. 'I'm DC Kincaide, and this is DC Goodhew. We understand your brother is concerned about one of the staff. Lorna Spence?'

Alice nodded. 'It's probably nothing, but we can't get hold of her.' She screwed up her nose and looked apologetic. 'Richard panics,' she added.

A year planner was pinned to the wall above the coffee station. Goodhew wandered over to inspect it. 'How long has she been missing?' he asked.

'She didn't turn up this morning. Or phone in.'

'One day?' spluttered Kincaide 'You mean she was in yesterday? That's not missing, it's throwing a sickie.'

Goodhew continued to read the holiday chart.

'I told you,' Alice sighed, 'Richard panics.'

'I am not panicking, I'm concerned,' snapped a man's voice. They all looked towards the open door and it was obvious that the voice belonged to Alice's brother. Richard Moran was a taut and angular man, his bone structure like his sister's but with less flesh to cover it. He was clean cut and clean shaven. He had her skin colour and the same dark hair. He dressed in chinos and an open-necked linen shirt and they looked close enough in age that they could have been twins.

He closed the door behind him and stabbed the on-off switch to kill the fan. 'Why do we need this bloody thing in here, Alice? We're running the air-conditioning and you make the place like an ice house.' He held a pen in his hand and twiddled it between his fingers, and although he was in effect standing still he shifted his weight from foot to foot with an agitated rocking motion.

Kincaide suggested he sat just as Goodhew opened his mouth to do the same. Instead of taking the spare chair Richard perched awkwardly on the edge of Alice's desk.

Kincaide spoke in an even, unhurried voice. 'Lorna was due at work this morning. At what time?'

'Between eight thirty and nine.'

'Why were you so concerned that you called her in as a missing person at eleven? She was less than three hours late.'

'I ... um...' His voice was tight with nerves. He coughed to clear his throat and started again. 'When I couldn't get hold of her on the phone I popped round to her flat. Then I heard you'd found a woman's body. I don't have any reason to think it's her. I suppose Alice is right, I am panicking. But the radio said she was all in black. Lorna wears black.'

'So do lots of women,' Goodhew pointed out. 'Do you have a photograph?'

Richard nodded. 'In my wallet, hang on.'

But Alice was already flicking through a small sheaf of papers that she'd taken from her handbag. 'I've got one here.'

She slid a colour six-by-four print across the desk; Goodhew picked it up and held it between himself and Kincaide. Three people leaning across a restaurant table for the benefit of the camera: Richard, Alice and this morning's corpse. 'I'm very sorry. This appears to be the woman we found today.'

There was a moment of nothingness, no reaction from either of them. It was just a second but it seemed to last longer.

Then Alice gasped and her hand shot up to her mouth to suppress the sound. Richard gave a grunt, like the air had been thumped from him, and he pressed his face into both his hands, as if suddenly desperate for privacy.

His shoulders rose and fell as he drew heavy breaths.

Kincaide looked at Goodhew, raising his hand in a 'wait' signal. Goodhew nodded and they waited.

Chapter Fourteen

The rest of the day passed slowly. It seemed like a huge contradiction; one person had killed, another had been killed, and yet there was no fast track past the everyday snags. No one filled out forms any faster, or made walking quicker, and the pavements never grew shorter. So while each point of the investigation was important the lines that joined the dots were the same old, same old.

Goodhew had accompanied Richard Moran to the morgue. Alice had waited with her brother, and from time to time took his hand. Richard stayed composed but Goodhew could see that there was a greater restraint in Alice. It didn't mean she was less concerned of course, in fact he guessed the difference between them had taken many years, possible a lifetime, to forge.

When Richard reached out for his sister's hand it seemed to be an automatic movement, a reflex. And just as his facial muscles seemed used to running through a gamut of expressions from doubt to fear, so hers ranged only from expressionless to a look designed to tell him to hold it in.

Clearly she wasn't the heart on the sleeve type.

And the silence had been heavy. Without any doubt they all knew that the identification would be positive and the certainty of it meant that Lorna Spence's flat was already being searched. But talking about it as a fait accompli seemed like wishing her dead. Even though she was.

Goodhew turned his thoughts to Lorna's flat. Kincaide would be there already, methodically working his way through her things.

Goodhew wished he could be in both places at once. He wanted the chance to absorb the feel of her before her death fully settled in a dusty layer. It often struck him that the last breaths of a life stayed in the home long after they'd left the body. And although in his conscious mind he knew it was illogical to assign human attributes to buildings and inanimate objects, his subconscious had never quite been able to let go of the idea that some places waited for a familiar footstep or scent or routine and that the last remnants of the person were only lost when the feeling of abandonment set in.

So he wondered what Kincaide was uncovering, but he also knew that he wanted to be present when Richard and Alice looked down at Lorna's face and made the leap from being told she was dead to actually absorbing the fact. He knew it was the moment when spontaneous emotional responses often illuminated the deceased and their nearest and dearest better than bright lights and an inquisition.

Eventually they were called in to view the body and afterwards Goodhew wondered what he'd really learnt. Alice stood further away as if three extra feet of floor space would be enough to leave her removed. Her spine was iron-bar straight and her arms were crossed Morticia-style. The only change the peeled-back sheet produced was the subtle movement of Alice's right thumb which flexed until it was pinching the soft flesh of her upper arm.

She fixed her stare somewhere beyond the sheet covering Lorna, and resolutely refused to make eye contact with either of the men.

Richard was different. At first he seemed unable to stand still and kept rubbing his palms against his thighs, but when he nodded that he was ready for the sheet to be lifted he drew one deep breath then managed to stop fidgeting.

His eyes bulged as if the conflict between not wanting to look and having a duty to was threatening to make them explode. He swallowed but didn't look away from her when he spoke. 'It doesn't look like Lorna,' he said.

Goodhew looked at Lorna too. 'But it is?'

'I can touch her, can't I? It is all right?'

'Of course.'

Richard ran two fingertips across the top of her cheek as if wiping away a tear.

'We had plans.'

'What kind of plans?'

Richard didn't answer, but instead turned to face his sister. 'We had plans, Alice.'

'I know,' she whispered. He reached out to her and she wrapped him in a tight embrace. 'I'm so sorry,' she murmured.

And the whole time Goodhew never saw her look anywhere apart from the blank wall on the opposite side of the room. He didn't ask about the plans, later would do.

Goodhew hadn't waited for another instruction, he'd just cleared off to Lorna's flat. He walked; the late afternoon traffic was already thickening and driving would save no time. But more than that he wanted to lose himself in Cambridge for a few minutes, to snatch a breath of fresh air and remind himself how the city outside the laboratory really smelt. He aimed to step into her flat with a clear set of senses and a chance of snatching a last metaphorical glimpse of her.

The sun was out and he realized that it was the first time since seeing Lorna's body on Midsummer Common that he'd been aware of anything unconnected with her. He would reach her flat with a brisk ten-minute walk along the edge of the pedestrianized shopping streets. He passed the

Cambridge Evening News kiosk on the corner of Sidney Street and Petty Cury; the hoarding announced 'Latest on Midsummer Common Murder'. People walked with the late edition under their arms or protruding from their bags. Soon her name would be announced and shortly after that the city would be on first-name terms with her.

A few minutes later he turned from the busy shops in Bridge Street down Rolfe Place and towards Rolfe Street. No one followed and ahead of him the pavements were empty. He could see two marked cars parked in the middle of an atypically empty row of parking spaces. A lone uniformed officer stood in a doorway. Goodhew knew that every activity would be watched from one house or another but he was glad that her home hadn't descended into a general gawping ground.

It was the type of street where the terraces had originally been functional and unglamorous but now existed in a new incarnation as desirable and fashionable city living. Few had not been 'modernized', the term which currently implied adding period features alongside state of the art gadgetry.

Lorna's flat appeared to have once been the living accommodation over a shop. The shop looked like it had ceased trading somewhere back in the 1970s when aluminium window frames and stone cladding or pebble dashing were still modernization options that left neighbours on speaking terms. OK, so the conversion from shop to ground floor flat had escaped the onslaught on the brickwork but the metal replacement windows and brown-glossed windowsills were a dead give-away and now it stood empty with a faded 'For Sale' board in the window. By contrast Lorna's front door was solid wood, and not one of those pseudo-traditional knock-offs but the real McCoy two-inch-thick type made half an inch thicker by a century of paint, and still with the original stained glass panel set in the top.

He was now close enough to recognize that the constable standing in the doorway was Kelly Wilkes. She smiled, stepping forward and to one side as he came within a few feet of her.

'Who's here?' he asked.

'Just a couple of forensics guys and Kincaide.'

'He's the only one?'

'Uh-huh. DI Marks was here but left Kincaide and DC Charles to finish off, then about twenty minutes ago Charles said he was off too. I think they've pretty much finished.'

'That's fast,' he commented as he stepped through the door. 'Must be a small flat.'

The hall had a floor tiled with the familiar year-dot uniform of dark red tiles, black and white diamonds and a few in cobalt blue for contrast. Four pairs of shoes had been bagged and left at the bottom of the stairs. Beneath the protective plastic laid down by the forensics team the stairs were carpeted. He climbed the centre of the flight, avoiding touching either wall. Above him the landing was partially open, banisters blocked in behind hardboard panels but still low enough for someone to look over to find out who was approaching. No one did. A single unlit bulb decorated with hand-painted swirls hung from an overhead light fitting, and if that counted as an artistic touch it was the only one. The top step was square and housed a small dark wood table. Goodhew's attention settled on it for a moment before being diverted by the sound of Kincaide's voice. But he had looked just long enough to see that the post was nothing more than a few advertising brochures.

Kincaide was close to the top of the stairs. 'That was on the mat when we arrived. At least we know she left before the post came.'

Goodhew looked past him into the flat: the curtains were drawn shut and the lights were on. 'How's it going?'

Kincaide shrugged. 'Just about wrapping it up. There's not much left to do.'

The living room was a reasonable size, and furnished with a few well-chosen items, mainly in pine. Both the chest of drawers and the bookcase looked like they'd been bought from local antique dealers, and the soft furnishings from a shop which specialized in neither cheap nor cheerful. Somehow he knew they weren't Lorna's own. By contrast the television, mirror and frame containing dried flowers had all arrived on a much more modest budget and were pack-up-and-go convenient. One remote control, two pens and a box of tissues were the most clutter she'd left. Perhaps she'd been hooked on those sell your home shows which preach depersonalizing the living space – anyhow, it wasn't hard to see why the search hadn't taken long.

Kincaide had moved on and Goodhew found him adding Lorna's bedding to the inventory of items being removed.

'I guess she rented?'

'Guess so,' Kincaide grunted. 'Haven't got that far yet. But who can afford to buy in the centre?' He glanced up, raised an eyebrow and added pointedly, 'Don't even know who can afford to rent in town, you'd have to be lucky enough to have it in the family.'

Goodhew ignored the dig. 'Nice bed.' It was a king-size with an asymmetric headboard made from wrought-iron gothic scrolls. Nice wasn't the right word, more like quirky with a touch of the Gaudi-esque about it.

'You serious?' Kincaide looked from Goodhew to the bed and back again, clearly unsure whether he was being had.

'Absolutely.'

'Really? I think it looks tacky, like a shitty art college project.' Kincaide couldn't wipe the distaste from his face, in fact he made no attempt to. 'It looks dodgy to me. Pervy in fact. And hideous.'

Kincaide wandered off again but Goodhew stayed behind, following the curves of the metal and trying to see it the way Kincaide had. He found himself pulling that same face but still didn't understand what there was not to like.

He walked over to the window and lifted the curtain, then dropped it again. He ran his fingers along the top curve of the bedhead then crossed the room, opening and closing the wardrobe. There was nothing left, no essence of Lorna's presence left to disturb.

Kincaide was in the kitchen, leaning on the worktop and sending a text with some fast and ambidextrous thumb activity. 'Hang on,' he grunted.

Goodhew flipped open an overhead cupboard: he'd found the crockery. Apart from two mugs the contents were all from a standard issue everything-proof rental set. The taller mug was cream with the word 'Chocolate' curling across it, the other was brightly painted with the name 'Lorna'. Not very revealing. He let the door snap shut.

Kincaide glanced up. 'I've done the cupboards.'

Goodhew took the hint and left the next one alone. 'What about that calendar?'

'Oh, yeah. Nothing much on it but it can go with the other paperwork. There's a box I've just moved to the top of the stairs.'

The calendar was the type with one square per day but no picture; it had come courtesy of Staples Office Supplies. The current month had only one entry, 'Hair – 12.00' on the 16th. If that was a good example of a month 'nothing much' really would be an accurate description. Goodhew unhooked it from the wall and turned forward the pages from the back. When it came to calendars people were either flip and keep or rip and bin. And he was pleased to see that Lorna had been with him on this one.

'Oh boy,' he sighed. Either her life was depressingly uneventful or she recorded her more interesting activities elsewhere.

He had turned back to the start of the year before any entry caught his attention: 9th January – 'Bryn to MOT car'. Goodhew read it just as Kincaide dropped his mobile back into his pocket.

'Seen something?'

Goodhew frowned. 'Don't know. Did she have a car?'

Kincaide took the calendar, 'I saw that too and checked at the Excelsior but they say no, she sold it apparently.'

Goodhew followed Kincaide and watched him drop the calendar into the document crate. And later, as he walked towards home, he reminded himself that there could be numerous people called Bryn in the area. More than just the Bryn O'Brien who'd sat nearest the paint cupboard in primary school. He was the class practical joker whom Gary couldn't even remember speaking to but had secretly admired. Bryn made light of education, never buckling under the weight of expectation, doing just enough to get by.

When Gary's mother had switched him to a private school at the end of Year 6 he'd found himself reeling from the shock of going from the top of his state school class to mediocre among his new peers. And for the first couple of years he gave Bryn credit for helping him through. Mentally he'd kept Bryn with him, imagining how Bryn would navigate the narrow ledge that was bottom of the class.

But the real Bryn was someone he knew next to nothing about. And the chances were it was a different Bryn, except that as he'd read the calendar his memory had conjured up a single item of O'Brien family trivia: Bryn's father had been a mechanic. And when he factored that in he knew that the odds narrowed dramatically.

The decision he made as he walked home was a simple one: he would track down Bryn O'Brien. With any luck he'd also be meeting someone on first-name terms with Lorna.

Chapter Fifteen

Goodhew walked across Parker's Piece towards home, a one-bedroomed rooftop flat in Park Terrace. The building had once been a four-storey townhouse, but since the nineties the basement and first three floors had been divided into office space and the only remaining living accommodation was Goodhew's. He glanced up to his window then walked down the short path and unlocked the heavy street door. It closed behind him with a solid and purposeful click: the sound that always reminded him he had the place to himself.

He took the stairs two at a time and on the final landing opened a second door, which led into his flat. He paused. Despite instincts telling him that nothing had been disturbed he let his eyes make their routine three-second sweep of the room. He began at the far end checking for three things, undisturbed bookshelves, his bedroom door still closed, and his beloved Bel Ami jukebox unplugged and unharmed. All OK. Finally he made sure that his pile of papers still lay on top of the closed case of his laptop. He concluded that nothing had moved, which gave him his cue to unwind one more turn.

He frowned, he found his own habit of double-checking annoying and acknowledged that it wasn't far from bordering on compulsive. But hell, everyone had their foibles and it wasn't like he wasted much time on it.

He changed into jeans and a shirt, poured a glass of orange juice and set his jukebox on free-play. The mechanism clicked and whirred before making its selection and dropping the single on to the deck. The arm swooped, giving the stylus a bumpy landing on the run-in strip. The 45 crackled then broke into the opening bars of Chuck Berry's 'School Days'.

How apt.

Gary slid his Sony notebook from one of the bottom bookshelves, pressed the power button and, as he waited for it to boot up, flipped open the Yellow Pages and scooted towards 'Car Repairs'. He had expected he'd need search engines for electoral rolls and credit checks and possibly even a visit to Friends Reunited but the notebook was never in the running – by the time it had loaded Windows, Gary had already drawn a blue Biro box around the name 'O'Brien and Sons'.

He checked his watch. Ten past seven.

He rang the number. No reply. No surprise there then.

But it was within walking distance, across Parker's Piece and then a few streets further on, behind the swimming pool. His curiosity had been stirred and he decided to go in any case. He waited for Chuck Berry to finish then pulled the plug from the wall and left his flat again.

Gary saw Parker's Piece as the no man's land between two distinctly different parts of the city. He lived on the historic side, the tourist trap brimming with distinctive buildings and enough magnetism to draw people from, literally, all over the world. The other side was certainly poorer and less distinctive, with a criss-cross of Any Town back-streets and a surfeit of struggling and vacant businesses. Personally he had no preference for either, knowing that, like backstage and front of house, neither could have functioned without the other.

He had no idea what to expect from a visit to a locked workshop, probably nothing more than a sign saying 'Closed' and another giving out the phone number that he'd already tried. He walked on anyway.

Bryn O'Brien had heard the phone ringing; in fact it was impossible to miss the sound of the extension which made an outside bell jangle in the eaves of the garage. But he made no move to answer it.

He was sitting within reach of it too. And knew without looking that the handset was on the bench, less than two feet from his left shoulder. Only one thing lay between it and him; a face-down copy of the *Cambridge Evening News*.

He stayed where he was, sunk into the improvised beaten vinyl settee that had once been the bench seat of a '62 low-line Ford Consul. He still wore his maroon overalls, and his steel-toed boots were planted squarely on the concrete floor. He had short blond hair and blue eyes, made brighter by the smudges of grease that he'd pushed on to his face during the day. One hand rested on each knee, and the first two knuckles of the right were grazed, pink circles left by a sudden departure of skin.

In front of him his current project was elevated

108

to full height on the ramps. It was another Mark II Ford, but this time a Zodiac, the fully equipped and subtly modified version of its deceased cousin. Bryn stared up at its underside. He'd replaced the 2.5 litre straight six with a rebuild V6 and the twin exhausts each branched into two, their four chrome tailpipes protruding from beneath the bumper. The car was a clean black underneath, with low profile tyres on Wolfrace wheels, wider than the originals had been.

He knew he'd created a retro-custom of an even more retro car. There had even been a phase when he'd been tempted to trade it for a PT Cruiser. But then he realized that could suck him into a scene full of all too earnest enthusiasts so he'd decided to stick with the little beast he'd created and he'd been glad. Especially at moments like these. He slid down in the seat and tilted his head back, still watching his car through part-closed eyes. It had the same effect as unwinding in the bath; his thoughts floated at their own speed, taking their own routes and pulling others along with them. He wasn't a deep thinker and he never had been. More than that, he was conscious of a distrust of contemplation and where it might lead. He wanted to release two particular thoughts, he hated the way they now seemed to be linked and kept coming back, hand in hand, to bother him.

He gazed up to his car and almost let go. If a face hadn't appeared in the small window of the workshop's concertina door he might have succeeded.

But probably not...

Gary found O'Brien's straight away. It was one of those places that he'd never noticed but equally knew he'd seen countless times before. It was brick-built with navy blue steel doors and an apex roof covered in something which looked suspiciously like corrugated asbestos. There was no 'Closed' sign, just a name and telephone number and a second board at one corner which read 'No Smoking'. Underneath there was a collection of stubbed-out cigarette ends; he wasn't sure whether that was a good sign or a bad one.

The workshop had its windows on the side walls near to the roof, only the six-by-nine Perspex pane in the door was within reach. He cupped his hands and tried to look inside. Sunlight and scratches had left it cloudy, and he knew that wiping it would make no difference, but he tried anyway.

Ever the optimist.

He stayed with his face close to the aperture for longer the second time and shapes began to pick themselves out. Weak daylight made it through the windows. He could see the roof of a white van, and a second car up on a ramp. In one of the lighter patches a year planner, and then, further across, the familiar red crate shape of a Snap-On tool kit.

Then he thought he saw movement; illogically he pulled back slightly. When he looked again a figure was approaching the door. He stepped to one side and waited.

Gary knew as soon as the door clanked open that he'd found his former classmate. It was a funny thing – if he'd been asked to describe Bryn before seeing him he may well have said, 'I can't remember.' In truth he had a vague recollection of fair hair, a slight build and perpetually scuffed shoes – hardly the stuff of positive IDs. But confronted with the man himself a whole barrel load of details flooded back, the eyebrows that always looked slightly raised, the single piercing in the right lobe – now unoccupied, the head tilted, in interest or defiance depending on interpretation, and the serious set of the mouth which accompanied it.

The slight build had been replaced by broad shoulders, but the boots he wore were still scuffed and he still had the habit of either pushing his hands into his pockets or leaning against something whenever he spoke. Today it was pockets. The teachers used to have a field day pulling him up on that each time they were busy pulling him up on something else – which had been often.

'We're closed.'

'I know.' He took a moment. Despite convincing himself that the odds of finding the right Bryn were good, he'd only visualized meeting the wrong one; now he knew he was about to hear something completely unplanned coming out of his mouth. He decided to steer clear of Lorna Spence. 'I went to school with you,' he began. How inane did that sound? 'At Chesterton Primary.'

'Congratulations.' Bryn raised one eyebrow very slightly but didn't smile.

Gary had recognized Bryn partly because he knew who he was looking for. Bryn, on the other hand, clearly didn't have a clue.

'I'm Gary Goodhew, you probably don't remember...' He left his words to trail off.

111

Bryn shrugged. 'Remember the name. What's up?'

Gary nodded towards the workshop. 'I need to ask you something, but not out here.'

'I'm just leaving.'

'Five minutes.'

Gary saw Bryn hesitate: he looked back into the workshop, then slid the door closed. 'Five minutes,' Gary repeated.

Bryn gave in. 'I've got time for a quick drink. The Salisbury's just round the corner.'

They walked in silence for the first hundred yards. Gary wondered how he should approach the subject; Lorna may have just used Bryn to repair her car, and if so, so what? But they'd been on first-name terms and Gary was well aware that anything he now found out should form part of a statement, not a chat over a pint.

Bryn spoke first. 'By the way, I'm not up for a school reunion. Not my thing.' He spoke in an easy way, the way Gary remembered, as though the answer didn't matter, except his eyes flickered as they watched for the reply and it was clear to Gary that the answer was very important.

Gary deflected the question. 'Maybe you need to hit thirty before you get nostalgic.'

The Salisbury was on the other side of the road. Bryn darted across in front of a car, leaving Gary a few yards behind. He figured there was no urge to hurry and reached the bar just as Bryn was being given change for his pint of lager. Gary ordered a Stella and followed Bryn to the table he'd selected at the far end of the bar.

The pub was traditional, not just styled to look

112

that way. The beams and old floors had really aged with the building rather than arriving as prefabricated panels. Bryn sat on a long bench, his back to the end wall. Gary chose a square chair that looked like it belonged in a dining room. The table had been converted from a treadle sewing machine and the word 'Singer' was curled into the metal footplate.

'Ever see anyone from school?' he began.

Bryn shook his head. 'I remember you though.'

'Really?'

'Yeah, I thought your sister was cute. Then you left and we were told you'd both got scholarships to some private school.'

Gary smiled, funny how rumours turned the truth into something else. Funny too how Bryn remembered his sister. 'Debbie probably was cute,' he conceded, 'but I think she was ten at the time.' They both paused to drink. 'I'm with the police now,' he added with no change of tone.

'Ah.' It was said with neither surprise nor alarm, but just as a matter of fact. 'I see.'

'Do you know a Lorna Spence?' he said quietly.

'A little, I think.'

'You think?'

Bryn rubbed imaginary sweat from his forehead with the flat of his right hand, further smudging the greasy streaks that already marked his skin up into his hairline. Gary noted the raw patches on Bryn's knuckles and wondered what he'd hit. Bryn thought for a few seconds then answered Gary's question with one of his own. 'Do you mean "do I know her", or do you mean "did I know her"?'

113

'What makes you think she's dead?'

Bryn dropped his hand on to the tabletop, covering a Guinnness beer mat with his palm then spreading his fingers out like he was trying to come up with five reasons. He had two. 'You lot found a woman's body this morning, right?'

Gary just nodded.

'It's been on the radio all day. Then you start to search a flat in Rolfe Street. Know how many flats I know down there?'

Gary didn't know but *he* hadn't noticed many, that was for sure. 'It's mostly houses down there, isn't it?'

'Maybe there's more, but I can only picture two flats, Lorna's and the empty one underneath. So when you turn up asking if I know her what else am I going to think?'

'Can you tell me when you last saw her?' Gary asked, wondering whether there was a record number of times for answering a question with a question.

'Am I making a statement or is this a "chat"?'

Gary decided to level with him, and with no question at the end. Letting people talk was a more accurate way of weighing them up than showering them with questions. 'I saw your name on Lorna's calendar, she planned for you to MOT her car back in January. I guessed that there might not be too many Bryns in the area so I thought I'd check out whether it was you or not. I'm part of the investigation team so you will be asked to make a statement, but for now I'm just trying to get some of the groundwork done.'

'Yeah, well, you always were good at homework.' He drained the rest of his pint. 'OK, hang on,' he added and headed towards the Gents.

Gary watched him go: nothing about him gave the impression of a man ill at ease, and yet Gary couldn't help wondering whether Bryn was heading out of a back door.

He went to the bar for another couple of pints, and hoped he wouldn't be drinking them alone.

Bryn washed his hands, squirting a large pool of liquid soap into his palm and taking time to work it between each of his fingers. Gradually some of the oil began to shift. But he wasn't fully conscious of what he was doing, most of his thoughts were on Gary Goodhew.

Gary Goodhew.

That was a name from the past, and it was true that at first he hadn't recognized his old classmate. But once the name had connected with the face, memories had rushed into his head. And he'd been surprised, not by the number, so far there had only been a few, but by the clarity.

Suddenly he could picture the whole class. Like the bulk of the kids, he had gone on to Chesterton Secondary School, but there had been others who had disappeared at the end of that year. He'd forgotten they'd ever existed until now. Suddenly he remembered Karen Jarvis and her frizzy hair, her book bag perforated with holes from a pair of compasses.

Steve 'Stench' Manning, who didn't actually smell, but just looked like he did.

Jon Wu with the skinny legs and scraped knees who wasn't bright but made masterpieces from papier mâché and poster paint.

And Gary Goodhew.

Goodhew's desk had been at right angles to the window. He'd mixed with everyone and no one. He was friendly enough, but seemed to spend most of his time staring out through the glass. Who knew what he found so absorbing in a car park, a few trees and a fence, but he never missed a trick. When Mr Mosley threw him a question, Goodhew never failed to pluck the right answer from thin air and throw it right back.

And if he'd matured into an extension of his junior self he wouldn't be missing much now, that was for sure.

Bryn dried his hands and took a deep breath before reaching for the door.

For someone who claimed he didn't like to think too deeply he had a great deal on his mind. He knew that saying nothing wasn't an option. Then again, he could see that saying too much might be dangerous. Enough is what he had to aim for. Precisely enough, at least until he'd had time to think.

Gary didn't read anything into Bryn's return to the table but was pleased about it nonetheless. He wanted their conversation to start up pretty much where it had left off so he made sure he spoke first. 'You said you *thought* you knew Lorna Spence a little. I didn't understand what exactly you meant.'

He saw that Bryn had relaxed: he leant back in his chair, his posture more open and his eye contact good. His speech was neither rushed nor overly hesitant. 'She brought her car in. It was a Rover. She'd been parked up further down our road and it wouldn't start. The alternator was on the blink, but it was a bit of a Friday car...'

Bryn paused and Gary knew he was looking appropriately blank.

'A lemon, a dog. A car turned out quick 'cos everyone wants to knock off for the weekend. You know, one that keeps throwing up so many niggly faults that you think the whole car must be a bit suspect.'

Gary nodded; he'd got it at 'lemon'.

'Well, she came in a few times after that. I think it suited her because we're so close to the town centre. Like I said, the car had mostly minor problems, but a couple of times we ended up having a drink afterwards. In here actually.'

'Her idea, or yours?'

Bryn screwed up his face, like he'd been asked a disproportionately difficult question. 'Can't remember.' He looked at Gary as if waiting to be told whether or not that was a reasonable answer.

'Fair enough,' Gary replied.

'I remember she asked if I fancied a game of pool and we ended up in Mickey Flynn's on Mill Road.'

'Is that the American place?'

'Yeah, that's it.'

'And what then?'

'That happened a couple of times too. She was funny, easy company. We saw each other a few times, but it wasn't ever planned. She'd turn up and if I was free we'd spend a couple of hours together.'

117

'Just as friends?'

Bryn smiled apologetically, like he'd just been caught with his fingers in a metaphorical jar of biscuits, then shifted his expression rapidly towards neutral. 'Sure,' he replied.

'OK.' Gary meant it as in 'OK, if that's how you want to tell it,' and he could see that that was what Bryn knew he meant. They both pretended he'd intended it the other way. 'So when did you last see her?'

'About the time she wrote me on her calendar, I guess. I MOT'd the car and she said she planned to sell it. Never saw her after that.'

'Did she mention friends or seem lonely, or unhappy? You know where she lived, what else do you know?'

'She mentioned people from work, said she had something going with her boss but we never got into it, think it might have been one of those on-off things. She never seemed like one of those women that can't handle being on their own and she certainly didn't seem like she wanted to settle down. I run a mile from those types.'

'Sounds like you knew her more than a *little*.'

That stalled Bryn, opening a route to somewhere he evidently had no plan to go. No matter, it could wait. Whatever composure he'd regained began to freewheel away. He slammed on the brakes and his earlier hesitancy reappeared; Gary knew that the productive part of the conversation was as good as over.

'Look,' Bryn said finally, 'maybe that's how it seems, but she was one of those people – you know, you see them a few times and really feel you're on the same wavelength, then suddenly you realize they've learnt plenty about you, but you know bugger all about them, so I don't know if I knew her much at all. I never had any romantic interest in her if that's what you're wondering. But I thought she was really genuine and sweet. And I liked her.'

Gary's gaze wandered towards the windows and settled on the sulphurous light pooling down from a streetlamp. He left his instincts to summarize the conversation and decided that what little he'd heard had been the truth; but he doubted it was the whole truth and was equally dubious that it had been nothing but.

Chapter Sixteen

Gary Goodhew left the Salisbury Arms at a few minutes before nine. The air was clear and still; it had hushed away the usual blur of background sounds, pushing its stillness between cars and pedestrians, leaving everyone to move in their own pool of solitude. He cut through the back alleys behind the houses, deliberately keeping his distance from any pockets of activity, heightening his feeling of isolation.

Even the sky had backed away, retracting the stars until they were just minute dots in the heavens.

The flatness of East Anglia kept the horizon low and the sky vast. When Goodhew had been about seven, his grandfather had told him to look at the ceiling, then to lie on the carpet and do the same. Goodhew knew that most things became smaller when you moved away from them, but when he lay down and looked up, the ceiling seemed to have grown. His grandfather had said that Cambridge was lying on the carpet and the sky was there to remind it that it was only a tiny corner of the world. Beyond that, Goodhew couldn't remember the exact purpose of the conversation, but he never failed to notice the sky.

By the time he was crossing Parker's Piece his thoughts had gravitated back to Lorna Spence. He was on the far side from Parkside station and he could see that the light was off in Marks's office. He'd spent most of the afternoon and early evening away from his boss, and therefore away from the latest thinking. He'd been with Richard for the identification and at Lorna's flat, but neither had given him any insight on the direction they would be moving. He probably wouldn't know until morning.

He guessed that Bryn had stepped beyond the boundaries of a mechanic–owner relationship. Too early to read much into it though – Bryn's reluctance to talk about it may have stemmed from one of many sources, like the desire for privacy or an aversion to the police. There'd be time for that kind of detail when Bryn made his official statement.

Goodhew felt wide awake, his mind buzzing too much for the confines of his flat. Without any plan he realized that he was drifting in an arc, away from the straight line taking him to his front door and left towards the centre. He began to think about seeing Richard, he wondered whether he could get away with visiting him. He tried to remind himself that it wasn't his place to be the first to know everything. Except that his obsession for knowing was what had pulled him into the job in the first place, he recognized the shortcoming and enjoyed giving in to it.

Goodhew glanced at his watch. He knew before he checked that it was around ten past nine, he just wanted to convince himself that it wasn't too late. Nine o'clock was the end of kiddies' bedtimes, the watershed where adult TV began and soaps mostly ended. News didn't air until ten; oh yes, it was early enough.

He'd already seen Richard Moran's home address and had immediately been able to pinpoint the house: it was the left-hand half of a towering six-storey semi, which stood next to a church and in a rare, elevated position looking down on Chesterton Lane and from there to the Cam.

It was a short walk through the town and out the other side, past the Excelsior Clinic, across the river and right at the next junction. He kept to the main routes now, walking with purpose, keen to reach Richard as quickly as possible.

He ignored the argument against his visit, only considering it might be a bad idea in between ringing the bell and seeing a shadow approaching the door from the other side of the glass. He hadn't decided what excuse to use for his visit, trusting himself to come up with something when the need arose.

It didn't.

Richard let him in without question: clearly he'd already got the hang of understanding that he'd lost his entitlement to privacy. Had Goodhew been asked to make a snap judgement, resignation personified would have summed up Moran; he looked hollowed out and punch-drunk, still standing but just waiting for the killer blow.

But once inside the light was better, and when Goodhew saw Richard face-on he knew that punch-drunk wasn't the phrase. Stoned more like. Yes, he looked out of it, broken even, but there was an unnatural energy in his stare.

Whatever. He looked like shit.

Goodhew opened his mouth to speak but Richard got in first. 'More questions? I'm glad, because I've got some for you. Plenty, actually.'

Goodhew followed him into the room nearest the front door. It was what makeover shows describe as 'lacking an identity', a study cum library, or TV room cum lounge. Or equally goods-in cum charity collection point. It all depended on which corner you studied. It had none of the pretentiousness of the Excelsior Clinic and looked to Goodhew like pure student flat.

Richard sat at one end of a settee opposite the door. Goodhew chose to sit at the other. The house was silent and, although a steady stream of headlights passed the window, nothing disturbed the stillness with anything greater than a low hum.

'You said you had plenty to ask?'

Richard nodded. 'I'm glad you came. I thought I wouldn't be able to speak to anyone this late, but I knew I wouldn't sleep either, not with so many unanswered questions.'

Goodhew knew the feeling. 'And these are things that have come to mind since you gave your statement?'

'Partially. I'd say they've been on my mind all along, but earlier I didn't stop long enough to distil them into clear questions. But now I have. Firstly, I want to know why suspicion is falling on us.'

'Us?'

'Me then. Me in particular.'

'You shouldn't feel it is–'

'Yes, yes.' Richard made a dismissive motion. 'You would say that, wouldn't you? What makes you think Lorna wasn't snatched by a stranger, or some passing acquaintance?'

Sometimes it was useful to be able to call up a stock answer to a question, half the time it was what a witness or victim expected to be told in any case, and that in itself brought with it a feeling of calm. 'Mr Moran, we are only in the first hours of this investigation and nothing has been ruled out...' One look at Richard's sour expression told Goodhew that he'd misjudged, but he plugged on with a second attempt. 'There are many routine questions that we need to ask, they aren't intended to make you feel that you are under any unreasonable suspicion but obviously it's important that we can construct an accurate picture of Lorna's habits and her relationships...'

Richard's expression hadn't diluted and Goodhew could see that he wasn't within a thousand miles of achieving the cathartic effect he'd hoped. The silence hung awkwardly for a long pause.

'Do you think I'm a dullard?'

Dullard. Goodhew found the word amusing but had no trouble not smiling, especially easy when Richard's mouth looked like it was stuffed with lemons. 'No. Of course not. What makes you think I'm not being straight with you?'

Richard's eyes were still glassy but they'd steadied up enough to scrutinize Goodhew. 'It's the problem of conventionality. You people ask all the standard questions and I've been making all the standard replies, so then you come back with all the standard responses. Now I have questions which I can't ask without making it clear that I've been giving you a misleading picture. Do you see?'

'In theory.'

'And?'

Goodhew felt a surge of good luck sweep over him; now he had the chance to catch up on everything that had already been said, and probably better it. He feigned a sigh and hoped he sounded cautious. 'Any discrepancies need to be corrected as soon as possible, and you may need to make a new statement – you understand that, don't you?'

Richard nodded. 'I wanted to keep my privacy.'

'But you were in a relationship with her?'

'Oh, yes. That part's true.'

'What's not then?'

'Nothing's untrue, I just put some spin on it.' He made a little snorting noise that was probably meant to be a laugh. It didn't work. But did succeed in demonstrating what he looked like while toppling out of his fragile comfort zone – naked, and without hope of being thrown even a small pair of briefs.

Goodhew just waited.

Richard licked his lips then finally committed with his opening gambit. 'I was out of my depth with Lorna.'

Goodhew waited some more, then Richard's words began to flow in earnest.

'Obviously I was in a relationship with her. On the face of it I don't suppose we seemed at all compatible – there was an age gap of over ten years, and our backgrounds were quite different. We didn't even look very well suited. But those are very outdated ideas, and neither of us took them as valid reasons for–' he drew a deep and weary breath and then let it out noisily, like it was steam forcing itself through a faulty valve – 'not pursuing each other.'

Without warning he rose and walked towards the window, stopping just before it. He stared down and Goodhew couldn't tell whether it was at the traffic outside or at the square work station which cluttered the floor space in front of the bay. Then his hand reached out, his thin fingers extending, the tips touching an item which lay out of Goodhew's view in the open top of a box marginally larger than a shoebox.

He brought the box back with him, and Goodhew saw that it contained books and magazines. *Men Are From Mars, Women Are From Venus* lay on top and it must have been its cover that Richard had stroked. 'These are Lorna's. She would sit in here, often in your seat, and read. Never for long, just brief snatches of books or magazines. She had a short attention span. She needed constant diversions, new things to do. To read. New people.'

Goodhew sensed that Richard was close to

making his point.

'She was lovely – please, that's one thing I don't want you to misunderstand. She was warm and caring and never set out to hurt me. I know that. And she wasn't unfaithful, not in her eyes.' Richard delved back into the box, lifting out a chunky handful of paperbacks. Mostly books in the category of 'Popular Psychology'. Goodhew spotted one called *On Kissing* and another entitled *Toxic Parents*. Richard dumped them on the cushion in between and carried on digging through the box. Goodhew flipped over *When Your Lover Is a Liar,* which promised 'practical strategies to stop them before they ruin your life'. He picked up the other books and shuffled it in between.

Richard was too preoccupied to notice. Finally he pulled his hand out and with it a bundle of seven or eight glossy magazines, which he spread out on the settee. 'These are the sort of things she would read.'

Goodhew looked. He was no expert on magazines and really had no idea what was supposed to be jumping out at him. Two of them were aimed at men, lad mags and certainly not top shelf. Middle shelf or thereabouts. The other five were women's magazines and he could see they were aimed at the younger end of the market; single independent girls, the so-called ladettes. Whatever Richard was showing him he wasn't getting it.

'I was out of my depth because this is what she embraced. Sexual freedom was part of who she was, she never wanted monogamy and told me so from the start. And like a mug I thought she'd change her mind, or wasn't serious, or... God, I

126

don't know, perhaps I thought I could handle it.' He flicked the mags with the back of his hand, making a brittle crack. 'Promiscuity is a fashion now, a must experiment necessity. I've read these articles and they're sick and vacuous.' Blotchy red patches were rising around his throat, like he'd swallowed his discomfort, just to have it break out through the skin. His voice quietened as he hit his stride. 'It's society going down the tube, turning decent women into whores.'

Goodhew guessed the word 'whores' wasn't one that Richard often spoke. Of course, he didn't know for sure. But he saw the way the word dried on Richard's lips, the way the mini-tirade vaporized as he registered what he'd just said.

'Sorry,' Richard muttered.

'It's fine,' Goodhew replied. 'So Lorna saw other people?'

'No, I don't think so. But she insisted she could if she wanted to. And that she would at some point, and tell me when she did. That's bad enough. No, actually, I think it's worse. On one hand she told me she loved me. And I know she did. But on the other...' He stopped speaking and gnawed his bottom lip.

There was something about Richard that reminded Goodhew of a teenage boy talking about a first romance. He should have been sitting on a tubular steel and canvas chair with his feet hooked round the legs as he leant over an old wood desk scraping something like 'LS 4 RM' into the hinged lid with his pair of school compasses.

'If she never followed it up perhaps it was only the fantasy of it that attracted her.'

127

'She was insecure. I told myself she did it to keep control, but I was getting to the end of my tether. I wanted it to be a phase, something she'd drop when she realized we were stable. We'd only been together since last December, but I couldn't stand the thought of being without her.'

'That's not long.'

'No, it's not. It's been strange, like time since I met her has moved at the wrong speed. Alice says I rushed into it, but it never felt like rushing.'

'And you met through work?'

'She started with us last summer, first of all as a temp, then we gave her a permanent contract.'

'She came through an agency?'

'Yes. Sort of. She was friendly with Victoria Nugent, who works for the dentist in our building. Lorna came in to meet her for lunch on several occasions and in the process started talking to Alice.' He paused and smiled affectionately. 'My sister was constantly frustrated with the temps we were sent, they often lacked basic written English skills and struggled to balance figures. When she found out that Lorna was job hunting she suggested that Lorna register with the agency we use, then hired her.' Richard nodded towards the ceiling. 'Ask her yourself.'

That threw Goodhew. 'Alice is here?'

'She lives here, I thought you knew. We've always lived together.'

'Always?'

For the first time since meeting him Goodhew saw amusement reach all the way up to Richard's eyes. But it didn't add warmth to his face, in fact it dropped the temperature to well below bitterly

128

cold. 'Lorna and I were very close. The point I'm trying to make is that Lorna could have been out walking on her own. It doesn't follow that she had to be meeting someone she knew.'

'No?'

'No. Not at all, sometimes she liked to be alone. She would go off for hours on end.'

'Even at midnight?'

'Yep.'

'She said that?'

'No, I made it up.' He sounded sarcastic but the words had come out too fast. A defensive reflex perhaps.

'Sorry, what I mean is, did you ever see her taking one of these walks?'

'It wasn't an excuse.'

'Excuse?'

Richard's eyes narrowed and he looked away.

Goodhew nodded. 'What happens when you reach the end of your tether, Richard? She told you she went walking alone and you wanted to believe her, but you had to be wondering how open she was really keeping the relationship.'

Richard continued to look away, and when he spoke he sounded distinctly pissed off. 'You've just twisted it right around. She was faithful to me,' he gasped, then stopped. The next couple of minutes ticked by and Goodhew watched Richard try to shut down the emotions that were suddenly clamouring to escape. Richard blinked. He swallowed. He tried breathing deeply. He pressed his hands over his mouth in an attempt to curb the quivering of his lips.

Goodhew cringed, he hadn't foreseen this, and

didn't know how to handle it either. He willed Richard to hold it together. Fat chance. Here was a man unravelling before his eyes. It wasn't a systematic unravelling either, more like a moth-eaten sweater dropping apart in many places at once.

A voice came from the doorway. 'Leave him.' He'd seen no movement but looked to find Alice glaring at him. One hand was on each side of the door frame, her hair was brushed straight down from a centre parting and she was fully dressed in a pale stone trouser suit. Apart from eyeliner under her lower lashes, her anger had taken all the other colour from her face. For someone so thin she made an excellent job of filling the doorway and Goodhew found himself on his feet, reacting to her words like a naughty Labrador caught with its nose in the shopping.

Her head tilted, directing him out into the hall. She moved one arm to let him pass. 'Go,' she hissed. He was happy to oblige; a swift retreat seemed like an all-round healthy idea.

He wondered whether there was anything appropriate he should say to Alice. But before he'd seriously begun considering the question, she had joined her brother on the settee. She sat close to him. Richard leant forward, burying his head into his sister's neck. Her chin rested in his hair and her arms curled him in, making a protecting shawl over his shoulders. She continued to glare at Goodhew, who mouthed the word 'Sorry' before turning away.

Each step he took sounded loudly on the hard floor, advertising both his intrusion and his retreat.

Finally, from behind him, Richard let out a whimper as the last of his self-control fractured. By the time Goodhew opened the front door Richard's hysteria was in full flow; it didn't sound attractive; too much snot, dribble and wailing.

Goodhew didn't look back at the house, he was too busy thinking about the conversation with Richard. It had been interesting, bizarre and not quite the laid-back, low-key chat that he'd had in mind.

Perhaps it was just a sixth sense, but he guessed that Marks would not be impressed.

Chapter Seventeen

Goodhew walked home the long way, alongside the river until he reached the footbridge that crossed above the gentle gushing of the small weir. A houseboat was moored below; one window was lit and he could see the silhouette of a woman and the book she read. The water barely moved, inviting him to dive in, but he knew the stillness was deceptive. A thought which stayed with him as he entered the long corridor of unlit trees crossing Jesus Green and leading towards the spot where he'd first seen Lorna's body.

There was no breeze, just the darkness of unmoving shadows. This would have been a more secluded place to commit murder. His gaze wandered over the grass beyond the trees; he seemed to be alone, but even so found it hard to believe that no one was watching.

He had felt unsettled since leaving Richard's house, dwelling on Richard's idea that Lorna had been murdered by a stranger. It was possible of course, but then there needed to be a reason why Lorna would have chosen to be alone near Midsummer Common in the early hours. Especially on a foggy night when someone could be waiting just out of sight.

Like Alice waiting in the hall.

He tried to imagine the relationship that Lorna and Richard had had, and wondered whether Alice had always been there either trying to suck Lorna into their claustrophobic clique or leaving her shut out of it. He wondered what Richard and Alice were like alone. He'd only seen them three times in twenty-four hours but they already reminded him of two halves of a panto pony. Next he wanted to know who was at the front.

He was pleased when he reached the end of the footpath. He kept to the road with the common on his left. At almost the eleven o'clock position he could see the ripple of the blue and white police tape cordoning off the southernmost corner. In the time it took to draw alongside the crime scene only two cars had passed. Neither driver seemed to notice him. There were no pedestrians either.

So much for thinking this junction would be less deserted; when this part of Cambridge slept it was virtually comatose.

He crossed the road, then stopped to look back at the taped-off area. Even without fog it was a dark corner, falling outside the nearest pools of lamplight and absorbing all natural light into its thick deep grass. In daylight he had found it impossible to believe that no one had witnessed Lorna's death, that the killer hadn't taken an enormous chance. At night, though, it was a very different place and he left with a more open mind. And glad that he'd taken the detour to see for himself.

In another ten minutes he'd reached home. Apart from the new message light blinking on his phone everything looked the same. He allowed it to blink a dozen times or more, wondering if he was about to hear DI Marks demanding an immediate call back. He considered not listening to it at all; if ignorance really was bliss then he could enjoy a decent few hours' sleep without having to plan out a conversation with his boss.

He sighed, then pressed 'Play'. May as well know what he was up against.

But the voice that spoke wasn't Marks's, it was his grandmother's. 'Gary. I'd like to have a chat with you, I'll ring you later. But perhaps if it's not too late when you get in you could ring me. I've come to a decision and it's time I put you in the picture.'

He checked his watch and decided it was too late to call back, then rang anyway; they were both night owls.

She had caller display on her phone and answered with typical directness. 'Can you meet me tomorrow?' she asked.

'After work?'

'Yes, latish if that suits you.'

'It would actually, there's a new case...'

'Yes, I saw the papers. I hoped you'd be on it.'

'But I don't know when I'll be free.'

'Doesn't matter. I'm having a late dinner at the Felix – call my mobile when you're on your way and I'll make sure I'm home for you.'

'What's going on?'

'Nothing to worry about, I promise.' She hesitated. 'It was just when we were at the Rock the other day, I suddenly realized how much you've grown up...'

'And?'

'I'll tell you tomorrow. It's too complicated for a phone call.'

'You can't just tell me half the story!'

'I haven't told you any fraction of anything actually.'

'Now I'll be awake trying to guess.'

'Well then, that's better than lying awake thinking about work. In any case, you'll never guess.'

Goodhew went to bed still curious. But as he drifted into sleep his thoughts ended up back with Lorna Spence and his unofficial visits to Bryn and Richard. There would be a team briefing session first thing; updating Marks beforehand was his best chance to avoid greater fallout later. In the end he was too tired to feel anything but philosophical, happy to make an early start and think about Marks then.

Chapter Eighteen

Goodhew was dressed again before it was fully light. DI Marks usually arrived around eight, therefore Goodhew decided to turn up half an hour before.

It was another clear but chilly morning. He made a quick and jacketless trip across Parker's Piece to the swimming pool, knowing that over an hour of swimming would leave him better able to withstand the cold than an extra layer of clothes.

He had the pool to himself, which wasn't unusual for very early mornings; most days he barely noticed other swimmers in any case. But today he appreciated the silence and fell into a rhythm based on his breathing and his hands plunging into the water, punctuated every twenty strokes or so by the turn and glide at the end of the length. Maybe it was the good rhythm that made him crack one hundred lengths fifteen minutes faster than usual. He stepped from the water and paused at the edge, burying his face in his towel just long enough for the chlorine sting to fade from his eyes. He felt like he'd made good time because he'd woken focused and that was how he was about to tackle the day. He slung his towel over his shoulder and headed for the changing rooms. It was either that, or he'd just miscounted.

It was seven twenty-five when he walked through the car park at the rear of the station. He was pleased and equally not surprised by the absence of Marks's Mazda. The car park was almost full, but quiet, too early for members of the public to be scrapping over one of the three visitors' spaces and too late for the upheaval of shift changes.

Goodhew glanced at the closest windows as he approached the double doors. As always he paid particular attention to the three coat hooks visible through the window directly to his left; today it was just out of habit as he expected them to be empty. Mel always wore one of four jackets to work, a red cut-off parka with a grey fur-edged hood on the coldest days through to a bleached denim jacket on the warmest, with either her brown bomber jacket or her knee-length red trench coat taking care of the temperatures in between. Hanging on the middle hook was her red mac: an early start for someone not due in until nine, and especially early compared to her normally clockwork arrival at three minutes to.

Mel's cubby-hole of a desk was buried too deep in the building to be seen from outside. Good-hew was happy to put his single-mindedness on hold, just for a few minutes, just to say good morning.

She wasn't at her desk, but he hovered for a few minutes anyway. He doubted she'd left her coat from the night before: her purse was next to the telephone and two empty polystyrene cups lay in the bin, post-cleaning lady and therefore post-8 p.m. the previous evening. And her chair wasn't tucked away either but marooned halfway between the desk and the gap where he stood. It looked like she'd executed one of those roll, rotate and stand-up moves that expert users of five-wheeled swivel chairs turn into something bordering on balletic. He pushed the chair away and tucked it back under its desk.

He guessed he heard Mel before he saw her, but he wasn't aware of any sound, just an instinct to turn around. 'Hi,' he said.

She wore a baggy jumper with sleeves that hung loose down to her knuckles but even with her hand closed he could see it was holding a ball of tissues. 'Hi,' she mumbled, and she did a funny up-down thing with the corners of the mouth, the one people do when they wish they could flash a sign-board saying 'Imagine I'm smiling back at you.'

'Doing overtime?'

'No.' The way she said it left no opening for conversation. 'What's up?' She looked up at him; her eyes weren't red but she'd been crying.

'That's what I should ask you, you're upset.'

'No wonder you made detective.' She pulled her chair back out from under the well of the desk and dropped on to it with her full weight; the gas-lift let the seat bounce down by an inch then recovered. She threw the ball of tissues into the bin. 'Looking crap and feeling crap, it's always a winning combination. Thanks for pointing it out.'

'You look nice, just upset.' He smiled. 'I mean, you don't look crap, even if you feel it.'

She studied his face for a while, saying nothing. 'I'm messing up, and I'm making choices that are meant to bail me out, and it's only once I've made them I see that I've fucked up again.'

'It can't be that bad, can it?'

Mel was still staring at him. 'Fuck-up on top of

137

fuck-up, that's me, Gary.' With no warning a new batch of tears rose and teetered, defying gravity to stay put until she had managed to blink them away.

To him the 'if you need to talk' offer always sounded like a line, but he said it anyway and then wasn't surprised when she shook her head.

'I don't think so. I'm not making any more choices. My new plan is to stick where I am, it's my anti-fuck-up strategy. But thanks for the offer.'

He started to say something but she stopped him. Her voice had suddenly become firmer. 'If you don't mind, Gary, I don't want to talk to you any more right now.'

Perhaps he showed surprise because she added a further explanation. 'You make me feel transparent.'

And whatever he'd expected her to say, it wasn't that. 'Like you're not there?'

'No. Not like that.' She looked impatient then. 'Transparent,' she repeated.

She looked at him as if saying it a second time would make it clear. No pun intended.

He wasn't just missing the point, it was invisible. 'Is that good, or bad?' he asked.

'Completely shit.'

'Oh.' He took a deep breath. 'I'm sorry, it's not deliberate.'

She pressed one eyelid closed with her right thumb, determined to poke away anything resembling another tear. Her voice had an edge to it now. 'If you were trying to do it, you probably couldn't, so there's no point feeling sorry, is there?'

He was lost. No point saying no just to be

agreeable, but he could also see that asking her to explain wasn't going help either. He moved both hands from his sides and then dropped them again, a kind of pointless penguin-thinking-about-flying type gesture. 'OK then.' He stood still for an awkward moment then tried for a belated but dignified exit. 'I'll leave you to it.'

She nodded and he turned away, but her voice followed him and caught him when he'd barely taken his third step. 'When I see you ... around, I mean ... you make me feel uncomfortable,' she said.

He turned to look at her. 'Sorry.'

'It's not your fault but I thought you should know.' She bit her bottom lip, then added 'Sorry' too.

'OK,' he mumbled, then inexplicably and without any trace of sarcasm added, 'Thanks.' He felt pretty dumb.

He took the stairs to the third floor to wait for Marks, wondering as he climbed the steps when Mel had noticed his interest. How long had she been aware that he watched her arriving at work and leaving in the evening? And did she know he'd been disappointed when she started wearing an engagement ring?

Her boyfriend was called Toby Doyle; he had two speeding convictions and one caution for being involved in a late-night disturbance. Apart from that he'd never been in trouble, but his father and older brothers were well known for lashing out. He thought she deserved someone better. And told himself it was none of his business. But still watched the way she walked, loved the sound of her laugh and made flimsy excuses to stand at her desk with his small talk.

He wondered when exactly he'd become the creepy guy from the third floor. As the whole picture sunk in, pretty dumb escalated to really, really dumb. People never saw you in the same way as you see yourself; he'd never seen himself as stalker material, but now he knew.

Up on the third Kincaide was already seated at one of the desks and spoke before Goodhew had even registered his presence. 'You're in early.'

'So are you,' he replied, and was pleased to have someone to take his thoughts away from his encounter with Mel. 'What's dragged you out of bed?'

Kincaide rolled his eyes. 'Don't ask.'

He wondered if that meant trouble at home, but considering Kincaide's well-known reticence where his marriage was concerned he didn't ask. Goodhew reminded himself what was higher on the agenda. 'Actually,' he began, 'I've been meaning to have a word.'

'Oh?'

Goodhew hesitated and the words clogged inside his brain. In the end he just held out his hand, and said, 'I'm pleased we're working together.'

Kincaide shrugged. 'Sure. Me too.'

'I just wanted you to know.'

'Good.' Kincaide's handshake was brief and hard. But he smiled. 'So why are you here so soon?'

'Oh, I need to see Marks. Think I might get a bollocking.' He explained his visits to Bryn and Richard.

Kincaide tried to look positive but couldn't pull it off without wincing. 'I'd just tell him about this O'Brien guy, you'll get Brownie points for finding him, then shut up about the Morans and hope they don't mention it either.'

Goodhew shook his head. 'No. I'll just get it over with. Coffee?'

'No thanks.' Kincaide pointed behind Goodhew. 'Marks just walked past.'

Goodhew reached Marks's office doorway before the inspector had even reached his chair. He sat but didn't invite Goodhew to do the same.

'If you have a minute, sir, I'd like a word.'

'I'm sure you would.' Marks tilted his head and raised his right brow, making one eye look bigger then the other. It wasn't his best look, but Goodhew guessed it wasn't done for appeal. 'And I'd like a few with you,' Marks added.

Goodhew waited.

'Get a chair,' Marks barked, 'then sit in it.'

He did what he was told, reaching for the nearest chair which stood against the wall. He began speaking straight away, hoping to pre-empt some of the conversation. 'I saw Lorna Spence's calendar, she'd booked her car in for an MOT with someone called Bryn...' He stopped midsentence.

Marks pointed at the carpet in front of his desk. 'Don't talk, just sit.' Marks picked up his Parker ballpoint and jabbed the button into his desk blotter a couple of times, making the pen retract and reappear noisily

When he was ready, he spoke. 'I suppose there was nothing on at the cinema last night?'

'Sorry?'

'Alice Moran rang to complain about your visit. Wandering around chit-chatting to witnesses is not how I expect you to find an evening's entertainment.'

'Oh.'

'Yes, "oh" indeed. Think I wouldn't find out? I'm supposed to be coordinating this investigation so I don't expect to arrive at work on day two to find I've been wheeled into kept-in-the-dark-corner. I want a full explanation, then I don't want it to happen again. All right?'

Goodhew nodded. 'Right.'

'Now then, start talking.'

An hour later Marks held a briefing session. He sat on the edge of a table with a pile of papers beside him. He scanned the faces of his team, noted some semi-vacant expressions and hoped it was just because they'd emptied their minds in readiness for the meeting. There weren't enough of them without compensating for any dunces on the team. Everyone would be stretched too far without more manpower.

Goodhew had arrived early with notebook and pen and was filling the page with a doodle resembling a spider juggling hoops. Marks thought it would be more appropriate to see him doodling a noose, considering the lucky escape he'd just had. It was fortunate for the young detective that they were so short-staffed, it made dropping him an impossibility.

Kincaide looked unusually distracted: wide awake, but his gaze periodically wandering towards the floor.

Marks hated meetings that dragged, and kept his direct and fast-paced; the sooner they were all active, the better. He cleared his throat and waited to have everyone's full attention, and started to speak when Kincaide's focus floated back up from the carpet. 'At the moment this is the whole team. As you can see you are very, very thin on the ground and this will mean two things. Firstly, you will have too much to do.'

Someone murmured, 'There's a surprise.'

He ignored the comment. 'And secondly, you'll be expected to handle elements of the investigation that many of you will not have experienced in the past.' He tapped his temple. 'None of you are thick, if you were you wouldn't be here, so use your eyes and ears, and most of all your common sense. Now, down to business.'

On top of the pile of papers lay a ten-by-eight photograph, face down. He turned it to face the group. It was a scene of crime shot of Lorna Spence. 'Preliminary information points to a time of death between 10 p.m. on Monday night and 2 a.m. yesterday morning. As you can see there is a ligature around her neck – this was used to secure the carrier bag. The cause of death has been confirmed as asphyxiation, not strangulation.

'However, there is no sign of defence wounds or any injury which may have incapacitated her. Nor evidence of any attempt by Lorna to free herself, so we are waiting for toxicology tests to determine whether any substances were taken or administered. We will not have the results of those until tomorrow. At the earliest.

'The same with the swabs. The victim was fully clothed except for knickers. We do not know whether these were removed or not there from the outset. There are no visible signs of sexual assault, some old bruising around the inner thigh region but nothing else that's recent in that area. Both her upper arms show some bruising, and this seems to be consistent with being gripped by someone facing her, while both parties were standing. Obviously there are detailed shots of all the injuries.'

He turned over the next photo and held it up. 'This is a close-up of her left hand. The same thing was written on both palms. It appears to say "I'm like Emma", or it could possibly be part of a longer message. The same person probably wrote both and the characters are better formed on the left palm. Lorna was right-handed and the current theory is that she wrote this herself.

'Why, and what it means, we have yet to discover. But I need to know of any connections she had with the name Emma.'

The next photo was a studio shot of Lorna. 'This is the photo that will be released to the press. Lorna Spence turned twenty-three on 6th February. She was five foot two. Single. Working as an administrator for the Excelsior Clinic. So far no relatives have been traced.'

Marks scanned the room. No one looked vacant now. Good.

He added the salient points he'd gleaned from Goodhew and assigned tasks to the team. Goodhew was, as usual, pretty damned unreadable but Marks noticed his interest peak as Bryn O'Brien's name was mentioned. He assigned O'Brien's interview to Kincaide, then informed Goodhew that he would be spending the day studying Lorna's phone bills and bank statements.

Goodhew opened his mouth to speak. Marks raised his hand in a halting motion. 'Is there something you don't understand, Gary? Perhaps the idea of sitting in the office and not moving is a bit alien to you?'

Goodhew shut his mouth again. He strummed his fingers on his knee a couple of times, probably in frustration.

Marks remained silent, letting the room settle, then dismissed the team. 'My mobile will be on.' He paused, making sure he had Goodhew's full attention. 'I need to know every development. Understood?'

Goodhew nodded. The officers filed past him. He could hear them breaking into conversation as they hit the corridor outside.

He glanced at Goodhew's notepad. The spider doodle had progressed and some of the hoops it juggled contained names. He saw 'Excelsior', 'Richard Moran' and 'Bryn O'Brien' written in neat capitals. The other hoops remained blank.

The spider's body had 'Lorna' written in the middle.

Chapter Nineteen

Goodhew wasn't the only person to think that a preemptive strike might be the safest way forward.

Bryn had unlocked the garage at eight but after forty-five minutes he found he had done nothing but fight the urge to bunk off. On one hand, with his father taking a month out to decorate, and only himself to answer to, it was never going to be an escape of Ferris Bueller-style proportions. But on the other...

He thought it over carefully.

On the other hand, there would be no joy in hanging round waiting for the inevitable visit from the law. He could see how that would go, probably with the unsubtle arrival of two uniforms in a marked car generating enough gossip to knock the business back more than a couple of days' skiving ever would. Better then for them to catch up with him away from work.

Or better still, for him to do the catching. And that was when he relocked the workshop and began walking towards Parkside police station.

He pulled a pack of Benson and Hedges from his pocket and lit up without breaking his stride. One packet usually lasted all week; three per day wasn't much of a habit. But this wasn't 'most weeks' and as he came within sight of the station he used the remains of the first cigarette to light his second.

He left two messages at the front desk, both times with his mobile number. After each he stepped out into the fresh air and lit up again. After the second he made up his mind to sit it out, and found a spot on the edge of the park that boasted both a bench and a bin. In the end he had no idea how long he remained there. His elbows rested on his knees, his hands rested, one in the palm of the other, about eighteen inches above the pavement. He lit each new cigarette from the last, but instead of putting any of them to his mouth he spent the time watching the ash growing, then falling on to the path.

He thought about Lorna. He wondered how much he needed to say. And how much he'd be able to leave out and whether he was pulling the lid on a can of worms. The Gary Goodhew he'd known from school had been quick-witted, logical and intuitive. It was a worrying combination. Bryn was realistic, he knew he wasn't going to be driving the conversation but he held on to the idea that it was safest to take a ride with someone you knew.

He decided against lighting another cigarette, and pinched the current one dead between the tip of his forefinger and thumb. He was about to toss the butt into the bin when he looked up and for first time realized he was being watched.

Gary was no more than fifteen feet away. 'You came in twice so I thought you might still be out here,' he said.

Bryn nodded. 'That figures. You haven't changed much, have you?' He threw the butt at the bin then, and for the first time missed. It bounced on to the ground in front of Gary who retrieved it and dropped it in.

'DC Kincaide is looking for you at the moment and I'm supposed to be doing something else. What's up?'

Bryn laced his fingers together, then loosened them again when he realized it looked like he was praying. 'There's a thing – a coincidence, I suppose. It was at the back of my mind when I saw you yesterday then I thought about it overnight. It's probably nothing but I wanted to point it out, then you can check, can't you?'

Gary looked back at the police station, then at Bryn. 'Sure. But whatever you tell me, you'll need to repeat, just to keep everything straight. It can't be unofficial, you understand that, don't you?'

Again Bryn nodded, but Gary still looked hesitant. Finally he sat and rested his elbows on his knees. Bryn knew that it was just one of those body language mirroring techniques, designed to put him at ease, but it made him feel more comfortable in any case. They both faced forward. For his part Bryn stared at the kerb across the road; it was the most mundane and commonplace thing he could spot and he knew it was what he needed to focus on as he deliberately exposed himself to police scrutiny. Sticking his neck out like this really went against the grain, so much so that when he started talking he took the long way round. 'I think it was in December when I first met Lorna, maybe the end of November. Well, not long before Christmas anyway. And like I told you last night we went out a couple of times to the pool hall on Mill Road. I was in there one night having a game and a drink with Colin, this bloke I knew. He used to do odd jobs and he'd done a bit of cash in hand for me, a couple of services and a few bits just helping me catch up with stuff. Well, Lorna turned up with a mate of hers and we ended up playing doubles.'

'Mate, as in another woman?'

'Yeah, yeah. Lorna worked with her, a girl called Victoria.'

'Victoria Nugent?' Gary still said it as a question even though he clearly knew the answer.

'Yes,' and Bryn paused a beat. He should have guessed that Victoria was already in the picture and it only made him more sure that this conversation was a good idea. 'I partnered her and we had a laugh. Have you met her?'

Gary shook his head. 'Not yet.'

'Feisty and flirty. We had quite a few to drink, all of us, that is. And Lorna spent as much time chatting to Colin as I did to Victoria, which was the first odd thing.'

'Why?'

'Well, to be honest Colin wasn't a nice bloke. I mean especially from a woman's point of view; he looked bad, smelt bad and was a bit of a scrounger. But they got on fine.'

'Unless Lorna was put out at you flirting with her mate?'

Bryn twisted around, leaning on the back rest for the first time and eyeing Gary with what he hoped looked like mild amusement. He waited for Gary to do the body mirroring thing before he replied. 'Trust me, as far as Victoria went, Lorna was just not the jealous type. As I said before, there was nothing going on between us.'

'Well then, what?'

'Yeah well, according to Colin they met again. He reckoned he was "on a promise". I thought he was having me on, but he was adamant.'

'But we're talking months ago, right?'

'Yeah, January.' Bryn could almost hear the tick, tick, tick as his bombshell counted down. 'Colin's dead.'

Only Gary's eyes showed a response. The pupils dilated and his stare made Bryn feel pinned down. 'And what was Colin's last name?' he asked.

'Willis.' His throat tightened as he spoke. No wave of relief followed, he felt no burden lifting. But what had he expected? His conscience was far from clear.

'You'll need to make a statement,' Gary said.

Bryn just nodded. He felt himself making a nauseating slide towards centre stage. It was for Lorna, he told himself. And as he walked towards Parkside police station shoulder to shoulder with his old classmate he couldn't help wondering how deep he was about to be buried.

Chapter Twenty

Marks still looked pissed off. But even if there was no mood change apparent to the naked eye, Goodhew was certain his boss would have mellowed during the day.

Marks repeated the essence of Goodhew's

request back at him. 'So, you've left Kincaide with this O'Brien guy and now you want to follow up this Colin Willis lead?'

'Absolutely.' Goodhew plonked a bulging folder on to the desk. 'I thought it would be a good idea to go through this. Just as a start. If there's a connection to Lorna Spence—'

'What happened to her bank statements and phone bills? You're not gallivanting off on anything else until they're done.'

'They are.' Goodhew slid a thin plastic wallet from inside the front flap of the larger folder. 'And there's not much to know. She used her bank account for paying bills and drawing cash, little else. Her bills were mostly on direct debit and aside from rent, rates, heating etc, she had one credit card and one store card. She doesn't appear to have been the type to bother about keeping paperwork, so we don't have a complete set of home or mobile bills.

'Without the detail there's not much to say, but I've requested a full set of both, as well as the calls relating to her office extension, a list of the incoming calls on her private numbers and copies of her credit card statements.'

'Nothing else?'

'Not yet, no.'

Marks held out his hand. 'Leave that with me, and you'd better hope I don't find something you have missed.' Goodhew was sure he spotted an encouraging gleam in Marks's eye. 'How're you proposing to look for a connection to Colin Willis?'

'Aside from the file? Maybe she mentioned him to someone at the Excelsior Clinic.'

151

'And while you're at it I suppose you could find out whether she ever mentioned Bryn O'Brien.' Marks leant back in his chair and surveyed Goodhew through narrowed eyes. He tapped his temples as he thought. 'And you may as well speak to Victoria Nugent, after all her name's popped up a couple of times now. And if anything else does crop up you'll be burrowing into that while you're there, I suppose?'

'Something like that.'

'Why did I send you off to trawl through Lorna Spence's paperwork?'

'Because–'

'Because I thought it was time you grasped the idea that I need to know where you are and what you're doing. I thought you'd be bored to death for a few hours, then you'd come back in happy for *me* to direct *you*. Instead of that you bounce in here bright-eyed and bushy-tailed like some frigging Disney bunny, then tell me you've got your whole day planned out. Look at my face, doesn't this look like a scowl to you?'

Goodhew tried to look apologetic. 'I thought that was concentration.' Marks gave him a poisonous look in return. OK, so he hadn't mellowed much after all. 'I could focus on the Colin Willis link and nothing else?' he asked hopefully.

Marks leant forward again and spread his hands out in front of him on the desk. Maybe to stop his fingers from tapping. Or maybe this time he really was concentrating. 'All right,' he sighed, 'but I still want regular communication, and don't go running off at obscure tangents without checking with me first.'

Chapter Twenty-One

Old habits die hard, or so they say.

Goodhew's favourite quiet spot at Parkside station had always been the desk on the third floor, in the corner nearest home. In the days when file servers and hubs had looked like extras from sci-fi sets the original layout had been modified to accommodate an air-conditioned IT room, eating into the open plan office space and leaving an almost useless little cul-de-sac where a redundant desk had been shunted.

Rather than pulling up a chair Goodhew sat on the desk. He leant against the wall and faced the window.

It was ten to two.

He opened Colin Willis's file and glanced at the first few documents, hoping to find the one that would suck him into this unfamiliar case. He knew the bare facts: partially decomposed body dragged from the Cam, no missing person report, ligature still around throat, car abandoned, suspected to be debt or drugs related. No leads. No progress.

His gaze wandered back to the window and towards the Avery, the pub on the far side of Parker's Piece.

That's when he admitted that old habits die hard. Mel was there, indistinguishable and Lowry-like in the distance but he knew her. She was with Toby. Even from that distance he could tell their body language wasn't good.

Get over it, he told himself, and looked back down to the file, flicking through until he felt the gloss of photographic paper. He slid out a clutch of prints. The first showed the water and the puffed-up clothes covering the torso. It looked like a guy, overstuffed and ready for a bonfire.

He glanced through the window again. They were closer now. Mel was heading back to work, or trying to. Toby stood in her path. Goodhew saw her speak, she pointed to her watch, then attempted to side-step him. He blocked. She stopped and spoke again. Toby reacted instantly, the flats of his hands flew up, simultaneously connecting with her shoulders. She took a couple of quick steps back.

Goodhew found himself on his feet, the photographs making a cracking noise as the edge of the pile hit the floor.

Mel pushed past Toby, and although he reached towards her, he made no attempt to grab her. He appeared to be shouting. He stood facing the police station. Goodhew was ready to move if Toby did, but in the end it was Mel who hurried alone.

Toby continued to shout but she didn't acknowledge him. She was about to cross the road in front of the station when she looked up at Goodhew. He had to be three or four feet back from the glass, yet he knew she could see him. Her stare was defiant; she was demanding that he back off, telling him to interfere at his peril. He didn't move for the first seconds, fixed to the spot by increasing discomfort. She glanced to her left. Checking for traffic.

He looked down at the splay of photographs at his feet and fixed his attention on the least pleasant shot of Colin Willis's unnaturally pale skin stretched across the bloated corpse. The last body Goodhew had seen recovered from water had been dead for over a year, weighed down and wedged beneath an abandoned jetty on the Ouse. Flesh underwater for that length of time reacts to form a soapy substance called adipocere. It stinks, worse than any normally decaying matter. Willis was nowhere near that far gone but Goodhew let memories of the stench seep back into his mind.

It was more than enough to jar him.

He bent on one knee to gather the shots, and once he had them back on the desk he started again.

The cause of death had been strangulation: the dog's chrome choke chain, still lodged around the throat, had exerted sufficient pressure on the windpipe to crush it. No one had missed Willis, and identification might have taken longer if Mill Road's community beat officer, PC McKendrick, hadn't recognized him from one of the morgue photos.

On the scale of parasites and predators Willis had been somewhere between house mites and head lice; a persistent but manageable irritation. He'd been a dabbler, he'd dabbled with handling stolen goods and with selling cannabis, and when money became short he'd even dabbled with work. Once or twice he'd tested the water by offering the police tip-offs but, despite his talk, Willis knew little and was in people's confidence even less.

An exact date of death had never been determined, but according to the pathologist the body had been submerged for several weeks. Willis's landlord hadn't received rent for all of February, not unusual, but he'd stuck to his routine of weekly visits to every tenant who owed him money He had not seen Willis since the first Friday in February.

On the 21st the residents of Fen Ditton had reported an abandoned vehicle and on the 26th the untaxed and inaccurately registered van had been impounded. It was only proved to be Willis's after his DNA was matched to the DNA found in the pick-your-own snot collection Willis had been accumulating in the driver's side door pocket.

This narrowed the date or dates of Willis's disappearance and death down to weeks two and three of February.

Goodhew searched the file for any connection to Lorna, or even any mention of Bryn O'Brien, but, much like the investigation itself, he drew a blank. The popular theory with the investigating team was that Willis had pissed someone off. Amazing what a couple of centuries of police training can produce.

Colin Willis had no friends or relatives pushing for progress and it was clear that the killing was being treated as a one-off. The perpetrator was expected to be someone busy committing other offences; the type of criminal that would either get grassed up at some point or drop himself in it with another unrelated crime. Therefore the case remained open and active. But not *that* open and not *that* active.

Once Goodhew was sure that there was nothing in the file to affect his immediate plans, he turned his attention to the first visit of the day: Richard Moran.

Chapter Twenty-Two

Twenty minutes later Goodhew left Parkside station for the short walk towards the city centre and another visit to Richard's home.

Faith Carver, the Excelsior Clinic's stern-faced receptionist, had informed Goodhew that Mr Moran had not been at work all day and had cancelled his forthcoming appointments.

Goodhew decided not to call ahead to the house but to take his chances on finding Richard home. He approached the front door and two scenarios flashed into his mind, one where Alice was home and he might struggle to speak to Richard privately, and the other where Alice was out and he was faced with dealing with Richard alone. As he waited for the door to open he tried to imagine how he would deal with Richard's histrionics if they kicked off again while they were by themselves.

Goodhew checked himself. Histrionics maybe wasn't the right word. It hadn't felt like watching an over-acting display; there had been nothing false about the amount of emotion that had

157

poured out, just perhaps its source. Richard possibly felt sorry for himself, and elements of the relationship had clearly troubled him, but did he really seem appropriately upset at Lorna's death? Goodhew had no answer to that.

The door swung wide and it was Richard who held it open.

Today he wore a suit. White cuffs, collar, and a small triangle behind his tie were all that showed of his shirt; it looked cleaner and better pressed than any new shirt Goodhew had ever seen.

Goodhew imagined Richard making meticulous efforts with his appearance, perhaps determined to keep control of the façade he put up between himself and the world. Did he know he'd failed? And failed dismally at that. He looked brittle, like he was suffering the human equivalent of metal fatigue and the next breath of bad news would make him crumble. And he also looked like he'd been crying and not sleeping; Goodhew was confident that his visit alone hadn't caused that amount of trauma.

Richard mumbled something about an office, then headed upstairs. Goodhew assumed he was supposed to follow. Neither of them spoke until Richard opened the door to a room at the back of the second floor and motioned for Goodhew to go in. 'Have a seat.'

The room was large, square, and the most true to life depiction of the Cluedo library that he could imagine. Bookshelves ran along two walls, mostly packed with sets of matching leather-bound volumes. The major item of furniture was a large oak desk positioned at ninety degrees to the window; it was bare-topped apart from an ornate letter opener lying near the edge. Goodhew didn't bother trying to spot the lead pipe, but thought he'd keep one ear open for revolving bookcases and secret panels, just in case.

Richard sat at his desk, leaving Goodhew to occupy a low chesterfield-style armchair on the opposite side. Goodhew's line of vision was somewhere level with the middle of Richard's chest, not ideal; it made Goodhew feel like he was supposed to raise a hand and wait for permission to speak. He left his hands where they were and waded in regardless. 'Does the name Emma mean anything to you?'

Richard was leaning with his weight on his elbows and his hands locked together at the fingers. He looked into his palms. 'Because of the writing?' He shook his head. 'No.' There was no sign he wasn't telling the truth but he still looked nervous.

'She never mentioned anyone with a similar name, maybe Emily or Gemma?'

'No, never.'

'And there's no one connected with you and not Lorna, a patient perhaps?'

'I've already been asked about this, and I've been through my files. There's nothing, I asked Alice too. But her friends and contacts are mostly the same as mine so she couldn't suggest anything.'

Goodhew changed tack. 'Has she ever been married?'

'No.' Richard unclasped his fingers and leant back in his chair, a gesture designed to exude relaxation. Perhaps he didn't realize that the fingers on his right hand were tightly gripping the edge of the desk, as if to stop it sliding away from him. 'If she had been serious about anyone she'd still be with them, that's the sort of woman she is. I remember my father describing her first encounter as an aberration, and that was the end of that.' He raised his head, jutting his chin as if to dare Goodhew to comment. Goodhew said nothing. One corner of Richard's mouth began to tremble.

'Parental pressure,' Richard added, as though just those two words gave a fully comprehensive explanation for all failed relationships in the Moran family.

'What sort of pressure?'

Richard blinked twice. 'The same sort I'd have been under if they'd been alive when I was seeing Lorna.'

'Which is?'

Richard was gripping the desk with both hands now. 'It doesn't matter now, does it?'

'I'd still like to know.'

'My father said Alice was precocious and he kept us all isolated from other families. Their rules seem ineffectual now. It's just when you're a child they seem omnipotent, you don't realize they're only human like the rest of us.

'This was my father's study. He was a well-known figure in his day, the umpteenth generation of Moran doctors, but the first to make a mark treating the wealthy of Cambridge. He achieved success through determination more than any exceptional medical skill. Not the type to take any prisoners, as they say. I found him a terrifying man and if I'd done something wrong he would summon me in here and I'd have to sit

160

in your chair, right there, and wait silently until he was ready to speak to me. Now I'm the one behind the desk, fancy that.'

If Richard was enjoying his seat on the throne it didn't show.

'So you've lived here all your life?'

'Yes. I even took my degree at Cambridge. We all grew up here and inherited it last year when he died. Alice and I are attached to the place.'

Goodhew empathized with the sentiment although he wasn't sure he'd want to live with his own sister – but then he only had one bedroom.

'Besides I'm not...' Richard stopped.

'Go on.'

Whatever Richard had almost said was now firmly shut away again.

'You were about to say something,' Goodhew pushed.

'It was nothing.'

'It won't hurt to say it anyway.'

'No, I was just rambling. I keep doing it, then mid-sentence I flash back to the way she looked at the hospital. Everything's become so insignificant since she died. I feel naive; plodding along thinking we were going somewhere together – I should have known.'

'That she was going to die?'

'That things would go wrong. Do you really think that anyone's life goes on the up and up?' Richard finally released his grip on the desk. 'You'll see, just when you least expect it.' He punched one fist into the other palm. 'Fair enough, you don't see it coming the first time, but once you realize that's what life's about it's naive

161

not to expect it.'

Goodhew raised his eyebrows. 'That's your philosophy on life then?'

'Absolutely.'

'Based on?'

'Everything, from the first time I was stamped on in the playground onwards.'

Ah, the Chicken-Licken school of positive thinking; no wonder Richard was a nervous wreck.

Goodhew tried another change of direction. 'Did Lorna have a dog?'

'A dog?' Richard repeated. His eyes flickered, his focus darting away and up, hunting for paw prints on the ceiling. 'Maybe as a child. I have no idea.' He kept his voice level and dragged his attention back to Goodhew. 'Why?' He sounded genuinely baffled.

'We have a possible lead, some dog hairs. They could be nothing.' He managed to stop himself from punctuating the sentence with 'Excuse the pun.'

'Do you know any more? What colour of dog, or breed?'

'At this stage we just need to know of any dogs she might have come into contact with.'

'I don't know of any.'

'Did she talk about anyone she knew having a dog?'

'Not that I remember.'

'No one at the clinic?'

'No. Still no.' Now he was starting to sound irritated, but every time Goodhew had seen him Richard had stayed permanently in the uneasy zone, uncomfortable, anxious or distressed. Goodhew couldn't read him well enough to identify which signs counted for anything. Not yet at least.

Deciding it was time to leave, he stood and extended his hand. 'I'm sorry if I was at all tactless when I visited last night.'

They shook hands. Richard's grip was firm. 'Thank you.'

'And I'm sorry for your loss.'

Richard managed a small smile. 'I know. I can see you have compassion. But then you're young. In fact about the same age as Lorna. She knew all about compassion too.'

'I didn't know it was age-related.'

Richard half turned towards the window. 'Do you know which way this faces?'

Goodhew took a second to get his bearings. 'North-west?'

'It faces towards Shire Hall and the site of the county jail. Between here and there is Castle Mound, know it?'

Castle Mound was a large grass-covered hillock which had been part of the original city defences in Roman times, and like every other person who'd been resident in Cambridge for more than five minutes he knew it. 'Of course,' he replied.

'You'd be amazed who doesn't.' Richard had become suddenly erect and firm-voiced. 'All right then, do you know what happened in 1855?'

'Got me there.'

'The last public hanging occurred over the gates of the jail. Castle Hill was crowded with spectators, including many women and children. A man and his sister-in-law were executed for poisoning his wife. That's her own sister. There

163

were estimates that thirty thousand arrived to watch. They packed the streets. You see, people want to see justice done, and they want to educate their children to see it too. My father used to stand at this window and complain at the abolition of the death penalty. He said it allowed people to get away with murder.'

'And you feel the same?'

'I agree with him, it is important to see justice done and that it's seen to be done. That's what I'm interested in for Lorna. As for compassion, I don't believe I have any left.'

Chapter Twenty-Three

Behind him Richard and his house were fading into the distance. Goodhew knew he hadn't learnt much, but at the same time he felt enlightened: for the first time he thought he'd been able to catch a glimpse of what, besides money and status, had attracted Lorna.

As he walked towards the Excelsior Clinic he wondered what else he would see in Alice if she were on her own. And as he approached Magdalene Bridge he realized he was about to find out; he saw her before she saw him.

She strode out purposefully and he guessed she was heading towards home. She wore a skirt and jacket and low court shoes that had just enough height to accentuate the curve of her calves. She had well-turned ankles, or so his grandfather would have said.

Her sunglasses were the only outward sign that she might be shielding herself from the world at large. Maybe they were her small guard against the risk of public curiosity. This was after all her part of town and she and Lorna would almost certainly have been familiar faces, especially amongst the local business community.

On the other hand it was a sunny day.

When she was a few feet away Goodhew raised his hand in greeting. 'Hi,' he said and smiled.

She smiled back but blankly at first, then as she shifted her glasses up on to the top of her head she registered who he was. 'Oh, hi. Were you coming to see me?'

'That was my plan. I have a couple more questions – we can sit down for a few minutes now if it's convenient.' She looked more attractive without the glasses and her eye contact helped. She was very good at eye contact. Very, very good. He told himself to curb the smiling, this was supposed to be a serious moment.

'Sure,' she replied and pointed to the nearest tea room. 'Is there OK or does it need to be more official than that?'

The café was small and almost empty. The table cloths were blue and yellow gingham and a row of brightly painted teapots were displayed on the low windowsill. It looked like the assembly point for the county's contingent of maiden aunts. 'That looks great,' he said.

They sat at the back, at the table furthest from the door. Alice visited the Ladies while Goodhew ordered a pot of tea then occupied himself by folding a paper napkin into a square and wedging it under one leg of the table to stop it rocking.

By the time he straightened up she had returned. 'Good to know we can still rely on the British police for the important things in life.'

'Like protecting the British cup of tea?'

'Exactly.'

She pulled her chair away from the table and positioned it at almost ninety degrees. She sat erect with her right leg crossed tightly over her left, her toe curled behind her calf. Her skirt draped over her knee and her hands rested in a neat clasp in her lap. Her hair was clipped in place too and a small amount of make-up covered her cheeks. Her appearance was composed but her voice was drained of the authoritative crispness he'd heard in it on each of their previous encounters. Each time she spoke now it was softly: he wondered whether events had cowed her voice into submission or whether the other sterner voice was only adopted in the presence of her brother.

The waitress arrived with the tea on a tray, which she balanced on one hand while reorganizing the space on the table and unloading it with the other. Neither Goodhew nor Alice spoke again until she'd left them.

'How can I help?' Alice asked.

'When I first visited the Excelsior Clinic both you and your brother carried photographs of Lorna Spence. I realize that she was more than an employee to your brother. It seems to me that she was more than just an employee to you too?' It was a statement but he let it sound like a question.

Alice poured the tea. 'Sugar?'

166

'Just milk, thanks.'

'I met Lorna after I returned to work at the clinic last year. We hit it off, which surprised me because on the face of it at least we had absolutely nothing in common. But she was nice company. When she started seeing Richard she behaved like one of the family, not in an imposing way, just like she was comfortable with our way of life. At first it felt like we were just friends, but then she began to feel more like a sister-in-law.'

'So you were close?'

'Close?' She tilted her head a little and her gaze wandered over to the bright rectangle of the window. Almost a minute had ticked by before she spoke again. 'I'd never considered it before, but I suppose we were.' She looked down at her hands in her lap, using them as a distraction whilst she reined in her thoughts.

When she looked back up at him Goodhew saw that uncertainty had replaced her usual assuredness.

Her voice was virtually inaudible. 'That's so strange. I've always thought of really close friendships as the ones you read about; best friends since childhood, or the living in each other's pockets kind. But that's not me. Lorna was the closest friend I had, but I had never seen it in those terms. She was more gregarious than me, and I'm sure she had other friends. In fact for a while Lorna was very close to another girl at the clinic, Victoria.'

'But?'

'They fell out.'

Goodhew waited for her to expand on the comment. She didn't. 'Do you know why?'

'It would be best for you to ask Victoria, but I think it was over a boyfriend. Lorna briefly saw Victoria's ex after Victoria had broken off their relationship. Lorna said that she was surprised it bothered Victoria, but that's all she said.'

'And this was before Lorna started her relationship with your brother?'

'Of course. As far as I'm aware Richard began seeing her just before last Christmas.'

'And did that concern you?'

'In what way?'

'In any way.'

'Career-wise they were in totally different places, but often that's no bad thing. Too much competition isn't always healthy. And there was an age gap, fourteen or fifteen years, but it didn't affect them as far as I could tell.'

'But you didn't approve?'

'You asked me if I had any concerns and I was only concerned that the gap might cause them some problems because it is the sort of thing that starts to worry Richard.'

'Because?'

She raised her palms towards the ceiling. 'Just because.'

Goodhew had a guess. 'Because he'd worry what people thought?'

'No.' She sighed. 'Because his glass is always half empty.'

'Ah.' Goodhew got it then. 'Because he might think that the age gap was going to put her off.'

'It was a possibility, but I didn't agree. For example I would guess that you're the same age as Lorna or marginally older. And I'm just a

168

couple of years older than Richard. No one that walks in here will know why we're talking, some may assume that we're together. We know it's not the case, but I don't think we would look ridiculous together at all. Would we?'

She said it in a totally matter-of-fact way, no hint of flirtation. And while he couldn't imagine that flirting was her style, he also wouldn't have minded if she'd given it a shot.

'No,' Goodhew agreed.

She glanced down at her hands then back up again as though she'd had a sudden thought. 'Actually,' she smiled slightly, 'I worried at first that their relationship might put a strain on my friendship with Lorna. But I was being silly. If anything Lorna and I grew closer.'

'And how about Richard and Lorna? How would you describe their feelings towards each other?'

'Happy. Not soulmates but perhaps not far short.'

'What else?'

Alice frowned. 'What are you looking for?'

'Tensions, things they rowed about. Not necessarily things that point towards a rift, but perhaps differences in attitude that would tell us more about Lorna.'

Alice refilled her cup, making a small ritual from the process. Goodhew wondered if she was trying to buy time or just searching for the right words. 'Lorna was quite a liberated type. It was something that I found was at odds with our upbringing, but it never caused me a problem. Lorna would be very outspoken, openly discussing everything from politics to women's issues. Sometimes Richard found her point of view difficult to comprehend, but he's told you that already.

'Lorna and I even talked about sex on several occasions, but sex in general, no specifics. I certainly wouldn't want to know about my brother's sex life; would you want to know about yours?'

Goodhew shook his head. 'Fair comment.'

For the first time Alice's attention drifted.

He left her with her thoughts for a few seconds more, then spoke. 'How are you feeling?'

'All right. Shocked. I don't know really.' She tilted her head back, trying to think. The muted lighting illuminated one side of her face, the first hints of crow's feet were traced around her eyes. The effect was strange, in one half of her face he could see how she looked ten years ago and in the other half how she might look in ten years' time; the twenty-nine-year-old Alice looked a little too earnest and the forty-nine-year-old a little too melancholy. He liked the current version best.

'Sad for Richard, I suppose,' she sighed finally.

'Not for Lorna?'

'Yes, of course, and for all of us who loved her. But mostly for Richard.'

He nodded and wondered if Richard was ever far from her thoughts. 'Does the name Emma mean anything to you?'

'No, we've been asked that already.'

'I know, just double-checking. What about dogs? Did she like them?'

Alice thought for a few seconds, then shrugged. 'No idea. I don't remember pets ever coming up in conversation. Why?'

170

'We have some dog hair samples that we'd like to identify. They may be nothing but we need to know if she had any connections to anyone with a dog.'

'I can't say for certain of course, but I don't think so.'

'I will need to speak to Victoria Nugent as well. Is she in today?'

'Most probably, although I haven't seen her.' A shadow passed across Alice's face. 'Actually, there's something you can do for me if you don't mind. I've explained why Lorna and Victoria fell out, and it was made more awkward by them working in the same building, but please try to take whatever Victoria says with a pinch of salt. She can seem very...' Alice hesitated as she fished for the appropriate word. In the end she settled for '...bitter.'

They were at the end of their conversation when Goodhew flashed back to the start. 'Earlier you said that you returned to the clinic last year. Where had you been?'

'I needed a break.'

'To do what?'

'Nothing. We'd had a loss. Our father died and I decided to spend some time sorting out the house.'

'Richard said it was left to all of you. Does that mean there are other siblings? Or were you and Richard the only two?'

She became very still, suddenly not sure which way to go next. He waited, knowing that she realized she had to say something. 'No, we weren't,' she said finally. 'There were four of us, myself,

171

Richard, then David and Jackie. David and Jackie were born during my father's second marriage.'

'And did they know Lorna too?'

Alice's eyes widened as if that was the exact route she had wanted to avoid. Her eyes locked with Goodhew's. He studied her face, gripped by the feeling that there was something more than just the words that she was either attempting to communicate or attempting not to. 'Not David,' she mumbled. 'We lost him years ago.' She rubbed her fingers into her palms, as though they were perspiring. But if anything was bubbling beneath her cool exterior it wasn't being allowed to break through. 'Jackie's nothing to do with the Excelsior Clinic. We don't see her often.'

'But she's local?'

Alice nodded. 'Fen Ditton.'

The name made the hairs rise across Goodhew's scalp.

'And Lorna knew her?'

'God, yes. They rode together on several occasions.'

'Rode? As in bikes?'

'Horses. Jackie's the country type. Lives in a cottage.' Alice chewed her bottom lip. 'With a dog.' She stood and brushed down her skirt. It was an abrupt movement, like the urge had come into her head and been translated into movement before her conscious mind had had the chance to be consulted. 'Can I go?' she asked.

Goodhew's thoughts were still on Jackie. 'Richard never mentioned any other siblings.'

Alice was staring at the door now. 'No,' she said quietly, 'I guess Richard wouldn't.'

Chapter Twenty-Four

Contrary to her prediction, Faith Carver's temping contract hadn't been terminated and she still occupied the reception desk.

She didn't look very happy, so he made sure he sounded positive, just to average things out. 'How are you, Mrs Carver?'

'Fine, thank you. Who would you like to see?'

'Victoria Nugent, if she's in.'

'Yes, she is, but she's just slipped outside.' Faith Carver lowered her voice to a whisper and gave one of her automatic scowls. 'Cigarette break, I think.'

'OK,' he whispered back. 'Tell me what she looks like.'

Faith stopped whispering and then answered in her usual businesslike voice. 'Tanned and skinny with very shiny black hair streaked with burgundy. Lowlights, I think they're called.'

'I thought she was a redhead.'

'That was yesterday. You won't miss her.' Faith cleared her throat with an awkward cough. 'Have you made much progress?' She rushed the words, clearly unsure whether asking was the correct thing to do.

'Some, I hope, but it's early days. I don't suppose you've thought of anything else?'

'No. But I only worked with her for one day.'

'No, that's fine, just thought I'd ask.'

He jogged back down the stairs and when he reached the pavement he knew immediately that Faith Carver had been right; Victoria was impossible to miss. The pavement tables were mostly unoccupied; she sat with her back to him and was the only woman with black hair. To describe it as shiny had been a gross understatement, it was straight and almost glasslike. The lowlights were in fact half a dozen chunks dyed a pronounced plummy red, incongruous against her white and green dental nurse's uniform. The lit cigarette she held in her right hand clashed further. Her elbow rested on the table and the cigarette smouldered close to her ear. The ash was about half an inch long and threatened to drop on to the pavement. She was using her left hand to stir an untouched cappuccino.

Goodhew hesitated. Either spring was in the air, or else Mel's observation that he was a prime candidate for stalker of the year had affected his frame of mind. Firstly he'd found Alice very attractive and he now couldn't help noticing that Victoria had her own unique appeal; she did for nurses' uniforms what Ann Summers had done for waitresses' uniforms ... and, er, nurses' uniforms. The stilettos helped. He imagined she made some of the male patients drool, which had to be a bit unpleasant for the dentist.

Goodhew drew a chair up to the table and sat a third of the way round from her. Her eyes were unnaturally blue, but then her skin was unnaturally tanned and it was hard to tell if either was genuine. The ash gave up and tumbled on to the cobbles.

'You're a detective, aren't you?' she said. Her lips barely moved when she spoke, but they parted enough to demonstrate that her teeth were straight and gleaming white.

Goodhew figured that working at the Excelsior Clinic had its perks.

He introduced himself properly. 'DC Gary Goodhew.'

She shrugged. 'Whatever.' She looked at her cigarette, stubbed it out and reached for another. 'I saw you here when she first went. Now I suppose you want to know more about dear Lorna?'

'We all want to know about her.'

Victoria blew a thin plume of smoke in the general direction of her coffee. 'That figures. Men all over the place, even when she's dead.'

'I heard you'd fallen out.'

'Lorna was a bitch.' She gave a bitter laugh. 'I'm supposed to say, "But I didn't want her dead." I can promise you, frequently I've wanted her dead. I imagined something less attention-grabbing though, quietly rotting away with an untreatable strain of syphilis. You know, something appropriate. Have I shocked you?'

'Did you want to?'

'Don't give a shit. Bet no one else says she's a bitch. Well, they wouldn't, would they?'

'Because she's dead?'

Victoria leant towards Goodhew and ran her forefinger along the edge of the table as if feeling the finish. He noticed her nail was pierced with a small diamond dangling from it. 'No, because they didn't know. I didn't know until we spent just a bit too much time together. She pinched my boyfriend, or did you hear that already?'

Goodhew mimicked her body language and leant a little closer to her. 'Yeah, I heard,' he said. 'That's all I heard though – they suggested I get it straight from the horse's mouth, so to speak.'

'Right. So either Alice told you or Richard did. They don't gossip, not really, they just stick to the facts.'

'How did they know you'd fallen out?'

'Oh, shit. The world knew, we weren't exactly subtle about it. Well, I wasn't anyway. That was a big difference between us. With Lorna it was all about getting her own way, and if that meant being two-faced she'd do it. I couldn't do that. She did the dirty on me and I wanted everyone to find out.

'I split up with my boyfriend, I'm the first to admit that. But she was in there, with him, in my bed, within hours. Not days, hours. Friends don't do that, do they?'

'I don't know. Perhaps he wanted to make you jealous. It happens.'

'Not with him. He screwed around while we were together, that's why I dumped him.'

'But you wanted him back?'

Her hand flew up into the air in irritation and remained poised by her ear as if she wanted to slap him. 'No, I fucking didn't. Wanker.' Goodhew wasn't sure if 'wanker' was directed at him or the boyfriend. Either way he decided not to take it personally and hoped she moved her hand before her nail decoration got tangled in her hair.

Goodhew sighed. 'I don't get it, you dumped him and didn't want him back, what difference did it make?'

'Do you have a gap in your education where women are concerned? She was supposed to be my friend.'

'Oh, I see, you decided he was a bastard and you needed your friend to think so too.'

'No!' she snapped indignantly.

'What then?'

She sat and thought about it, then corrected herself. 'You put it across in a tactless way but, fair enough, that is one way to look at it. Just not the way I see it.'

'Fair enough,' he echoed. 'What was his name?'

'I'm not prepared to say.'

'You can't do that. We need to know. This is a murder investigation.'

'OK then. John.'

'John what?'

'Smith.'

'Seriously?'

She didn't answer, just glared at him with full-throttle disdain.

He decided to come back to the name question later. 'And when did you last see him?'

'Don't know.' She thought for a minute. 'I really don't know. Way back, I guess.'

'I'll need to contact him. Can you let me have his address?'

'No, sorry. Like I say, I haven't seen him and I lost touch ages ago.'

'No phone number, email address even?'

'That's right. Nothing.'

'And he stopped seeing Lorna?'

'He wasn't seeing her. It was a sex thing. That was Lorna and men all over. One sex thing after another. By rights she should have been the VD capital of Cambridge.'

'But her relationship with Richard was different?'

'Why? Because it's lasted a few months? Or because he's richer than most? Or perhaps because he was strung out with jealousy and she liked watching the frenzy it sent him into? Have you asked him about the phone yet?'

'What phone?'

'The mobile he bought her. He pays the bill, gets it itemized and sent to his office so he can check on her.'

'How do you know?'

'It's a small place with thin walls, easy to know what's going on if you set out to.' She half closed her eyes and stared at the froth spinning on the top of her coffee. 'Lorna's old phone, the one she lost? It's in Richard's office. You know, I think he's a good bloke, she just screwed him up. But on the other hand I'm a shit judge of men.'

He kept his tone casual, hoping the question would catch her with her guard down. 'And how well do you know Bryn O'Brien?'

Victoria's expression remained unaltered.

'Ah.' She blew out another column of smoke, this time with her head tilted back, sending it straight upwards. 'I suppose it depends on how you categorize what's relevant. I don't know his mother's maiden name or his date of birth if that's what you mean. But if good sex and superficial conversation qualify then I'm in. Or should I say, he was.'

'But he'd seen Lorna as well.'

'And?'

'Why was Bryn fair game when John wasn't?'

'No one was going out with Bryn, were they? Lorna was seeing Richard and I was enjoying being single.'

'Now I'm confused.'

Victoria was unimpressed. 'I can imagine. Free-spirited women must be quite an anathema to someone like you.'

'At this moment, you're quite right.' She was grating big time now and he was annoyed with himself for being unable to keep it from his voice. He forced his speech to slow and lowered the volume to make her pay better attention. 'Let me explain why I'm confused. You and Lorna were out with Bryn in January, correct?'

She lowered her eyelashes in a slow blink. 'Yup.'

'But you fell out with her autumn last year.'

'If you say so.'

'Well, did you, or not?'

'You figure it out.'

'Well, if you did it would imply you patched things up, yet now she's dead you're happy to admit you hated her. So either you never fell out in the first place or you fell out for a second time. And if you really did fall out over this John Smith you've seen him far more recently than "ages ago".'

Victoria ran her tongue across the front of her upper teeth. If it was supposed to look at all sexy it didn't work. Her eyes hardened and she pointed towards the river. 'Look over there.'

Goodhew did and saw nothing.

'I think I see your next promotion coming over

the horizon.' Victoria stood abruptly, her cappuccino still untouched. 'I know nothing that can help, so let's just leave it there.'

'What about Colin Willis?'

She looked at him in irritation. 'Who?'

'The bloke you and she and Bryn played pool with.'

'I never even spoke to him.'

Goodhew glanced around to make sure there was still no one within earshot. 'Did Lorna sleep with him?'

Victoria lowered her face closer to his. 'Lorna wanted something but not sex. I know that much.'

'How do you?'

Victoria straightened. 'Is my tan fake?'

Goodhew didn't answer.

Victoria rolled her eyes. 'It's obvious. But then we've already established that you're a bit retarded on the women front, haven't we?'

Chapter Twenty-Five

The Boat Race stood on the corner of East Road and Burleigh Street and had once been Cambridge's best-known live music pub. But in the eyes of the planning office, the arrival of Robert Sayles's new department store and Burleigh Street's subsequent revamp hadn't left room for such a venue. It was now called the Vine and every trace of its former persona had been eradicated. It was just a few minutes' walk from Parkside station and where Michael Kincaide had suggested they meet for a drink.

Although Goodhew found its new wine bar guise about as dynamic as a house full of magnolia walls he still felt nostalgia for the building and tried to superimpose his memories of local bands like the Frigidaires and Jump, Bump and Boogie over the anaemic pop trickling from the new but gutless sound system.

Kincaide had arrived first and sat near the door with a glass of red wine and a copy of the *Cambridge Evening News*. Goodhew just got a coffee.

He had managed to stay true to his word and had contacted Marks with each new development as the day went along. His penultimate call revealing the existence of Jackie had coincided with Kincaide ending his interview with Bryn. So it had been Kincaide who'd been assigned to visit her. Goodhew had been disappointed not to join him, but then again that had left him with time to see the charming Victoria.

Hmm.

As Goodhew reached the table Kincaide held up the front page of the paper. 'Have you seen it?'

Goodhew tilted his head to match the angle of the paper, but he didn't really need to: there were only three short words in the headline, easy to read even upside down, 'Who is Emma?'

'I'd like to know how they got it,' Kincaide said and passed it across to him. Goodhew started reading as he sat down. The story was simple; the paper had been tipped off about the message on Lorna's palms, stating that the main line of the police investigation was the theory that Emma

181

was someone known to both Lorna and her killer. Therefore, find Emma and find the murderer. 'Marks went ballistic, I think he wants to slaughter whoever leaked it.'

'It might flush out the answer though. I mean, if I were called Emma I'd certainly stop and think about any connection I might have with Lorna.'

'You approve then?'

'No, I'm just saying that with some luck it may work to our advantage, that's all. Any idea who did it?'

Kincaide shook his head. 'Marks said there'd been too much anonymity already and it had to stop.'

'Whatever that means.'

'You know what that means, he's going to be flushing out whoever posted him the evidence on the Airport Rapist and probably demote or sack him over this.'

'Oh, I think he'll calm down.' Goodhew slid the paper back to Kincaide. 'How was Jackie Moran?'

'Not at home, and neither were the immediate neighbours.'

'But the house looked occupied?'

'Oh, yes. And I checked at the local paper shop, she has *The Times* delivered three times a week and she's bang up to date with her bill. I couldn't find out where she works, if she does. Did you ask Alice?'

'Shit, I should have. We could go over now, though – to Jackie's, I mean. More likely to catch her at home in the evening.'

Kincaide checked his watch. 'Haven't you got a life outside work? Tomorrow morning first thing will be good enough. We can both go. How was it with Victoria Nugent? Your mate Bryn called her feisty.'

'He's not my mate.'

'OK. But that's what he called her.'

'Well, that's one way to describe her. I think I'd go for scary. The dates of her falling out with Lorna just don't add up – right in the middle of it they seemed to have patched things up enough for Bryn to think they were close friends when they all went out together.'

'Unless he's lying.'

Goodhew screwed up his nose. 'Why would he? No, that doesn't make sense, he would have to have concocted the story with Victoria.'

'And?'

'They don't know each other that well.'

'Or so they say. And the only other two people who were supposedly there are both dead. Then there's this business of Victoria hating Lorna. No one else admits to hating her but in Richard Moran's own words he felt jealous because she was a slapper.'

'No, no, he didn't actually say that.'

'OK. He said she wanted a more–' Kincaide paused to make little quote signs in the air – 'open relationship than he did. What bloke is going to buy into that one? The only reason he's not going to say anything against her is self-preservation; we'd be breathing down his throat if he owned up to how he really felt about her. In fact we should be breathing down his throat.'

'So if it's that simple how does "Emma" fit in?'

'Worry about it tomorrow. We'll start with

183

Jackie Moran first thing.' From within his pocket Kincaide's mobile bleeped. 'You need sex,' he added as he fumbled for his phone.

Goodhew looked down at his coffee. He didn't like Kincaide's phraseology but had to admit that it was a fair point.

He glanced up in time to see Kincaide unlock his phone then smirk as he read the message. 'And speaking of which,' he said, dropping it back in his pocket, 'I'd better go.'

Somehow Goodhew knew that Kincaide's text hadn't been sent by his wife. He took his time finishing his coffee and he wondered how it was that the Bryns, Kincaides and Victorias of the world seemed to have no qualms about entering into casual liaisons, whereas he couldn't seem to separate the physical from the emotional.

He guessed that those were the signals he gave out too; the women he attracted weren't the one night fling kind. And even looking back at school he could see that the 'just say no' anti-drugs campaign had been wasted on him; he oozed so little irresponsibility that until he was eighteen he'd never even been offered a cigarette.

He counted the months back to the last of the half-dozen or so dates he'd shared with Tasha, a gap student from Sydney. More time had passed than he'd realized; no wonder he'd had a moment of finding Victoria attractive. And the idea of a quick fling had a certain appeal, but he knew it wouldn't be happening; he couldn't imagine a time where it would ever be his thing.

On top of that he couldn't totally grasp the concept of opening up that much to just anyone, and for the time being at least he knew that any desires were illogically attached to Mel.

He checked his watch and saw it was time to track down his grandmother; perhaps he could admonish her for saddling him with a rogue sexual ethics gene.

He dialled her mobile and as it rang it occurred to him that she was far more likely to tell him to make the most of being single. In which case the gene must have come from his granddad, because it certainly had never been located growing anywhere near his mum's side of the tree.

Chapter Twenty-Six

His grandmother lived on the first floor of a two-storey art deco block of eight flats on the Fen Causeway. The building was white with curved windows, sweeping balconies and rooms so large that they would have dwarfed even the bulbous deco furniture they'd been designed to house. Connaught Villas lounged across a plot big enough to accommodate two streets of 'affordable' housing and although the road outside was often clogged with city-bound cars the main view was the lush marshy fields of Newnham Common. This was high quality city dwelling.

Goodhew arrived within ten minutes; he had his own key and let himself into her apartment. A small lobby led into the single large reception room. 'Hello, Gran, it's me,' he called. The room was warm, slightly humid, but not in an unpleasant way. A yucca tree thrived in a large pot halfway between the kitchen door and the french windows, enjoying the steam from the kitchen and the sun from the south. He draped his jacket across the back of his favourite armchair and checked the time on the grandfather clock as it clunked through the seconds.

It struck the hour a single dainty chime. As a child he'd wondered why it didn't count out the hours like every other chiming clock, and that began a thought process that led him to wonder why most things in his childhood seemed to be so different to other childhoods.

Then he'd grown up and discovered that his best friend was his grandmother and if that was unconventional it really didn't matter.

And on cue his grandmother appeared in the kitchen doorway with a tray of tea and biscuits. She was still wearing the black cocktail dress that she'd obviously worn to the Felix.

He smiled at her and settled back into the cherry leather wing-chair. 'You're looking well.'

'Good quality meals on wheels,' she joked.

'Really?'

'Yes, my favourite Chinese has started home deliveries.'

She placed the tray on the coffee table and sat in the chair facing him. She reached underneath and produced a black box from the magazine shelf. 'Backgammon?'

'Of course.' Goodhew opened out the board and slid the red and black counters into place. He held out the red dice for her, and she opened her hand for him to drop them in. 'Oh, and before I forget...' He pulled an envelope from his back pocket. 'Your rent.'

'Thanks,' she said and pulled an expression that he couldn't place but suspected was in the region of 'You're not going to want to hear this.'

The flat was hers, in fact the whole building was, and Goodhew guessed that, apart from her own apartment, it was the last of his grandparents' assets. Paying market rate for renting the flat was something he'd insisted upon, and he assumed that if she ever started to struggle financially the logical step would be to rent out the floors below his. 'Is it about my flat?' he asked.

'In a roundabout way, yes.' After that she fell silent and Goodhew guessed there was something that she was waiting for him to say.

'If you need the building back, I can easily move. I don't mind,' he added, hoping he wasn't the completely useless liar that she claimed he was.

She took one of the dice and twiddled it between her thumb and forefinger. He smiled to himself as he noticed how precisely its colour matched her nail polish; she had a talent for detail. 'I know,' she said, 'but it's nothing like that. I visited Mason, my solicitor, and I've come away with some documents. I'd like you to look over them.'

'Sure.'

'I'd like us to play first.' She offered him the plate of biscuits.

They fell silent for a few moments, each picked up a dice and threw them simultaneously. He scored six, she scored one. He moved the pieces, then looked up.

'How's work?' she asked.

'Fine. Why?' A mischievous smile darted on to her face.

He grinned. 'What?'

'I think romance often blooms in the workplace, don't you?'

He shook his head. 'Only when it's mutual. And if anyone ever shows a flicker of mutual interest I'll be sure to let you know.'

'But you like her?'

'I made something out of nothing. I didn't even misread the signals, there weren't any. And now I don't know what I was thinking, she has a boyfriend, she wouldn't be with him if she'd had enough.'

'Some people don't leave.'

'She's made it clear she's not interested. Even if that wasn't the case that's not the way I'd want to start a relationship.'

'So that's that?'

'Absolutely,' he replied firmly.

Goodhew leant over and took his tea while his grandmother set hers to one side, preferring to concentrate on the game.

'Sometimes,' she said, 'things don't work out the way we want them to.'

He glanced across at her and found her shrewd gaze waiting to meet his. 'We're not still talking about Mel now, are we?'

'No.'

He shook his dice on to the board and took his turn.

She turned over the doubling dice. 'I'm doubling the game,' she said. She liked raising the stakes.

He waited until his turn before speaking and turned the doubling dice again. 'Nothing ventured, nothing gained,' he said. 'Your turn.'

'I notice the boundaries you set for yourself, Gary.'

'Such as?'

'The terms on which you're prepared to start a relationship. Or work on your own initiative. Or refuse to judge Kincaide. The way you push yourself to stay fit. I could go on and on.' He was aware that she watched him as he stretched across the table to move pieces from her side of the board. 'It is clear to me that you're ready–' she threw her dice and took her move, tapping the pieces on the board as she counted – 'to inherit your grandfather's money.' She kept her tone casual but it was obvious to both of them that her smile was an apologetic one. Without further explanation she reached behind a cushion and pulled out several sheets of paper then tried to pass him the top copy. Her voice was hushed. 'I can take you through all the major assets in detail, but this is a summary.'

Goodhew refused to look at it. 'No,' he said, then realized how sharp his voice sounded. 'No, thank you,' he said more softly.

'One of your properties is the house in Park Terrace.'

'I own my flat?'

'Yes, and the rest of the building beneath.'

'This is ridiculous.'

She selected a different sheet and tried to pass it to him. 'This is the current valuation.' She waved the paper. 'I know you're phobic about money but just read it. Please.'

189

'I'm not phobic, I just don't want it,' he said quietly.

'It's already yours. And it's part of your grandfather's legacy. Not taking it would be letting him down.'

'What about Debbie?'

'That's your half. She'll receive a similar settlement when I think she can deal with it.'

'I don't understand, everything was left to Mum and Dad.'

'No, only some of it. We couldn't trust that it would reach you and your sister.'

'Because of my mother?'

'It doesn't matter why.'

Goodhew collected the dice and returned them to the backgammon box. It was obvious that they would not be completing the game. He fought to overcome the lump in his throat and waited until it felt safe for him to try to speak. 'I interviewed a witness yesterday, his name's Bryn O'Brien and we were at primary school together. As we were talking I suddenly had this huge flashback. I was in maths. I loved maths but I couldn't concentrate and I knocked my pen on to the floor. I watched it bounce then roll under the next desk. I went to get it then looked up and the headmistress was at the classroom door. I knew something terrible had happened and I was sent home because Granddad was ill.'

His grandmother nodded as if she remembered too. 'And you never went back.'

'Then you went away.'

'It was the best way for me to deal with his death.'

'We understood that. Yesterday reminded me of how much damage that money caused. Once Mum started spending she stuck us in that school. Debbie and I barely saw each other, and when I did manage to speak to her she just cried all the time. We were homesick and didn't fit in with the other kids.'

'But that's just it, Gary. It was your mum in combination with the money that caused the problem.'

'We lost touch with all our old friends, then at the end of term we came home to find Dad on the edge of a breakdown while Mum and the money were getting up to who knows what. I'm sorry, I know this isn't the response you wanted, but I'm very conscious of the parts of my life that are going well and I'm not going to jeopardize them for money.'

'It doesn't have to change anything,' she said.

But her expression betrayed her, they both knew that wasn't true. He scratched around for the right words and in the meantime heard himself say, 'You hid it from me.' It was a thought he shouldn't have spoken, he already knew she knew how he felt and already knew she was sorry.

She placed one page on the table and left him alone then. Afterwards all he could remember was the clock ticking and his stomach growing tighter and tighter. He rested his elbows on his knees and pressed his face into his cupped hands. He stayed like that for almost a minute, then blew out a long breath and looked at the paper. As far as he was concerned, money was trouble.

He remembered Ratty's theory about trouble,

Touch it and it stains you.

He pushed the paper away; it slid off the far side of the table and drifted to the floor. He let himself out of his grandmother's flat and headed back to work; right now the only person's trouble he was interested in was Lorna Spence's.

Chapter Twenty-Seven

Colin Willis's file had been left on Goodhew's chair and a sheet of paper lay on the desktop. He dumped the file next to it and the down draught sent the page floating towards the edge. He caught it before it fell. The message was written in marker pen and the note was headed 'Gary Goodhew', and underlined twice.

'10.15 p.m. Faith Carver called, wanted to speak to you only. Please call her.' Followed by her number.

He glanced at his watch. She was likely to be asleep, but that was tough luck. Murder was murder.

He took the cordless handset from his desk and dialled, then flipped open the front of the Willis file, expecting a wait while Mrs Carver stirred. A photograph of the inside of his flat was on top; it was in a similar state of decay as the body.

Faith Carver answered on the first ring, in the old-fashioned way with a recitation of her number. Goodhew closed the file.

'It's DC Goodhew here, I'm sorry if I've

woken you.'

'No, no, it's perfectly all right. I decided to wait up for you to call.' Her voice had an official crispness. 'I wanted to speak to you directly because I hate gossip and what I want to say sounds as if it's exactly that. I'm hoping I can trust you to be discreet if this turns out to be irrelevant.'

'Of course.'

'Good. Victoria Nugent seemed very agitated after you left today Obviously I only met her for the first time this week, I know she can be petulant, but she's never seemed the nervous type. So I made a point of keeping an eye on her and after about fifteen minutes she slipped out of the building.'

'Did you see where she went?'

'Yes and no. She walked to the far side of the punting station and stayed there for ten minutes or so. I couldn't see her but I would have noticed if she'd gone anywhere else. When she reappeared she was in the process of closing her mobile phone so I assume that she'd been making a call.'

'And how did she seem when she returned?'

'Back to normal.'

'And that is?'

'Cold, borderline rude.'

'But a moment ago you described her as petulant.'

'I said I know she can be. She was on Monday. She had a bad atmosphere hanging about her like a robe, she was not pleased when I told her that Lorna was late in.'

'Do you know what she wanted?'

'That's what Lorna asked. She seemed put out

193

when I didn't know. The gist of it was that it was urgent.'

'And no idea what?'

'Nothing.'

'You said Lorna was late in. How late?'

'Just before ten, between quarter to and ten to. I know because I checked the clock.'

'Why?'

'I don't like lateness. I believe you can tell what sort of person someone is from their timekeeping. Someone who's consistently five minutes late is quite different from someone who's consistently five minutes early. That may sound like rubbish to you but it's what I think and I do like to know the sort of people I work with.'

'OK. And what sort do you think Lorna was?'

'Now she's dead it seems she had problems...'

'But what did you think at the time?'

Faith Carver deliberated for several seconds, long enough for Goodhew to ask her if she was still there.

'Yes, I'm here, I was just thinking.' She paused again, this time for longer. Goodhew waited while she gathered her thoughts. 'There are little things I never considered to mention,' she said. 'Lorna was late, as I said, and by the time she'd arrived people had been trying to get hold of her. Victoria of course. But Richard and Alice Moran had also both asked for her, work-related I guessed.

'Then when she first arrived Lorna seemed friendly, but a little tense. Maybe because she was late, I don't know. But she was certainly talkative later on, she told me about the clinic, the different treatments and how much they cost.

You know, general chit-chat really.

'On balance, I think she seemed outgoing and popular, perhaps not very professional turning up late like that, but that doesn't seem to matter much these days. Maybe she had a good reason. I must admit, when she wasn't in by nine yesterday morning I was starting to draw conclusions. But then as it turned out they would have been the wrong ones, wouldn't they?'

Goodhew had scribbled notes across the original message, trying to keep up with the rush of observations pouring from Faith Carver. 'I've taken notes but we'll need to take a statement from you too.' Goodhew arranged it for the following morning.

Faith Carver went through the formality of confirming the arrangement and was just reaching the goodbyes when she gasped, 'Oh yes, there is something else. I nearly forgot to mention it. Lorna slipped off to lunch at twelve and didn't come back until one thirty, and before she went I heard her mobile phone receive several text messages.'

Goodhew replaced the handset. He hadn't realized that a second person had entered the room and jumped when he heard a cough. Marks stood in the open doorway. Expressionless.

'Why are you here?'

Goodhew shrugged. 'Nothing on TV.' But Marks wasn't about to be moved by flippant comments, so he added, 'I was going to take another look at Colin Willis's file but I've just spoken to Faith Carver instead; how soon will we have Lorna's phone records?'

'Coincidentally, just about now.' Marks held

out a wodge of faxes. 'They're the up-to-date listings from all the phones you're checking, from the last bill until yesterday and including Lorna's extension at work. Don't stay too late. I'll be in my office.'

Goodhew settled down to study the pile of paper. But he knew he was getting tired when he stared at the lists of numbers and found them totally meaningless. He wandered round to the drinks machine and downed two coffees in quick succession then returned to his desk with a slightly clearer mind.

Lorna had made many phone calls and, judging by the variety of numbers, made them to many people. Then, two weeks and two days before the end of the bill, the calls stopped. So that fitted with Victoria's claim that Lorna had changed her phone and left him with no way of checking who she'd been texting on the morning of her disappearance.

His extension rang: it was Marks. 'Go home, Gary.' Marks sounded tired, his voice gravelly.

'It looks like Lorna Spence was using a second mobile. Victoria Nugent said much the same, reckons the old one is at the Excelsior Clinic. Could the new one be at her flat?'

'I doubt it, the flat was searched.'

'I know, but perhaps it was missed.'

'Read me the number.'

'I don't have it, but I have a list of mobiles that she was in the habit of texting. We need to know who they belong to and whether they started texting her on a new number.'

'I'll get that checked. What other progress?'

'No, apart from that, nothing really. We're visiting Jackie Moran first thing in the morning.'

'You and Kincaide?'

'Yes.'

'Good. Now go home, get some sleep and start fresh tomorrow.'

Chapter Twenty-Eight

Goodhew managed a fitful doze from just after three until five thirty-five and awoke to the sound of incessant rain and the silence of birds. He lay on top of his bed, bare-chested but still wearing jeans; a slight improvement on a fully clothed crash-out on the settee.

He sat on the edge of the bed until his head cleared then crossed to the window wanting to see the downpour; some days the rain sounded worse than it was, amplified by the water gushing through downpipes and dripping from the guttering.

But today it was as wet as it sounded, if not wetter.

The rain fell in sleet-thick sheets, and the sky was bruised and grey like a battered lead lid nailed down close above the rooftops.

He made the few hundred yards to work much longer by detouring via Parkside pool. But he stopped swimming after ninety lengths, worried that he might keep Kincaide waiting, and so arrived at his desk promptly on the dot of seven.

Forty-five minutes after Kincaide had been due at the station there was still no sign of him. No answer on his home phone and his mobile diverted to voice mail. Goodhew told himself there was probably a good reason for it and refused the temptation of dropping back into anti-Kincaide mode.

But equally he hadn't felt like wasting any more time waiting so he'd left without him and now stood alone on the doorstep of Jackie Moran's cottage. The rain had not slowed and drove at a forty-five degree angle at the unprotected front of the house. The front garden consisted of one raised stone bed planted with a couple of dozen petunias and, at the end furthest from the front door, young sweet pea plants growing up the sides of a black wrought iron obelisk. The garden was hardly ambitious but both sets of plants were being battered by the weather and only a few minutes passed before Goodhew deteriorated from damp to equally bedraggled.

It was a strong Suffolk accent that snapped him out of his moment of rain-muffled solitary confinement. 'You won't catch Jackie this late.' The voice belonged to a postman who was walking towards him from the property next door. 'She's like clockwork; gone at eight every weekday.'

'To work?'

The postman poked a couple of items of what looked like junk mail through Jackie Moran's letterbox before answering. 'I dunno.'

'Damn,' Goodhew sighed. 'I needed to speak to her this morning.'

'Well, I can tell you where she'll be, at the

stables at Old Mile Farm, just out towards Quy. But I don't know if it's work or not, 'cept I s'pose anything involving horses is work. Worse than kids, they are. Probably why all these females love 'em so much.'

Goodhew had been vaguely aware of seeing the farm's signboard on one of the routes to Newmarket, but the postman was happy to give him precise directions before waving goodbye from a distance of about three feet.

Newmarket: the home of flat racing, the sport of kings. Many of the racing yards were positioned near the centre of the town, tucked just out of sight of the main through roads. Or more likely, in a town where horses had right of way, the roads had been developed afterwards, deliberately planned to avoid disturbing the town's main industry.

Further out from the centre, the surrounding villages remained horse rich, acres and acres of pristine post and rail heaven.

And it was with that amount of local knowledge that Goodhew drew himself a picture of what to expect at Old Mile Farm and added in a younger version of Alice Moran to represent Jackie.

The signboard for the farm was the only thing visible from the road; it was wood and nailed to a telegraph pole. The words had been carved out and painted white. He turned down the unmade track alongside and immediately wrote himself a mental note advising against making assumptions in the future. He was not driving towards a smart racing yard and none of the three horses turned out in the field bore any resemblance to a thoroughbred; Heinz 57s of the horse world. Two of them were bay, standing at about fourteen hands and looking like they were at least fifty per cent native breed, and the third was a heavy-set skewbald closer to sixteen hands. One of the bays trotted alongside the fence, its mane and tail sodden and steam rising from its back even as the rain continued to fall. It reached the far corner then stretched its neck over the top rail, pricked its ears forward and whinnied.

Goodhew drove past. The track opened out to a small area of uneven hard standing, just big enough to park half a dozen cars; a RAV4 took up one corner, but although his was the only other vehicle, Goodhew still found it hard to park and avoid the puddles.

In front of him was a fenced-in menage and facing on to that was a row of ten loose boxes. The air smelt of wet earth and manure. A muck heap steamed and a water butt caught the rain as it spurted from a broken strip of guttering on the overhang of roof above the last stable. The butt was overflowing and the loudest sound was the sploshing of water falling into the butt then bouncing out and on to the concrete floor below.

A rug hung over the door to the third loose box. It was open and he walked towards it. 'Hello?' he called.

No reply.

He looked inside but it was empty. He walked along the row. The seventh stable was the only one occupied; a chestnut gelding with the name Jester on his head collar poked his nose over the door. Then in the distance Goodhew heard the bay whinny again and was soon able to pick out the sound of hooves. Unlike the others, the horse that was ridden into the yard was a thoroughbred. She was a grey and definitely no youngster, walking towards the boxes with the reins hanging loose around her neck. A border collie trotted alongside, inches from her hooves.

Her rider wore a crash hat and a wax jacket with its collar turned up, making it impossible for him to catch more than a glimpse of her face. 'Jackie Moran?' he asked doubtfully.

'Yes, that's me. Give me one minute to sort Suze out.' She patted the mare's neck then swung out of the saddle, landing lightly on the balls of her feet. She led the horse into the third box. The collie sat with its back to Goodhew in the middle of the doorway and watched the untacking. Jackie Moran rugged up Suze then hauled the saddle on to the door and hooked the bridle on a nearby peg. Neither animal attempted to move until the collie was forced to get out of the path of the closing door. 'Which way today, Bridy?' The dog chose the stable and Jackie Moran slid the bolt behind her. 'She's a lazy old girl, sleeps half the day now.'

He guessed she meant the dog.

'They're both the same,' she added, immediately making his guess irrelevant. 'How can I help?' Before he'd had a chance to reply she corrected herself, drawing an end to her initial informality. 'I suppose what I should first find out is who you are and what you want.' She pulled the crash hat from her head and ran her fingers once through her brown hair as if that would be enough to unflatten it.

He introduced himself and her expression remained unaltered: cooperative but not up for having her time wasted. She didn't need to say 'Get on with it,' it was written on her face.

'I'm here about Lorna Spence.'

'Thought you might be,' she said. Perhaps she'd taken stock of him taking stock of her and she deliberately paused before adding, 'You're very young, aren't you?' like it was the only thing she'd found worth a mention.

He just shrugged.

'We can sit in there.' She pointed towards the first stable in the block. 'Will that be OK?' She looked hopeful; whatever was in the horse box cum lounge clearly appealed to her. 'It's dry.'

'Fine.' He gave her the 'after you' gesture. 'Go ahead.'

She unbolted both halves of the stable door and he followed her inside. The horse box cum lounge was more horse box cum storeroom with bales of hay and straw, two feed bins and a pile of buckets. She closed the bottom half of the door – perhaps to keep in the pretence of warmth – and moved two bales so they could sit, almost side by side facing the door.

'I take the tack and grooming kit home each night, to reduce the chance of break-ins. When I was a teenager I used to bring a sleeping bag and camp out in here so I could get up early and ride, but I'd never do that now.'

They each sat on a bale, Jackie with her feet planted squarely in front of her and one hand on each knee; she looked like she was bracing herself.

'Lorna Spence?' He let the name hang in the air, hoping she'd conjure up the question that went with the name. She did.

'We weren't close friends you know. But I liked her and we seemed to get on OK. She helped exercise the horses once or twice each week.'

'She rode well?'

'Very riding school.' He looked puzzled, she explained. 'She'd been taught well, but obviously hadn't ridden enough to be an unconsciously competent horsewoman. I think she would have struggled with Suze, but she was fine on Jester. Suze looks docile now, but she's smart, she'd have played up. She always sees through people.'

'Is that a hint?'

A defensive note slipped into her voice. 'I don't hint, I either say it or keep it to myself. Lorna was competent but not expert. Suze is a retired racehorse, she was highly strung in her day, and animals like that are well aware of who they can take advantage of. And that was all I meant.'

Goodhew tried to read behind her defiant look. He had the distinct feeling that she chose to keep her thoughts to herself far more often than she vented them. Reticence was no ugly trait, just one he didn't have the luxury of letting her indulge in.

But she seemed to open up when she talked about her horse and if that meant he had to take a metaphorical canter round the paddock to get over each metaphorical hurdle that was fine by him.

Jackie ran her nail up and down the double-stitched outer seam of her jodhpurs. It was the kind of action that reminded him of a schoolgirl

203

chewing a pencil or twirling her hair. Distracted. And insecure.

'Tell me about Suze,' he asked gently.

Her gaze darted up and looked into his. Her face softened and for the first time he saw what appeared to be a genuine smile. 'She's really called Souza Symphony, that was her racing name. My dad owned part shares in her but she only ran a few times. She wasn't quite quick enough. She was fast actually, but we're talking about a tenth of a second here and there making all the difference. That picture behind you...' She pointed to the back of the stable door where a photocopy of a press clipping was pinned. 'That was the only thing she ever won. Beginner's luck, my mother said.'

There were two people pictured with the horse. One was the jockey. Goodhew read the caption: 'Souza Symphony, winner of the 5F Yearling Handicap, pictured with jockey Brendan Quinn and owner Mrs Sarah Moran.' If Jackie Moran had tried to dress up as a grinning *Dynasty* extra this would have been the result. 'That's her?'

'I remember Mum took us on summer holidays to Bournemouth then abandoned us at the hotel for the day while she drove to Brighton to watch her run. Dad came down a few days later and they had this huge row about it.'

'When was it?'

''82, can't you tell by the clothes? Suze is a real old girl now and I'm glad Mum went, she was so thrilled. Suze went on to have a couple of foals then I talked Dad into letting me keep her. I suppose it's silly to have two horses myself but it's how I like to spend my time.'

'Do you work?'

'I inherited this place and my cottage, so there's no rent. I'm paid to look after the three horses in the field and I give riding lessons at the weekend. That's it. I'd love to do this place up but I don't think it'll happen somehow. I'm not one of the family's high-flyers, am I?' Her smile reappeared but he thought it now looked artificially bright.

'Why didn't you come forward?' He threw in the question, hoping to catch her more off guard now.

Her eyes narrowed and the smile hardened. 'Time to get down to business?'

'Something like that.'

'Well, first off, thanks for letting me chat about Suze, I needed an ice-breaker. I find it hard to get started with people.' She was quite obviously stalling. 'I'm not good with them, I suppose that's why I like it here.' She paused, her stalling stalled. A few more seconds passed before she spoke again. 'I can cope, one to one like this. But not with big groups of people. Or in unfamiliar places. It's pathetic.' She said it in such a matter-of-fact way that at first he wondered if there was any truth in what she said.

'And secondly?'

'Secondly, I didn't want to waste my stress and time on you lot if you were going to squander it so I decided to let you find me if you thought it important enough.'

'That could be withholding evidence.'

'That's bollocks.'

'Bollocks?'

'There's nothing to withhold. We rode horses together sometimes. Big deal.'

'How did you meet – was it through Richard or Alice or the clinic?'

'No way. Lorna found me by accident, she wanted somewhere to ride and called in here.'

'A coincidence?'

'In theory. But I don't think so. I'm sure she engineered it. That would be very much like Lorna, you know. She liked to make things happen – by chance, if you see what I mean.'

'And you were friends with her?'

'It sounds worse than I'm sure it was. I think she thought she could bring us all closer together. She hoped to marry Richard and maybe she was picturing being nice and close to her new "sisters" too.'

'Was it working?'

'It was a non-starter.'

'Why?'

'I guess we're just not that kind of family.'

'Richard and Alice seem very close.'

'Yes, I've always thought they seemed like a healthy example of siblingdom.' She smiled at her own sarcasm, then shook her head and looked away. 'But not my thing.' She changed the subject quickly. 'Do you have brothers or sisters?'

'One sister.'

'And do you live together? Thought not. They live together and work together.'

'I know.'

'And I couldn't imagine either of them marrying somehow. Wouldn't it just make the status quo wobble too much?' She shifted topic without pausing. 'The stables belonged to my mother. And as well as the cottage I was left a third share of the family house. Have you been there yet?'

He nodded. 'Interesting property.'

'It's a monster. My mother never liked it. Perhaps I'll sell up, start over somewhere else. It's not like Alice and Richard would miss me, they'd probably love to buy me out. I know it's what my dad wanted for me. Secretly I think he would have liked it if I'd been more of an academic, but he let me carry on down here. He'd drop by sometimes, bring a flask with him. When it was raining we'd sit in here, or in his car, and we'd talk.

'He'd always ask me loads of questions, he was always checking if I was happy. I knew he was dying, though, before the others did – ironic when they work in medicine, don't you think?

'He came here last June and it was a perfect summer's day. Warm but breezy. Leaves rustling, fluffy clouds. All that shit. In fact just the way they make England look in adverts. And I looked at him and realized his skin had that horrible greyness, the one people get when they're seriously ill. I had the feeling then that it wouldn't be long.'

Goodhew's mobile bleeped and he quickly read the new message. 'My colleague DC Kincaide will be here in a minute.'

'Why?'

'Nothing to worry about, we were originally coming together but he's just running late.'

'That's overkill.'

'It's just procedure.'

'No, just to talk to one person about a dead acquaintance? It would definitely be overkill. So you want me for more than that, don't you?'

Astute.

Goodhew couldn't decide how to answer, but she didn't seem to be waiting for a reply.

'I don't know who Emma is, by the way,' she said.

'How...' He stopped himself there, realizing the answer. 'Last night's paper?'

She nodded.

'Are you sure?' he checked.

'Absolutely.'

She stood and moved to the half-open door, resting her elbow on top. She was looking across to the car park. 'So what's your partner like?'

'Why?'

'No, I mean what does he look like? There's a bloke getting out of a dark blue saloon. He's in a suit.'

'That'll be him.'

'He won't want to sit in here in that suit, will he?'

Goodhew rose to his feet and joined her in the doorway. 'Good point.'

She returned to sit on her bale. 'Actually, I'd like to stay in here if you don't mind.'

He knew that so far his meeting with her had been casual, unstructured and nothing like training recommended. He also felt it had as much potential for being productive as any other approach.

Goodhew waved at Kincaide to show him where they were. Kincaide carried an A4 document wallet and he held it over his head as he made a dash for the shelter of the stable overhang. He half walked, half ran, trying to avoid splashes on his trouser legs. The suggestion that he sit on a hay bale was going to go down very badly.

Jackie had seemed to relax and Goodhew didn't want to lose that opportunity to talk to her. He guessed with Kincaide's arrival her earlier stiffness was set to return. There was no more than ten seconds before Kincaide would make it through the door. Goodhew turned to face Jackie, his voice little more than a whisper. 'Tell me about Colin Willis.'

The guard she'd begun to drop flew back into place. But for a split second she looked betrayed. Her whole body gave a sharp and involuntary jolt; if words were bullets she'd just been shot.

Kincaide had drawn to a halt next to the RAV4. He'd driven slowly down the track, trying to avoid mud splashes on the paintwork, only to find the so-called car park was nothing but mud ruts full of silty water. No doubt the air would be hanging with the stench of horse shit.

He spotted the manure heap; it was at the other end of the yard, but it was large and steam was rising from it at an unhealthy pace. He opened his door and found that curling up his nose did not improve the smell. Yep. Definite shit in the air.

One look at the place told him that he'd be adding a dry cleaning bill to his expenses.

He grabbed an empty plastic folder from the pocket at the back of the passenger seat and, using it as a makeshift brolly, dashed towards the semi-dry area at the front of the stables. Goodhew waved at him from one of the boxes. Inwardly he groaned; what a fucking dump, not even an office.

He hoped there was no horse in there.

There wasn't, thank God, but Goodhew and Jackie Moran were sitting on straw bales and it didn't look like the place possessed a chair.

'Are we really in here?' He deliberately injected a note of disgust into the question. He knew it didn't do to undervalue yourself and he wanted to give out a clear I-deserve-better-than-this message.

In all honesty neither of them seemed too concerned for him. But Goodhew was still new to the job and would be pissed off with him arriving late, and if this Moran girl spent most of her time down on the farm she probably didn't know better.

She was one of those women who wasn't unattractive but did absolutely nothing to improve her looks. Her hair was unsightly, Plain Jane brown and unkempt. And why did some women think that make-up wasn't important? No wonder she was single with just a herd of donkeys for company. Aside from that though she wasn't in bad shape – petite but with nicely rounded breasts and the sort of all-over lack of flabbiness that he approved of.

'Everything OK?' Goodhew asked.

'Yeah, absolutely.' He stared at Jackie Moran for a moment or two: she looked sly. Hiding something. He made no effort to smile. 'How far have you got, Gary?'

'Just idle chit-chat. We thought we'd wait for you. Miss Moran's been telling me about the horses. One of them used to race.'

Whoopee fucking doo. He made no comment

but couldn't stop his eyes from rolling. There were times when moments of blinding dimness like this made him wonder if Goodhew was just putting on an act. Didn't the bloke have a single ounce of initiative?

Kincaide shook Jackie Moran's hand, making sure he pressed hard to assert his authority. 'I'm sure DC Goodhew managed to explain that we're investigating the murder of Lorna Spence?'

Jackie Moran just nodded. He cast a glance in Gary's direction but Gary was avoiding looking him in the eye. Jackie continued to stare.

'I'd like you to come into Parkside to make a statement.'

'Is that necessary?' she asked.

He was gratified to see that, on cue, her eyes widened and imagined that the accompanying gulp must have been close to audible.

'Firstly, I'm not prepared to sit in here. Secondly, I expect to be questioning you for several hours. Especially–' he paused, adding a mental flourish – 'the part where you explain your connection to Colin Willis.'

Her expression remained unchanged and, more disappointingly, she didn't even go pale.

A bit of a let-down. He sniffed. Maybe he'd played that card just a bit too early. 'We'll bring you back for your vehicle when we've finished.'

'I can drive. I can't leave my dog here.'

Kincaide felt his forehead wrinkle, he wasn't up for having some scabby dog in his car. 'OK, follow me. And when we get there bring it in with you. We'd like a fur sample while we're at it.'

He smiled: this time she had gone pale.

They drove in convoy back to Parkside station. Kincaide led and Goodhew brought up the rear. Jackie's dog stared at him through the back window of her car. He stared back but really his thoughts were on Kincaide.

In Goodhew's opinion there was nothing about Jackie Moran that had needed an aggressive approach, then Kincaide had come along and really rattled her.

Bridy turned from the glass and walked around in a circle before flopping out of sight. If this was the dog whose choke chain had last been used to kill Colin Willis it might be enough to justify Kincaide's approach.

By the time they arrived the rain had stopped and Cambridge was in the process of drying out. The puddles in the police station car park weren't muddy, they lay on the tarmac and reflected the surrounding glass and concrete building. A rainbow of oil floated on them for an additional urban touch.

Kincaide walked two yards in front. Jackie followed with her hands in her pockets and her head hung low. And – like owner, like dog – Bridy trotted behind looking as if she was heading for an appointment with the vet. Mud was caked on the dog's legs, and the same splatters covered Jackie's jodhpurs and jodhpur boots. Goodhew had already noticed that her hands were grubby. Her hair still lay flat from her crash hat.

He lengthened his step for a few strides and tapped her on the elbow.

'What?'

'I realize you weren't expecting to be here. If you want to take a few minutes to freshen up that's fine.'

She nodded and as soon as they'd passed through the exterior door he pointed her towards the ladies' toilet. 'I'll wait here.'

The spring door creaked shut behind her, making Kincaide turn. He scowled. 'What are you doing?'

'She's on edge.'

'That's good.'

'We're not here to traumatize people.'

'We are when they deserve it.'

'Oh right, and she's a career criminal, I suppose?'

'She's a potential suspect.'

'For killing Lorna Spence?'

'Yes.'

'Because...'

'Because if it was that dog's chain found around Colin Willis's neck then she may have killed once – that makes her at least an interesting possibility. And look how the Spence woman died.'

'Drugged and asphyxiated?'

'Neck, neck. Bit of a coincidence.'

'One strangled, one suffocated. Yes, I see your point. Until we have proof that she was involved in one, let's just keep an open mind about the other.'

'Yeah, always.'

Goodhew took a breath. 'Look, I just have a different approach to you.'

'It's fine. You'll learn, we were all new once.'

Jackie re-emerged with clean hands, tidy hair and surrounded by the strong smell of anti-bacterial soap. She followed Kincaide to the interview room, her boots making loud and hollow footsteps and Bridy's claws clicking away like a midget tap dancer doing a warm-up routine. Apart from that they were silent.

The only available room was small and chilly. It had one frosted window set high in the wall as though, in the original plans for the building, this had been intended as a toilet. Condensation left the glass wet and the area smelling like damp paper. Goodhew would have thought that spending days at a stables would have left Jackie acclimatized to the cold, but nevertheless she began to shiver as soon as they settled into the two chairs opposite her.

Bridy slunk under the table, circling twice before lying against her mistress's feet.

Kincaide spoke first. 'What do you know of the death of Colin Willis?'

Again his name failed to startle her. 'I thought you wanted to ask me about Lorna.'

'Didn't you know they're connected?'

She shook her head. 'I don't even know who this Colin Willis is.'

'You must remember a body pulled from the Cam in March?'

'Vaguely.' She blinked slowly, her eyelids swooping gracefully down and up. She maintained an emotionless expression. 'Was that his name then?'

Kincaide moved on. 'He was strangled. Did Lorna mention him?'

Goodhew cut in. 'Along with the body we recovered a dog's choke chain. We'd like to take a hair sample from Bridy.'

'Fur,' Kincaide corrected.

'For elimination?' she asked.

Kincaide spoke again. 'We will insist if you don't volunteer it.'

'Really?' She sighed. The interview was still in the first twenty minutes but each time she spoke she sounded increasingly weary. 'On what grounds?'

'For elimination,' Kincaide replied. His response was a deliberate echo of her own earlier question and that seemed to amuse him. He leant back in his chair as he waited for her to speak.

She turned her head towards Goodhew but kept her eyes on Kincaide for a beat before slowly shifting her gaze too. If that was supposed to convey any kind of message it didn't reach him. As soon as she'd emerged from the ladies' toilet she'd switched into a partially catatonic state. Goodhew wondered whether she was inwardly reciting a deep relaxation mantra. Her calmness was now bordering on unnatural. She spoke slowly, showing mild interest and zero anxiety. He didn't believe her. Either through strict self-control or as an involuntary reaction to the situation she had deployed a huge and effective layer of emotional insulation; their questions didn't appear to be making a dent.

Goodhew decided to give her an opening. 'Have you lost a choke chain at any point? Or could someone else have used it?'

Again she blinked before replying. 'I'm happy for you to take a sample.'

'Thank you. Colin Willis was a distinctive-looking man, I'd like to show you a photograph.'

'Of him dead?'

'We have a couple of older shots. I can find one of those.'

'I'd prefer it.'

Goodhew flicked through until he found the two-year-old mug shot and passed it across. He put the file back on the table. Kincaide picked it up. 'I'll find the other one,' he said.

Jackie did the slow blink thing again before raising the photograph into her line of sight. It took a couple of seconds before what she was viewing connected with her brain. The change in her was minuscule; her pupils dilated. 'He was a criminal then?'

Before Goodhew had a chance to respond Kincaide spoke. 'Have you seen this?'

She looked and so did Goodhew. Kincaide was holding up a morgue photo of Willis's head and torso. It was one of those shots that gave a very good idea of how the room must have smelt. It wasn't pleasant.

Chapter Twenty-Nine

Marks caught Goodhew as he walked back from the canteen with a sandwich. It had been the last one that looked vaguely edible; turkey salad according to the label. The two slices of bread had already begun to curl, no sign of even a lettuce leaf, and the uniformly thin slice of too-pink filling looked more like a play mat for salmonella than anything that had ever had feathers.

The sandwich failed to rouse Goodhew from the vicinity of depressed/embarrassed.

Depressed because he'd failed to notice that his fledgling relationship, far from being one-sided, actually didn't exist, and embarrassed because it was now crystal clear to everyone concerned what an idiot he was.

He gingerly lifted the corner of one slice. He hadn't eaten since breakfast and although he didn't feel very hungry he'd decided that missing lunch reeked too heavily of self-pity. He looked up as soon as he heard Marks's voice.

'Follow me.'

Marks headed towards the stairs. Goodhew hurried behind, risking a bite of the sandwich. It tasted of bread. He decided not to think about it any further and kept eating. Marks led the way down the stairs and across the car park towards his maroon Mazda. He pressed the remote and the doors clicked.

'Are we going somewhere?'

'I can see how you made detective,' Marks replied drily.

He slid a folded sheet of paper from his pocket and passed it to Goodhew, who waited until he'd buckled himself into the passenger seat before opening it out. At the top was the name 'Martin Reed' followed by a Bedford address. The remainder of the page just listed directions for the journey from Cambridge.

'We're going to Bedford then?'

'Is it your day for stating the obvious? I thought I'd bring you along in the hope I'd get some intelligent input. Is that going to be too much to ask?'

Goodhew assumed the question was rhetorical and kept quiet.

Marks reversed out of the parking space and simultaneously waved his hand in the general direction of the piece of paper. 'That's one of the possible Emma connections.'

Goodhew knew that some of the officers on the investigation had been dredging both physical archives and various databases for any possible explanation of the writing on Lorna's palms. He'd spoken to DC Charles and PC Wilkes who'd both been dragged in; they'd assumed their mission would be fruitless, a soul-destroying exercise in investigative box ticking.

'So they found something?'

Marks raised an eyebrow slightly in an are-you-taking-the-piss way and managed to stop short of saying, 'No, we're off to Bedford for fun.' 'Charles came across it, a missing girl called Joanne Reed, called herself by her middle name, Emma.'

'Doesn't ring a bell. Was it suspicious?'

'You won't remember it because it was 1996. Martin Reed is her father. The nationals ran reports early on, but there were no clues and no sightings so it dropped out of the news pretty quickly.'

'No body?'

'Absolutely nothing.'

'So why are we interested?'

'You've spoken to Jackie Moran and she doesn't know an Emma, right?'

'Yes.'

'Well, Jackie and this Emma were in the same year at Northampton University. Jackie Moran was still a student when Joanne Reed disappeared.'

Within fifteen minutes they were on the sliproad joining the A14 and Goodhew knew they had a good hour's drive ahead of them. The road was busy and Marks accelerated then cruised at a steady sixty-five. It was fast enough to overtake lorries but slow enough to be overtaken by almost everyone else. And it gave Goodhew plenty of time to think about Jackie Moran.

Martin Reed's house was the right-hand one of a pair of ex-council semis. The exterior was cream, and saucer-sized bedding plants lined one side of the driveway, running in an arrow-straight strip equidistant between the parallel lines made by the three car-lengths of concrete and the square-edged tightly cropped lawn. The front of the house had three windows, two up and one down, made bright white from the set of matching nets. The front door itself was old style, aluminium-framed with leaf-patterned frosted glass, and it too glinted with obsessive cleanliness.

In normal circumstances Goodhew hated ringing door bells; you press the button and if you can't hear the bell from the outside you're left with the dilemma of whether to wait or whether to knock. If you do knock it seems to be almost guaranteed that the door will then be opened by someone whose first words are 'OK, OK, what's the rush' or similar.

Goodhew pressed the bell once. The usual

worry was not after all an issue; they had yet to cross the threshold but it was already obvious that this was not a home that tolerated neglect.

The door was opened within seconds by a grey-haired woman in her early fifties. She managed to look exasperated and welcoming at the same time.

'Mrs Reed?' Marks asked.

'Yep. But not the first one. I'm no good to you, it's Martin you want.' She spoke slowly, as though reluctant to engage in conversation. 'He's round the back,' she said. 'Whatever you're here about I hope it's worth it. He's already gone into one of his moods. I'd rather you stayed away than stir everything up, especially if it's going to be for nothing again.'

They found him standing at the top of a stepladder cleaning the already transparent windows, working a cloth up into the top corner of the glass, making small and dedicated circles.

His hand stopped moving and he turned his head, oh so slowly, to look over his left shoulder. His attention dwelt on Marks for a full thirty seconds, then with a lethargic blink he lifted his gaze and set it down again on Goodhew. No one spoke at first and the effect was like a slo-mo moment in a movie where he read their faces and they read him.

Martin Reed was a giant of a man, at least six foot four and weighing in the region of twenty stone. His hair had receded, leaving him with just a dark wavy clump on top. The sides were short, as though he'd once sported a flat-top and had never quite grown out of it. He'd been good-looking when he was younger, and he'd never quite grown out of that either.

He stayed at the top of the ladder, clearly in no rush to invest his time in descending. 'How can I help?' His voice was deep but soft.

'We'd like to ask you about Joanne,' Marks replied.

'Well, I realize that.' There was no sarcasm there, just an acceptance that the police would always ask about his daughter. 'You haven't found her, have you?'

'No, I'm sorry, we haven't.'

'OK.' He came down from the ladder then, and led them into the house. They stood in the kitchen and waited while he put the window cleaning cloths and sprays back in the cupboard under the sink. He put the items away one at a time, folding the chamois and placing it on the shelf, leaving the sponge squarely on top, then straightening the bottles on either side.

Goodhew glanced around the room: every surface was clean and devoid of clutter. The washing-up sponge was precisely located in the middle of the gap between the two taps and a tea towel folded into quarters hung from a drawer. It looked ironed.

A lone pen had been left on the windowsill; he guessed it didn't count as clutter because it had been placed exactly parallel to the edge. There were good odds that the rest of the house would match. Martin Reed washed his hands and dried them on the tea towel then replaced it in precisely the same position. Here the pristine and symmetrical ruled as the big man struggled to keep control of his surroundings. He reminded Goodhew of a child on best behaviour, trying too hard, concentrating on every small task and almost imploding with the strain. Instinctively Goodhew knew that this was a man who rarely left home.

They were led into the front room where Mr Reed invited them to sit on the settee. 'You met my wife, Mary?'

They nodded.

'She won't be joining us unless you really need her to.'

Marks replied. 'No, that's fine. She said you'd "gone into one of your moods". What did she mean?'

Reed did the slo-mo blinking thing again. 'She knew what I was like when we married. She keeps me sane, I suppose. Even now I get keyed up when you come. I tell myself not to be disappointed but I can't help wondering if this time... I try to put the thought out of my head, but it sneaks back in. I kid myself that I have no expectations left but in the hour before you're due to arrive I'm counting down the minutes. It would be easier for me if you could tell me the gist of it by phone each time. Is that possible?'

'I'm sorry, Mr Reed, but we're working on a different case. There's a slim possibility of a link, but that's all. Just the name Emma.'

'That's it? Emma?' Martin Reed shook his head, sagging as if the disappointment had winded him.

'The case notes say that Joanne was known as Emma. Is that correct?'

Martin Reed spread out his large hands, palms up. 'It was nothing. She'd always preferred her middle name and decided to be known by it while she was at university But Emma's not a rare name and it was never a big deal to Jo as far as I could tell. She used it briefly. As far as I could work out it seemed to be about–' he paused to make the quotes sign with his fingers – 'self-discovery. Some kids go spiky-haired, or dabble with drugs. Sometimes she changed her name. One of the detectives on the original team came up with the idea that it was a pseudonym she used for something dodgy. As if. She was a very contented teenager. We waited for her to be the typical rebel but it never happened.' It sounded as though his words were practised, that he'd said them over and over in the last ten years, but that made them no less accurate.

Marks plugged on. 'We also have some photographs we'd like to show you. Just let me know if anyone looks familiar.' Marks slid the shots from the file then put it on the cushion between himself and Goodhew. He handed the pictures to Mr Reed one at a time.

The five-by-sevens looked tiny in the man's huge hands. At each one he shook his head. 'These are recent.'

'Fairly.'

'So I could be trying to recognize people I knew ten years ago?'

'Possibly.'

'No one looks familiar. But if I stare long enough they all could. Do you have any idea how many people I've met since Jo vanished?'

Goodhew lifted the front cover of the file. Plenty of sheets. Words and more words. But hearing one person's perceptions always had more resonance for him than a whole file of facts.

He was aware that Marks was mentioning names and continuing to probe but getting nowhere. He was drawing their visit to a close. Goodhew kept his eyes diverted from Marks, knowing that his first words would derail his boss's line of questioning. He placed his hand on Joanne's file, like they were at risk from it opening itself. 'We have all the details but would you be prepared to tell us what happened – just as you remember it?'

Mr Reed looked at him like he'd just noticed him for the very first time. 'Why? This isn't your case.'

Goodhew didn't have an answer. Morbid curiosity or nosiness? Had he just asked an inappropriate question without thinking it through? So far Joanne appeared to have zero connection to Lorna and that made it out of line.

He continued to avoid looking at Marks and simply replied honestly: 'Just in case.'

Whatever Martin Reed's opinion, he started talking in any case. 'I used to fear the progression of old age and I was scared of dying. I imagined turning into first my dad, then my granddad, as the most depressing descent into oblivion. The thought of watching my children turn into adolescents, then adults, then become middle-aged – watching them peak then decline – I used to feel repulsed at the idea. Now it seems like heaven. Joanne would be thirty. I don't do what-ifs about anything except her age. Annie, my wife, did. She what-iffed until it killed her. She didn't just mourn her daughter, she pined for the wedding Jo might have had, and the children and the career and on and on.'

'Was she an only child?' Marks asked.

'Oh yes.' The happy-sad nerves at the corners of Martin Reed's mouth gave a flutter of involuntary twitches. 'Imagine having three, four, five kids. You couldn't watch them all, but we only had one and we didn't keep her safe. Logically we knew it wasn't our fault, like logic makes a difference.

'Somewhere between the first and second anniversaries I accepted she was dead. Not consciously. But I knew she wasn't in any TV crowds, or in front of me in the checkout queue, or on the other end of a ringing phone. My wife felt differently, though, and to Annie I'd done the unforgivable: abandoned our child.'

Martin Reed picked up the TV remote from the arm of the chair, licked his thumb then rubbed at a small area on the side of the control. The silence between them lengthened. Goodhew spoke first.

'Mr Reed?'

Martin Reed snapped back into talk mode. 'The very night before Jo vanished Annie and I watched a documentary about parents who'd lost children. It said how high the divorce rate was. And I couldn't understand it, I thought they'd need each other, imagined them clinging together through their grief. After all, I thought the parents would be the only ones who could understand.

'In reality, I think of that as the last night of our marriage, and I don't mean that to sound melo-

225

dramatic but until Jo disappeared we'd had a charmed life, twenty-odd years of home and family with nothing more serious than every other household round here.

'You lose a child and you do understand each other's grief at first, but if you get out of step it's all over. Suddenly each of you is alone; I'd have a good day and Annie would have a bad one. Then she would resent seeing me coping when she couldn't. And vice versa.'

The next time he fell silent nobody interrupted. Goodhew felt he ought to coax him into speaking but the only thing he could think to do was to ask Martin Reed whether he was all right. And very clearly he wasn't, so they just waited out the silence while more imaginary grime was scratched from the remote control.

'You can't share any happy memories with your partner without feeling like you're deliberately trying to cause them pain. I'd faced everyone and talked about Jo, pretty non-stop sometimes, everyone except Annie. Between us Jo became the biggest taboo.'

This time Martin Reed seemed to have finished but Goodhew waited for a few seconds until he was sure it really was his turn to speak. If there had been a clock in the room this was the point where it would have ticked loudly. 'From your point of view, how well has the investigation been handled?'

Martin Reed drew a steady breath and leant back in his chair. He looked up at the ceiling for a while. 'I'm not a bitter man,' he said, 'but I find it painful to accept that whoever is responsible may never be caught. I'm not wishing I could blame anyone. In my heart of hearts I believe she was dead before the alarm was even raised; Tanya her room-mate rang on a Wednesday, halfway through *Morse*. Jo hadn't been seen since the previous Friday.'

'Why did she wait so long?'

'Apparently Jo had spent several other nights away and Kelly just assumed that Jo was seeing someone.'

'But Jo never said so?'

'No, but that would be typical, she was guarded in that way.'

'What about the police?'

'They never found anyone. They asked a few questions about her sex life.' He shook his head, still feeling disbelief. 'She was twenty, and we were her parents. Do you think we wanted to talk about our child even having a sexual history never mind any "kinky habits", as one of them put it? Let's just say we weren't surprised when it turned out to be a dead end.'

'You never thought of anything that wasn't followed up?'

'No. We never felt left in the dark. Never. You may not be on Jo's case but I still appreciate your time. I don't stop, you know.'

Goodhew wasn't sure what Reed meant. 'Thinking about her?'

'No, I mean I don't stop. I don't like going out, I find it easier to stay in and keep busy. But a visit from you gives me hope, lets me unburden a bit too. Even visits like the last one, essentially nothing more than a courtesy call, but it let me know you hadn't forgotten.'

Goodhew flicked open the file and scanned the most recent details. Martin Reed continued to talk, Goodhew kept listening, punctuating the gaps with an appropriate grunt or 'hmm'. Finally, when he was certain that he wasn't making a mistake, he said, 'And the last visit was when exactly?'

They'd made phone calls, checked and double-checked. Whoever had visited Martin Reed had not been a policeman. Mr Reed was vague, he remembered him as a man in his late fifties. But no name. Said he hadn't asked for ID. But then he hadn't today either.

They drove away.

Marks shook his head. 'Talking about it obviously helps him.'

'Poor bloke. The best result he's ever going to get will be bad news.'

'You did well though.'

'Did I?' Goodhew hadn't thought so.

'The mystery visitor was interesting.'

'But possibly irrelevant?'

'We'll see.' Marks pulled out, taking a right on to a busier road. 'While I was on the phone I was briefed on the initial forensics report.' He glanced across as if checking that Goodhew was listening before continuing. 'As we know, death was by asphyxiation but she'd also been drugged with GHB. Heard of it?'

Goodhew nodded. 'Gamma hydroxybutyrate, usually a liquid. Colourless and odourless but with a slight salty taste. Causes dizziness, confusion and memory loss.'

228

'Very good. Well, Lorna's was administered in coffee. The report estimates that she ingested about four times the amount that would be expected to cause incapacitation. It's a drug often connected with date rape cases.'

Goodhew scanned the report. 'Had she been raped?'

'Semen was present but nothing to indicate anything conclusive either way.'

Goodhew thought for a moment then spoke. 'I'd like to go back to Lorna Spence's flat.'

Marks cast a sharp glance in his direction. 'Why?'

'To search again.'

'And I assume you have a good reason?'

'Three actually. Firstly and secondly we've found out about Joanne Reed and Colin Willis since the flat was searched.'

'OK. Thirdly?'

'The search was conducted very quickly. I think something's been missed.'

'Kincaide would say you're trying to show him up.'

'I'm not.'

Marks stared at the road in front of him but far too intently to be concentrating on his driving alone. 'Do you know anything about how the "Emma" story was leaked to last night's paper?' he said.

'No.'

'Sure?'

'Absolutely.'

Goodhew had no idea how the two topics could be linked, but his reply seemed to prompt his boss's decision.

Every hint of warmth had dropped from Marks's voice when he replied. 'I don't want you going near Lorna Spence's flat, Gary. If there is to be another search it won't involve you.'

Chapter Thirty

For the second day in a row Goodhew met Kincaide at the Vine. They sat at the same seats at the same table, Kincaide with his red wine and Goodhew with coffee. But it didn't feel the same as it had twenty-four hours earlier.

Goodhew diverted himself by watching the foam swirl around on the surface of his freshly stirred café-au-lait. Kincaide was talking, or rather bragging, about his interview with Jackie Moran and Goodhew had all but stopped listening; one day of working closely with Kincaide had taught him that they had nothing in common. And more frustratingly he knew he could have saved himself the trouble because Kincaide was just the way he'd struck Goodhew on their first introduction.

He reminded himself that he wasn't the one that needed putting straight and made the effort to tune back in to what Kincaide was saying.

'Did you see her face when I showed her the photo of the corpse?'

Goodhew tossed the spoon on to the saucer and coffee splashed over the table. 'What was that about?' he snapped. 'You obviously thought it was clever. Did it achieve anything? No. Do we look crass, insensitive, stupid? Yes, I think so.'

Kincaide swigged from his glass, downing half. 'What's put you in a shitty mood?' He sounded indifferent.

Goodhew lowered his voice again. 'I was embarrassed to be sitting next to you.'

'But happy to come for a drink?'

'Don't even think the word "hypocrite",' Goodhew cut in. 'I came to tell you how I felt. I thought you were out of line and I can't find a rational reason for you treating her like that. And since we've been sitting here you've just been gloating about bullying a witness.'

Kincaide emptied his glass. 'Jackie Moran is a suspect, and I thought you were being way too soft with her. I was just evening things up. If you want to call that bullying that's up to you.' His voice was impassive. He stood and looked down at Goodhew. 'This mood you're in is pissing me off.'

The door closed after Kincaide, and Goodhew gave his half-cold coffee another stir. He followed it with a bottle of Stella. The sound system was doling out a cover version of a Ray Charles number; take a great song then murder it – it had to be a ploy to make punters drink more. He drank his beer and let his annoyance subside, but still didn't buy Kincaide's excuses.

Twenty minutes later Goodhew left the Vine and turned down Burleigh Street and then Fitzroy Street, walking up the middle of the pedestrianized shopping area. There were still plenty of people around, mainly moving in small groups.

One group of girls waited for their friend as she used an ATM. Two more had their heads together, giggling as they both read a text message. A couple walked side by side, locked together by holding each other around the waist. One girl walked alone. It seemed so safe, yet he wished she wouldn't do it. She glanced away as she saw him look at her. Once she was beyond him he guessed she may have looked back again to double-check that he wouldn't turn and follow; even when people swore they were safe their actions contradicted them.

He had always been in the habit of checking doorways and alleys. Even front gardens sometimes. And it was his automatic custom of checking in all directions that led him to look far down a side street and spot a Vauxhall that he recognized.

It was parked sideways on, with its passenger door closest. Even if he had been facing the front or back bumpers it was too far along the side road for him to see the registration. But he'd long known that identifying cars can be like identifying people. A person can be spotted by their gait, or stance, or distinctive dress style, a car by the way its suspension sags, or its aerial sways, or even the unique fingerprint of stickers in the back window. This one he was certain he knew from the combination of flashy non-factory alloys and the shape of the suit jacket hanging on the inside of the rear door.

It wasn't Kincaide's part of town, but it was his car.

Sitting in a bar with Goodhew fell well short of Kincaide's idea of a good evening out. He checked his watch, and mentally double-checked that he'd left his mobile switched on and in his pocket. Goodhew was still banging on about Jackie Moran; sometimes he just couldn't fathom the bloke's logic. Yesterday, the nostalgia over some old pub and the urge to track a witness down at eight in the evening. Today, and he was complaining that the same witness hadn't been treated like their new best friend. As far as Kincaide could see, Goodhew spent too much time fretting about work. In fact Goodhew never seemed to think about much else. Kincaide tried to flash back to the time when he'd had that level of commitment to the job.

Instead his thoughts returned to his mobile; he wished the text would arrive.

While he waited he decided he'd made a more than adequate job of keeping his side of the conversation flowing. And while he wasn't one for enjoying anticipation, by the time the phone bleeped he wouldn't have been surprised if just the sound of it had given him a hard on.

He looked at the first new message in his inbox: '10 mins usual place.' That was about the most it ever read. Part of him wanted to show Goodhew and to own up to what was going on. But another part of him, and arguably the better part, resisted the temptation; Goodhew was still idealistic enough to disapprove of affairs. But he also didn't have enough first-hand experience to see how they could negate some of the frustrations of marriage.

Kincaide made his excuses and left the Vine.

He'd parked at the rear of Dreams bed show-room, halfway between the police station and the pub. It was usually a good spot, a small yard that was deserted once the shops had closed for the night and a discreet place for her to meet him.

He arrived first and realized that a second car occupied the car park. Its windows were already steamed, he'd need to park up somewhere else. He sat in the driver's seat and waited; within two minutes the other door opened and she slipped into the seat beside him. She smelt flowery, like she'd just sprayed herself with one of those cheap body sprays that teenagers use before they discover real perfume. He liked it. A lot. More than enough for him to feel the first stirrings of an erection.

'I got here as soon as I could,' Mel said.

He'd been meeting her at least twice a week for over a month. He pointed at the other car. 'We need somewhere else.'

'We could leave it here and go for a drink. It would be nice if we could just talk tonight.'

He grinned and reached across, taking her hand and pressing it hard against his crotch. 'Are you kidding? I can't walk around in this condition.' She tried to slide her hand away but he held on to it. 'Hey, I'm just teasing, and I was listening this morning. We'll park up somewhere else and talk.'

The ideal spot was about half a mile away where part way along a cul-de-sac there was a right-hand spur which had been blocked off to cars. At most there would be an infrequent passer-by; the alley was a poor shortcut to any-where apart from the backs of the houses.

He glanced across at her as they drove. Her

skirt came to a couple of inches above her knee, further up now she was sitting, and she fiddled with the hemline. Her legs were bare and catching a glimpse of the smallest area of the soft skin between her thighs was enough to keep him hard. She turned him on in a way his frigid wife Janice never could nor ever had. 'How's your head?' he asked.

Her expression softened; as always she appreciated his concern. 'It only feels bruised if I touch it.'

'You know you should press charges.' He knew she wouldn't, but said it anyway. Toby had slapped her around several times before, and he was sure that Mel was already acclimatized to the routine of receiving aggression and offering forgiveness. He'd noticed that some women had a thirst for abuse and he had no intention of being sucked in with her. One day Toby would be ready to move on and it would be typical if Mel then went on to another violent relationship. In the meantime the issue of his marriage wasn't going to be a problem when she had a psycho boyfriend to keep secrets from.

'If I tried to leave him he'd come after me.'

'Not if he was under arrest.'

'He'd come after you if he knew.'

From the corner of his eye he could see that she was studying his face and it made him feel as though he was being tested. He kept his voice level. 'And how would he know? That sounds like a threat, Mel.'

Nothing else was said until he'd parked. Then he looked and saw she was fighting back tears. 'All I was going to do was tell you that Toby's been hanging around at lunchtimes, that he's suspicious, but your first assumption is that I'm trying to pressurize you. What sort of person do you think I am?'

The evening was morphing into aggravation, so he tried to sound soothing. 'Hey,' he whispered, 'you know I didn't mean to upset you. We're getting very intense and I thought you were forgetting what we'd agreed.' Her tears didn't recede or increase, they sat on hold. 'Sometimes I want to just blurt it out to Jan, but I know I mustn't.'

She bit on her bottom lip and said nothing.

'We both agreed on it, didn't we?' She nodded, and he leant forward to kiss her. His timing was right; her lips parted and after the first tentative moments he felt her hand cup his upper arm and her thumb gently rub his bicep. He pulled away first, just far enough that there was nowhere else for her to look but into his eyes. 'That's still OK with you, isn't it? I don't want you to be uncomfortable with this.'

She leant forward to kiss him then. It was funny how setting limits on their relationship always seemed to produce results. He guessed it might be one of those contrary things; tell a needy woman what she can't have and that's what she'll chase.

He pulled her closer and slipped his tongue between her lips. He found the waistband of her skirt and from there slid his hand up and down her spine, marvelling at the tautness of her soft bare skin. Her back arched as if to let him know that her breasts were available to him, but instead of undoing her bra he traced his middle finger over the sheer fabric, around her body until he

236

was stroking her right nipple.

Her tongue dipped into his mouth with more urgency and this time when he pressed her hand against his trousers she didn't pull away He encouraged her fingers to find the zip. Her hands were small but dextrous, and as ever, it took only seconds before she had him in the firm grasp of her delicate fingers. He stroked her hair as they continued to kiss and waited until her massaging was rhythmic before beginning to tease their mouths apart and gently nudge her face towards his penis.

He settled back into the corner made by his seat and the door. She ran her tongue along the shaft then drew him into her mouth. God, she was good at this. He adjusted the rear view mirror to give him a good view of anyone coming from the driver's side of the car and split his attention between it, the rear of the car and the passenger side.

No other vehicles entered the street and at first the only pedestrians were those passing the end of the road. He stopped bothering to check the mirrors but continued to watch in that one direction, now through lazy half-closed eyes.

Inadvertently Jan slipped into his thoughts and he felt a pang of guilt, but he also knew that a small dose of guilt was preferable to a bucketload of her indifference. So she was just an impostor and he pushed her out again.

Another minute passed and he ceased to care whether anyone saw them. He watched the gentle bobbing of Mel's head, and felt the regular movements of her mouth by stroking the tips of his fingers against the side of her cheek.

He wanted to climax slowly.

It was only a semi-conscious decision to walk towards Kincaide's car: Goodhew's feet were heading that way before his brain had time to consider whether there was any reason to.

He could see that Kincaide was sitting in the driver's seat, partially facing in Goodhew's direction, but although Goodhew raised his hand no acknowledgement came in return. Kincaide was stock-still, perhaps concentrating on a phone call or the radio.

Goodhew slowed, feeling suddenly as though he'd done the wrong thing, that he was intruding. Apart from some houses between him and the car there was nowhere to turn off and doing a 180 degree about-face would look pretty stupid.

He slowed some more. He had picked out something else now and an uneasy feeling was crawling up his spine. The moment between seeing it and recognizing it as Mel's red mac stayed in his head like a mangled bit of Super 8 footage.

He chose to take the about-face option in less than a second, but somehow in that time he saw Kincaide look, then jerk upright. Kincaide's lips moved. Then the back of Mel's head appeared. She turned towards him as he turned from her.

The car slewed out of the edge of his field of vision and he hurried away, far faster than he'd approached.

Chapter Thirty-One

He knew as he walked away that there would be
no early night. He went to the cinema and caught
Kirsten Dunst's latest film. He'd never heard of it
before he arrived, and by the time it had finished
he had forgotten what it was called, but that
didn't matter; in his opinion Kirsten was one of
the two movie stars who could chuck out their
scripts and still deserve Oscars.

Kirsten had stared into a mirror, feeling sorry
for herself. She'd cast Goodhew an empathetic
glance. He'd sighed and wondered how he'd
allowed himself to be blind to Mel and Kincaide's affair, why he felt let down by Kincaide,
and what gave him the right to feel hurt. Finally,
he saw that despite wishing things were different,
they weren't, and it was really none of his
business. He'd left before the end credits rolled.

When Goodhew let himself back into his flat it
was ten minutes past ten. There were no
messages on the answer-phone. He stood by the
window for the next few minutes, wanting to call
his grandmother and hating himself for hurting
her, but still unable to ring.

Beyond the shadowy expanse of Parker's Piece
the police station was quiet; a few lights on
around the building and a few officers on duty.

Marks was right, a fresh start in the morning
would be the best thing.

Goodhew padded out to the kitchen, a narrow room with all the appliances on the right and the units on the left. A small sash window and a red drop-leaf table occupied the far wall. Two items stood on the table, a portable TV and a calendar of Hawaiian sunsets propped against it.

Goodhew decided to make an omelette. He used his last four eggs, then threw in ham, cheese, milk, butter, and a sprinkling of black pepper.

He switched on the portable TV and flicked through the channels while the olive oil heated in the pan. Sport, sport, relationships. He kept flicking. Cop show, game show, black and white film. He paused. He recognized Veronica Lake and he didn't turn over.

Veronica and Kirsten on the same night, it should have felt like his lucky day, but seeing Kincaide and Mel had thumped the scales down in the opposite direction.

He turned back to the pan and finished cooking, then he leant against the worktop with plate in one hand and fork in the other and tried watching someone else solve a different murder.

He knew before the second mouthful that it wasn't enough to keep him home.

Chapter Thirty-Two

It took Goodhew fifteen minutes to walk from Parkside pool to Rolfe Street, Lorna's little road, where gentrified townhouses squeezed together in neat order with their single front steps like children's feet, lined up and waiting one step back from the kerb.

Midges danced in the glow from the street-lamps, parting to let him pass as he strode through their light pools. His footsteps beat a crisp rhythm on the pavement. It was late enough for the streets to be empty and early enough for his sounds to be masked by the television sets, one turned up louder than a speaking voice in almost every home.

Except Lorna's of course.

Her flat was still and silent, her letterbox sealed from the inside and the windows strapped with striped police tape.

And the flat below hers was silent too, un-occupied and for sale when she died. Now un-occupied and unsaleable and Goodhew was glad. The last thing he needed was a neighbour reporting footsteps overhead.

He reached in his pocket and wrapped his fingers around the key. He rubbed his thumb along the teeth and as he did so he silently prayed that the lock had not been changed. He slid it in and turned it. The door opened, and he sighed with relief; walking up the stairs was a far better prospect than up the drainpipe and across the ground-floor flat roof.

This way at least there would be no evidence of forced entry.

He closed the door behind him and felt his way up the stairs. Dust and mustiness had already invaded, pushing out any breath of Lorna from the air.

He found the landing and groped around identifying first the door frame, then the door, then the handle. The door opened into a large all-purpose living area; enough light trickled through the sash window to pick out the shape of a settee and coffee table and circular dining set.

Both kitchen and bathroom were at the rear of the flat, overlooked only by houses in the road running parallel to Rolfe Street; turning the lights on in these two rooms was still a risk, but a calculated one, and by his reckoning, worth taking.

He chose the bathroom first, and closed the door behind him before pulling the light cord. The suite had been changed circa 1978, he guessed, the days when green toilets, in any shade from lichen to avocado, were still considered desirable. This one was sage, with marble effect tiles, pine fittings and cream walls. It was clean and well kept, but not attractive. All the surfaces were bare. He clicked open the mirrored door of the medicine cabinet: that too was empty. He hoped the kitchen yielded more.

He switched off the bathroom light and ducked from there into the kitchen. Again he shut the door behind him, and this time he twisted the blinds shut before flicking on the overhead strip light.

Before beginning his search he opened and closed each cupboard, weighing up the size of the job. Plenty had been removed from the kitchen: the bin, tea towels, fruit from the bowl and perishables from the fridge. But plenty had been left: glasses, china, cutlery, and jars and tins of food.

The units were fitted, more modern than the bathroom, beech veneer with a polished granite top and thin chrome handles. He started by tapping and tugging at the four-inch fascia running around the bottom. It was secure and bore no sign that it had ever been disturbed.

Two bar stools were tucked under a tiny breakfast bar; he grabbed one and stood on it to inspect on top of the units. He checked inside each appliance and in the pots of odds and ends under the sink. He wished he knew what, if anything, he hoped to find.

It was fifteen minutes later when he started on the food cupboard.

He guessed she'd eaten out a lot, or hadn't eaten much at all; her cupboard catered for breakfast and snacks. One shelf was filled with tins of soup, and not just plain old Heinz Tomato like his own kitchen. There were at least a dozen varieties, from asparagus to lobster bisque. He lifted and shook each can, and when he was content that each was full and unopened he moved to the rows of spreads on the shelf below.

Most of the jams were unopened and stood with the labels facing forwards. The two jars of peanut butter, one crunchy, one smooth, told a different story. Their glass sides were scraped clear, and only a few helpings remained at the bottom of each. Behind the peanut butter was the familiar fat-cheeked shape of a Marmite jar. People either loved it or hated it, Lorna must have been in the 'loved it' camp as she had three jars of the stuff on the go. Goodhew picked up the first jar: liquorice-coloured stains streaked the black glass. He unscrewed the yellow lid and glanced inside. Just Marmite with a couple of flecks of butter.

He replaced the lid and licked Marmite from the tip of his gloved finger. The seal was gone on one of the other two jars. He felt a kick of excitement and snatched up the jar at the back; it was too clean. He unscrewed it quickly, it felt light enough to be almost empty. Under the lid was a ball of cotton wool.

When he'd been a kid his mum had kept cotton wool in the top of vitamin bottles. He never understood why, but now he knew he'd find tablets in this bottle too.

There weren't many of them, he estimated about twenty. And they weren't all the same, a mix of red capsules and torpedo-shaped pills. He replaced the cotton wool and returned the jar to its place at the back of the shelf.

He ran his gaze along the shelf below. The lid of a vinegar bottle protruded from behind a coffee jar. He pulled it out and immediately saw the liquid was clear. He removed his glove and dripped a splash on to his finger. As soon as it hit his tongue he smiled. Jackpot.

Later on he'd wonder how different things would

have been if he'd just replaced the bottle and left, but he couldn't have done that.

Not really.

Not when the rest of the flat beckoned.

He checked the bedroom curtains, making sure the heavy red velvet overlapped to seal in the light. Then he used his torch to search the room. Her wrought-iron bedstead had been stripped of its sheets. Her stereo stood beside the bed, accompanied by a stack of a dozen CDs. He ran the beam of light down their spines. The last one was *The Best of Blondie*, the rest were modern chart compilations.

He moved his torch around the room and went over to Lorna's wardrobe. The door creaked as he opened it. He stopped and listened. Had he heard something else too?

No. He'd just been in the house too long.

Time to leave.

'In a minute, in a minute,' he whispered to himself and shone the torch into the cupboard.

Most of her clothes still hung from the rail, though some had fallen. He knelt to check the bottom of the wardrobe. Then froze. He heard a creak on the stairs then a whisper. Shit. There was only one option; he clicked off his torch and felt his way into the cupboard. From somewhere near the landing a woman's voice hissed, 'I'll start in the bedroom.'

Goodhew pulled the doors to within an inch of shutting. Above his head clothes swayed and the hangers click-clacked against each other. Footsteps entered the room and he froze.

'You do the kitchen.' This time she spoke clearly

and he recognized the voice as Victoria Nugent's.

'OK,' a man replied.

Goodhew could see nothing so he half closed his eyes and just listened. She was wearing stilettos and she moved with short steps that echoed on the bare boards. He heard the curtains open and shafts of moonlight slipped into the cupboard. Not good. Then her shadow fell across the crack and he knew she was about to open the door.

Victoria had spent a giddy afternoon riding on an adrenalin surge. She had made a mistake. No, it had been an oversight. But now she had a plan. In her mind's eye she'd visualized every move. Especially the finale.

As they entered Lorna's flat she realized she was rushing up the stairs too quickly and checked herself. She had to be convincing. She would fail if she let her motives become transparent.

He followed, more heavy-footed, less enthusiastic. But that would change.

'Where will it be?' he asked.

'I don't know.' She led the way across the living room; she knew the route, even in the dark. She made straight for the bedroom, but turned back to him at the doorway. 'I'll start in the bedroom.'

He stopped in his tracks, not sure what she was asking him to do.

'You do the kitchen.'

Her heart thumped but she didn't allow herself to think about how dangerous it all was. It was good that he seemed more nervous than her, even though she had no doubt that she could lead him where he didn't want to go.

She crossed to the window. The curtains rasped as they were hauled back on their tracks. That was better, she could see the room properly now.

She knew she had at least a few minutes while he poked around in the kitchen units.

Directly across from her was the room's only wardrobe, that would be the logical place to start. She opened the doors simultaneously. Then without even a glance inside she made a point of slamming them. Then she loudly opened and closed the chest of drawers.

Finally she retrieved a tissue from her sleeve and lay on the edge of the bed. She kept the tissue pressed to her lips and did her best to feign emotional exhaustion. She was no great actress, but she firmly believed that people noticed only what they chose to.

It didn't take him more than a few minutes to search the kitchen then he came to find her. He stopped in the doorway and nodded towards the open curtains. 'Someone will see us,' he said. Then he looked at her. 'What's wrong?'

'You didn't find it, did you?' Her voice was thick with emotion. 'It's not here either.'

He stepped into the room, but stopped halfway, next to the bed. 'Where will it be?' he repeated.

'I don't know, most of her stuff has gone.'

'Perhaps the police have it then?'

This was good. 'Do you think I hadn't worked that out?' She raised her voice just enough to threaten hysteria. Then she sighed and raised both hands with a 'just hang on' gesture. 'I'm sorry, I know it's not your fault. But Bryn, I don't know what I'd do if anyone saw it.'

'Why would it be so bad?'

She bit back the urge to scream. He was so thick. Even this simple fictitious scenario was beyond him. If she'd really lost a diary in Lorna's flat why would she need to spell out why she didn't want every Tom, Dick and Plod poring over its steamy pages?

Did Bryn think she was that brazen?

Her voice wavered with irritation as she spoke, but she was sure he would interpret it as raw emotion. 'I just don't know what I'd do.'

Her body sagged and she buried her face in her hands. He was quick to sit beside her. 'It'll be OK,' he whispered. She reached out and found his hand. She pulled him nearer. She felt his arm slip round her shoulder and she nestled closer still. She shivered and her skin tingled against the silky fabric of her blouse.

A minute of silence passed.

'I bet you miss her,' she said.

'I didn't really know her.'

'But you were sleeping with her.'

'You've got it wrong, it was very casual. We weren't having a relationship.'

She turned her face up to his, and kissed him tentatively.

He jerked his head back but she could already tell that there was no way he was about to bolt. 'What are you doing?' he asked.

He started to say something else but she pressed her fingertips to his lips. 'Shhh.' She kissed him again, and slid her hand around to cup his neck and keep him close. The kiss lingered and became deeper as she teased his tongue into her mouth. Her lips were soft and her mouth tasted of spearmint. He wasn't a bad kisser, just a little too eager, too adolescent. But that was a good thing.

With her free hand she started to unbutton her blouse. Pulling the buttons apart, letting him think their kissing had reawakened the chemistry between them. She knew the exact moment when his focus on her became total, and then she pulled back. He looked surprised. She ran her hand across his lap, pretending it was a casual touch, but they both knew it wasn't.

She stood in front of him. Her nerves had calmed, she'd stopped shivering, suddenly the room felt much warmer. She dropped her blouse to the floor and watched his intense gaze fall to her cleavage.

She paused to run her hands over her breasts. She pushed her bra down and cupped her breasts, massaging the nipples with her thumbs.

Her stare was unwavering.

She saw him rub the palm of his hand on the hip of his trousers and she knew she was making progress.

'Why not?' she asked lightly and let her skirt drop to the floor.

She unhooked her bra and let it fall, then stepped back and pirouetted slowly in just her black G-string and high heels. Her skin was tanned and taut. She knew her body was better than Lorna's.

'You look good,' he said.

Her lips parted and she ran her tongue across her teeth and smiled.

'But we're not doing it here,' he added.

She knew she was committed and held his gaze. 'Why not? You're hard, aren't you?' She reached down, took his hand and guided it between her legs. 'It's what I really need right now.'

'But not here.'

'Why not?'

'What if we're caught?'

'We won't be. But it's the risk that's turning me on. I don't even think I'd mind if someone were watching.' She bent forward and kissed him again. His fingers travelled up, across her stomach to her breasts. Her skin was warm, her nipples erect. She tilted her head back, encouraging his lips to kiss her neck. 'Come on,' she breathed. 'Come on.' She pushed his hand back down to her G-string. 'Pull it off,' she gasped.

Obediently he yanked it a couple of times. On the second the flimsy elastic snapped. He paused to mutter, 'I'm sorry.'

'It doesn't matter.' She rolled on to her back on the mattress, using all her weight to pull him with her. His left hand yanked the zip on his trousers. His legs pressed between hers, his hips pushing them apart.

She squeezed his arm with her fingers and wriggled, as if trying to escape, but in his ear she breathed, 'Come on then, fuck me.'

He was heavy and enthusiastic; it felt like being humped by an eighteen-month-old Labrador. His mouth moved to her neck and he sucked on the skin over her jugular. His hips pushed her legs further apart. She wrapped her ankles around his thighs. He penetrated her and pushed himself in

250

deep. Her neck was burning as the blood rushed to the skin, her lower body throbbing as his body ground against hers. Credit where it was due; he was more Dobermann than Labrador.

Even so, she gritted her teeth and stared at the gloom of the ceiling, counting the thrusts. For something to do. There were always three hundred or so.

Blokes: it was the monotony of them that got to her.

As the wardrobe door opened Goodhew braced himself for discovery only to see the door bounce back at him in the same instant. For two or three seconds he was in darkness, then, as though the wardrobe suddenly relaxed, the doors popped back open by a good inch and a half. He hoped he wasn't as exposed as he felt.

He watched Victoria positioning herself on Lorna's bed and knew what she had planned long before the other guy had a clue. Goodhew wished silence wasn't obligatory at that moment; he had a major urge to groan. Why hadn't he just left?

Then he recognized Bryn's voice and he knew his only real option was to sit tight and wait for the situation's inevitable climax.

He leant back and stared upwards into the darkest part of the cupboard, probably up the skirt of one of Lorna's little black dresses. The bed springs were creaking along in the key of F and he didn't dare look out through the gap in the door.

When he'd sat in the same class as Bryn and the teachers asked them what they thought they'd be doing in fifteen years' time he hadn't pictured

251

this. Strange really.

He wondered how long he'd been sitting there: this must be one of the moments in life where time dragged. After about five minutes they fell silent and he sneaked a glance. He was just in time to see Victoria climbing astride Bryn and off they went again. The springs changed key and picked up in tempo. A few seconds later they creaked faster still; it was starting to remind him of the end of 'Come On Eileen'. Victoria and Bryn didn't exactly try to outdo Kevin Rowland's vocals, but it was fair to say that Goodhew knew when it was safe to look. Or safe-ish.

Bryn was lying on his back with his trousers still tangled down around his calves. Victoria had slid off the bed and was reaching for her skirt.

'I'm getting dressed, I'm cold,' she said quietly.

Bryn stared at her but didn't move. She picked up her underwear. She slipped her feet into her shoes and began buttoning her blouse.

He watched, unblinking.

'That lived up to expectations,' she said.

'What?'

'I got what I expected. Mediocre.' Bryn didn't move. 'I'd stick with the cars,' Victoria continued, 'you've probably got some talent for *tinkering* with them.'

Bryn stiffened. 'What are you on about?'

'Lorna.'

'Lorna? What about her?'

Victoria stood with her feet planted shoulder-width apart and her body full on to Bryn. 'I fell out with her over you. But now I've proved she never mattered to you. For your information, I was so over you when we did this.'

'Bollocks.'

'I'm sorry?'

'It's bollocks. You must think I'm stupid. Lorna wasn't interested in me any more than you were. What's the big deal about proving you can shag me on Lorna's bed?'

Goodhew wondered what reaction Victoria had expected. Bryn had gone as far as rolling on to his side and raising himself on one elbow; if she had expected him to be irate she would be disappointed. 'What's the real reason then?'

Victoria turned sideways, with the wardrobe close to her left hand. When she turned her head away from Bryn, Goodhew knew he was in her line of sight and prayed her attention was elsewhere.

'Believe what you want, but I'm telling you, she was jealous. And I'm glad we did it in here. I don't miss her, in the end I hated her.'

'There wasn't any diary, was there?'

'So now I'm a liar? You're sick.'

'I'm sick? You got me in here with the sole idea of trashing Lorna and I'm sick?'

'Like you weren't up for it,' she sneered.

This time Bryn sounded like she'd gone too far. 'Enough.' He growled and began to pull up his trousers. 'I admit it, I was up for it. You offered, I accepted, that's the whole story. But you. You're in a whole other league.'

'You slept with Lorna, I got jealous,' Victoria goaded. 'I slept with you and she was the jealous one. Looking at you now, no, I don't understand it, but that's how it was. I like to settle scores,

Bryn.' She hitched her skirt up a few inches with one hand and rubbed the other between her legs until it was wet and shiny, with his semen across her palm and fingers. She smeared it across the mattress.

'What the hell are you doing?' Bryn spluttered.

Victoria, her back to him, faced the wardrobe and appeared to be staring straight at Goodhew. Suddenly her hand flew towards the doors and slammed them shut. 'That was a message for Lorna and you.' Her voice was sharp enough to pierce the plywood doors. 'A fuck off message.'

Goodhew heard her stride away. She sounded close to running as she darted through the heart of the unlit flat and down on to the street.

Goodhew listened, he'd only heard Victoria leave. Was he alone yet? His legs were seized with cramp and his right arm was numb; he was desperate to move but emerging to find himself face to face with Bryn didn't appeal either.

Victoria had made a good job of sealing the cupboard. Goodhew pressed his hand against the door, testing how tightly it fitted. Opening the wardrobe was easy; opening it silently and by just a few millimetres would be a damn sight more difficult. He dug the tips of his fingers into the join between the two closed doors and pressed, gently at first, then harder. It creaked and the doors parted by quarter of an inch, just as Bryn dragged the curtains half shut.

Goodhew moved his eye as close to the opening as he could without having to move his body. The only illumination came from the streetlamp outside, still drizzling just about enough light into the room to leave his old school pal Bryn O'Brien bathed in anaemia. Bryn was too busy frowning down to the street to sense he was being observed.

He buckled his belt, and brushed down his thighs and the front of his shirt. He wore noticeably unscuffed brown lace-up shoes and the light from the window shone in little pane-shaped domes on the leather. He reached in his pocket, checked for his keys, then stepped into the dark core of the flat.

Goodhew didn't move, just listened.

Bryn moved slowly through the sitting room, feeling his way from door frame to chair, and from chair to wall. It was slow but uneventful until he reached the landing. A stumble. A clatter. 'Oh, fuck. What the hell is that?'

He must have kicked something away; wood cracked and an object bounced on the stairs. He ran down after it. The door opened, then slammed, and Goodhew scrambled from the cupboard and staggered to the window as fast as his numb legs would carry him. Bryn strode out of sight. There was no way of telling whether he was driving or where he was heading. Goodhew sighed in disappointment, but what did he expect? Bryn wasn't going to park outside, was he?

Goodhew used his torch to light his way across the flat; he knew he risked someone outside seeing the light dancing on the walls but he just wanted to get out.

Fast.

The narrow beam caught something shining on the landing. He knelt down and directed the light down the stairs. Bryn had tripped on a side table, then kicked it, sending it crashing down to the hall.

And before it had fallen it had been the home to a small pile of junk mail. Brochures for holiday parks, lawn-mowers and orthopaedic mattresses in clear envelopes. There were four of them, inconspicuous and easily overlooked. None read 'L. Spence'; they were addressed to the wrong people.

The first two names he recognized: 'V. Nugent' and 'J. Moran'. The other two were new: 'Miss H. Sellars' and 'W. Thompson-Stark'.

They'd all been opened, cut with scissors by the look of the neat seams.

He rescued the table from the foot of the stairs, leaving it resting on the landing wall to hide its broken leg. He scribbled the names on a scrap of paper and replaced the brochures, then left to vanish into the night.

Suddenly he had much to do.

Chapter Thirty-Three

Victoria scuttled from Lorna's flat on to the street. She ran, clattering along the pavement as fast as her spiked heels could carry her. Everyone thought she was tough but her brittle coat of bravado had just chipped and shattered.

Yes, she'd played it out pretty much as she planned. But Bryn wasn't the pushover she'd expected him to be; instead of recoiling at her big finale he'd become infused with rage. The room had filled with it and she suddenly wondered if she'd been terribly wrong about him. She hadn't finished their encounter with an arrogant trounce out of the flat, instead she'd bolted.

Now she didn't care if anyone saw her, the only thing on her mind was fear of being caught.

Fear of Bryn.

She clutched her small handbag: it contained her phone, keys, money and cigarettes, none of which she could afford to lose.

She darted through a back alley and was out of sight of Lorna's flat before the door opened. Ahead of her was a dark tunnel of unlit back fences and high gates, and at the end she knew she'd find a narrow gap taking her on to the footpath beside the Cam.

She was furious with herself, she'd been so excited by the prospect of humiliating him that she'd been too vague with the details of what would happen afterwards. She had planned this route but only thought about it as it was in daylight. She'd accepted that it would be muddy, but now she couldn't see the thick puddles. Silty water slopped into her left shoe.

There'd been another oversight too; she'd come in Bryn's car and now she was cold, with no underwear and no jacket, but more importantly he could still drive and she had no means of reaching her flat first.

The moon vanished behind a shifting cloud, she could only inch forward until it reappeared. She needed to run, but not in these shoes and not in the pitch black.

She found the path beside the river and hurried towards the illuminated restaurants on Magdalene Bridge, wondering whether she should hail a taxi. But the lights were only on while staff cleaned up; the clientele were long gone. She glanced up and down the street in case a cab was parked up waiting for a job from its dispatcher. Nothing but an already booked car. The driver and his passengers all looked towards her as they rolled past.

She looked down at her tarty skirt and mud-caked shoes and imagined what they must be thinking. She hurried away from the kerb. Any driver would be disgusted at carrying a passenger such a short distance and, anyway, the wait would be longer than the journey.

She walked away from the centre towards home. She kept to the pavement for a few minutes, checking over her shoulder and ducking into doorways as she saw the beams of car headlights. But none of them were Bryn's.

Victoria rented a small flat in the annexe of a large Edwardian house. The approach was impressive even if her flat wasn't. A wall ran round the gardens, waist-high, like an immovable girdle keeping the conifers pinned to the house. Movement sensors controlled security lighting and she could see it glaring from a hundred yards away. She kept low and close to the wall, peering over between the low straggling branches.

Bryn's old Ford waited in the driveway.

Lights off.

Engine silent.

Windows steamed.

She hugged herself and waited. A passing taxi

flashed its lights on her, but drove on. She wondered whether they'd think she was loitering and perhaps call the police.

Five minutes later and she heard the Zodiac start. But it didn't move and several minutes on she heard the fan running, kicking warm air into the interior and clearing the windows. Bryn was planning to wait.

She lit a cigarette, not a conscious decision, just one made by her agitated fingers. She drew a couple of quick breaths with her eyes shut and a scowl pressing her forehead into a crease. She opened her eyes as the taxi returned; this time he slowed and rolled down his electric window.

'All right?'

'Yeah,' she nodded. 'Just waiting for someone.'

'You don't want a lift then?'

'No.' She shook her head and he pulled away. Before he'd travelled fifty yards she wished she'd answered yes. She watched the taxi's tail lights shrink to dots. And she wanted to be somewhere else.

She felt in her bag, to check for her purse and phone. Both there. What the hell? She had the money, it made sense to spend the night in a hotel. She could use their room service, laundry service and buy a change of clothes in the morning.

Fuck Bryn. She pictured herself bathing, getting warm and clean then sliding between smooth cotton hotel sheets and drifting off to sleep while Bryn slept upright in that aging piece of scrap.

She hoped its radiator boiled over and spewed its guts out over the gravel drive.

She turned and strode back towards the city

centre; she'd stay at the Garden House Hotel. She'd stayed there once after being taken to Grantchester and back by punt. Before Bryn and Lorna and all of this mess. She'd had a romantic night, they'd ordered dinner in their room and watched the last punts return just before sunset. Then they'd cuddled in bed and watched *Sleepless in Seattle* on the TV.

A night of escapism was what she needed. Forget about Bryn and Lorna and all but one of the Morans.

She reached the traffic lights on the junction of Castle Hill and Magdalene Street. She hurried back towards the bridge, but this time it was a welcome sight. She had a plan and she didn't care what any bystanders thought she looked like.

On her right was a row of matching shops, two- and three-storey buildings painted a sombre battleship grey with the window and door frames in black; every name over every door painted in the same black script.

On her left the walls of Benson Hall were high and dark. Sooted and glassless, with bricked panels in stone window frames.

These were the street scenes that in daylight artists captured in watercolours. They were old and genteel and never seemed threatening.

So Victoria continued down the dark conduit that whisked her towards the centre.

The lights were mostly out on Magdalene Bridge, but two high streetlamps still operated, diffusing light across its span. Shops and restaurants left small courtesy lights glowing but nothing more. The last diners and drinkers had long since dispersed and the only sounds were the rippling of the Cam as it slithered beneath her, and her feet clacking on the pavement above.

She didn't realize that she had stopped shivering; her next small victory was in sight and all her thoughts were on the hotel, not on the chilly night licking at her bare ankles, or her fingers stiffening with cold.

And worst of all she hadn't felt the goosebumps climbing her scalp, trying to tell her she was being watched.

Ahead the road narrowed and a shadow moved.

But Victoria didn't notice.

Chapter Thirty-Four

The Round Church stood at the top of Trinity Street, like a sentry marking the start of the next part of the city. As she hurried towards it, a little nervous butterfly darted around her stomach. For the first time she noticed gateposts topped with statues of eagles. They had books at their feet. She glanced at them, and they glared back. Looking ready to fly off and scatter pages into the streets of Cambridge.

The walk seemed further through empty streets than it did during a hectic lunch hour. She wished again that she'd stopped the cab, but she wouldn't find one now, not in the deserted pedestrian area. She followed the grounds of St John's round to the right and into Trinity Street.

261

Somewhere in the adjacent streets running footsteps echoed.

She hurried, skipping into a trot every few paces. Past the feet of St John's College Chapel.

The road darkened and she tried to keep a picture of the street in daytime at the front of her memory. The ornate railings were just pretty. The blackened stone was just old. She drifted towards the kerbside, then quickly sidestepped a low bollard. Stupid decision to paint them black.

Another entrance to St John's came and went, and in a fleeting moment she considered finding the porter's lodge and demanding assistance. But she didn't need the night to be any longer and in just another five minutes she'd reach the hotel.

Ahead of her, though, the road became darker still; she passed a little park and for a few yards the only illumination was from the moon and the eerie glow it cast as it shone on the white blossom of the chestnut trees. Their branches waved at her from over the railings.

She passed Trinity College and forced herself not to look up at its medieval elevations, remembering the gargoyles and grotesque stonework. Instead she fixed her sights further ahead to the start of the shops and began to feel relief that she was back in safer territory.

The street made a slow curve to the right. A cash point machine flashed, winking at the facing pink and blue geometric display in Jaeger's window. Even in the dark the shops were designed to appeal.

But the diversion they created was to be short-lived.

She slowed again when she saw the figure ahead; a shadow moving out of a doorway. Seeing one person was worse than seeing none. She kept walking, but she had no choice, there was nowhere to run.

She was feet from passing when she risked a glance. Instantly her apprehension disintegrated. 'Oh hi,' she beamed.

'Victoria?'

She exhaled in relief. 'Yes.'

'Why are you walking on your own?'

'I had a row with a boyfriend, I was walking to the Garden House to spend the night there and I was getting a bit spooked walking through town in the dark. I'm so glad it's you.' She knew she'd never been this friendly before, but suddenly hoped it sounded genuine enough to get her out of trouble. 'And what are you doing here?'

'I just needed to get out. Get some fresh air. Is he in your flat?'

Victoria lit another cigarette. 'Waiting outside.'

'What's his name?'

'Bryn.'

'I didn't know you had a boyfriend.'

'It's a casual thing.'

'Not ready for anything serious yet?'

'Something like that.'

'But it's been several months since...' The sentence died and they both gave it a moment to be laid to rest. 'Do you want me to go back with you?'

Victoria puffed out a thin stream of smoke. She was wondering whether the opportunity for a free bed for the night was about to present itself. She sighed and tried to sound weary. 'I can't face him right now.'

She made a few half-hearted steps in the direction of the hotel. 'He scares me,' she moaned.

'Scares you? He's sitting outside your flat. He can't do anything from there.'

She lowered her voice like she was confiding a secret. 'He's angry with me, he thinks I'm coming back tonight and he's waiting for me.'

'But you're leaving him there to teach him a lesson?'

'That was the idea,' she said, 'but I've gone off it now.'

'No, you should. I'll help you.'

Victoria shrugged. 'I'm not sure.'

'You have your mobile, don't you?'

Victoria reached in her bag, pulled out her phone and unlocked the keypad. 'He'll know it's my phone.'

'Yes, but he won't know the text is from me and I know how to make him squirm. Remember, it's because of him you're out here cold and vulnerable.'

Victoria nodded.

'So it's a good idea?'

Victoria shrugged, then nodded again. 'Why not?'

'Text this...' The words were recited slowly to give her enough time to spell them. "You'll be sorry in the morning and..."'

Victoria prodded the keypad with both thumbs. 'And what?'

'That's it.'

'Send?'

'Yes.'

She pressed the send button and watched until the message icon had flown from the screen. 'Do I send him the next bit later?'

'Why not?'

'And how's it going to work?'

Her companion sighed and stared skywards, and she looked too. The moon was a cold yellow and the small clouds were racing fast enough to give the impression that the chimney tops were moving. A few yards further down Trinity Street a building stood on the corner of Trinity Lane, carvings protruding from both sides of the roofline. They matched, and appeared to be like ships' figureheads sticking out about two feet from the guttering and giving the effect of trying to rip the structure in two different directions.

No one would have noticed them unless they'd happened to look up like that. It was impossible to make out the detail in the starlit sky, they were just silhouettes.

'Why will that scare him?' she persisted.

Her companion sighed, exhaling the breath with a deep hiss of theatrical exasperation, then looking down again, gaze dropping in a straight line, like it had fallen from the roof. 'When I first found out you were seeing our father I felt uncomfortable, but I didn't begrudge him some company. We all know what it's like to be lonely. You weren't what I expected at first, but you deserve our thanks for sticking with him right until the end. I thought it showed a kind and generous side to your nature.'

They began to walk again, slowly this time, but within yards they'd stopped once more. She shifted her weight from foot to foot. The cold was biting now and the conversation had slid into more difficult territory. It was uncomfortable to stay still but neither was it the right time to walk away. 'I wanted to be with him,' she said.

'I'm surprised he didn't leave you something, a token of his thanks perhaps.'

'I didn't expect anything.'

'Oh, come on. If he'd lived you would have been enjoying his money, why not once he's dead?' There was a pause. 'Or did you think one of us would look after you?'

And it was the pause that made her hesitate. In that three-second silence there was a shift, a mutation in the mood between them that told her finding the correct answer had just become imperative. But she couldn't think of anything at all to say.

She felt a hand grab at her sleeve. She looked bewildered and pulled back, but not enough to break free. The fingers gripped too tightly.

She looked from left to right, hoping for even one pedestrian. In one direction rows of chained-up riderless bikes and in the other windowless walls and a solitary glowing lamp in the shape of a barber's pole. But no people.

Her eyes widened, she still wanted to be mistaken. 'No. I don't know why you're getting angry with me...'

'I'm angry with myself. Why didn't I see it sooner? You took something from my father.'

'I didn't.'

'You took something from my father,' the voice repeated.

'It wasn't about you.' Victoria gasped as her back slammed against the damp stone wall, her body weightless, swimming nowhere against the pain.

The hands released her, and she staggered forwards, trying to regain her balance and clear her head. She stumbled four or five steps, hoping she was free to go.

She felt a hand on her shoulder and shrugged it away, but it wasn't there to spin her round, just to pass something around her neck. She was hauled back in like a toy mouse on the end of a string.

Her shoulders hunched and she threw herself from side to side, snapping her nails on the webbing belt savaging her skin. Her bag hit the path, spilling its contents in all directions. Her feet flailed, fighting to grip. Her left foot trampled a lipstick and her ankle rolled, dropping her weight against the ligature.

And in response to her struggle it tightened. She felt her mouth gaping and her tongue arching as it gagged against her tonsils. No one came running to save her and the last thing she did was piss herself.

And the last thing she felt was it overtaking the semen already trickling down her cold bare thighs.

Victoria slumped to the ground, and after a couple of seconds her leg kicked once, like a dreaming dog. But that was all.

There was no attempt to retrieve her handbag or its contents, but the phone was slipped into a pocket.

Above her body there was a square bay window set across the corner of the building. And about ten feet from the ground there was a man's face carved under the windowsill. He was black with pollution, except the dome of his head where the cream stone was exposed and looked like his skull.

Victoria's face was distorted but still intact. It didn't look right.

So she was rolled on to her front. Fingers twisted through her hair and held tightly. Then her head was lifted and her face slammed against the ground. Again and again. Pummelled against the stone pavement until it grated tracks into her skin.

The killer walked away towards the river, still carrying Victoria's phone. It was time Bryn had another text.

Chapter Thirty-Five

Bryn glared at the message. 'What the fuck's that supposed to mean?' He threw the phone on to the passenger seat. He guessed one thing: there was no point waiting for her.

The drive was big enough to turn without reversing, but even so he backed up closer to her door before flooring the accelerator. The car seemed to crouch before leaping forward, the fat tyres spitting flint chips at her windows.

He shot out through the gateway on to the deserted road, leaving just the growl of the engine and quickly dispersed vapour trails billowing in the disturbed air. He guessed he would have annoyed someone.

He hoped so anyway.

Instead of heading for home he took the road out of town. He needed thinking time and the best way to think was to drive. He rested his right hand on the top of the steering wheel, and his left on the column change.

His speed crept up, passing forty in the thirty zone, then nudging fifty a few seconds after that. He was touching sixty as he swung around the last bend before the motorway when he suddenly remembered the speed camera. He touched his brakes too hard, the back end wobbled then straightened just as a familiar flash exploded in front of his eyes.

'Shit,' he snapped. This was all he needed. Everything was going from bad to worse, he just hoped there was no film in it, but looking at the way the day was turning out he doubted luck was with him at all. It wasn't like he could afford any more speeding convictions. 'Shit,' he repeated and kept just under the speed limit as he coasted down the slip road and on to the M11.

The traffic was thicker, overnight lorries heading to the docks and late night businessmen heading for London; even so he kept to the speed limit and let them thunder past. He needed to calm down. Let it go.

He'd known he wasn't Victoria's type, not in anything other than a casual way. But hey, originally it had been fun. Now, though, she was playing a game and he didn't understand what it meant. Gary had wondered if Lorna had been jealous, but there was no way. Even if Victoria pretended there was. So what was her motive?

His brain meandered around the issue.

And soon his speed was drifting downwards, and the same aggressive wide tyres that had churned Victoria's gravel were stroking the tarmac as they floated towards the edge of their lane.

Bryn started, jerking his eyes open as the car shuddered on the ridged white line separating the lanes from the hard shoulder. He didn't think he'd been sleeping. Or perhaps he had. What time was it anyway? Twenty to two. Fucked for work tomorrow, that was certain. He could sleep in the car. But not now. Not now.

He opened the quarter-light, turning it backwards so that the air gushed into his face; he took deep breaths and blinked. He leant across and opened the glove box, keeping one hand on the wheel and managing to hold his head up enough to look over the dashboard.

His fingers groped around, locating first an A to Z, then sunglasses, mints and finally a packet of cigarettes. He tried to grip it with the tips of his first two fingers but instead flipped it to the back of the glove box, somewhere behind the ring-bound spine of the road atlas.

He could do without this.

Bryn pulled on to the hard shoulder, taking the car out of gear but leaving the engine running, then he stretched across and grabbed the packet. He slid one cigarette out and pushed the dashboard lighter in and waited. He rarely smoked in the car and wasn't even sure the lighter worked.

After a few more seconds it clicked and popped back out; at least something was going right.

He lit up then tossed the packet back, slamming the glove box. He knew he was tired and wished he'd never decided to drive. He would double back at the next junction, get home, think again in the morning.

He kept the window open, but just to be certain he shuffled his backside back until he was sitting to attention, put the car in first and signalled. One pair of headlights appeared in the rear-view mirror and he waited for them to pass.

He used the hard shoulder to gain speed and was doing forty by the time the other vehicle, an articulated lorry, caught him. Bryn's car wavered as it was buffeted in the slipstream.

He pulled out into the first lane. A horn bellowed and he swerved back off the road again as a second lorry thundered by.

How the fuck had he missed something that big?

He checked behind him once again and this time made doubly sure that the road was empty. He levelled his speed at seventy-five; no one got speeding tickets for less than ten per cent over the limit. Well, he didn't think so and with thirty-plus miles until home he didn't want it to take a minute longer than it had to.

With twenty-eight miles to go he turned up the heater. Just a little. No point in freezing.

Twenty-five miles to go. Tail lights suddenly appeared two car lengths in front of him. He swung into the second lane, out round the other car dawdling at sixty.

Twenty-three miles to go. Still in the middle lane and Victoria didn't matter. Getting home mattered. Sinking into bed. Drifting into sleep.

Twenty-two miles to go. The tyres sounded like a ticket machine as they bumped over the cat's eyes between the middle lane and the slow lane.

New ticket, new ticket, new ticket.

Then like knuckles on a washboard as they rumbled again on the raised white line between the slow lane and the hard shoulder. First the passenger side tyres. Then the driver's side.

All at a perfectly uniform seventy-five miles per hour.

One hand lay in his lap.

His eyes were closed and staying closed, not seeing the bridge support rising from the verge ahead. And his other hand rested on the wheel, doing nothing to stop the car's gentle trickle away from the road.

The bridge dealt the car a glancing blow. Buckling the corner of the front bumper, twisting the front wing inwards. The headlamp shattered, the surrounding chrome bezel springing from its mounting and smacking the window. The car bounced away, back towards the carriageway.

But only for a second.

Bryn jerked awake. He heard the crash. And opened his eyes enough to see the road slewing under him. He felt the car careering right. He slammed on the brakes and yanked the wheel left.

The Zodiac left the motorway front nearside first. It slid on a narrow strip of mud then bounced through the furrows and deep grass further off road, coming to rest at an unnatural tilt.

Bryn yanked on the inside door handle and stumbled out on to the verge. His shaking hands gripped his mobile and he managed to dial 999. He walked around his car once then decided he'd seen enough. He sat back in and knew he was going to cry. He also knew that it was entirely his own fault.

When his phone beeped and he saw Victoria's name on the incoming message he had no desire to read it. He'd been dragged into more trouble than he'd had in a lifetime.

So he never saw the three little words which said 'PS IM DEAD'.

Chapter Thirty-Six

Mel sat in an armchair, in the front room of her flat. The upholstery was tired, but she'd been sitting in the same position for hours and the sagging cushions seemed to have wrapped themselves around her. She was warm and feeling cosy; a comforting place in a worrying home.

Toby was out. Probably at Mickey Flynn's potting Aftershock faster than pool balls.

Her mobile silently vibrated on the arm of her chair: she checked the number before answering. It was Michael Kincaide. She pressed 'end', then switched it off.

It was time to think, not time to talk.

Kincaide switched off his mobile. He pulled off

his tie and plodded up towards his bedroom. His wife was already in bed, asleep. Or pretending she was.

'Jan?'

He brushed his teeth, undressed and slipped in beside her. 'Jan?' He nudged her between the shoulder blades.

'What?'

'Roll over.'

She sighed and turned to face him. 'I've had a long day, Mike. I don't feel like anything.'

'It's been ages.'

'Ages since the weekend? Don't be pathetic,' she grumbled and turned away again. 'And next time try something more creative than "Roll over."'

Marks couldn't sleep. He was drinking coffee and staring at the unlit windows of Goodhew's flat when DC Charles brought in an envelope.

'Sorry to bother you, sir, but it's just been delivered and I thought you'd like it straight away.'

Marks stared at it before taking it from the detective. He knew what it was, just not what it said. 'I don't suppose you know if Goodhew's in the building?'

Charles gave a tut. 'You've just missed him, sir, he was looking up stuff on the computer till about ten minutes ago.'

'And he's gone?'

'Yep. Saw him get into a taxi out the front.'

When Charles had gone Marks opened the envelope. He wouldn't bother with fingerprinting it. Firstly, he knew there'd be no point. Secondly, if by a fluke there was a point then he didn't want

274

to find it. He'd given up debating the ethics of receiving these anonymous tip-offs; he preferred instead to treat them with suspicion but follow them up anyway.

The words were typed in the usual way, vertically centred on a sheet of A4.

What did Lorna keep in a Marmite jar and
a vinegar bottle?
Why does she get other people's junk mail?
Ask Victoria Nugent why she visited
Lorna's flat tonight.

Had Marks looked for Goodhew half an hour earlier he would have found him with one hand resting on the open pages of the telephone directory and the other on his mouse, directing the flow of data scrolling up on his PC screen.

Goodhew was watching for 'Sellars'. There were a few, but none with the initial H., and in the phone book there were too many, at least too many to call at this unsocial hour.

He moved on to 'W. Thompson-Stark'. He guessed with a name like that, any match would be the only match.

He typed 'Thompson', in case the Stark had been added later. The screen filled with Thompsons, so he started at the bottom and there, one entry below Z. Thompson (Shoplifting) was W. Thompson-Stark (Sexual Assault).

He double-clicked the entry and waited a painfully slow one and a half seconds for the data to appear on the screen.

The W. stood for Wayne, who was now twenty-six years old.

And the case dated back six years.

Goodhew's gaze scanned the information.

Rape charge brought. Reduced to sexual assault. Assault occurred on 9th July, reported after five days. No forensic evidence. Defendant denied charges but sentenced to three years, released after two.

Goodhew flicked on to the next screen. Two words jumped out at once. 'Lorna Spence.'

He let go of his mouse like it was hot.

He held his breath, reading the details slowly, making sure he read them correctly. His heart pounded.

He printed the details and called a taxi.

Wayne Thompson-Stark lived in Cutter's Path, Ely, a pretty development of townhouses running from the river back towards the canal. The cab dropped Goodhew at the edge of the estate.

'I'll drive you round if you want,' the driver offered. 'I just don't know which road it'll be, not with it being too new for the maps an' all.'

Goodhew shook his head. 'Don't worry.' He preferred to find it on foot.

The houses were too new for most of them to even display numbers and it took several minutes for him firstly to find an entrance to Cutter's Path and secondly to work out which direction to walk for Number 71.

The Path part of the name was appropriate: the cul-de-sac end of the road opened out on to a mock village green complete with winding foot-path. Cobbles of course, and lit by faux Victorian lamp posts. Goodhew guessed it would stay looking pretty until too many new owners began improving with white plastic doors, porches and innovative garden features.

Number 71 was the last on the left and like most of the other houses its lights were out.

Tough. Murder and sleeping comfortably didn't belong together.

From his side of the front door there was little that showed of the inside, one distorted pane directing his gaze up towards a black blur of darkness. He gave the bell a firm press and heard it chiming from the hallway; an upstairs light was switched on in a second and he knew he hadn't woken anyone.

The little pane of rippled glass revealed a view of a white handrail, pointing to the top of the stairs. A man stepped into view. He stood on the landing while he felt his way into some sort of dressing gown. He tied the belt around his waist. He was big built and when he finally banged down the steps it was as if he let gravity do all the work.

He opened the door to halfway. He didn't bother with the chain, if he had one, so perhaps pre-dawn callers didn't worry him. The light shone from behind him, making it hard to see his face. Goodhew looked in the general direction of the man's eyes and caught sight of a shadow moving upstairs. The man didn't speak.

Goodhew flipped out his ID. 'DC Goodhew. I expect you've heard of a recent murder in Cambridge...'

His sentence trailed away to nothing, the word 'murder' had opened the door.

Wayne Thompson-Stark was at least six feet two and broad, like a rugby player but with a straighter nose.

'Who else is in the house, Mr Thompson-Stark?'

'It's just Thompson. My girlfriend, she'll be down in a minute. Gone to the bathroom.'

'You weren't asleep?'

Thompson shook his head as though the bags under his eyes hadn't answered for him. He probably hadn't slept well for days. He spoke in a gruff voice which made him sound older. But then he also looked older than twenty-six. 'Go through, sit down.' He patted his towelling robe. 'You don't care if I stay like this?'

The front door opened into the sitting room, but Thompson led the way through to a narrow dining room at the back of the house and they chose chairs at opposite sides of a Formica drop-leaf table.

Upstairs a door creaked and footsteps padded across carpet. Goodhew whispered: 'You know I need to ask you questions about Lorna Spence, don't you?'

Thompson looked surprised. 'You don't need to whisper. Do you think she wouldn't know?'

Goodhew shrugged. 'Can't assume.'

Thompson reached to his left and pulled a chair alongside his own ready for his girlfriend.

'We don't have secrets,' said a woman's voice.

She stood a few feet back from the door, as if weighing up the situation before deciding whether to step into it. Her hair was in bunches and she wore pyjamas, pink winceyette covered in a pattern which appeared to be a jumble of numbered sheep. The fabric was tight across her belly and she looked about eight months pregnant. She turned to Thompson and he held out his hand for her to join them.

'This is DC Goodhew.'

She nodded and sat in the waiting seat.

Goodhew waited for her to be introduced, then realized they had no intention of bothering. 'What's your name?' he asked.

This time it was her turn to look startled. 'Hayley,' she said.

'Sellars?' Goodhew replied and she nodded.

Thompson chuckled. It was short and humourless. 'I thought you knew. Like you said though, you can't assume.'

Hayley reached out and slipped her hand into Thompson's. He gave it a squeeze.

Goodhew's gaze wandered across to the clock ticking towards 3 a.m. then it drifted back to the couple facing him.

Thompson didn't look aggressive; Hayley looked neither scared for Thompson nor scared of him.

But they both looked sorry. For what though?

Goodhew wiped his eyes. Something was clouding his vision and he needed to push it away. 'I'll be honest,' he sighed. 'Hayley, I don't know what connection you had with Lorna Spence, I just know there was one. And Mr Thompson, I need to know about your relationship with her too, about the assault and your conviction.' He sighed again. 'I know it's the middle of the night but if you could explain it to me I'd be very grateful.'

Their fingers were entwined, which seemed

their only need for communication. She wanted him to speak first and he knew it too.

'It was the week I was twenty and I had a vague idea who Lorna was. I'd seen her and her mate Vicky around, I just knew their first names, that kind of thing. I was out with some old school mates, having a few drinks, playing pool, and I noticed her having a row with her boyfriend. This was early in the evening, not much after seven and the next time I looked round she was on her own. She looked choked up.

'Later on she stood near the pool table, then asked if one of us would let her play. My mate played her and between shots I got talking to her. She'd split with her boyfriend, or that's what she said. She seemed all right, I had no reason to think she was lying.'

Hayley was glaring at her hands and chewing her lip. Goodhew wondered whether she was listening or had drifted somewhere else. Thompson released her hand and wrapped his arm around her instead. 'By about ten we were getting on fine and when the others moved on we decided to stay and talk for longer. I remember the bell rang for last orders and she asked if I could take her home. I didn't even own a car so I walked her back. Just before her house we started kissing and I honestly don't remember whose idea that was, we just had one of those moments when we both paused and knew it was about to happen.

'We were there for a while, and she was pressed up to me, knew I s'pose that I was turned on.' He paused to shrug in apology. 'I was nearly twenty, that's what I spent most of my time thinking about.'

He paused again.

'And then you had sex?' asked Goodhew.

Thompson nodded. 'Not sex like I expected. Not that I expected it, what I mean is she had weird ideas. We went into the kitchen because she said everyone would be in bed and no one would hear if we did it there. And it started off OK, just basic messing around. But then she took my hand and wanted me to shove it inside her, said she wanted it to hurt.'

Hayley kept silent, her eyes turned away, her cheeks turning hot.

'I didn't like it, so I didn't do it but when we started having sex she wanted me to fight her for it, pretend I was raping her.

'Now when I say it sounds too weird, it's obvious I should've stopped then and there, but she made it seem that I was being dull. And we did do it, and it was rough, but that was what she wanted. Oh, fuck it. I don't mean because she wanted it rough it was OK. I just mean it wasn't rape, or assault, or anything against her will.'

'So why did she press charges?'

'Because...' Thompson's voice was replaced by Hayley's.

'Because Lorna made everyone suffer.' She looked up at Goodhew and tears brimmed in her eyes. 'When we heard she'd been murdered I wondered whether Wayne had done it and he wondered whether it was me. That's how much she still affects us.' She sniffed and pressed away the tears with the heel of her hand. 'I wrote to

Wayne when he was in prison, I asked him to let me visit him, and he did. That's how we met.'

'But you knew Lorna?'

'Oh, yes. I was on my lunch break, decided to go down town and grab a sandwich. I swallowed the wrong way and stood outside Marks and Spencer's having a coughing fit. Next thing I knew she was banging me on the back and sorting out a glass of water. We met for lunch a couple of days later and before long she was my best friend. We went everywhere together, told each other everything too. I knew about the rape, the trauma she'd been through with examinations and the court case and the fear she felt at the thought of Wayne being released. And I believed it one hundred per cent.'

'We went out one night though and somehow I ended up drunk, too drunk for what I'd ordered. It didn't even occur to me that I'd been drugged, and I stood at the bar happily leaning on some guy. Probably telling Lorna how lovely he was for all I can remember. Well, that's what she said I said anyway. She said she felt hurt then went home.'

Hayley drew a deep breath and new tears appeared and slipped silently on to her cheeks. 'He broke my nose, and four fingers. I had six stitches, an Aids test, a tetanus shot and a dose of the clap. And then they never caught him. And Lorna...'

Her voice trailed off as her face screwed up with pain. Thompson held her closer and he kissed her hair.

Goodhew wasn't sure what to do. 'I can arrange for you to talk to a female officer if you prefer.'

Thompson gave his head a small shake; it didn't just mean 'no' but 'be quiet, wait.'

'No,' she whispered. 'It isn't the man that bothers me. Lorna was racked with guilt, distraught that she'd left me with him. She kept me company, helped me deal with the police procedures and cope with the medical problems.

'The drug I'd been given left me with only bits of memory. Every day I tried to recall more about the attack. I had a vague picture of an alley littered with beer crates. Oil stains on the tarmac, grit and sludge in the puddles. And not looking at him, turning my head away towards the narrow end of the alley where it's only wide enough for bicycles and pedestrians. I was pleading for someone to come and save me.

'Every time I thought about it I remembered looking towards the narrow end of the alley, not the other end where people actually would pass by. Why would I do that?' She didn't wait for an answer. 'I'll tell you, it was because I knew someone else was in the alley.

'Then after that I couldn't get the idea out of my head that Lorna had been there. Hidden. Watching. And that's been the greater battle – having that idea in my head and not being able to get it out again.

'I didn't even know if I'd just invented that part. I stewed on it. I had no proof and I told myself I was being hysterical. But I couldn't dismiss it. The feeling of those eyes on me... In the end I accused her. She was outraged. But she would have been, wouldn't she? I didn't see her after that.'

'So you had no proof?'

She shook her head. 'None. Women's intuition maybe.'

'But why would she?'

'Why would anyone want to watch a friend being raped? I don't know. It makes her worse than him. Can you imagine what this has done to my friendships? I couldn't get over this feeling that I was raped by her too, then I remembered everything she'd told me about her rape. That's when I started to wonder whether she'd made that up as well.'

It wasn't much to go on. Perhaps Thompson had understood what Goodhew was thinking. 'It may not sound much evidence, but when Hayley came to see me I'd already spent months trying to grasp what had happened to me. I knew she'd come with the answer.'

'Where were you when she died?'

'Here with Hayley.'

'Just the two of you?'

'You're asking the wrong questions. What you need to know is Lorna's objective. What was she chasing and who was she prepared to damage to get it?' Thompson leant closer to Goodhew. 'Lorna only did things for Lorna. She was the centre of her universe. Everybody else just spun around her, she made sure it happened that way.'

Thompson fell silent and the two of them looked across at Goodhew. He didn't know what he'd expected, but it hadn't been this. Maybe they were lying, concocting it all to cover for whichever one had killed her, but he threw out the idea at once. Instead he saw the truth of the situation: a light had been shone into one of the dark corners of Lorna's life, and there she stood, quietly manipulating the people around her. The drugs at Lorna's flat fitted the picture. Lorna had already sent one man to prison and manipulated a situation until a woman had been raped. How much further had her game-playing needed to go before it had become an extreme and deadly sport?

The only sound came from the hand-me-down fridge freezer which gurgled and hummed from its cubby hole behind the door.

Goodhew shuddered.

'Are you OK?' Hayley looked genuinely concerned.

'Just tired,' he answered and hurried to stand, keen to leave behind the foreboding which had just draped its leaden arm across his shoulders.

Chapter Thirty-Seven

Goodhew had lost all track of time, he had no idea how long he'd been awake. He wasn't even sure when dawn was due, although he could see from the light seeping in from the east of the sky that it was on its way.

The taxi hurried from Ely, past flat farmlands, and into the edge of Cambridge. There was one thing Goodhew had known: he was too tired to drive.

As the cab approached his flat he realized that his attention had swung towards Parkside

285

station. At the last moment he directed the driver away, and several minutes later was on the doorstep of his grandmother's apartment.

She took what seemed an age to open the door, and when he saw her he wondered whether she'd stopped to apply make-up or if she slept in it every night. Her housecoat looked newly ironed too, and he felt more dog-eared than ever.

He frowned and she didn't look too happy either. 'You look like shit,' she said.

'You swore.'

She held open the door for him and he stepped through. 'It's called communicating with the younger generation,' she said drily. 'I was making a point.'

'Oh, I see.'

'Besides at 4.30 a.m. I'm entitled to swear.' But she didn't sound at all tired, was clearly more awake than he was. 'What's up? And why didn't you use your key?'

'Sorry, it's at home. Look, I can't sleep.'

'Not about your phobia, I assume?'

'No. I need to talk.'

He slumped into his favourite chair, and she perched on the edge of the cushion of the chair facing his.

'Well, well, I never thought I'd hear that from you, Gary. Not that I'm surprised that you do. You've pushed yourself to make detective in almost record time and now, correct me if I'm wrong, you seem to put pressure on yourself by feeling responsible for every serious crime you touch.' She paused. 'I'm right, aren't I?'

'Not exactly.'

'No? You have yet to master the art of leaving work at work – it seems to follow you round as if it's hiding in your back pocket.'

Goodhew shrugged. 'Yeah, well, actually it is the murder,' he said finally.

'Explain it to me.'

'The case? Sure.' He settled back in the chair, and she did the same.

She listened without interruption.

'I feel,' he said finally, 'as if we just don't know anything. It's too random, just a fog of possibilities and no direction through it.'

'Of course there will be.'

'Go on then, infect me with optimism.'

'Of course you know things, the problem is you have too many little gems of information and you can't distinguish the ones that matter.' She beamed.

'Case closed then,' he muttered.

'Gary. Just pull in the slack.'

'I'm sorry?'

'All these little gems – perhaps they're all threaded on to the same bracelet. Pull in the slack and you'll see how they all sit together.'

'Oh God. Optimism and analogy. Sorry but I really am too tired.'

But she was now on a roll. 'What do your instincts tell you?'

'Nothing. That's why I came to see you. I haven't got a clue any more.'

She gave the chair's armrest a decisive thump. 'I'm putting the kettle on. If you were ten years younger I'd say you were over-tired and send you to bed.' His grandmother retreated and Goodhew closed his eyes until he heard the kettle boil then followed her into the kitchen.

'I thought getting it off my chest might help.'

His grandmother raised an eyebrow. 'Are you turning over a new leaf?'

Goodhew laughed but without humour. 'No, just a one-off.'

'You know the bracelet analogy? Maybe the gems are in the wrong order.'

'And I suppose you already worked out what the right order is?' He took three tea bags from the canister and dropped them into the pot.

'I haven't the foggiest.' She pulled out a tray and he loaded it with the milk, sugar and mugs. But she wasn't about to drop the problem either. 'If Lorna's death was planned, why do it in such an open place? Even at 1 a.m. there must've been a good chance of someone seeing them.'

'Someone put the GHB in Lorna's coffee. How quickly it worked wasn't entirely in the killer's hands, so perhaps the plan was to kill her down one of the footpaths.'

He paused, aware that his grandmother's train of thought had wandered down an obscure footpath of its own.

'Was she promiscuous?'

'Possibly no more so than many single people. What I am discovering is that she was a manipulator. She has pulled strings in several people's lives, then been there to pick up the pieces. The letters I found at her flat, junk mail really, but they were addressed to people she was connected to.'

'Who?'

He listed them: 'Jackie, Victoria, then two I've just visited, Hayley Sellars and Wayne Thompson. I wonder if the killer had them sent. Maybe Lorna had done something to hurt each of them.'

'Does that make them your list of suspects?' she asked.

'I don't think so,' he mused. 'The killer would hardly include themself in the mail shot.'

'Who knows?' she replied. 'The best place to hide is in a crowd.

'And what's it got to do with what's written on her hand?'

'Lorna probably wrote the words herself, you know, maybe the killer didn't put her up to it.'

'Maybe,' he muttered, as he abruptly found himself down another stagnant backwater. 'That's the problem, too many pissing maybes.' He took the tray back through to the sitting room and his grandmother followed.

'Now you're swearing,' she observed.

He sank into the chair again, and his tiredness returned. He smiled wearily. 'I'm entitled to, it's a belated attempt at misspent youth.'

She just changed the subject. 'Could Bryn have killed her?'

'Definitely not.'

'Why not?' she persisted.

Goodhew shrugged. 'Gut feeling.'

She pressed him. 'You're adamant?'

'Absolutely.'

She beamed. 'And ten minutes ago I thought you were banging on my door because you didn't know whether you could trust your own judgement.'

Goodhew smiled too. 'Touché.'

His mind wandered and he stayed uninterrupted with his thoughts. Ten minutes later his grandmother left the room, although he barely noticed. He had suddenly reached the point of sleep and in his mind he was reading the fronts of the junk mail envelopes, flicking through them one by one.

Jackie Moran.

Victoria Nugent.

Hayley Sellars.

Wayne Thompson-Stark.

He added more envelopes, one for Richard Moran, another for Alice and a third for Bryn. That made seven.

He knew the police would soon swarm over Hayley and Wayne's lives, dragging up their worst memories. Hayley's words drifted back to him; he remembered her voice, quiet but determined. *Lorna made everyone suffer.* Her words rang with truth. Perhaps she was wrong, but she believed she wasn't.

He flicked through the envelopes again, but now there were ten. Colin Willis had one, but so did Kincaide, and the tenth was for Mel.

Shit. It was like a Rubik's cube, coming together in one place only to be jumbled up somewhere else. Jumbled and blurred.

He shut his eyes and pictured the cube levitating and unravelling itself.

In the kitchen Goodhew's grandmother stared into the eye-level grill, where the bread lay face up like a row of sunbathers catching afternoon rays.

She loved seeing the golden tan creep across the white loaf, something she'd made a habit of watching since the days of rationing when, as a child, she'd taken pride in never singeing a crumb.

When the toast was brown she stacked it on a plate before glancing into the sitting room. She watched him until she was sure he really slept, poured his tea down the sink and took her mug to her bedroom.

She turned on the bedside radio, just loud enough to pick out the banter from the Q103 DJ; at five to six she wasn't going back to sleep.

Ironic when she wasn't the insomniac.

She glanced over at her late husband's photo, then at the photo of Gary and his sister. What did he want to prove anyway? But she knew his trouble; he had inherited a little too much of his grandfather's conscience. He had to learn to let go of the things he couldn't put right.

She heard the jingle for the start of the news and turned up the volume.

'A woman's body has been found in the centre of Cambridge in what looks like a shocking new development to the Midsummer Common murder of Lorna Spence. A student made the grim discovery in the early hours of this morning, and although police have not issued a statement, early unofficial reports are refusing to rule out the possibility that the deaths are connected.'

She swung her legs back off the bed and muttered under her breath, 'So much for your sleep, Gary.'

Chapter Thirty-Eight

As Marks spoke to the coroner's office on his mobile he turned away from the murder scene and found himself facing the window of a gift shop. A teddy dressed as a Beefeater smiled back at him. Marks wandered out of the bear's line of vision and instead stood at the end of Rose Crescent; his favourite street in the city. Such a shame for him that for some considerable time he'd be picturing Victoria Nugent's crumpled body at the end of it.

Marks hung up just as Goodhew came into view. He glared but Goodhew was too busy looking past him to the cordon surrounding the body for it to have any effect.

Marks held on to most of the dirty look and managed to sound caustic. 'Oh, it's you, Gary. There's definitely a problem when I find it easier to identify murder victims than to recognize an approaching member of my own team.' He immediately felt a stab of guilt; Goodhew wore responsibility like a second skin. He lived with it and Marks doubted that he could shake it off it he tried. If Goodhew wasn't around it wouldn't be because he was shirking.

'Who?' Goodhew asked.

'Victoria Nugent.' Marks saw no surprise in Goodhew's eyes, just a final, almost apologetic glance in the dead girl's direction. 'Preliminaries say dead between eleven thirty and two thirty.'

Goodhew looked for a second as though he was working on some kind of mental arithmetic, but all he said was, 'How?'

'Beaten and strangled. Actually it might be the other way around. The killer pummelled her face into the ground, there's not much blood but what there is has stayed in one spot, like she wasn't capable of struggling by then.'

'Bryn?' Goodhew didn't often dabble with one-word sentences but he was struggling to collate his thoughts. He hadn't expected another death, and he was kicking himself because the one thing his limited experience should have taught him was to expect the unexpected.

Marks looked quizzical.

Goodhew rephrased it into something more comprehensible.

'Has anyone spoken to him?'

'Spoken to who?' Marks still looked quizzical.

'Bryn O'Brien.'

'Where the hell did you get that from?'

'Must've been mentioned. He was the guy that dated Lorna a while back.'

'I know that, and he made a statement after Lorna, remember? I still don't remember a relationship between him and Victoria.'

Goodhew shrugged. 'Might be worth cross-checking the semen ... if there is any, I mean.'

'You irritate me–' Marks said, then stopped mid-sentence. He deliberately used his most matter-of-fact voice, making sure he sounded so emotionless that Goodhew would start to wonder whether he'd misheard and, for once, pay complete attention.

Goodhew asked another question to fill the silence. 'Did the murderer leave a message?'

Marks held up a hand in protest. 'You irritate me,' he repeated, still sounding placid, 'because I need you as part of the team. I had forgotten about your disappearing skills, you fire off like a bullet when an investigation starts and ricochet around the case until you hit a target. I only know–' He stopped as PC Kelly Wilkes hurried over holding a folded sheet of A4. 'What?'

'Sorry to interrupt, sir, we've found the dead woman's mobile phone. It was handed in to PC Sheen on nights and he's been trying to get hold of you. Here's his number. It appears to be registered to the dead woman and he had a play around with it, says she was texting another mobile early this morning. He's checked the number and it is registered to a Mr O'Brien. I said I'd ask you to ring as soon as possible.'

Marks's eyes narrowed as they studied first the note then Goodhew's impenetrable expression. Finally he sighed. 'I was going to say that I only know where you've been by the sound of the ricochet.' He held up the sheet and flicked it with his finger. It gave a sharp crack of surprise. 'That's today's ricochet, isn't it?'

Chapter Thirty-Nine

Ignoring his boss was not a deliberate ploy, and Goodhew was well aware that Marks had a point, but just as Marks was making it Goodhew stopped listening. Instead his attention focused about two hundred yards further towards the city centre, and he watched as a familiar figure turned and walked away from the police cordon.

Marks asked something about a ricochet but when Goodhew checked his DI's expression he knew that asking Marks to repeat the question wouldn't be a wise option. He hesitated, but couldn't find any appropriate bluff so just said, 'I'm sorry, I'll only be a minute,' and ran towards the cordon before Marks had the chance to order him to stop.

A couple of heads turned as he passed and he heard Marks shout his name but he pretended not to hear, he was only interested in catching up with the man he'd just seen. He made it past the barricade and on to the market square in time to see Bryn O'Brien vanish behind the striped canvas of the organic fruit and veg stand.

Goodhew ran along between a row of stalls; Bryn walked in the road along the perimeter of the market, on a parallel path. He didn't hurry and never looked back. But when Goodhew emerged from a gap to his right Bryn didn't seem surprised either.

He stopped squarely in front of Goodhew. Bryn's smart clothes were gone and the scuffed boots were back, but this time teamed with jeans instead of overalls. That still meant he had two deep front pockets ideal for stuffing his hands into, which was what he immediately did. 'What do you want?' he said.

Bryn looked defiant, like he was trying to win the Year 6 staring contest, but Goodhew wasn't ten any more and could see it was just a defensive bluff. Goodhew turned away and began to walk, only speaking when Bryn caught up with him. 'You came to find me,' he said. 'So what do you want?'

'I want to know who's dead.'

Goodhew kept walking, just looking straight ahead and making Bryn do all the work. 'Don't you already?' he asked coolly.

'Why would I?' It could have been indignation in Bryn's voice, but it sounded more like panic.

Goodhew slowed slightly. 'What are you afraid of, Bryn?'

'I don't know what you mean. I just want to know who it is.'

'But the only one you knew connected to Lorna was Victoria. So–' Goodhew halted abruptly and spun to face Bryn – 'are you afraid that she's dead or afraid of having the police on your back?'

'It is Victoria then?'

'That's right.' Breaking news of a death should have involved more sympathy but Goodhew felt strangely detached. 'Why were you looking for me?'

'I told you.'

'No, why me? Why not call the station, or ask the PC at the cordon, or, come to that, wait for the *Cambridge Evening News* like the rest of the general public? Were you hoping I wouldn't be suspicious just because I vaguely know you?'

Bryn scowled. 'No. I just thought you'd tell me.'

'So you thought I'd treat you differently.'

'Gary, what's your problem?' Bryn held up his hands in 'I surrender' mode. 'I'm sorry you've got a bit of an issue here. The bottom line is you did tell me, so you did treat me differently. But you're right, we're not mates and we don't know each other so whatever I've done hasn't let you down, has it?'

'That's bollocks.'

'Oh yeah, I suppose you react like this with everyone you don't know?'

This time it was Bryn who started walking. Goodhew watched him tramping towards the corner and knew Bryn had a point. So Goodhew did the catching up. 'Including Colin Willis we now have three deaths and as far as I can tell you are the only person who knew all of them, so you're right in the middle of this.'

'I'm not in the middle,' Bryn argued. 'I just look like I am.'

'OK, so when did you last see Victoria?'

'I don't know.'

'Don't know? Not last night then?'

Bryn shook his head.

Goodhew persisted. 'Did you see her last night?'

'No.' It sounded as though Bryn was testing out the word at first and he must have thought that it sounded all right because he immediately

297

repeated it again with more confidence. 'I didn't see her,' he added.

Anger surged through Goodhew. All at once it punched him squarely in the gut, shoved him between the shoulder blades and flung him forward. He grabbed at Bryn's shoulder, spinning him around and back into a recessed shop entrance. 'Do I have gullible stamped on my forehead or something?' he growled.

Bryn paled. 'What are you on about?'

'You're a liar.'

'I didn't see her.'

'I know you were the last person with her.' There was no way they were about to debate this and he rammed it home with a prod of his finger. 'I *know* you were with her at Lorna's flat. Do you really think that we wouldn't have the place under surveillance?'

Bryn groaned. 'Who else knows?'

'Let's just say it depends on how soon the swab results come back from the forensics team.'

Bryn took a couple of seconds to digest the comment, acknowledging that it had sunk in by groaning again. This time the sound definitely had more parts gurgle to it. And he wobbled too.

Goodhew reached forward and hauled Bryn back out of the doorway. Bryn half walked and was half dragged around the corner into Petty Cury's pedestrianized arcade, then immediately left again and in through the newly unlocked doors of a sandwich shop. A surly woman in a cheerful gingham apron was too busy wiping the work surfaces to even look in their direction. The glass counter was still empty; it was fortunate that they had no desire to place an order.

Aside from the counter the place had a token table and two chairs. They both sat. They were on opposite sides of the table. Goodhew rested his elbows on the table and leant forward. Bryn did the same but spoke first. 'What happens now?' he whispered.

'I need to take you in. You have to make a statement.'

'So why are we here?'

'I want to ask you some questions.'

'Off the record?'

'You're just telling me first. And I wouldn't be economical with the truth if I were you, it has a way of coming out in the end.'

'That's what my mother says.'

'Yeah, well, that's what I think.'

Bryn shrugged. 'OK then.'

'You made out you barely knew Victoria and said there was nothing going on between you and Lorna. Why lie?'

'I didn't.'

'You had sex with both of them.'

'But there wasn't anything going on.'

Goodhew rapped the table with his knuckles. 'Hello! Most people call that more than nothing.'

'Why? If we'd only been to the same gym or restaurant then it would be fine to say there was nothing. We just happened to ... you know ... that was all.'

'Just happened to? And how did you just happen to break and enter into Lorna Spence's flat?'

'Victoria had a key, and she said she'd lost something.'

'The diary?'

Bryn shook his head. 'What don't you know, eh?'

'At the moment I'd say everything that matters. She called you, I assume?'

Bryn nodded. 'Yeah, she phoned me yesterday, said she wanted to meet up. I didn't mind, actually.' Bryn pulled an apologetic face. 'I did fancy her, she looked just like August off last year's calendar. It was still pinned up by the kettle until recently.'

'Then you met her and threw it out?' Goodhew couldn't believe he'd said anything to perpetuate this strand of the conversation, even sarcastically.

'No, I met her and moved it next to the phone.'

'This is a murder.'

'I know, I know, and I'm sorry but I was just being honest.'

Goodhew decided that a better truth barometer would be the accuracy of Bryn's description of the inside-flat activity. 'OK. When did you decide to go to Lorna's?'

'Victoria suggested it as soon as I saw her. She said she had a key and we'd be in and out in a minute. I didn't like it, but she argued that it wasn't a crime scene and we weren't breaking in. I thought that made sense until we got there, then I knew straight away that we were doing something we shouldn't.'

With only minor prompting Bryn described everything Goodhew already knew with enough accuracy to push the barometer needle up near one hundred per cent. 'So,' Bryn concluded, 'even I can see that the diary was invented, which means she wanted me there for some other reason.'

'And?'

'I don't know the answer.'

'It's common knowledge that Lorna and Victoria fell out, but supposedly over a man. You're the only one I can find who has slept with both of them, but you are also the only person who disputes this theory.'

'So?'

'So, Victoria has tried to straighten out the story by making you think there was jealousy between them after all. She should have left it alone, because now it looks like you were telling the truth in the first place.'

'Hey!' The voice belonged to the surly woman and her gingham apron. They both looked up. She had her hands on her hips. 'This isn't a bus shelter, it's a business. Are you ordering or not?'

It was a not. Goodhew jerked his head towards the door. 'I'm going to walk you to Parkside.'

Bryn liked to think he could take things in his stride – tackle new obstacles running – roll with the punches. Fine theory, but the last twenty-four hours had demonstrated that his everyday life hadn't until now been very challenging. It had been hours since his Zodiac had ground to a halt, but it was only as he and Gary stepped back out into Petty Cury that his world finally stopped spinning. And it felt better that way.

'I'm sorry I lied,' he said. He retrieved his mobile from his pocket and hoped that sharing it with Gary would keep the brakes fully engaged. 'I had a text from her last night.'

'From Victoria?'

'It arrived while I was waiting to be towed, but I was too pissed off to look at it until I'd got the car back.' Bryn opened the message but couldn't bring himself to read it again.

He passed the phone to Gary. 'You didn't take it seriously?' Gary asked.

'I didn't know what to make of it. I never thought it really meant she was, you know...'

'Dead?'

'Yep.' Bryn tried to push the thought away. He wanted to ask how she'd died but at the same time he guessed he didn't really want to find out. He shoved his hands into his pockets and stayed quiet.

'I suppose your trip down the M11 is your only alibi?'

'Won't that do?'

'It depends on the timings.'

Bryn felt his stomach make an uneasy shift. 'I wouldn't hurt anyone.'

Gary smiled, but Bryn wasn't too blind to see the melancholy behind it. 'I want to believe you.'

'Sure, and I want you to. I also want the patron saint of panel beaters to pop the dent out of my Zodiac's wing, but things only happen when you make them.'

'You mean you make your own luck?'

'Exactly.' Bryn said it with more bravado than he felt.

Gary seemed to be thinking it over. 'Good theory,' he concluded. 'What was supposed to be in Victoria's diary?'

'She called it "intimate" and said it would be humiliating if anyone else read it.'

'And you believed her?'

'Why not? She wasn't very inhibited, I'm sure she did some wild stuff in the past.'

'But she didn't seem the apologetic type. I can't imagine her feeling humiliated.'

They were within a couple of hundred yards of the police station and Bryn was aware that he was walking more slowly. He didn't want to sit in some soulless interview room sharing the details of his last twenty-four hours with a complete stranger.

'Anyway,' Gary said, pointing ahead, 'we're here now. It doesn't matter about the diary, it was only theoretical. I was more interested to see whether your reasons for believing her held any water. And I think you've been gullible.'

That stung and Bryn suddenly felt indignant. 'No, she worked with the Moran family on a day-to-day basis. I think she would have felt humiliated if it had all come out. Most normal people would find the situation pretty kinky.'

Gary scowled. 'What are you on about?' he said just as his mobile rang. He made no move to answer it.

Bryn hesitated, then replied just as Gary reached into his jacket after all.

Bryn wasn't sure whether Gary had heard him; the mobile was still held to his ear, but he was staring at Bryn with a new expression which wavered between bewilderment and brainwave.

Chapter Forty

Bryn's words grabbed Goodhew's attention; they echoed something else that he'd heard, he just couldn't place what it was. He struggled to clutch the thought, but it was wedged on the edge of his subconscious and he was still diverted by Bryn's first comment when he was floored by the second.

And his mobile was ringing. He wanted to let it ring, but knew he would find it too distracting. He answered, planning to promise to ring the caller back and nothing else. But the voice at the other end was Mel's and his words caught in his throat just long enough for her to start to deliver the message.

She sounded awkward, or he imagined she did. 'You have an urgent message from a woman. It's personal and I said I'd pass it on straight away.' She paused. 'OK?'

'Uh-huh.'

'She says you must ring her on her mobile about a horse called Suze.'

He waited for more, but there wasn't any. 'That's it?'

'What were you expecting, something about a boy called Sue?'

'What?'

'The song? Oh, never mind.' She sounded embarrassed now. 'I was being silly. Sorry.'

'It's fine. I'll call her.' He knew he sounded

304

brusque but he couldn't help it. 'I'm dropping off a Bryn O'Brien at the station. Ring Marks immediately and let him know.'

He slipped the phone back into his pocket and concentrated on Bryn. 'Did you just say "Victoria and the dad"?'

Bryn managed a what-have-I-done-now combination of shrugging, nodding and looking apprehensive. 'Victoria went out with old man Moran till he died. You didn't know?'

'No one mentioned it. What else do you know about them?'

'Nothing except he was rich and she was gorgeous, I think it was what's called mutually beneficial.'

'Right.'

'Ask the Morans.'

Goodhew nodded. He was still fighting to grasp the original thought. 'And what did you say just before that?'

'No idea.'

'Come on, I said you'd been gullible, and you said...'

'Oh yeah, yeah, I was just saying that working with the Morans would make any sexy stuff between her and the dad more embarrassing, especially as her best mate was shagging his son.'

Goodhew snapped his fingers, he'd got it. 'No, you didn't say "sexy". You said "kinky".'

'And?'

Goodhew tapped Bryn's arm. 'And we've been loitering outside for too long. Get in and help us with our inquiries.'

Chapter Forty-One

All Goodhew did was to accompany Bryn as far as the door; he wasn't sure how far he trusted him yet, but felt confident that Bryn wasn't stupid enough to abscond through the rear entrance.

Goodhew rang Mel again. 'One more thing,' he said without any preamble. 'Marks has the Joanne Reed case notes in his office. I'll be back shortly, please get them ready so I can grab them on my way past.'

'OK,' she said.

'It's urgent,' he added.

'Fine,' she replied, probably thinking he was lazy for not doing it himself. He thought he probably was. He had nothing else to add so just hung up. Now he'd be arrogant as well as lazy.

He was still standing at the top of the steps outside Parkside station when he rang Jackie Moran's mobile. He looked towards the city centre as he put the phone to his ear and for the first time noticed that her RAV4 was parked in the nearest of the metered bays to his right. He could make out the shape of a person sitting in the driver's seat; he couldn't tell if it was Jackie Moran, but as the phone began to ring he saw the figure move. He saw her step on to the pavement in the same instant as he heard her voice. 'Thanks for phoning me,' she said.

'Stay there,' he said and hung up.

306

Today she was wearing navy blue jodhpurs and a dark green pullover; he wondered how often she dressed for anything apart from a trip to the stables. She was holding a large manila envelope which was pressed to her chest with her arms wrapped around it the same way that high school girls held their books in 1950s teen movies.

Two things had altered. Firstly she was dogless and secondly, even from a distance, he could see a marked change in her body language. She stood in the middle of the path, feet planted squarely. As he came closer he saw she had a resolute expression to match her stance.

'Why the coded message?' he asked.

'I didn't want to be fobbed off with anyone else.'

'Look, it depends what you're going to say, but I can't promise that I can deal with it.'

'I've made a decision, now all I want is some moral support. I think I can trust you?'

'Sure, but...'

She took a deep breath. 'Don't spoil it. I want support, not an accomplice.'

'All I was about to say is that my authority is practically zero. I'm a junior officer.'

'Determination outranks rank, you know.'

Goodhew gave a short laugh. 'Everyone's a philosopher today. Let's sit somewhere, you can show me what's in the envelope and then I'll either take a statement or stay with you while you repeat it to my superior. Is that suitably supportive?'

'Absolutely.' She started to walk towards Parkside station. 'I think I may as well talk to you in there. I don't think this will be quick.'

Mel must have seen him arrive because she was waiting with Joanne Reed's case notes. She passed them over and he thanked her. He tried to make eye contact too, but she just turned away again.

Two rooms along the corridor from Mel's desk was an unoccupied office. It contained nothing but two chairs, a small desk and a large window overlooking the rear car park. Goodhew decided that it was the ideal place to meet: the window had clinched it.

One long side of the desk was against the wall and they sat along the other side, with chairs facing. 'Before we go any further,' Goodhew said, 'I need to know about Joanne Reed.'

Jackie looked towards the ceiling as if trying to recall where she'd heard the name. 'The girl that disappeared from university?' She was trying to sound vague or surprised, or both. In fact she managed neither.

'Did you know her?' Goodhew asked.

'No.' The 'no' was of the not-up-for-debate-definitely-not types. He didn't believe her but decided to move on. His folder was on his lap, Jackie's envelope tantalizingly close to him on the desktop.

'OK then,' he said. 'Fire away.'

'I've heard about the new murder.'

'What do you know?'

'That there's a connection to Lorna.' Colour flushed across her cheeks, and then was gone. 'Is it Victoria?'

Goodhew gave a small nod. 'Yes.'

'I'm sorry. I didn't know her too well but...' Her sentence drifted into silence. 'I've realized it's time to talk to you because I killed Colin Willis.' She put her hand on the envelope, not to pass it over, more to hold on to it. 'Your tests would have shown that the fur was Bridy's in any case.'

'So why not tell us at the time?'

Jackie turned her face away; she seemed to be frowning at the desktop. Her expression remained unchanged through several minutes and even when she looked up at him again. 'I was trying to understand it,' she said. 'I thought it was over, so I didn't realize that there was any urgency. Then, with this other death, I knew I was wrong.'

Goodhew suspected that her earlier show of confidence had been brought on by nothing more than the decision to act. Since entering the room her skin had lost its colour and her expression changed with the sluggishness of perpetual shock. He wanted her to keep talking so that her resolve to tell all didn't diminish. 'How well did you know Willis?'

'I didn't. I'd seen him hanging around on the footpath beside the river several times. I only noticed him in the first place because his presence made me feel slightly uncomfortable. But you know, by the time he attacked me I'd convinced myself that I was being paranoid. I walked past him and he suddenly grabbed my throat.' As if to illustrate she put her hand to her own throat. She closed her eyes as she recounted the attack unfolding. By the time she had described Colin Willis's body disappearing into the Cam she was still clenching her own neck and was breathing hard.

Goodhew reached forward and gently pulled her hand away. She opened her eyes and gulped in just enough air to calm herself. When she spoke she sounded hoarse. 'I'm not sorry I killed him because I don't think I had any choice. But I'm sorry I didn't wait for help. I should have made a statement at the time. I have nightmares about it. I have nightmares about everything. And I've regretted it so many times. I know I should have told you when you took the fur samples from Bridy.'

'Why didn't you?'

'For the same reason I slid his body into the river.'

'I thought that was an impulse?'

'It was – when I saw the knife I realized that he'd been planning to kill me. It didn't seem at all random, it was like someone had put him up to it and that's what I couldn't deal with. And I thought if I came forward no one would believe me. In that moment I thought that just by getting rid of him I wouldn't have to face up to the truth that someone, and probably someone I know, actually wanted me dead.'

'Like who?'

'I don't know.' Jackie bit one side of her bottom lip and stared at him.

Goodhew felt as though she was weighing him up, having second thoughts about telling him. 'But you have some information?'

Her gaze moved away from him and fixed itself on the envelope. For the first time tears welled in her eyes. 'I've had it for weeks.' She passed him the envelope. 'But I didn't know it would lead to all of this.'

'You had it before Lorna died?'

She nodded.

'And when she was murdered you still didn't think you needed to come forward?'

Again colour rose in her cheeks but this time spread with enough intensity to reach her temples. 'I didn't think there was a connection. I just thought, oh, I don't know, maybe that she was the victim of a random attack.'

'Until you heard that there had been another death?' He slid his hand into the envelope. It was the kind that had gusseted sides and it had been slightly puffed out, fat enough to contain a sheaf of papers so he was surprised to find only one sheet.

She nodded again and rubbed her face with the heel of her hand. 'I'm sorry.'

He put the page on to the table in front of him; it was A5 and made from a flimsy cream paper, the sort that sounds like a crisp hundred decibels when it's the only sound in an empty room. It had been written on by a dark blue ballpoint pen. The handwriting was angular and erratic and had been applied with sufficient force to cause the imprint of the words from the back of the page to interfere with reading the words on the front. 'Do you recognize the writing?'

'Read it,' she whispered. 'You'll see.'

It started mid-sentence:

so drained. All these successive entries of 'nothing to note, nothing to note'. I watched the hare and ignored the tortoise.

Alice was full of anger today. It is the same cold

temper that she's always had but today was the first time I've noticed it directed at her sister. I should have known, her love for Richard… Jealousy is a dark and irrational beast.

I have been obsessively documenting one scenario, thinking that I can contain the problem when in reality I may have given free rein to the genuine demon. Only circumstance and not my intervention has stopped further deaths occurring.

When I face God I hope he forgives me, I have been so selfish.

Then there was a small gap, before the writing continued.

Despite yesterday's low I have made the decision to continue this journal. I love them all, regardless of any flaws. I believe I have been right, and wrong, in equal measures.

Of course I'm just as scared for Jackie as I've always been, but I will speak to Alice, I'm sure she would never harm her own sister.

Goodhew read it twice. There were no dates and no clue to the author's identity. 'Your father?' he guessed.

She nodded. 'He was a compulsive list scribbler, one of those people that seemed unable to think without a pen in his hand.'

'And this was the only page?'

'Yes. I don't know what it was torn from either.'

'How did you get it?'

'I found it at the farm the day Colin Willis tried to kill me. I suppose I was in shock, but I still had to see to the horses. It was in the stable, the one with the bales where we sat. I took Suze out for a couple of hours and found it when I returned.'

'You think someone left it while you were out with her?'

Jackie's left elbow was resting on the table and her left palm was the cradle, propping up her head at the temple. He wondered whether her brain was starting to hurt. His certainly was. 'It may have been there already, I really don't know.'

'What does he mean by further deaths? It implies someone has already died.'

She blew out a long slow sigh. 'I don't understand.'

'OK. Are you saying that you think Alice may have hired Colin Willis?'

She dropped her hand away from her face and sounded surprised. 'No, of course not. That's not what I meant. The note implies that she hates me, and it's true we're not close, but I think it was left there to frame her. If I had been killed it would have been found at the farm and she would have been investigated, wouldn't she?'

'Undoubtedly, so the next question is who could have taken it from your father?'

Her eyes opened wider. 'I don't know about any casual visitors, but I'd say the main people would have been the three of us–'

'You, Richard and Alice?'

'Yes, and Victoria.'

'So you knew your father dated Victoria?'

'Of course. It was common knowledge.' He saw a glint of amusement spring on to her face. 'They even went out together *in public*.'

313

'You never mentioned Victoria and your father.'

'Because you were investigating Lorna's background – why would I?'

'So how did you feel about her?'

'In what way?'

'She was about your age and having an affair with your dad, wasn't that weird?'

'No, I barely knew her. In any case my father would have told me to mind my own business.'

'And what about Richard and Alice, they worked with her?'

She shrugged. 'I doubt they were bothered – but even if they were, Richard's never had my father's ear so he couldn't have influenced anything, and Alice would have kept her thoughts to herself.

'It's only because I was so much younger than them that it was different for me. They've always had each other, they wouldn't care about what he was doing. It affected me the most, but Dad made the rules in our house and we stuck to them.'

Chapter Forty-Two

Grey areas were always the most difficult to navigate and as soon as Goodhew had finished talking to Jackie Moran he found himself in the middle of one; he didn't know what to do with her. He wasn't about to sit with her until Marks returned, but didn't want to leave her alone either. Arresting her didn't seem appropriate, but on the grounds that she'd just admitted to killing a man, perhaps it was. In the end he spotted PC Kelly Wilkes arriving back in the car park. As soon as she'd locked her vehicle he tapped on the glass, but when she saw him at the window she pointed at him and gave him the stay signal. By the time she arrived in the corridor she had her mobile phone in her hand and was waving it in his direction like it was on stun mode. She sliced her other hand backwards and forwards across her throat.

'You're dead,' she whispered, then louder: 'DI Marks is on the phone.' She slapped the phone into his palm.

Goodhew guided her through the door to Jackie. 'Look after her till I come back,' he said, then shut the door behind her and tentatively raised the phone to his ear. 'Sir?'

'You walked away from me. You were insubordinate in front of my team and in public.' His voice was icy. 'Furthermore you then refuse to respond to your mobile.'

'It was off.' Goodhew bit his lip; there was no point in saying anything, he knew from Marks's tone that he'd gone far too far.

'Go to your desk, sit there and don't move a muscle until I get there. I might not get back for quite some time. Do you understand?'

'Yes, sir.'

'Good, because if those ants in your pants take you anywhere at all I'm going to be treating it as gross misconduct. Where's Wilkes?'

'With Jackie Moran. I was about to ring you.' Goodhew brought his boss up to date and hoped that news of the progress made with Bryn and Jackie would defuse the worst of Marks's anger.

Goodhew apologized to PC Wilkes and left her keeping Jackie Moran company, then returned to his desk with a coffee in one hand and Joanne Reed's case notes in the other. Even with the challenge of sitting still he had plenty to do and began searching for the reference to anything that could be construed as 'kinky'. It didn't take long, and in fact he wondered how he'd missed it the first time, but on the second page of the inventory of items found at her flat were the contents of her wardrobe.

Item 6 - S and M whip.

One person's kinky was another person's bland, but to him there was nothing else on the list that seemed any racier than lacy knickers. Whoever had picked that description for the item had had one lad's mag too many the night before.

He pressed the 'on' button on his PC then drained his coffee cup and wandered off for a refill; when Marks had said not to move a muscle he was sure that he hadn't meant it literally.

By the time he returned it had completed booting up and the hard disk was silent after chugging through its endless stream of security programs. It was always so much more efficient when he didn't watch it: if only Marks would accept the same excuse from him. Goodhew went on to the internet, ignoring his new emails and making straight for Google where he typed *Dr Moran Cambridge* as his search criteria. The usual long list appeared, headed by a link to eBay where items on both doctors and Cambridge were popular. One day he would investigate an effective way to use search engines, but for now expert scroll bar control was his limit. At the bottom of the first page the word 'obituary' jumped out. He double-clicked and in an impressively small number of milliseconds was viewing a recent photograph of Dr Alex Moran, Cambridge – physician, father and founder of the Excelsior Clinic.

Goodhew stared thoughtfully at the photo. The face in the photo stared back enigmatically. It was, Goodhew decided, fair to describe him as a man in his late fifties. He right-clicked the photo and selected copy, then pasted the picture into a new email. He added only his mobile number and the words 'Call me if this is the man.'

On his phone he arrowed 'up' through the list of last dialled numbers until he recognized Martin Reed's, then he pressed 'dial'.

Mrs Reed answered with just 'Hello.'

'This is DC Goodhew,' he replied. 'Is Mr Reed there?'

He'd gone for a walk and she didn't expect him home for another hour. She began to fish for the reason for his call.

'I'm sorry, there's still no news of Joanne, but I do need to send him an email. Do you have a computer?' They did, and Goodhew gazed at the screen long after the 'sent' message had disappeared.

Mel had gone to Marks's office almost certain that it would be empty. It was, but that left her with a dilemma. She turned the envelope over and over; the DC who had brought it in had insisted that it must be given to Marks, not kept for him in admin, and no way was it to be left on his desk. As far as she could see, that meant hanging round until Marks returned.

Then she saw a second option, hand it to another detective working on the investigation. And so what if the only one in the building was Goodhew, wasn't it time they cleared the air?

She found him sitting at his desk seemingly oblivious to everything apart from his PC. 'Just the person.'

'Jump to the front of the queue.'

'What queue?'

'Never mind, go for it.' He sat back in his chair. There was no urgency in his expression and she sensed his interest in her had evaporated.

'Kincaide and I...' She stumbled over her words, took a breath and began again. 'Look, I know you saw us and it's obvious you don't approve.'

'It's none of my business.'

'Well, actually, that's my point. You don't have the right to take it out on me. I'm sorry if you feel personally affected by my relationships...'

'I don't. I was surprised–' he paused then corrected himself – 'more than surprised actually. When you were crying the other morning I thought it was because of Toby, and I thought that was the mess you were trying to untangle yourself from, not a relationship with Kincaide.'

There was something in the way Goodhew worded things that made them sound far less complicated than they were, like unmessing her life would be as easy as pressing a button marked 'reverse'. She flopped into the nearest vacant chair and they spent the next couple of minutes in a strangely amicable silence.

In the end it was Goodhew who spoke first. 'I had no right to be upset with you and I'm sorry if you feel I've been sort of stalking you.'

'Stalking?'

'The whole transparent thing.'

Mel smiled and it felt like the first time in days. 'That's not how I meant it and I've decided it's good to know someone who can see the real you.'

'Is it?'

'What's the point otherwise?' She held out the envelope. 'This is for Marks, I'm not supposed to leave it lying around, would you pass it to him?'

'Sure, what is it?'

'Some sort of book, I don't know exactly, it came from Victoria Nugent's place. DI Marks phoned them and asked them to look for it and they found it almost immediately.'

Once he was alone again Goodhew opened the envelope. If his guess was correct he was about to see the book from which Jackie Moran's page had been torn.

The best lies, the most convincing ones, are grounded in truth. When Victoria took Bryn to Lorna's flat she pretended she had lost a diary. There were countless other stories she could have concocted but she chose one she could visualize and subsequently remember. One that was connected with something true.

All this was obvious now Marks had worked it out. At some point in the morning he had called the team at Victoria's, asking them to make a special search for anything resembling Alex Moran's journal, and bingo.

Goodhew slid it out on to the desk.

It had a navy blue hard-backed cover, a red linen spine and looked like it had once been part of the stationery supplies of a government department circa 1972. The pages were sewn in place rather than glued and Goodhew immediately saw that the cream paper matched the loose sheet. The book was just over a quarter of an inch thick. He opened it at the back and thumbed forward until he located the last used page. The book was almost empty. He continued to flick forward, turning a total of eleven pages before he reached the front.

A date and the number '56' were written on the inside of the cover. Did that mean there had been another fifty-five of them? Moran had started this one a couple of months before he died, so fifty-five of them would probably be going back at least twenty years.

There were no dates but it seemed as though he'd written in it every day, commenting that there was 'nothing to note' or in some cases abbreviating it to 'ntn' rather than skipping a day. His style was rambling, and initially it was difficult to grasp his purpose. He frequently mentioned Jackie. He felt she had been in some kind of danger, and as on the one loose sheet wrote that he was scared for her. When Goodhew turned each new page it was her name that jumped out, but the function of the journal only hit him as he reached the end of the fifth page and read:

I have always thought that two things keep me from handing her over, my fears for her safety and the slim-

mest doubt that I am mistaken. But now I think I have been kidding myself. There will be no one to monitor Jackie once I am gone. I don't know whether I can ask Richard and Alice, they have isolated themselves from her, it is as if they know. I only ever know on a day-by-day basis that all is well, I cannot be sure she won't do something again. I made excuses for her when David died, but she isn't a child now. It may be better that she languishes in an institution rather than risk another innocent family suffering. I think I must visit Martin Reed.

Goodhew's stomach lurched. One page had appeared to point at Alice, but the rest was her father's documentation of his other daughter's guilt. He turned the next page and scanned the words, looking for any reference to the visit to Martin Reed. He spotted it on the opposite page and he pointed the words with his index finger to prevent himself from rushing ahead too quickly:

Why did I visit him in the first place? Did I think that I could learn to sidestep the occasional waves of guilt that even swamp me at this late stage? I know my shortcomings and loving Jackie as I do has made me a victim of her.

I think he is a braver man than me; he wants to face the truth and despite my intentions to do so I am incapable of making myself tell him. I prefer to think that I am being kinder by keeping the rotten truth from him. If her body turned out to be somewhere else I would have made things worse again, although in my heart of hearts I know I am correct. There are only so many good places to hide a decaying corpse.

By the time Marks returned to the building the journal was back in its newly sealed envelope, and the photocopies were safely hidden in Goodhew's inside jacket pocket.

Chapter Forty-Three

'My office,' Marks growled. He didn't wait for a response, but from out in the corridor barked the additional command, 'Now.' Goodhew grabbed his phone, the envelope and Joanne Reed's case notes and darted after his boss.

Marks sat at his desk, but with no paperwork in front of him. In fact all that was in front of him were his crossed arms. Body language experts claimed that folded arms were a sign of ill ease, but from where Goodhew was standing he was going to be the only one suffering from that. In fact it looked like Marks's folded arms might be the only things preventing him from exploding in rage.

Goodhew approached the visitor's chair. 'Is it OK if I sit?'

His backside had barely touched the cloth seat when Marks spoke. 'When I saw you this morning I had the distinct impression that you were not taking your responsibilities seriously.' His voice wasn't raised, but he was spitting out the words in succinct volleys and it didn't sound as though interrupting, or even attempting to answer, would be wise.

'You,' he continued, 'are the youngest DC we have ever had in this department. You may think you are acting on your own initiative. In fact you have nowhere near enough experience of life, never mind the police force, to even begin to comprehend what initiative is and how to employ it effectively. I need people who follow orders. Who follow protocol. And most of all who follow things through. You may be bright and talented but I thought I'd made it clear that I wouldn't hesitate in getting shot of you if you kept pissing me around. Do you think that I have somehow given you a mandate to do what the hell you like?'

Marks glared. Goodhew said nothing.

'In case you're confused, that was not one of my rhetorical questions, Gary.'

Goodhew shook his head then. 'No, sir, I don't.'

'I have a technique I apply when I want a really clear idea of how an individual is affecting my team: I imagine that the team consists entirely of clones of that person. When I visualize a team consisting of Gary Goodhews it is anarchic, inappropriate and intolerable. I will concede that you do have moments of brilliance but you took your choice. When I said the anonymous notes had to stop I was serious.'

Goodhew tried to interrupt but Marks rode over him.

'You're right, I can't prove a thing. But I know.' He tapped his forehead just above the left eye socket. 'I tell the team that we now have DNA from the so-called Airport Rapist, next thing I get the match I need. Lorna's flat was searched within hours of me telling you not to. And what the hell was the idea of tipping the paper off with the "I'm like Emma" connection?'

That caught him out. 'I didn't,' he answered, but Marks was already rolling on.

'It was not information that the papers should have received at that point in the investigation. In a mad moment I considered turning a blind eye to all of this, but pow-wowing with the press combined with your behaviour today has forced my hand. Do you have anything to say to me?'

'I didn't contact the paper.'

'Wrong answer.' There was a long pause before Marks spoke again. 'I am not prepared to work with you any longer, Goodhew.'

Goodhew nodded to himself. Hadn't he asked for just that?

His mobile rang, its relatively sober ring tone sounding like a crass interruption. He glanced at Marks who nodded for him to answer it.

The call was less than thirty seconds long, and he relayed its contents to his boss knowing that he would salvage at least something from the meeting. 'That was Martin Reed. He rang to confirm that the man who posed as a detective was in fact Dr Alex Moran.'

'How...?'

'I emailed him a photograph.'

'So what's your theory on the page now?'

'I don't know.' Goodhew bit his lip.

'No, not good enough. You had enough insight to show him the picture, so tell me more.'

'It was just the mention of "further deaths". I think he knew he was dying and went to see Martin Reed in an attempt to "put things in order". I don't know what connection he had with Joanne Reed. He sounds as though he was feeling guilty when he wrote that page so perhaps he thought seeing Martin Reed would clear his conscience.'

Marks raised his eyebrows. 'Like I said, moments of brilliance but that's just not enough.'

Goodhew took a deep breath and managed to speak. 'What happens now?'

Marks's tone was cool and final. 'Go home, take annual leave for the rest of the week. By Monday you'll be in another department.'

Chapter Forty-Four

Kincaide had already spent the best part of the day working through Jackie Moran's statement with her. She'd made it transparently clear that she didn't like him much, or at all in fact, and it was probably because he wasn't letting her prattle on about her flock of animals. She showed more concern for them than any people she mentioned, particularly the one she'd strangled. At this rate he'd be stuck in her company for a few more hours yet.

He glanced at his watch and wondered whether he could engineer enough of a break to sort out the Mel situation. He didn't like the way she'd cooled off. He had no idea what had caused it, but neither did he think that she'd need much coaxing; a little attention went a long way with her type.

He realized Jackie Moran was staring at him.

'You didn't write anything down,' she said. 'If you've finished I'd like to go. I need to see to the horses.'

'Sorry.' He smiled as he said it and decided that he'd definitely take a break, even if it achieved nothing more than delay her departure.

But before he could say anything the door opened and Marks appeared and beckoned him into the corridor.

'How's it going?

Kincaide shrugged. 'I don't buy that self-defence argument of hers.'

'But she's sticking to it?'

'Not budging.'

'Might be worth picking it up again in the morning, arrange for her to come back first thing.'

Kincaide wasn't about to argue and made a swift exit. As he walked towards the stairs he thought of Mel and grinned. Now there'd be plenty of time to get her back on track. With any luck he'd still be home in time to remind Jan that their own weekly routine had slipped by a few days. Perfunctory it might be, but it was still worth doing.

Chapter Forty-Five

It was almost nine o'clock before Goodhew met up with his grandmother.

'So is that a suspension or not?' she asked.

'One step short. I don't think Marks would

want to try to explain why he never took an official line on the anonymous notes, especially if he suspected they were an internal issue. He's not happy though.'

Goodhew had finished explaining the situation to his grandmother. They were seated by the window in the Galleria, a small Italian restaurant by the river. Goodhew had chosen it, and it was no coincidence that it was within sight of the unlit Excelsior Clinic. The waiter returned to the table with the pepper mill and ground some on his bolognese. His grandmother had ordered salad and he had no doubt that her pale blouse would stay unblemished; his white shirt wouldn't be so lucky.

Goodhew waited until they were alone before he spoke again. 'But to be honest, it's not as bad as I thought.'

Her fork hesitated a couple of inches from her mouth, and then descended. 'I thought you'd be devastated.'

'Of course I'm upset, but on the other hand, what's really changed? As long as I'm in the building I'd still have access to information on various cases so I can still do things in my own time.'

'Gary, that's the part you're suppose to curb. You've had a lucky escape. Imagine if you were caught.'

'I'm learning, I just need to be more careful and I'm proud of the things I've done. The one that's caused more hot water with Marks than anything else was the one I didn't do.'

'I'm confused now – which one didn't you do?'

'I never tipped off the paper.'

'You didn't? I thought you were bluffing.'

'If I'm such a useless liar why can't you work out when I'm telling the truth?' Goodhew frowned and twirled some spaghetti on to his fork but instead of eating it he kept on twirling then said, 'Marks thought I'd done it. That's why he never asked any of us to look into it. We need to know who tipped off the papers, and more importantly work out why.'

'We? You and me or you and your colleagues?'

'Either – does it matter who comes up with the answer?'

'It's just one big rush for the truth, isn't it? Doesn't matter who gets there first just as long as it gets uncovered.'

'And what's wrong with that?'

'You watch too many old movies. What's it going to take to tuck you safely back under Marks's wing?'

If she'd seen the finality in Marks's dismissal of him she wouldn't have even bothered asking the question. In truth he knew how bad he'd feel if he was left to follow the rest of the case via press reports and snippets of canteen chat.

For the last couple of hours he'd been bloody-minded and unrealistically upbeat about it and that had suited him fine, but now, as he stared across to the Excelsior Clinic, he knew he had to face the reality of his situation. It would take much more than a sympathetic ear or the diversion of their surroundings to buffer him from the sick and empty feeling currently hollowing out the pit of his stomach.

He excused himself and left; he needed to be alone, just like he was alone with the mess he'd created for himself. He walked towards the centre of the city, knowing that the feeling wasn't going to disappear, but somehow hoping that walking past the places where Victoria and Lorna had died would numb it.

In the end, when he was no closer to any peace with himself, he gave in to the illogical compulsion to hail a cab and drive past every other address connected with the case.

He sat directly behind the driver, and chose not to engage in any conversation. The roads were almost empty and the car made unhampered progress back and forth across town, slowing past one destination before transporting him towards the next.

If the driver thought the job was a strange one he didn't comment.

Victoria and Lorna's flats were pitch black but numerous lights were on in Richard and Alice's house. A security light illuminated the hard standing outside Bryn's workshop, and a single light shone from Jackie's hallway.

This time the 'where next' question was the easiest to answer. Jackie's RAV4 hadn't been parked anywhere near her house. Unless there had been a major development Goodhew doubted she was still making a statement. They drove by Parkside station on the off-chance and once he was certain that her car was nowhere on site he instructed the driver to head for Old Mile Farm.

Chapter Forty-Six

Goodhew paid the driver and asked to be dropped at the roadside by the gateway to the farm. The track down to the stables was unlit but he wanted to walk into the yard unannounced. The moonlight was just sufficient for him to be able to pick out the shape of the post and rails fencing running beside him, but it still took him several minutes before he came within sight of the car park.

A tree marked the end of the track and he stopped while he was still within its shadow. Jackie's car was parked in the same spot as it had been the last time he'd visited. From where he stood it looked empty. There was no sign of life from the stables either; not even the horses moved.

He crept across the yard, pausing long enough at the vehicle to confirm that it really was empty, then quietly making for the stable where they'd sat before. Both halves of the door were closed. He felt his way over the bolts, checking that both were locked from the outside. They were, and he was about to check the other loose boxes when he heard her voice behind him. 'I'm here.'

He spun around but couldn't see her. She sounded about fifty feet away from him.

'Put on the floodlights,' she called.

'Where?'

'In the corner, to your right.'

He felt his way to where the short side of the L-shaped stable block met the long side and found three switches.

'It's the middle one,' she added, as if she had seen him hesitate. He turned towards her voice as he flicked it on. Four halogen lamps burst into life, drenching the menage in cold white light. Jackie was on a travelling rug in the middle of the arena, leaning on her left hand, holding a mug in the other. Gone was the stable girl look, instead she wore strappy sandals, jeans and a baggy green and white cotton shirt.

'What are you doing?' he asked.

'Come here.'

He climbed the railing then jumped down on to the sawdust and walked towards her. The scene looked like an arty photo shoot; her clothes were far too flimsy for night time, her cheeks were red, her lips damson and glossy. She didn't look cold and her smile was unnaturally luminescent.

'Would you like to talk to me?' she asked.

'That's not why I came. I just wondered where you'd gone.'

'No, I mean, please talk to me.'

'Sure.' Goodhew sat beside her. 'Are you warm enough?'

'Yep.'

'Good.'

She lowered her voice. 'I'm a bit drunk.'

'I can tell.'

'Really? I'd offer you a drink, but I've only got what's left in the mug.' She swigged another mouthful. 'Do you know the point when you're so unhappy that you're not scared any more?'

'Scared of what?'

'Of anything, because if it got you, so what? What can it do to you when a bullet in the brain would be a relief. That's what I've been doing, lying here and thinking so what. So what. So fucking what.'

'What is "it"?'

'It. You know, the "it" that comes into your room when you're a kid, that makes you scared to open the wardrobe or look under the bed.'

'The "it" that might jump out and get you?'

'Yes, that's the one. But not "might", it will.'

Goodhew reached out and wrapped his fingers around the mug. He gave it a gentle tug and she let go.

'Your father knew about Joanne Reed, so why did you pretend you didn't?'

'You're not at work now, Mr Detective.' She reached for the mug but he held it away from her.

'Why not tell me? I know you knew her,' he persisted. 'What really scares you, Jackie?'

'Nothing.' She glared at him, but the woolliness of drink left her unable to remain intractable. She leant towards him, breathing out brandy fumes and wafting something that smelt like Paco Rabanne. She touched his cheek, then ran her hand down and inside the breast of his jacket. 'My father didn't allow Richard to bring women home so he and Joanne came here for sex.'

'Richard told you?'

'No, I saw them.'

'How often?'

'They came here several times but I only saw it once.'

Goodhew thought he'd misheard. Jackie laughed. 'They were in the end stable and I watched them through the window, both stark naked, not the tiniest bit aware that they could be seen.'

Goodhew looked across to the dust-covered window and pictured Jackie watching her brother and his girlfriend, possibly even standing on the edge of the muck heap to gain a better view. Jackie's fingers began fiddling with the top button of Goodhew's shirt; he pressed his hand on top of hers to keep it still.

'Is that true?' he said.

'My father said I should say nothing...' She paused and tilted her head towards the stables. 'We could ... you know, I could show you what I saw.'

He ignored the suggestion. 'Your father thought he knew what happened to Joanne Reed. What did he tell you?'

'Not much. He drove down here one lunchtime, jumped out of his car and started shouting at me. He kept saying, "What happened? Tell me what happened to her. You should know by now that I'm not stupid." I had no idea what he meant. He walked round the place for about ten minutes, ranting to himself. Finally he said, "Very clever," and just drove out again.'

Goodhew thought about Alex Moran's journal and his search of Old Mile Farm. It only took a minute, then he lifted Jackie's hand away from his shirt and up to his lips. He kissed her fingers. 'Thank you for telling me. Now, I'm going to drive you home.'

333

'Then pull me in in the morning?'

'I'd prefer it if you just showed up.'

'Why not take me straight there now?'

'Go home and sober up. You can't go on like this.'

'Stay with me then.'

'No.' He stood and pulled her on to her feet but didn't release his hold on her hands. 'Why were you here tonight?'

'Honestly? I missed Alex.'

'Oh yes, Alex who knew you so well.' He felt her tense.

'What's that supposed to mean?'

'What did he mean when he wrote that he made excuses for you when David died?' She tried to pull away from him but he wouldn't let go. 'Did he think you were responsible for killing your baby brother?'

He knew she was going to cry before the tears fell, but he could also see that it wasn't sadness that made her cry. Frustration maybe, or more likely anger. She still squirmed and he still refused to release her. He tried again. 'Jackie. Is that what he thought? Is it?'

'Is it? Is it?' she mimicked. 'Did you put the pillow on his face? You can tell me. Is that what you did? Is it? Is it? All right, I'll tell you what scares me, the "it", the fucking "it" that's controlled everything I've done every fucking day of my life. I never chose to be a bad person.'

A breeze ruffled the sawdust and puffed out the fabric of her shirt. Suddenly Goodhew realized that the scent wasn't just like Paco Rabanne. It was Paco Rabanne. Impregnated in a man's

334

unwashed shirt. Her heightened sexuality hadn't been solely the result of alcohol, and Goodhew suddenly knew a whole lot more than just where Joanne Reed's body was buried.

Chapter Forty-Seven

Goodhew arrived home in the early hours, but didn't bother kidding himself that trying to sleep would be anything but a wasted journey to the bedroom. He switched on the jukebox, and selected what he guessed would be enough tracks to keep him company until Marks arrived at work. He turned the volume up high, amplifying every hiss and scratch on the old 45s, filling the room with obscure fifties doo-wop.

He made coffee then settled by the loft window and watched Parkside police station until he saw his boss arrive. He stopped to unplug the Bel Ami, then hurried from the building and across Parker's Piece, only slowing as he approached Marks's office door. Inside a phone rang twice before being answered. Goodhew knocked anyway then stepped away from the door to wait. It was almost five minutes later when he heard his boss order him to enter.

Marks leant forward with both elbows resting on the desk. He didn't smile, but he didn't look angry either.

Goodhew stepped just far enough into the office to give himself space to close the door. 'I'm not ignoring your instructions, but I do need five minutes with you.'

'Being in the building at all is ignoring them.'

'OK, I'm ignoring them slightly, but totally respect the spirit in which they were made.'

'For pity's sake,' Marks sighed, 'just get on with it.'

'I think I know where Joanne Reed's body is hidden.'

It was easy to see he'd grabbed Marks's interest, but even so his boss remained cautious. 'Go on.'

'That's why I need five minutes.'

Marks gestured towards the nearest chair. 'Make it good.'

'When you called me insubordinate earlier you were right. There have been times when you've placed your trust in me and I value that. I didn't tip off the *Cambridge Evening News*, so someone else had a motive for doing that.

'What I did do though was to look at Alex Moran's journal while I was waiting for you to return yesterday and I think he guessed where the body was hidden – he talks of the "rotten truth" and there being "only so many good places to hide a decaying corpse". Actually I photocopied some of the pages, which is even worse, but I'm capable of more than I'm being given the chance to do. My intentions have always been to help, never to undermine you. And if that's what I've done, I'm sorry, sir, genuinely sorry.'

'So where's the body?'

Goodhew gave a slightly filtered version of the previous night's events.

'So now she admits seeing Joanne Reed there

with her brother?'

'That's right.'

'And you think the body's where?'

Goodhew told him.

Marks looked sceptical. 'And that's based on the father having a look round then saying "Very clever"? He must have been talking about something else, you don't pat your kids on the head and say well done for hiding a corpse.'

'Not in normal families,' Goodhew conceded.

'She only offers information when we've pretty much worked it out for ourselves. All I see is a woman who's constantly covering her own back.'

'I don't agree.'

'I see,' Marks said, then let the words settle for several seconds. When he finally spoke again his first question surprised Goodhew. 'Do you know what motive Jackie Moran might have had for killing Lorna Spence?'

'None that I know of. I don't think she did.'

'And that's your unbiased view?'

'Absolutely.'

Marks frowned. 'Personally? In her position I would have gone for help rather than dumping Colin Willis's body. I suspect that anyone who kills then covers it up is hiding something. But go on, tell me your theories.'

Goodhew had some of course, plenty in fact. They'd only been a jumble of seedling ideas until the last hour, but talking to Marks had stimulated his thoughts and some of the ideas had flourished, they'd sprouted tentacles and now seemed to be intertwining quite effectively. The next step would be to try them out loud. He took a deep breath, then jumped in. 'Firstly,' he began, 'we know that both Victoria Nugent and Lorna Spence met Colin Willis, therefore it seems too coincidental that he just happened to target Jackie Moran. Either he picked her after becoming interested as a result of something Victoria or Lorna said, or he was hired to kill her by one of these two.'

'Which one?'

'Lorna. From what Bryn O'Brien said, it was Lorna who spent time alone with Colin Willis, Victoria wasn't interested.'

'So why would she want Jackie dead?'

'Perhaps she didn't. Maybe she hired Colin Willis on behalf of someone else. Once it was obvious that the plan had failed, killing Lorna would have broken the link between Colin Willis and whoever wanted Jackie dead.'

'The diary page left at the stables was obviously just planted to throw suspicion on Alice.'

'And we only know it was planted because Jackie Moran survived, otherwise it might have looked like she'd owned it all along.'

'Actually,' Marks corrected, 'we only know it was planted because Jackie Moran told us so.'

Goodhew didn't like the implication. 'Even if it didn't turn up as she said it did, I'm sure it's genuine.'

'OK. So if it was planted that would be by Lorna?'

'But ultimately for the benefit of whoever hired Willis.'

'Who then goes on to kill Lorna when Jackie survives.'

'I guess.'

'And this same person will be Victoria Nugent's killer too?'

Goodhew nodded but suddenly felt his ideas drifting off course – or wilting, to use his earlier analogy.

'So you're saying–' Marks was hitting his stride now – 'that behind all of this is a very efficient killer who has murdered both Lorna then Victoria but felt it necessary to go through a third party and hire an amateur like Willis in a half-hearted attempt to kill Jackie Moran? And when the first attempt on Jackie Moran fails why wasn't there a second? So why the "I'm like Emma" message? And who sent Lorna the junk mail?'

Goodhew didn't answer.

'You see, Gary, ideas are all fine and good but they need to hold water. If you spend too much time working on your own you will lose sight of the real objectives.'

Goodhew nodded dumbly. Marks was right, of course, and he felt stupid for letting himself colour the facts, even if he hadn't realized he was doing so.

'Do you want another chance in this department?'

'Yes. Please.'

Marks sent him to get coffees and when he returned Goodhew found his boss sitting with Alex Moran's journal in one hand and his phone in the other. His attention was with the phone. After another minute he replaced the receiver and took the coffee.

'Do you know what leads are like?' he said.

This was one where Goodhew knew the answer. 'Buses?'

'Exactly. I've got a bundle of them.'

'Not a fleet?'

'In the hours before Lorna's death she'd had intercourse with two men, Bryn O'Brien and Richard Moran. It was easy to determine who Victoria Nugent had had intercourse with because up pops our friend Bryn O'Brien again. And due to the chaotic nature of the attack there are hair and fibre samples in abundance. Luckily for Mr O'Brien she died at just about the same time as he was flashed by a speed camera out near the M11.'

Marks sipped his coffee then turned his attention to the journal, flicking through the pages. 'Imagine wading through fifty-six books of this stuff, he's cryptic beyond belief. And obsessive. And I worry about someone who can't be honest in their own notes.'

'Perhaps he's the unstable one.'

'But somehow, I doubt he killed Lorna and Victoria from beyond the grave,' Marks replied drily.

They still didn't know nearly enough about Lorna, but it was obvious to Goodhew that the people who liked her the least would turn out to be the ones who knew her the best. He remembered a quote that seemed to sum her up and realized that it led them towards a different line of thinking. 'Lorna only did things for Lorna – it's what Wayne Thompson-Stark and Hayley Sellars said.'

'And what are you saying?'

'If that's the case Lorna didn't hire Colin Willis on anyone's behalf except her own.'

'And if Jackie Moran knew that, it would be a motive for revenge.'

Goodhew stiffened; he hadn't intended to throw greater suspicion on Jackie Moran. He reined in his feelings. Just because he hoped she was innocent, it didn't mean that she was. 'That's not what I meant, but yes, you're right.'

He closed his eyes to help him concentrate. Eventually Marks prodded him in the arm. 'Are you feeling all right?'

Goodhew opened his eyes. 'If I come up with another possible scenario will you shoot it down in flames again?'

'Only if it's crap, Gary. What are you thinking?'

'We know that Lorna had a history of playing games with people's lives, she was an arch manipulator. Say, Lorna hired Colin Willis knowing about the contents of the journal. If she had successfully framed Alice, and with Jackie gone, she would have had Richard and his money all to herself. Lorna took the page from her friend Victoria who'd been having the relationship with Alex Moran and that's what they fell out over, not a boyfriend. Wayne said Lorna's friend was called Vicky – if that's Victoria Nugent it would have been her that sent all the junk mail because she was the only one who had known Lorna long enough to know about Wayne and Hayley.'

'Apart from Wayne and Hayley themselves.'

'Yes, I suppose so,' Goodhew admitted.

'OK,' Marks said slowly. 'It makes sense so far. You're saying that when Jackie Moran survived the attack she would have realized that Lorna, and therefore Victoria, had access to Alex

341

Moran's files. You realize your scenario still makes Jackie the prime suspect?'

Goodhew pulled a face. 'I know that, but I can't imagine her killing anyone.'

'Apart from Colin Willis?' Marks shut the book. 'I'm not quite as trusting as you, Gary, so I sent a car out to bring her here. You have half an hour to plan your interview then we'll speak to her together.'

Chapter Forty-Eight

Marks deliberately arrived at the interview room fifteen minutes before Goodhew. He'd wanted a few minutes alone to assess Jackie Moran.

She was withdrawn and reminded him of children he'd interviewed in the past, the ones whose lids were so tightly sprung that they stayed snapped shut. A crowbar might prise them open but only patience ever budged them without permanent damage.

He wondered what was going on inside her head. She kept it all secret but he'd noticed a response when she'd heard Goodhew's name. A quick blink. A move of the hand. Two tells that let him know that he'd been wise to have Gary back.

He and Jackie Moran sat in virtual silence for the ten minutes it took for Goodhew to join them. Marks didn't even try to guess what was going on in her head, he was too busy trying to corral his own thoughts. He knew he'd been inconsistent: throwing Goodhew out of his team then having him back within hours made no sense. And formally disciplining him would have been the right thing to do, not treating him as if the normal rules hadn't been written to include him. Police work was a science and Goodhew could not be allowed to run around working to his own agenda. And Marks knew that failing to stop him would ultimately be no one's responsibility but his own.

And yet.

And yet.

And yet.

Marks knew that what Goodhew possessed was a talent, a gift for people and truth and logic that didn't come with any amount of training. Marks knew he'd be a fool to condone it, but trying to extinguish it ultimately seemed the greater crime.

In that long ten minutes he knew it was time to decide.

Chapter Forty-Nine

Goodhew reached the interview room door and took one deep breath before pushing it open; he silently thanked Marks for giving him another chance and equally silently promised not to mess it up.

Marks didn't acknowledge his arrival but Jackie Moran wriggled in her chair when she saw him, not in a restless way but with a shift of weight that made it look like she was settling down ready for a long interview. He didn't wait for Marks to speak. 'How are you?' he asked.

'Tired,' she said.

'Can I make a suggestion?'

'Go on.'

But Marks interrupted. 'Wait,' he said quietly. He stood, then rested his hand on Goodhew's shoulder. The touch was brief but handed him every opportunity he'd hoped for. 'Carry on without me,' he added unnecessarily.

When the door closed behind Marks, Goodhew spoke again. 'I'm sorry I made you cry.'

'Don't worry about it.'

'Can we start by clearing the air – we can put all the other times we've spoken to one side. I understand why you didn't tell me about Colin Willis, or knowing Joanne Reed. Whatever you've said so far doesn't matter.'

'But you know things about me.'

'Tell me your version.'

'What about my father's journal?' She tried to look defiant but there was the ghost of a quake in her voice and he wanted that to be the real Jackie Moran.

'No. Forget your father, just for now. You don't have to live under the shadow of everything he wrote, especially when he was wrong. Imagine nothing had happened to David or Joanne, imagine you could have the freedom to do whatever you wanted with the rest of your life, what would you do?'

'It's a stupid question.'

'Why?'

'Because.' She tried to leave it there but he waited longer than she could. 'Because, that's not where I am.'

'You're wrong, it's exactly where you are. How old are you?'

'Thirty, but you know that.'

'Thirty. Well, in ten years' time when you're forty and in the same place you were at thirty, which was the same as at twenty, you may as well assume the pattern's set for the rest of your life.'

She looked unimpressed. 'If you were at least forty I might buy it, but you're younger than me so I'm sitting here thinking, What do you know?'

Goodhew had a flash of clarity, the kind that he knew from playing chess where he could read the board and mentally jump three or four moves ahead. It largely depended on how well you knew your opponent and understood their game plan.

Jackie wavered between looking stubborn and depressed: as far as Goodhew was concerned, that amounted to one hundred per cent defensive play. 'What if I come up with a really good answer?' As she thought he was so young he thought he'd try a burst of boyish charm and managed a cheeky flicker of the right eye that stopped just short of being a wink.

She snorted and one corner of her mouth twitched. 'Go on then.' Good, that was move one, sudden release of excess tension.

'OK, I know this is very important, but I'll need a minute to think. What do I know?' he pondered. He watched her watching him pretending to concentrate. Once their eyes had locked like that it was easy for them to keep on staring at one another and he let the moment stretch out until it began to feel silly, then he said, 'Can you give me a clue?'

Perhaps it was involuntary, perhaps just a burst of nerves, but, as he'd hoped, she giggled.

Make her laugh. Move two, complete and straight into move three.

'If I can't convince you about being forty, try this,' he said quietly. Their eyes were still locked. 'If no one believed me when I told the truth I'd be pretty upset. If I was six and it was my parents who didn't believe me I'd be devastated. And it wasn't as if they were remote people. You loved and admired your father.' Jackie's face reddened but she didn't look away, he guessed she wanted to but it was like she was witnessing a car crash and she couldn't. 'If that was me and he died still thinking the worst of me I'd be heartbroken. I wouldn't expect anyone to believe me, not when my parents didn't.'

Jackie opened her mouth to speak but nothing came. Still she watched him.

'You should have told us about Willis and Joanne Reed but it just hurts too much when everyone thinks you're lying, doesn't it?'

This time she tore her gaze away from him. She hid her nose and mouth behind her hands and tried to hide the tears forming in her eyes.

'It hurts, doesn't it?' he pressed, knowing he was at the point where he couldn't afford to take no answer as any sort of reply.

But he didn't need to ask again. Her hands didn't move, making the 'yes' more like a muffled grunt. But they both knew what she'd said. She opened her eyes and tears fell on to her cheeks; she was totally still and they trickled down in twin tracks, pausing at her jaw line before dropping and vanishing into the mesh of her jersey.

'I'm not trying to catch you out,' he said.

'I know,' she said finally The stubbornness had left her – so, strangely, had her depressed expression – and in their place was acceptance. 'I haven't lied to you, I've just kept things back until I knew you'd believe me.'

'And I do, so no more, OK?'

'OK.' She spent a single minute collecting herself: it felt more like the entire afternoon. 'My father wasn't just educated,' she said at last, 'he was by far the most intelligent and inspiring man I've ever met. And yet he spent nearly all of his life thinking that I killed my own brother. If he could be so wrong, how could I be sure of anything? I actually *know* nothing.'

'But you think you do,' Goodhew persisted.

She opened her mouth to speak, but he could see the tears threatening again. She blinked them away and took deep breaths until she looked confident that they weren't going to choke her words. 'I know I saw Richard with David...' She paused. 'Richard was in David's room, sitting on the floor at the foot of the cot. I wasn't very old, of course, but I remember thinking it was odd.' She frowned. 'Maybe it was later that I thought it was odd. I don't know now.'

'What was odd?'

'Odd that Richard was in the room at all when he had never shown any interest in the baby. No interest whatsoever. He had a pillow on the floor beside him and there was poor little David. Lying in his cot. Looking all wrong. Not even like a baby somehow. I could tell it was all wrong, he was like a toy. Like alabaster. Richard said nothing, just stood up then walked right past me and out the door. I didn't go any closer but I couldn't leave either. I don't know how long it was before my mother came and found me there. She said something to me, but I don't know what, and when she saw David she began to scream but I can't remember any sounds, just a huge silence. I only know she was screaming because of her face. She was holding him and he was limp, I remember thinking that it looked like there weren't any bones left in his body, then there were people everywhere. My dad of course but I don't know who else, they were in and out of the house. And they took his body away and my dad kept asking me what had happened.'

'What did you tell him?'

'Nothing.'

'You didn't tell him about Richard?'

'I tried to talk to Alice but she said I was wrong, called it a stupid story, and I never told anyone else.'

'Why not?'

'Oh God!' She shook her head. 'I've asked myself that so many times. My dad kept asking me what had happened. Over and over. By the time I realized he thought I'd killed David the truth would have sounded like a lie.'

'And he really thought you'd done it?'

'Absolutely, he even explained to me how children can create false memories. To be honest there are times when I've doubted myself.' Jackie dug a tissue from her pocket and blew her nose. 'As he pointed out, I was a small child, I might have been taken into care and that would have finished my mother. But she drank herself to death in any case so I'm not sure what difference it would have made. I regret I didn't push things further, it could have saved Emma.'

'Emma not Joanne?'

'I didn't know her well, but yes, I knew her as Emma. We had what you could call a fledgling friendship – a group of us had gone to watch the racing at Newmarket and Emma and I seemed to hit it off. We talked about spending a day with the horses. We were enjoying ourselves until she met Richard. He spotted us and made a beeline for Emma and I didn't see much of her for the rest of the evening. I don't know what went on between them. In fact I didn't know that anything went on at all. Until a few weeks later when she disappeared.'

'You never came forward.'

'To say what? I would never have thought anything of it if it hadn't been for what happened with David, so I spoke to Alice again. You know they're really close, you've seen it. Alice was furious with me, said I had to promise to keep quiet, that it was too late to stir things up about David, and too cruel to my parents. She promised she'd deal with Richard and said it was my duty to show some loyalty to them both.'

'So you are saying that you think your brother was responsible for Joanne Reed's disappearance.'

'I think so. It's his jealousy. He gets these rages, he kind of burns up with them. If there had been proof that Emma was dead I would have come forward.'

'And when "I'm like Emma" appeared in the papers? Did you consider that it might be a message for you?'

'I didn't know what to think. I'd never thought Lorna was in any danger.'

'Did it scare you? Wasn't it a threat?'

'What do you mean?'

'You told me about your father turning up at the farm and shouting, "Tell me what happened to her" – who was he talking about?'

'Emma.'

'And what was he looking for?'

When Jackie hesitated, Goodhew cut in. 'Don't make me tease it out of you one sentence at a time, Jackie. You know where this is going.'

She nodded. 'He never told me what he meant by "very clever", but I walked everywhere that I'd seen him go. There was only one place that would have hidden Emma's body and that was the manure heap, which, if you think about it, is pretty cunning. I assumed he said "very clever" to me because he thought it was all my doing. I didn't even try to convince him that it wasn't me. I thought about digging it over just to see, but I never did.'

'In fact you never did anything.'

'No, I didn't.'

Chapter Fifty

Goodhew stepped outside the interview room and wasn't surprised to find someone waiting in the corridor. It was PC Kelly Wilkes. 'I'll go in with her,' she said. 'Marks is next door.'

That made sense. Goodhew had deliberately ignored the camera in the corner of the room because he didn't want to be put off, but at the back of his mind he'd been certain Marks was in the adjoining room and with him for every second of the interview. Marks opened the door from the inside before Goodhew was even close. 'She agreed to the search then?'

'Yes, sir.'

'I've requested everything that's available on David Moran's death. Richard and Alice Moran are already on their way. We're picking them up together. We don't want to raise his suspicions until he's on his own. I'm going to keep out of the way, let him think it's all low key, then I'll join you at the appropriate moment.'

'I'm going to interview him?'

'Why not? Your interview with his sister made very good TV.'

For the nine to fivers in the city the day had only just begun. Schools were ringing their bells for morning break and the traffic had settled down after rush hour. Goodhew looked out from the nearest window: heavy clouds were heading in Cambridge's direction and he guessed it would be another wet twenty-four hours. Already he wished the day was over. He was fuzzy with tiredness and had spent the first few hours of the morning propping up his brain with a succession of cups of coffee. He'd reused each polystyrene cup until it cracked, but even so was about to ditch the third of the morning. He took his latest half-drunk cup to Interview Room 3 where Alice and Richard Moran sat side by side.

Alice was slightly tidier than immaculate. Goodhew had never before understood the school marking system that awarded an A* as a mark above the highest possible mark of A, but now he saw it. On previous occasions her appearance had been A grade faultless, but today she deserved an added star for extra endeavour. Richard on the other hand had crumpled further and now looked as though he were the shorter of the two. It gave the impression that they shared the same reserves of energy and emotional strength and just passed them back and forth by osmosis.

Marks held up the journal. Richard's gaze did a skittish jig from one person to the next, whereas Alice just said, 'Oh.'

'Do you know what this is?' Marks asked.

Richard nodded and Alice said, 'Yes, of course. My father kept journals for as long as we can remember. Burgundy for work and the dark blue ones were about our–' she took a breath – 'our family.'

'I see, and why didn't you tell us that one was missing?'

'I didn't know.' She turned to Richard. 'Did you, Richard?'

He shook his head. 'No. They were packed away with the rest of his possessions.' He looked down into his hands. 'Jackie's here, isn't she?'

'She's been making a statement. This diary was found at Victoria Nugent's house.'

'Is Jackie under arrest?' he asked. Alice was watching him closely, but didn't seem unhappy that he'd decided to do the talking.

'Not yet,' Goodhew replied. 'Tell me about David.'

Richard's gaze met his sister's then. From his imploring expression Goodhew guessed it was some kind of SOS, and it was Alice who replied. 'Because of what my father wrote?'

'I can't comment.'

She scowled. 'Well, it wouldn't have come from anywhere else. David was the youngest – I think I told you that before – and he died. He was a small baby, but not ever ill as far as I can remember. Our stepmother had put him down for an afternoon nap and she found him dead a couple of hours later – cot death, they said.' She looked toward her brother. 'Except our father couldn't accept it, could he?'

Richard shook his head and picked up the story; the handover had been seamless. 'Our stepmother wasn't a healthy woman, she suffered from post-natal depression after Jackie was born and by the time David arrived she'd started drinking heavily too.'

'And your father blamed her?'

'No, no. He felt he needed to protect her. You

353

see, he thought Jackie had killed David because she was jealous of him. But she was only six at the time and he felt that she wouldn't have understood what she'd done. If she'd been taken away our stepmother would have been devastated, Jackie was all she had.'

'Apart from you two?'

Richard shrugged. 'In any case, who would hand over their six-year-old child even in that situation? She probably would have been institutionalized and for what result? I can quite understand why he kept quiet.'

Alice took over again. 'But that's when he started keeping his notes. He told us that he wanted to know he had a record of her behaviour in case she showed signs of doing it again.'

'And you all knew about this?'

'We knew he made all these notes, but we had no idea of the contents,' Alice said. 'He kept it entirely to himself until near his death, and it was only then that he told us what he suspected.'

'And you both thought it appropriate to keep it secret from this investigation?'

'Our father wanted it kept in the family.'

'Even if there was another murder?'

Alice stiffened. 'You misunderstand us. We think our father's suspicions were wrong. He was a complex and intelligent man but not infallible. He was devastated when David died and for some reason that we'll never know he directed the blame on to our sister. He was obsessed with his notes, but why would we connect those to Lorna's murder?'

Goodhew ignored the question. 'In his notes he

also mentions Joanne Reed. Did you both know her?'

Alice shook her head, but Richard nodded. Goodhew found the sight of them responding independently of one another slightly startling. 'I met her,' Richard said, 'through Jackie. I saw her twice, or maybe three times, I don't remember now. Dad knew because I'd told him, and after she disappeared he asked me about her and Jackie and what they'd done together.'

Goodhew spoke without realizing he'd planned to, and his voice sounded sharp. 'What did he mean?'

'How do I know? Joanne was uncomfortable with Jackie hanging round at the stables, and Dad asked me if I'd seen Joanne the weekend she disappeared.' Goodhew studied Richard; he didn't seem to enjoy the attention, though, and quickly added, 'But I hadn't, I swear.'

'Then why not tell us all of this before?'

'We told you, we promised our father that we'd look after her.' There was an audible shake to his voice.

'Yes, and Alice just told me that you both thought your father's suspicions were incorrect. Do you share that opinion or not?'

He wavered, then replied, 'Yes.' Perhaps it was the wrong answer, or maybe he'd been distracted by an unexpected thought. Goodhew waited. Richard stared, his eyes unnaturally focused on the bridge of Goodhew's nose. When he spoke his voice was low and ponderous, as though he was articulating unfamiliar thoughts. 'But now I think about it, my life was perfect before she arrived.'

'Goodhew?' It was Alice who'd cut in. She sounded calmer than ever, supporting Goodhew's theory of osmosis. 'What can we do to help Jackie?'

Goodhew's initial response to Alice's interruption was relief; her simple question had redirected her brother into a calmer state, possibly saving them all from another emotional eruption.

Then he rethought and decided to remove Alice to another room.

By the time he returned PC Wilkes was waiting in the corridor again.

'This is becoming a habit,' she said, and handed him a single sheet of paper. 'That's all we've come up with so far. I've got a mate in the County Records Office and she scanned it for me. Lucky we got anything, I guess.'

The copy was pale and Goodhew had to turn it to the light before he saw it was the death certificate for David Joseph Moran. He glanced at the dates: born in August, just after Goodhew's first birthday, and dead before Goodhew's second. The cause cited, 'natural causes'.

A dead-end urge to protect the child manifested itself by a series of 'if only' thoughts. Pointless, except as an incentive to win justice for the child.

It was the mention of the County Records Office, housed on the site of the former jail, which reminded him, that and the word justice…

Goodhew had left Richard alone for what he hoped was enough time to make him wonder whether he'd been abandoned. He folded the copy of David's death certificate in half and returned to the interview room with it in his inside pocket. He sat back down, this time pulling his chair much closer.

'We were talking about Joanne Reed. Where did you meet her?'

Richard slid one hand under each thigh. Goodhew had heard teachers yelling, 'If you can't keep your hands still, sit on them,' but he'd never seen anyone over the age of about eight actually do it. 'Newmarket...' Richard began, then started the sentence again but speaking more clearly the second time. 'Newmarket races. Dad and I went to watch the racing, and Jackie was there with some other girls and one of them was Joanne Reed.'

'Who else was there?'

'Just Dad and myself.'

'Not Alice?'

'No, she didn't feel well.'

'How can you still remember after ten years?'

'I just do.'

'And you saw Joanne again after that?'

'Of course not.'

'But you liked her?'

'From what I saw of her, yes.'

'Did you want to see her again?'

'I thought it might happen but nothing was arranged.'

'Did you ask her?'

He hesitated, then 'No.'

Goodhew paused.

Richard took a deep breath. 'I asked her if she'd like to come racing again and she said yes. But it wasn't a specific invite. I gave her my number, she called the following week and we met for a drink.'

'Where?'

'The Eagle, Cambridge.'

'Then what?'

Richard pulled the sort of awkward expression that Goodhew guessed was supposed to signify a mix of discretion and candour.

Goodhew decided to fill in the gap. 'So you went somewhere private?'

Richard nodded.

'For sex?' Goodhew waited for another nod then continued, 'If you were already in Cambridge why go to Old Mile Farm, why not just go home?'

'I took her to the stables on the pretext of see-ing the horses, in the hope that things would progress once we were there.'

'I see. So you didn't meet there for sex because your father wouldn't let you bring women home?'

Richard hesitated. 'Well, there was that too,' he admitted.

'We know of two women with whom you've had a sexual relationship, one is dead and the other has been missing for a decade. Doesn't make you single of the week, does it?' Richard looked away, and Goodhew changed direction. 'A few minutes ago the word "justice" came up and it made me recall a conversation we had earlier in the week.'

Richard looked curious but said nothing.

'You told me that you thought it was important to see justice done, and that it's seen to be done. You said that's what you wanted for Lorna.'

'That's right.'

'Did you mean Lorna as the victim, or Lorna as the condemned?'

Richard leant back in his chair and crossed his legs. 'Now you've lost me.'

'Her death was carefully orchestrated. She had plenty of experience of controlling people but she went too far with you, you weren't going to let her walk away, you needed to punish her. There was a risk you'd be caught but it had to be out in the open like that, otherwise it wouldn't have felt like she'd had a public execution.'

'And what was her unforgivable crime exactly?' Richard said as he sat straight again. There wasn't much more fidgeting he could do without breaking into a sweat, but there again, he looked pretty close to breaking into a sweat in any case. Goodhew could see he wasn't scared though, the nervousness was just the bubbling by-product of a rage that was nearing boiling point. Richard still had the lid on it, but it was rattling loudly.

'Perhaps she found out you killed Joanne Reed. Was she trying to blackmail you?'

'I never killed Joanne.'

'Come on, you admit you have a problem with jealousy. And a temper. What happens when you lose control? Did Joanne end up like Victoria, with her skull caved in? You didn't have a chance to hide Victoria. And we're looking for Joanne's body right now.'

The first visible bead of sweat appeared at Richard's hairline. It reminded Goodhew of condensation running down the inside of a saucepan. Richard wiped it away, Goodhew kept pushing.

'She's buried at the farm, isn't she, Richard?'

'Don't.' Richard hissed.

Goodhew smirked. 'Don't what?' he said coolly.

'Don't.' Richard said it like it was a threat, but Goodhew remained unmoved, refusing to let it grow beyond the impotent, orphaned word it really was. Without warning, Richard pushed his chair back, the metal feet squealing in protest. 'Don't try to trick me.' He pointed his finger at Goodhew, prodding the air as if to emphasize a point, but the words would not come. Then he realized his hand was shaking and dropped it back into his lap, clasping it with the other to keep it still. 'You don't know anything, you're playing games.'

'No, no, you're wrong. Your sister's making a statement as we speak.'

The colour drained from Richard's face and he slumped backwards. 'You're lying. She wouldn't do that to me.'

'Why not?' As far as Goodhew was concerned Jackie should have made one years ago. Goodhew stood and reached in his pocket. He held the baby's death certificate close to Richard's face. 'Jackie says you killed David.'

Richard gasped and his expression altered, travelling from disbelief to dismay with a brief but unmissable stop-off at did-anyone-notice. 'I see,' he said, trying for finality, desperate to make them the last two words of the conversation.

For Goodhew it was more than just illuminating: he'd accidentally tripped the switch that activated the floodlights, and Richard was the only one basking in the glare.

Chapter Fifty-One

The first revelation was so blinding that Goodhew was almost too dazzled to see the second.

Marks was already out in the corridor, but talking on his mobile. He made the 'one minute' sign
and turned away so he could concentrate. Goodhew didn't want to wait, this was the wrong
moment for him to slow down, the right moment
to barge into the room at the other end of the
corridor. It was as if Marks could sense his im-
patience: he turned back briefly and repeated the
gesture.

OK, OK, Goodhew thought. He leant back on
the wall then slid down until he was squatting. He
refolded the death certificate and fanned his face,
then unfolded it and held it like a wobble board,
rippling it up and down, hoping the noise would
irritate Marks enough to make him hang up.

It didn't.

The only person's attention it was grabbing was
his own. He stopped moving it as the significance
of David's date of birth suddenly hit home.

'Shit,' he muttered, and rushed away from his
boss towards the nearest photocopier. It took
three attempts before key details on the next
generation copy were clear enough to read.

He got his mobile and rang Mel's extension.
'Have you left your desk in the last half-hour?'
'No.'

'Marks sent someone out to Old Mile Farm – any idea who?'

'Kincaide and Charles.'

'Thanks.'

Goodhew rang Charles, hurrying towards his desk as he spoke. 'Are you there yet? Good. One of the loose boxes has a press clipping on the wall – photograph it with your phone and text it over. Make sure the picture and the date are both clear.'

His fatigue had fled, replaced by vigour and clarity. He still had only a single purpose but now he knew where his efforts were converging. He booted up his PC, plugged a USB cable into his mobile and waited for the double-beep that announced each new message.

It arrived without a hitch. He enlarged the image and sent it straight to the laser printer. It was still warm when he slapped it on to the desk in front of Jackie Moran.

'That's the newspaper clipping from your stable.' It wasn't a question and she didn't nod. He followed it with the photocopy. 'And that is David's death certificate. If I can put the two of them together and see it, so will any jury.'

She opened her mouth to speak but Goodhew held up his hand. 'Enough. This very minute I'm not listening, especially to people who think I buy every lie and half-truth that's thrown at me.'

He almost left without saying more, but turned back just before reaching for the door handle. 'Think about it before I get back. I am this close–' he held the tips of his thumb and forefinger a millimetre apart – 'and this investigation is finishing today.'

Chapter Fifty-Two

Marks was in the viewing room next door, sitting at a PC. The individual CCTV screens were on an adjacent desk but Marks was watching via his monitor where the images were running in separate windows on his desktop.

Alice leaning forward with her elbows on the table.

Richard leaning back with his hands cupping his neck.

Jackie staring into the camera.

Marks had a fourth window open; a paused image of Goodhew's earlier interview with Richard. Marks had played it twice before seeing what had rattled Goodhew and he would have replayed it again, but before he had a chance his young DC reappeared in Jackie Moran's room, this time shoving photocopies in front of her.

Marks leant closer to the screen.

Goodhew's demeanour had changed; he seemed cold, with every movement measured, his conversation terse and his exit from the room equally abrupt. Jackie Moran stared at the back of the door for several seconds after it closed, then she placed the two sheets of A4 side by side and perfectly symmetrically in the centre of the desk. She sat so still that she looked like the shot had been freeze-framed.

Marks continued to watch her until he heard his

363

own door open. At first glance he thought Goodhew was enraged; his jaw was set, his eyes bright and unusually intense. Goodhew looked at the paused footage of Richard Moran and then at Marks.

Marks sensed he was being challenged, then he understood. Goodhew was angry, but more than that he was brooding with determination; he had seen the way to the end of the investigation and felt compelled to follow it through. The challenge was not to put the brakes on Goodhew or, more specifically, to give him the keys and let him drive.

Marks reached forward and tweaked the two sheets of paper out of Goodhew's hand. 'Is this what you just gave Jackie Moran?'

'Yes, look.' Goodhew pointed to the dates.

Marks studied both pages, his gaze pacing around each page then flicking back and forth between the two. He saw the closeness of the dates almost at once; the subsequent deduction came more slowly. Then it dawned on him. 'Oh, I see,' he said slowly. 'And how do you suggest we proceed from here?'

Chapter Fifty-Three

There was no room for compassion now. Any Goodhew had felt, or might have felt in a less heated moment, had been displaced by his rising fury. He threw open the door. She was standing at the window and turned to look at him. She was just as good at eye contact but now he wondered how he'd ever found her attractive.

'I know who killed Lorna Spence.' He left it as a blank statement of fact. No discussion. Neither was he going to be drawn into any prolonged gazing. He sat on one of the two chairs and motioned for her to sit on the other.

'I'm fine standing,' she said.

'Suit yourself, just don't expect to intimidate me with any of that "I'm higher than you" body language crap.'

She pulled the chair back. 'It's no big deal, I can sit if it bothers you that much.'

'What do you know about murderers who kill in teams?'

'Nothing.'

'Teams can include pairs.'

'Like I said, nothing.'

So many thoughts were raging in his head that it would have been easy to open his mouth and release a disjointed battery of accusations. In fact the words which came were dispassionate and as steel-edged as any he'd ever spoken.

'Team killers follow common patterns. They are strongly attracted to one another, or even related, and one is dominant, making decisions, controlling their partner. Whereas the submissive one feels guilt and fear, their temperament may include aggressive outbursts. The dominant one decides what they do next. Does any of this sound familiar?'

'Frankly, no.'

'That's the best thing about killing teams,' he said. 'Mostly it's the submissive one that controls the final outcome, like now. It seems illogical, you'd think it was the dominant one that steered it all the way, but no, sooner or later, when they've had enough, the weaker will take drastic steps to escape.'

Jackie Moran opened her eyes. The papers were still on the desk and she was still in the interview room. On the face of it nothing had changed, but for the first time she could see the world, or more specifically her world, for what it was.

In front of her was proof of a lie. It was proof that it wasn't the first lie she'd been told, and proof of the many other lies that had rained down on her ever since. Here was conclusive evidence, the gas and canary test, whose verdict found all of her relationships to be tiny featherless corpses.

She recalled one of Goodhew's questions: imagine you could have the freedom to do whatever you wanted with the rest of your life, what would you do?

It wasn't a stupid question now, in fact it was the only little bird that still hopped and sang. Its voice was clear and insistent. All she had to do was open the cage.

She knocked on her door until he came to see what she wanted. He held it a few inches ajar and spoke through the gap. 'What?'

'I know what I was afraid of.'

His eyes were at their most vivid, concentrating on her, looking for subtext. He said nothing and the space between her and Goodhew became hot and airless, slowing the seconds and constricting her chest. She drew a deep breath and spoke first.

'Finding out it was all lies, and facing up to it.'

'And?'

'No choice now.'

He gave a half nod and she saw his expression soften. 'What do you want to do?'

She looked beyond him to the interview room along the corridor. 'Go in there.'

'One to one?'

'No, with you.'

Goodhew opened the interview room door and let Jackie walk through first. Part of her wanted to hang back and make him take the first step, but the rest of her knew this was the right way to go.

'Jackie has been cleared of any involvement,' he said, 'and she wants to talk to you. I said you'd already expressed the desire to help her in any way possible.'

Jackie picked up a chair and placed it directly across from her sister. She sat and took her time to study Alice; her expressions were always hard to read, and in the end Jackie categorized this one as an attempt at indifference. But she could also see that Alice was just trying much too hard.

Goodhew had moved his chair three or four feet back from the table. This was the only time he had seen them together. Jackie considered it from his point of view; there was certainly a family resemblance, but Alice was taller and wiry, more self-assured. And they both knew she was the smarter of the two. Jackie stared at her big sister, and could still feel the lingering residue of childhood awe. She hoped Goodhew wouldn't intervene, hoped he wouldn't need to.

Jackie wanted to broach the first question, but the thoughts wouldn't crystallize into an opening line. She hesitated too long and Alice spoke, looking only at Jackie. 'What are you are doing?'

'I need some answers.'

'What answers?' Alice frowned, the space between her eyebrows drawing into two deep vertical creases.

'Ones that will make everything add up.' Jackie heard the defensive note in her voice, she knew she needed to stop and regroup.

'What are you talking about?' Alice persisted. So far she'd been the only one who'd asked any questions.

Jackie let Alice's words hang in the air until it was clear that she had no intention of answering. Goodhew watched her, steady and calm. He was the true strength in the room, not Alice.

And when Jackie spoke it was with all the authority that she'd hoped her voice could find. 'You have manipulated me and you have all but ruined my life. I came to you for help and you dismissed everything I said and I thought it was all because you truly believed I had killed David. Then later when Emma disappeared I thought you were blindly protecting Richard. You are such a liar.'

Alice said nothing.

'My God, you really don't get it. I see through you now, you can't fob me off. When Colin Willis attacked me, I came to you to warn you. You have betrayed me.'

Alice looked away, but Jackie jumped to her

feet, forcing herself into her sister's line of sight.

'I need to know what I ever did to you, Alice. Why hate me so much? Why let me be the one that my whole family thinks is a killer? Why, Alice? I thought we were close once. Don't I deserve the truth from you? Don't I deserve to know why I've spent my whole life terrified?'

A cold smile touched Alice's lips. 'No, you don't.'

Jackie settled back into her seat. Did Alice really think she had anything to negotiate with? 'Remember it was me who comforted you each time you miscarried...' She saw her sister's surprise. 'That's right, Alice, how many times? Four? Five?'

Alice was quick to answer, her voice hushed. 'Five.'

Jackie heard her own voice change. *All we want is our own baby, Jackie.* ' She repeated the words she'd heard her sister say so many times over the years, but a cruel and sarcastic note pierced her impression. 'But you had him and you let Richard kill him. You never cried that on my shoulder, did you?'

'Jackie!' Alice snapped the name, expecting it to produce instant silence.

'Alice!' Jackie mimicked. 'My mum was photographed the week he was born, thin as a rake. David was your baby, Richard killed him and you let him get away with it. You never gave a shit.'

'Jackie, I'm warning you.'

'No, Alice, you have nothing to threaten me with. Everyone lied to me. I was the only one who thought that David was my brother. It wasn't post-natal depression that my mother was suffering, it was the burden of covering up your pregnancy and your affair with Richard. You weren't her children yet she was still trying to protect you. And Alex was protecting you too.

'But me, I've been cheated out of my whole family. Because of you my parents thought I'd smothered David.'

Something changed in Alice, less than a muscle move, an invisible nuance that made Jackie react. 'What's funny?'

Alice shook her head. 'You really are laughable. Do you honestly think Alex would have grieved over a child that wasn't his? Alex was creeping into my room and your mother was too busy drinking herself stupid to notice.'

'But you and Richard...' Icy shock flushed Jackie's veins, flooded her brain, orphaned her thoughts and left them staggering in numb circles.

'Alex always knew you never killed David. Did you really think I chose to have a relationship with my own brother? I turned to Richard because of Alex.'

Jackie heard herself make a sound, half gasp, half cry. But no words came.

'Come on, Jackie, we both know we are the products of a disturbed home.' Alice reached forward and stroked Jackie's hand. 'No point shaking your head like that. Your mother died and I had Richard. You weren't special, Jackie, you were just there. It was inevitable that Alex would want sex with you. He never loved Richard, but he always loved his girls. You deluded yourself into thinking he felt something for you and in return you loved him in that first-big-romance way of yours. You were never enough for him though. Never. He saw other women, like Victoria, and all he had to do was make sure you stayed quiet. That's why he kept his journals, that's why he pretended you had killed David and Joanne Reed, they were ways of discrediting you.'

Jackie's voice was barely audible. 'No, he loved me.'

Alice leant closer. 'No, he didn't. He was perverted and corrupting. He abused you and you have twisted it around in your head into something it never was. It suited him to have you all to himself. It was convenient for him to make you the scapegoat for David.'

The shock left Jackie as quickly as it arrived. She knew that Goodhew was still in her corner, ever patient, never judging. He saw her as more than just a string of sordid revelations. She would come to terms with those later.

Right now all that mattered was Alice and the verbal grenades being hurled at her.

Jackie levelled at her sister, then took her best shot. 'But not for Joanne Reed.'

Alice stumbled, tried to rewind the conversation, but couldn't quite make sense of Jackie's comment. 'What do you mean?'

Jackie spelt it out, her voice quiet but dogged. 'Alex knew I'd never killed David so he never believed I killed Joanne Reed. He would not have kept up the pretence just for Richard. You said yourself he never loved him, even as an adult Richard could never step out of line. Richard had nothing to negotiate with, but you had everything.'

'No,' said Alice quietly.

'Why not? Surely you're not saying Richard killed Joanne Reed?'

Alice began to shake her head, then stopped.

Jackie leapt on the moment. 'Now you're stuck, aren't you? It's you or him, Alice. I went to the races at Newmarket and that's when Richard met Joanne. You weren't there because you'd had another miscarriage. Then a few days later I saw Richard and Joanne together, having sex up at Old Mile Farm. When she disappeared I thought Richard was behind it. And I warned you, but you wouldn't listen. You told me to keep my distance. You played me and Richard off against each other, you made him think I'd killed Joanne Reed, knowing that I would stay away.

'Then what about Lorna? You introduced her to Richard, you wanted them together. Lorna told me how you encouraged her to get pregnant and you told me last summer that you'd lost hope of having another successful pregnancy. It must have knotted you up hearing them in the next bedroom. Would you have killed her once she'd had the child? She never wanted one though, did she? When I told you about Colin Willis you realized that Lorna wanted both of us out of the way to get to Richard and it turned into a classic battle of two women chasing one man. Or did Richard kill her because he found out she was sleeping around?

'And what was Victoria? An impulse kill by Richard or an opportunity to tie up your loose ends?' Jackie stopped abruptly and sat back in her seat. 'It's you or him now, just tell the truth.'

Alice ran her tongue over her teeth and narrowed her eyes. It was a look that Jackie recognized from as far back as she could remember: it preceded her sister's most calculated game play and appeared just as she contemplated making any key move. In this instance there was only one move available.

'OK,' she sighed. 'It was Richard, he killed them all.'

Jackie smiled. 'Jealous, was he?'

'Irrationally jealous. I tried to reason with him but he's not well.'

'I don't believe you.'

'Neither do I,' Goodhew said, then added, 'Just wait,' with no further explanation.

Five minutes passed and Jackie was beginning to wonder whether something had gone awry, then the door opened. A female officer stepped through, accompanied by Richard. 'I want to speak to Jackie,' he said. He seemed oblivious to everyone else, even Alice.

Jackie nodded. 'OK.'

'You're wrong about Alice.'

Jackie blinked. 'How?'

'She didn't make me think you'd killed Joanne, she told me she'd done it. I killed David to give us a fresh start but it left me in an impossible situation. We were in it together. I knew she had killed Lorna, it was only Victoria's murder that I knew nothing about. I've agreed to make a statement, I just wanted to tell you to your face.'

He was many things she despised, and so many things she recognized in herself. And some that were both. He left the interview room and

Goodhew ushered her out too. At the last second she turned back to find Alice white-faced and staring after them.

Goodhew stopped Jackie in the hallway. 'Will you be all right?'

'Yes, I think so.' Jackie thought there ought to be something deeper she could add, something more profound. But the only words that flashed through her mind were forward and inappropriate. In the end she shook his hand, and 'Thank you' was all she said.

Marks studied the TV; he'd just finished watching the tapes of Richard and Alice for a second time. Finally he turned his attention to Goodhew. 'That was impressive,' he said.

'Thank you, sir.'

'And that's the sort of inspired chaos I'm missing when I don't keep you fully occupied?'

'Possibly, sir.'

'Heaven help us with you in the department.'

'I don't have to stay.'

'Yes, you do, even if keeping you turns out to be the only reckless thing I do before I retire. But here's the deal: I keep you challenged, you keep me informed. Anything else is on your head. I will never cover up for you. Understand?'

'Thank you, sir.'

'Never.'

'I know.'

'Right. I expect you've heard, they've started searching at Old Mile Farm.'

Goodhew nodded and imagined the forensics team swinging into action, taking measurements and planning their assault on the mountain of manure. The tactic would be a slow and thorough sift through the site and not the occasion to use the term 'fingertip search'. 'Can I go?' he asked.

Marks shook his head. 'Not this time. It could take days and once you've caught up on your sleep your paperwork needs you. I'll let you know as soon as anything turns up. If it does.'

'It will.'

Chapter Fifty-Four

It was two days since Alice and Richard Moran had been formally charged. It was early afternoon and Goodhew had a call to make. The phone was in his hands, but he hesitated and looked across Parker's Piece from his quiet corner on the third floor.

Ratty had finally been in and made a statement. It contained nothing new, but involved supplying him with three hot drinks and a plate of sandwiches. Goodhew watched Ratty walk away, back into his life of sleeping rough.

Just beyond Ratty, Mel was returning from lunch; the two passed within feet of one another. While Mel chose dangerous relationships he wondered whether her life was much safer than Ratty's. He hoped so, but he also knew that caring about someone wasn't enough to keep them safe; there was nothing Martin Reed could have done.

He dialled the number from memory. For the

first time in many weeks Goodhew had woken after a decent night's sleep, reborn in a mood of reflection; the calm after the storm had finally arrived and this was the last gust blowing its way out of his life and into someone else's.

Goodhew's call to Martin Reed was short. The phone rang twice before it was answered.

'Mr Reed?'

'Yes.'

'This is DC Goodhew.'

'I know, I recognized your voice.'

Goodhew wouldn't have recognized Martin Reed's. It was taut, hoarse even.

'We wanted you to be aware that we've recovered an unidentified body.' He was careful to stress the word 'unidentified'. 'We will be conducting tests and as soon as–'

'But it could be Jo?'

Goodhew hesitated. 'It could, yes.'

'And you'll ring.'

'Yes, as soon as we can.'

'I'll just wait then,' he said and put down the phone.

Murder was a very big stain to leave on the world. He guessed it marked even those on the periphery, like Faith Carver and Bryn O'Brien. He knew that both Martin Reed and Jackie Moran would be scrubbing away at it for years to come.

The pile of typing on Mel's desk had grown to about three inches thick, most of it urgent and illegible. She didn't mind. She'd just shared a sandwich and a packet of crisps with Toby: neither of them had spoken much, but the silence had been without any trace of bad atmosphere and that was progress.

On the way back she'd glanced up at the third floor, knowing where Goodhew liked to sit. She couldn't see him up there but almost waved, just in case. She hoped they'd talk properly soon, but she wasn't going to push that one either. She wanted to thank him for helping her find the gear that would reverse her out of the mess she was in, but first she had to be sure she could use it.

She snapped off another row of squares from her half-eaten bar of Dairy Milk. Thank God for chocolate.

Behind her the door opened and she knew without looking that the footsteps belonged to Michael Kincaide. She'd avoided him for two days and now hoped that if she ignored him he'd go away, but she felt him sneak up on her. He planted a ticklish kiss on the bare skin at the back of her neck, making goosebumps.

She swung her chair around and looked up at him. He was wearing a suit which made him look all of his twenty-seven years. Was that an age gap big enough for him to be a father figure?

His aftershave was Calvin Klein, and it used to smell good, just a splash too strong, but still good. She wasn't sure when she'd gone off it.

'I'm sorry if I've upset you, Mel. I've missed you,' he said. 'Meet me later and we can talk.' He was so sincere that he was starting to remind her of the double glazing salesman who had persuaded her mum to replace a perfectly good set of windows.

'I've grown out of you, Michael. Go and find

someone else.' She sounded more assertive than she felt and was pleased when he didn't hang around to argue, banging the nearest door open with the heel of his hand.

It was caught by Goodhew coming the other way. 'Have you upset him?'

'I ended my date-a-married-man phase.'

'Oh, I see. And Toby?'

'I'll see.' She changed the subject. 'Where are you going?'

'Early finish, I'm meeting someone at the pub.'

Then it was her turn to say, 'Oh, I see.' He left through the back door and she watched him until he disappeared from view.

Bryn sat in the bench seat in his workshop making a pointless examination of the end of his five-eighths spanner.

For a while he had felt he was in the path of the investigation. It had been a juggernaut thundering towards him, headlights blazing, horn blaring. And he had been transfixed, seemingly unable to step out of the route that lined up with its front grille. But now it had passed him. It had thrown up dust and confusion and buffeted him with its slipstream before he realized that he was back in his usual quiet spot at the side of the road. He guessed he'd hear it rumble on for some time yet as it manoeuvred across town. The whole experience had introduced him to the unfamiliar territory of deep thought, definitely not somewhere he wanted to stay for long, but he gave a few minutes to Willis and Lorna and Victoria. Death had never touched him before, and now, as if to prove things came in threes, they'd all died in the space of weeks.

He didn't know how he was supposed to feel. He had had a passing closeness to each of them but in reality he knew less than nothing about any of them. And that was kind of how it was with everyone he knew. Therefore his deep thought for the day was really to ask himself if that was enough.

He wondered about Gary. Perhaps just the knowledge that they'd been classmates gave them something of a bond, or maybe he'd only imagined they'd been on the same wavelength.

Bryn gave a small chuckle. He was hardly going to track Gary down and ask if they could be friends. What next, swapping football cards? Besides, a mate in the police force – didn't seem likely.

But, even so…

Bryn threw the spanner back in the toolbox and grabbed his jacket. It wouldn't hurt to ask Gary for a drink, then they'd see.

There was one more thing that Goodhew knew he needed to do before the end of the day. The Avery pub stood on Parker's Piece, at the opposite end to Parkside police station and a few hundred yards from his flat.

Inside the pub his grandmother was waiting for him with two halves of lager. 'I thought champagne would be inappropriate – besides, I don't like it much.'

'What are we celebrating?' he asked, then before she could reply he spoke again. 'Tell me in a minute. First, though, I am really sorry I gave you a hard time over the inheritance. I know it's not your fault, and in normal circumstances it would be appreciated.'

'Gary, I understand, though I doubt most of the rest of the Western world would... It shouldn't be a crime to hate money. Just do your best.'

'I will.' He smiled. 'You make it sound like a spelling test.'

'It's probably not quite that bad.'

'So what are we celebrating?'

'End of the case.'

They clinked glasses. 'End of the case,' he repeated.

'And you weren't fired, I was very proud. Did you work out why you don't like Kincaide?'

'Oh, he's just sexist, racist, big-headed, narrow-minded, spiteful and arrogant, but beyond that ... a really good bloke.'

'Mel?'

'Who knows? We'll see.'

'And Bryn?'

'Gut feeling? I guess I think he's OK. Why?'

'He's standing outside your house right now.'

They both watched him for a second. 'D'you want to meet him?' Goodhew asked.

His grandmother smiled. 'Yes, actually, I'd love to.'

Author's Note

One of the pleasures of completing a book is looking back at the list of people who have helped in some way, many of whom I have only met through the book itself. I'm therefore grateful for the process of writing which can, at times, be wonderfully isolated, but is also a source of rich and rewarding human contact. Among the people I will always associate with this book are DI Neil Constable, Kimberly Jackson, Laura Watson, Christine Bartram and Barry Crowther, Paul Johnston, Mark Billingham, Simon Kernick, Imogen Olsen with her eagle eyes, and Lisa Williams and Laura Clift at Cherry Bomb Rock Photography.

I would also like to make a special point of acknowledging Richard Reynolds and Roger Ellory, who have both been generous with their time and expertise.

Thank you to Krystyna Green and all the staff at Constable & Robinson. I may be biased but this book looks fantastic.

Finally, I've seen lots of authors thank their agents and I now have first-hand experience of what a special role an agent plays and how much they deserve appreciation. Thank you, Broo.

A.B.

The publishers hope that this book has given you enjoyable reading. Large Print Books are especially designed to be as easy to see and hold as possible. If you wish a complete list of our books please ask at your local library or write directly to:

Magna Large Print Books
Magna House, Long Preston,
Skipton, North Yorkshire.
BD23 4ND

This Large Print Book for the partially sighted, who cannot read normal print, is published under the auspices of

THE ULVERSCROFT FOUNDATION